T0326036

G J BONHAM

LONG ROAD
TO HAPPINESS

She thought she had left her past behind –
until it came back to haunt her

G J BONHAM

LONG ROAD
ROAD

TO HAPPINESS

She thought she had left her past behind –
until it came back to haunt her

MEREO
Cirencester

Mereo Books

1A The Wool Market Dyer Street Cirencester Gloucestershire GL7 2PR
An imprint of Memoirs Publishing www.mereobooks.com

Long Road To Happiness: 978-1-86151-073-0

First published in Great Britain in 2014
by Mereo Books, an imprint of Memoirs Publishing

Copyright ©2014

The address for Memoirs Publishing Group Limited can be found at
www.memoirspublishing.com

Cover design - Ray Lipscombe

The Memoirs Publishing Group Ltd Reg. No. 7834348

The Memoirs Publishing Group supports both The Forest Stewardship Council® (FSC®)
and the PEFC® leading international forest-certification organisations. Our books carrying
both the FSC label and the PEFC® and are printed on FSC®-certified paper. FSC® is
the only forest-certification scheme supported by the leading environmental
organisations including Greenpeace. Our paper procurement policy can be found at
www.memoirspublishing.com/environment

Typeset in 11/16pt Plantin by Wiltshire Associates Publisher Services Ltd.
Printed and bound in Great Britain by Printondemand-Worldwide, Peterborough PE2 6XD

This novel is dedicated to Series 36 Class, who joined the Royal Navy on May Fourth 1959 at HMS Fisgard.

To my husband, who was one of them.
He died 26 December 2011.

Chapter One

1936

When she arrived home from school, fourteen-year-old Susie Caddy found the dirty little house where she lived with Ma and her half-brother Erik empty. A note was pinned on the scullery door written in Ma's scrawled hand, ordering Susie to clean the front room. Susie sighed. She had to clean the front room every Wednesday for Ma's customers. Rolling up the sleeves of her well-worn cardigan, she went into the smelly room and made a start.

Susie was humming loudly to herself, so she didn't hear the door open. She never heard a sound, until she was seized from behind by a pair of hands that felt like steel. Their owner swung her around until she was facing him. He was a big brute of a man.

'Get your hands off me! Leave me alone! Leave me alone!' she yelled.

Susie struggled to free herself. The attacker's hands seized the front of her blouse, ripping it open with such force that she fell backwards to the floor. Moving quickly, he straddled her body and started tearing at the rest of the material, exposing her half-developed breasts. Then he lowered his head and started sucking and nipping her flesh. Eyes wide with terror, she let out a piercing scream. 'Leave me alone you, filthy beast!' she gasped.

She was silenced by a blow to her chin. Terror-stricken and with tears running down her face, she fought back, tossing her body from side to side, trying to get his bulk off her. Her punches to his body had no effect at all; he seemed to be made of stone and was deaf to her constant pleadings. Her struggles only seemed to make him more determined as he shifted his massive weight, pinning her more securely to the floor.

'You're not a bad-looking lass' he said. ''Bout time you were on the game like yer ma, earning a few quid. Now open yer legs and be nice to Uncle Bob or I'll give you something to yell and scream about.' He growled at her, an ugly threatening sound, which made her fear for her life.

He tried to cover her mouth with his, and Susie shuddered. The stench of alcohol from his breath made her gag, and her skin crawled as she felt his big beefy hands on her legs. In desperation she thrust her mouth close to his and bit down as hard as she could on his bottom lip. He let out a loud howl, followed by a fierce blow to her head which made stars float before her eyes. A sick feeling swept over her and foul-tasting bile coated her tongue. The punch almost knocked the fight out of her. She lay there shaking.

Then she gathered herself together. Gritting her teeth and drawing on a reserve of strength she had never known she had, she fought back against both the brute trying to rape her and the blackness that threatened to engulf her. Pounding his body with clenched fists, she screamed and screamed. He ignored her, covering her mouth with a beefy paw, which muffled her screams. She lunged again and again, finally managing to lift one of her legs to kick him. Each futile attempt to try and free herself was followed by a blow. His heavy rasping voice filled her ears as he forced himself upon her. She knew her bruised body was weakening.

Suddenly she gave an agonising scream. She had felt his hands part her thighs and his fingers enter her between her legs. She realised she couldn't escape, and with the realisation came more tears. She was fastened to the floor by his massive weight, and could barely breathe. She lay there desperately hoping that someone would stop this monster. She knew she was at his mercy, and nothing and no one could save her from what was about to happen.

A sharp, bitingly cold blast of air swept over Susie's bare thighs, the coldness and the memory of his fingers inside her making her shudder. Someone had opened the door. Her mother stood in the doorway.

'She's a mite young for you, Bob' she said.

The man grunted, rolled off Susie and got to his feet. 'I've been waitin' an age for you, Ethel, and this young 'un offered herself' he said. 'She ought to be on the game – old enough.' He sucked in gulps of air while buttoning his trousers.

'Next year mebbe. Now off yer go. I'll be with you in a tick' came her mother's reply. Bob harrumphed and headed towards Ma's bedroom.

Thank God her mother had come home. Susie brought her sore and aching body upright and pulled her knickers up and her skirt down. With shaking fingers she tied the remnants of her torn blouse together while brushing away tears from her eyes with the back of her hand.

'Thanks for saving me, Ma.'

Her mother advanced on her and gave Susie a smack across the face with the flat of her hand.

'What's that for?' Susie cupped her face and her eyes began to water.

'For trying to steal Uncle Bob offa me, that's what for.'

Standing motionless and staring at the grotesque face before her, Susie wondered if her mother had lost her mind. She had already lost most of her other assets, Susie reckoned. Ethel had been a good-looking woman before the gin bottle had taken its toll, but now the whites of her eyes were opaque and streaked with red while the bags underneath grew darker. Her nose was bulbous, and two hideous pouches hung from each side of her jaw. How could she take that devil's side? A closer look gave Susie the answer: Ma was drunk again.

'Well? Cat got yer tongue?'

'I didn't. I didn't steal anything. I hate him, and I hate you for…' Another stinging blow smashed into Susie's face.

'Don't you talk to me like, that, you little bitch. Yer uncle's money feeds 'n' keeps you. Truth to tell, you egged him on, didn't yer?'

Cupping her face with both hands, Susie tried to explain.

'No, I didn't. I was cleaning up as usual when he came up behind me and grabbed me. Look at my bruises.'

'Uncle Bob's rough, I'll give you that, but you asked for everything you got. Now get out of my sight.'

'I'll go, and I won't be back!' Susie cried out in anger, running past Ethel. She grabbed her one and only coat from a nail in the scullery and ran out through the yard, slamming the back door behind her. Her whole body was aching and sore from being repeatedly punched by the man and slapped around by her mother. 'I'll get out of this stinking place somehow,' Susie vowed through her tears.

She hated this dockside town where she'd been born. The smell, squalor, dirt and filth of the overcrowded hovels bred all kinds of diseases, with shared lavatories blocked up with sewage mixed with vomit from drunks in the gutter and the stench of bilge from the docks. The smell made the stomachs of grown men heave. Added to this were bedbugs, fleas and lice in hair and clothing, and the drunken sailors in street brawls. Susie hated living in this horrible place. The cloak of darkness brought more terror with night-time predators – women and children disappeared off the streets, never to be seen again – pickpockets who'd steal anything, and gangs of young lads armed with knives and looking for fights.

Susie loathed Water Street, where they lived, and hated her mother for going with dockers and sailors for money and spending it a large part of it on gin. Suzy and her half-brother Erik were left to look after themselves, mostly getting by on bread and dripping or occasionally fish and chips bought with the pennies they stole from Ma's money tin when she was blind drunk. Not only had Susie grown up without knowing who her father was, she didn't even know his name, and was marked as Ethel's bastard in the dockside slums. The prospect of remaining in Sunderland and ending up like her mother terrified Susie. Ma's words echoed in her ears: '*Next year, mebbe.*'

As she was hurrying to the top of the street, Susie suddenly stopped. Where in the world could she go? The only friend she had was her schoolteacher, Mrs Elliot, but she lived a bus ride away and Susie had no money; nor did she have any friends she could ask for help. In this town, if you were born a bastard you were at the mercy of school bullies, but a whore's bastard was treated much worse. All the kids at school spat at her whenever she passed them and cruelly taunted her by calling 'You're a baddy, Susie Caddy'. Other kids yelled 'You'll be a whore just like yer ma.' She loathed the kids in her class and kept well away from them.

Mrs Elliot was the only person who had shown her any kindness. She was nice and clean and smelled of peppermint, and she encouraged Susie to do well at school. Mrs Elliot gave her instructions on how to keep both herself and Erik clean and told her how to get rid of head lice and school sores. Susie had taken cash from the money tin that she had discovered under Ma's bed and bought lotions and creams to get rid of their lice and sores.

She admired her teacher and was a regular visitor at Mrs Elliot's house during school holidays. Susie loved being served tea on a clean table, with clean cups and plates and delicious homemade cakes. It was during these visits she learned that Mrs Elliot had been born in London, although her husband hailed from the north of England. Her teacher never mentioned her husband's relatives, nor did she speak of any children. In fact, she knew very little about her favourite teacher, except that her husband had died in the Great War. Mrs Elliot kept a picture of him in his uniform on her mantelshelf.

'Susie, Susie!'

Swinging around, she saw her seven-year-old half-brother running towards her in great excitement. 'I've got thruppence! I've got thruppence!' Erik stopped in his tracks and looked at his stepsister. There were black and blue bruises on her swollen face, her lip was bleeding and she had a big shiner. 'What's the matter? Is Ma drunk again?'

'It's nothing. Who gave you that?' she asked, eyeing the coin in his grubby hand. 'Did you pinch it?'

'No, I didn't. I got it off Uncle Bob. So there,' he said, poking out his tongue.

Susie glanced fearfully down the street and shivered inwardly. Ma insisted that her children call all the male visitors 'Uncle', and she wondered what Erik's reaction would be when he found out where and how Ma got her money.

'Lend us a penny, Erik. I'll pay you back, I promise,' she coaxed.

'I'm going to get some chips and then I'll give you a penny' he replied. 'C'mon, slowcoach, or you'll have the chip shop closing.'

Sitting on the bus licking her fingers, Susie finished the

last of the chips Erik had given her. The little devil wanted her to pay back the penny he had given her for her bus fare plus a penny interest. She would have to pay him back somehow or she would never hear the end of it. Erik's father had been a Swedish sailor in port for a night or two, just as Susie's father had been, only he had been Spanish and his ship had been a freighter called the *Cadiz*. She had gleaned this information only a few months before, when Ethel had rambled on in a drunken stupor.

She could not count the number of times she and Erik had arrived home from Saturday night markets to find Ma drunk on the scullery floor clutching an empty gin bottle. She would throw a blanket over her while Erik threw the bottle on the pile in the backyard. Then they would make their own meal, usually bread and dripping washed down with a mug of weak tea or hot water if there was no tea. If there was no bread they ate the fruit they had pinched from a barrow at the market. After playing Crown and Anchor, a dice game given to them by one of the sailors who visited Ma, they would go to bed, leaving their drunken mother snoring her head off.

When Ma had a man to visit, she would send Susie and Erik outside to play, or if it was dark they were ordered to bed, where they would lie on the bug-infested mattress listening to Ma's bed springs twanging and grunts and groans coming from her room. Sleeping next door to her mother's bedroom left Susie with precious few illusions about what happened between a man and a woman. To get away from the terrible bedroom noises, Susie would stick her fingers in her ears and escaped into her dream world. It was always the same dream: belonging to a nice family, with a mother who was kind and cooked beautiful pies and cakes and kept a clean house. Susie longed to have a mother and father who would take her to the country for picnics, or perhaps on a seaside holiday. In the festive season, they would all sing carols around a fir tree with lots of flickering candles, and on Christmas Day they would eat roast turkey, or goose, with a huge plum pudding. But most of all, Susie wanted to be surrounded by nice, clean, happy people.

Stepping down from the bus, she almost slipped on the wet pavement. The light rain which had started earlier now poured down. Her thin shoes, which she had constantly repaired with pieces of cardboard, looked ready for the rag and bone man, but they were all she had.

Pulling her coat high over her head, she began to run. Mrs Elliot's house was just off High Street. In her haste and because of her leaky shoes she slipped and slid all the way there. Opening the wooden gate that surrounded the small garden of the semi-detached house, She hurried up the path. She had no idea what her teacher would say, or even if she would invite her in. Feeling a little nervous, she knocked gently on the door and sighed. Mrs Elliot was her only hope.

'Who's there?' a familiar voice enquired.

'It's Susie Caddy.'

Opening the door wider, Mrs Elliot cried, 'Why, you're wet through, lass.' Margaret Elliot knew instantly that the girl was in trouble. 'Come in, take off your coat and I'll dry it in front of the fire' she said. Margaret prattled on, observing that the girl had several bruises and a split lip as well as a black eye. She sighed sadly; her young pupil had been beaten again. Noticing the girl's torn blouse, she produced one of her own for Susie to wear while she got busy with the salve.

Sitting back in a chair next to a small table, now warm and dry, Susie looked over at the woman she most admired. She was standing next to the fire, toasting bread on a long pronged fork and passing the cooked slices to Susie, who was busy spreading the warm toast with butter and jam.

After eating three slices of toast and two pieces of fruitcake with hot tea, Susie smiled. 'That's the best I've had to eat since the last time I was here' she said. 'Did you make the fruit cake, Mrs Elliot?' Susie hesitated, and when she received no answer she added, 'S'pose I'd better tell you why I've come.'

Margaret turned and looked into Susie's eyes, reading some of the anguish the girl was feeling. 'Yes, I baked the cake and I'm glad you like it,' she said, smiling at the bruised girl. 'Take your time, Susie, and only when you feel at ease tell me what happened.'

This was not the first time, Margaret reflected, that the young girl had been beaten by the mother. There had been other times when Susie's mother had staggered home drunk and lashed out at her. She also knew that there was very little food in the Caddys' house, and Susie often went hungry as her mother spent the money she made from her sordid trade in the pub. But Ethel Caddy had gone too far this time, Margaret decided, seeing the terrible bruising on the girl's face, neck, arms and legs.

Susie drew in a deep breath. 'I was cleaning the front room when a man came in and grabbed me. I knew he had been drinking 'cos I could smell his breath as soon as he swung me around to face him. I told him to leave me alone and he grabbed me by the collar of my blouse. I ended up on the floor with him on top of me.' Tears rolled down her cheeks. 'It was awful, Mrs Elliot, awful!'

Margaret handed her a clean handkerchief. 'I can well imagine how terrible it was, lass. Please continue.'

'Well, he tore open my blouse and started licking and biting my chest. The more I struggled, the worse he got. He spread my legs apart, then he put his hand up my skirt and pulled my knickers down and stuck his fingers in my private place. Then Ma came in and he stopped, but you'll never believe this, Mrs Elliot, he said I'd led him on, and Ma took his side and smacked me.'

Margaret could believe that, and more. The dockside area on the other side of town was a dirty little slum where the down-and-outs lived, scraping a living any way they could. Ethel Caddy was well known in the pubs along the dockside streets. Margaret had heard the gossip about her from the women's group at the church hall where she helped out at weekends. The volunteers gave out good quality hand-me-downs and food to the poor, but never money, as it was always squandered in the pub, rather than on the neglected children.

'I have to get away from here' Susie said through shimmering tears.

'But where will you go, lass? Where will you live?'

Susie flung herself out of her seat. Kneeling down in front of her teacher's chair, she begged, 'Please help me to get to London, Mrs Elliot. I can find work there, and in London nobody will know about Ma.'

'Perhaps if I talk to your mother and…'

Sobbing, Susie interrupted her teacher, 'I can't go back there. I can't! I just can't! I'll end up just like her. I know I will. All the kids in class say so. Ma's going to send me to the docks, to bring sailors home, maybe next year. Honestly, that's what she said. You're the only person who can help me. Please, Mrs Elliot, please!' she begged, tears falling down her cheeks and washing away the salve which Margaret had gently applied earlier to the girl's cuts and bruises.

Studying the forlorn girl who squatted tearfully before her, Margaret thought how cruel the world was. She would have given anything to have had a child, but her husband, Jack, had volunteered for the Northumberland Fusiliers two months after their marriage in 1916 and had been killed six weeks after arriving at the front.

Margaret mentally shook herself and focused her attention on the girl kneeling before her. In a year or so, this poor girl would be sold to drunken sailors and dockworkers by her mother. Her rich dark curls would be drab and matted, and her skin would be pockmarked. She might even have some teeth missing. Margaret guessed

Ethel Caddy knew how to handle men, but a young girl like Susie would not and she would be pushed around and probably beaten. Margaret had made up her mind to help. How could she leave this unfortunate girl to the mercies of a gin-swigging mother who would use her daughter's youth and profit by selling her to men?

She was convinced that in time and with proper care, Susie's lovely complexion would heal. Her eyes of deep violet complemented the shoulder-length hair that curled naturally around her face. Although she was a trifle small and painfully thin, Margaret knew that with regular, nourishing meals she would grow and fill out. With her Mediterranean hair colouring and skin like an English rose, Margaret did not doubt that this sad, unfortunate girl would soon be a pretty young woman. Men would adore her, and with her looks she might just find a man who would cherish her. Margaret was in no doubt that if she refused to help the girl, Susie would be passed from one man to another and would inevitably end up like her drunken mother.

After delicate questioning, Margaret was relieved to find that the brute had not penetrated the young girl, but she had been manhandled and roughly mauled. She knew she could not make Susie go home.

'Please dry your eyes,' she said gently, offering the teary young girl another handkerchief. 'I will help you.'

'You're the best teacher in the whole world,' Susie cried, hugging her.

'First, sit in your chair and let me explain,' Margaret

ordered, in her usual schoolteacher manner. Susie instantly obeyed and sat very still with an expectant look on her face.

'I have an old school friend who lives with her husband in London. She has a cake shop in Fulham Road, and I'm going to write and ask if you can help in the shop. Her husband works in an insurance office in the city. I'm sure that if my friend thinks you can be of some assistance she will let me know by return mail. However, she may not be able to give you lodgings, so…'

'I'll be…'

'Susie, it is rude to interrupt when someone is speaking. Please stop sniffing and use the handkerchief I gave you. You will have to learn this and much more if you want to work in a shop, but far more important, you will have to be polite to the customers. As I was saying, I will ask my friend if she knows of a suitable boarding house nearby. All this will only come to pass if she has some work for you or if she knows of a reputable shopkeeper who has a vacancy. We shall wait and see. However, while we await her reply you can remain here with me and sleep in the spare bedroom. So take that awful frown off your face and please stop sucking your bottom lip. You do not have to return home. I doubt very much that your mother will report you missing to the local constabulary.'

Margaret took a deep breath and pressed on. 'And as it is almost Easter and you are of an age, I see no reason why you cannot leave school. Perhaps working in a cake shop you may in time meet a nice man and marry. So I will help you to go to London to find a better life.'

Susie waited until she knew her teacher had finished speaking before saying, 'I promise never to interrupt again. Mrs Elliot, will you please tell me some more about your friend and her cake shop?'

Margaret relaxed in the chair with a faraway look in her eyes as she started to speak about her school days in London.

'Miriam Carter and I were best friends at Clementine College for young ladies. Her name in those days was Miss Miriam Blore. She was never a studious girl, but she had a flare for cookery and far outshone any of the other girls. The cake we have just eaten is one of her recipes. Miriam has a brother and a sister, both of whom are in business. The brother, Percy Blore, owns three butchers' shops and their sister, Grace, owns a small hotel called the Carrington, where I understand she has several guest rooms and serves meals. I used to know the Blore family quite well, but I have not been to London for many years and have lost touch with them, except my dear friend Miriam. She is a genius at making cakes and tarts, and her little shop serves Londoners of every kind and even some of the gentry, too. People travel miles for her strawberry and gooseberry tarts. Why, she was telling me in her last letter, that she had made some tarts for a big reception and Lady So-and-So - I can't remember the name – had sent a note to the shop saying how exquisite the strawberry tarts had been. Lady, er...' Margaret hesitated.

'Lady So-and-So,' Susie supplied. Margaret started laughing and Susie joined in.

After a hot bath Susie snuggled down between the crisp white sheets. She knew there would be no bugs in Mrs Elliot's bedding. Unable to sleep, she tossed and turned, not because of her painful bruises, but because she was thinking of ladies and gentlemen in London eating delicate strawberry tarts. She promised herself that one day she would be a lady and serve strawberry tarts at a reception. Mentally, she reminded herself to ask Mrs Elliot what a reception was. Susie fell asleep.

Two things happened over the following weeks to delight Susie. For her birthday Mrs Elliot bought her a new black woollen coat, shoes, stockings and matching hat and gloves, and a letter from London arrived offering Susie a place to stay and work in the cake shop. This news sent her dancing around the room. She had never had new clothes before, only hand-me-downs from the church. Susie hugged Mrs Elliot to thank her for the gift, but the best present of all was the promise of living in London.

Margaret lectured her pupil on how to behave, especially when serving customers in a shop. Susie's table manners improved under Mrs Elliot's critical eye. She was told not to slouch, speak loudly or use slang words. She was taught how to tell the difference between polite gentlemen and rough men. Mrs Elliot even advised Susie on aspects of personal hygiene that every woman should know, and bought her both a toothbrush and a nail-file and instructed her on their use. 'Respect your body and nurture it!' she commanded. Susie was glad that the tell-tale bruises had faded and the cut lip was healing nicely.

She begged Mrs Elliot not to tell her friend Miriam about her mother or the beatings.

The day she was catching the train to London, Mrs Elliot gave Susie a slip of paper with a name on it. 'This lady teaches deportment, elocution and healthy skin procedures', she told her. 'You may want to use some of the money Miriam pays you to further improve yourself.'

After picking up some sandwiches and fruitcake, they set off to catch the bus that would take them to Durham to connect with the London train. It was gloomy and rainy when they arrived at the station, with Susie clutching a small brown suitcase that Mrs Elliot had given her, and her benefactor carrying a small box of provisions for the journey.

'Miriam and her husband Cyril will meet the train at Kings Cross and take you to Fulham' she said. 'Do not go wandering around if the train arrives early. Do not forget to write to me and tell me how you get on in London, as I will be anxious until I hear from you. And please give Miriam and Cyril my fond regards.'

Margaret Elliot was having difficulty holding back her tears. Over the last few weeks she had come to love this girl. She would miss the sound of her soft laughter around the house, and the evenings they spent together reading stories and poems or teaching the young girl needlework and showing her how to make Miriam's famous fruit cake. Margaret had tried to prepare the girl as she would her own daughter.

After settling her favourite pupil in an empty

compartment, she gave Susie an old purse, containing some coins and the train ticket.

'This money will see you through the next week, or until you receive a wage from Miriam' she said. She gave Susie a swift peck on the cheek, but could no longer hold back the tears. She left the train wiping her eyes, just as the guard was blowing his whistle.

Susie took tuppence out of the purse and leaned out of the window. 'Please, Mrs Elliott, can you give this to Erik, my stepbrother, when he joins your class after Easter?' she called. As the train started to move she waved and blew Mrs Elliot a kiss, leaving a tearful teacher behind. But Susie did not shed a tear as the train slowly inched its way out of the station; she was far too excited to cry. Susie Caddy was on her way to London.

Chapter Two

When the train stopped at York, Susie hurried along the platform to buy a cup of tea from one of the British Rail trolley ladies. She was informed as she waited for the hot beverage to be poured that tea ladies were employed at every mainline station throughout the British Isles. Returning to her carriage after being instructed on the best way to brew tea, Susie sipped the hot liquid and had sunk her teeth into a piece of fruit cake when the carriage door opened and a tall, lanky boy in a smart school uniform entered.

'You can't come in here, this is a private carriage,' she mumbled through a mouthful of cake.

'Oh, who says?' he asked, sitting down opposite her.

'My auntie chose this carriage for me. I'm going to London,' she replied, trying to adopt Mrs Elliott's tone and hoping to impress the skinny boy seated before her. His eyebrows shot up and a smile crept across his face, as if he knew she was exaggerating.

'So who's your illustrious aunt, then? The Queen of Sheba?'

'She's a very important schoolteacher, and rich, too' Susie stated in a matter-of-fact tone, reminding herself to call her teacher 'aunt' rather than auntie.

'I'll bet she smells minty, wears horned-rim specs and tweed skirts, and is very prim and proper. And if your aunt is so rich, why are you travelling second class? Don't you know first class is far superior?'

Always quick on the uptake, she countered with, 'There was no room left in first class, so my aunt booked this carriage for me.'

Suddenly the train lurched forward, throwing both of them off-balance and spilling Suzy's tea. She was amazed; he had described Mrs Elliot to a T. His comment about first-class and second-class seats on trains was interesting, too, and she stored the information away.

'I'm in first class and there are heaps of empty seats' he said. 'I'll take you and show you, if you don't believe me.'

'Did you get on the train at York?' she asked, changing the subject. She didn't want to leave her suitcase in the carriage rack and follow him. Mrs Elliot had warned her about thieves and unattended luggage.

'No, Inverness. Changed at Edinburgh. I board at Gordounston.'

'You do what?'

'That's the school I go to. We play lots of sports. I'm in the cricket team and my friend Philip is the captain. He's a Greek prince, you know.'

No, she didn't know nor did she care, but she was interested to hear about his school. 'Do you travel to Scotland every day?' she asked.

He rolled his eyes at the ceiling of the carriage. 'What a country girl you are! I couldn't take the train to Scotland every day. My home is in Kent. We a have a town house in London too. Mummy is extremely busy with charity work, and Papa travels abroad for the government. They are too busy to look after me, so I board.' Her puzzled frown caused him to add, 'That means I sleep at school.'

Susie shifted awkwardly in her seat. Mrs Elliott had not told her that some people have two houses or that children could sleep at school. There were still lots of things she wanted to know.

'Please tell me about yourself and your family' she asked. 'Is your father rich? I mean your Papa?' Her schoolteacher had told her that most people measure happiness by how much money they have, and this boy looked very happy.

'Not, rich, or poor, I really don't know how much money my family have. As for me, I suppose when I finish my schooling I will do military training. Our family have been enrolling at Sandhurst for years – tradition, you know. After my passing out I will be posted abroad for several years. Then perhaps I will get married and raise some little perishers. That's what Papa calls children. Although, personally, I would like to be an MP like my grandfather.'

'A what?'

'A Member of Parliament. Do I have to repeat myself all the time?'

Susie ignored his remark. 'Sounds like you have your life planned' she commented.

'I haven't. My parents have. Now it's your turn to tell me about your family.'

'I have no family, only my aunt.' The lies rolled off her tongue effortlessly.

'Are your parents dead?'

She nodded. 'They died when I was a baby, and my aunt looked after me. My father was an officer in the Spanish Navy and my mother was an English beauty.'

Susie sighed. She was slowly becoming an accomplished liar, but she would do and say anything to be treated politely and with respect.

'It must have been difficult growing up without parents. Why are you leaving your aunt? What is your name? How old are you? Why are you going to London?'

He was firing question at her like darts. Susie's mind started racing to find plausible answers. 'My aunt can't look after me any more, so I'm going to stay with a family friend and work in their cake shop. That's why I'm going to London. My aunt once told me that a lady never reveals her age to anyone. So I'm not going to tell you how old I am. I am called Susie Caddy, but I don't like it.' She paused. 'The kids at school always make fun of me and my name. My father was an officer in the Spanish Navy and his ship was called the *Cadiz*.' That was what Ethel had led her to believe.

'If you don't like your name then change it. My grandfather always said if one does not like the situation, then one should alter it.'

She had absolutely no idea what he was talking about,

and asked shyly, 'What would you do if you disliked your name?'

'We are talking about your name, not mine. Susie, I suspect, is short for Susan, but if you really want my advice I would stick with Susie. It suits you. If you don't like your surname, change that too.'

'I do like the sound of Susan better. Could I use Cadiz for my surname? That sounds really nice. Susan Cadiz! Can you call me that?

'Yes, if you like. Susan, you can do whatever you want. It's a free country.'

'What's your name, and how old are you?' she inquired.

'Harry Fortescue, and I'm almost seventeen. Chaps like me are not concerned with keeping our age a secret.' He laughed aloud, and it was so infectious that she laughed, too.

'You know, for a pipsqueak you have the most unusual colour of eyes' he said. 'Are they blue or violet?' He leaned forward in his seat and peered into her eyes as if he were examining an insect. 'Yes, they are definitely violet. They should have named you Viola.'

'Viola? Who's that?'

'It's from Shakespeare's *Twelfth Night*. Great show.'

She would have to try and see this show in London. Harry seemed a nice boy, well-dressed and well-mannered, even a little rude at times. Nobody had ever called her a pipsqueak before. It sounded nice to her ears, and she made a mental note to find out what it meant.

'Would you like a piece of my aunt's fruit cake?' she asked him.

'Rather! I'll bet it's heaps better than the one our cook bakes.'

'Your mother doesn't cook for you?'

'Good lord! Mother, in the kitchen! Not, a chance. We employ a cook. She's been with us for years.'

Susan was fascinated listening to his accent, and she tucked away in her mind his manner of speaking. She just had to keep him talking to try and commit to memory the rhythm and flow of his lovely voice. They talked non-stop for over an hour, Susan asking the questions and Harry supplying the answers. Susan wanted to know everything, from his favourite subject at school to what he ate for breakfast.

Eventually she had a mental picture of what his life was like, and she had to admit to herself that it was very different from her own. He lived a veritable prince's life, while hers had been lower than that of a pauper.

'Soused herrings or poached kidneys for breakfast, fruit cake for elevenses, muffins and honey for afternoon tea, all served by housemaids. Fresh salmon for luncheon and roast baron of beef for dinner with French wine,' he told her.

'Elevenses?'

'Mid-morning tea.'

She nodded. 'Do you have…'

Suddenly the carriage door opened, revealing a middle-aged man in a striped suit and homburg hat, looking anything but pleased, Susan thought, as he addressed Harry.

'So this is where you have been hiding, Master Harry!'

he said. 'I have been looking all through the train for you. Now please come back to your seat and study your Latin verbs.'

Harry gave a deep sigh and stood up. 'Harper, this young lady is travelling alone to London, and I've been keeping her company. May I introduce Miss Cadiz to you? Susan, this is Mr Harper, my travelling companion and tutor.' Harry winked at her. Mr Harper removed his hat, tweaked his necktie and gave Susan - a weak smile.

After Harry and his tutor had left, Susan sat back and closed her eyes. She had never been called a lady before. Remembering all the things he had told her about his family, she just knew she was going to enjoy her new life in London. Harry Fortescue was the second nicest person she had ever met, Mrs Elliot being the first. She hadn't even minded when he had joked that she was dumb, but she vowed she would not remain dumb for long; she would visit the elocution school that Mrs Elliott had recommended to improve herself, and as soon as she had some money she would buy a dictionary. 'Susan Cadiz' she whispered to herself. It sounded very grown up.

At the next station the carriage filled with other passengers. Some of them gave her quick looks and then studiously ignored her, but one or two produced friendly smiles. She glanced around the compartment, trying mentally to slot her travelling companions into life's little boxes, as Mrs Elliot called them. A heavily-built man with a pleasant face, doing the newspaper crossword, chewed the end of his pencil – a businessman, perhaps. A soldier was reading a comic called 'Tom Mix Rides Again'. An elderly woman was furiously clacking knitting needles – maybe a cardigan for her grandchild – while a younger woman was writing in a book, her pen rapidly skipping across the page.

Susan idly wondered why these people were travelling to London. Surely they could not all be starting a new life, as she was. Perhaps they were visiting family or taking a holiday – or just enjoyed train rides.

She dropped her eyes when the older woman looked up from her knitting; Mrs Elliot had told her it was rude to stare. Susan quickly turned to look out at the growing darkness, and to her surprise found that the interior of the carriage was reflected in the dark window. Now she could stare at them without being rude.

As the train was entering Kings Cross Station she stood up, eager to get her first glimpse of London, and opened the carriage window, much to the annoyance of the other passengers. As a burst of smoke filled the carriage, she turned to face them.

'I'm sorry' she said, 'I wanted to see the city. This is my first visit to London.'

'There's not much to see from here, lass, except smoke and steam,' replied the man who had been solving the crossword puzzle. Leaning past Susan, he closed the window.

As the train slowly rolled along the platform and came to a halt, screeching wheels and belching steam mingled with noises of slamming carriage doors, rattling railway couplings and people's voices splitting the air. Susan stepped down from the train and stood transfixed. The hectic pace of station porters ferrying luggage and the hustle and bustle of people arriving and departing captured her attention. Never had she seen or heard anything like this before. People hugged and kissed each other as they met or exchanged tearful farewells. Well-dressed men and fashionable ladies mixed with people in ill-fitting coats and unpolished shoes. There were women with heavy baskets selling flowers, young lads hawking the evening edition and tea ladies pushing trolleys with everything from sandwiches and pies to iced buns and cakes. The whole place was alive with activity. It was so exciting. She stayed riveted to a large Gothic pillar, where she watched and waited with her small brown suitcase at her feet.

'Is your name Susie?' a smartly dressed middle-aged woman asked.

'Yes, yes, Susan really' she replied.

'Lord be praised, Cyril, I've found her!' the woman called out to a thin-looking man who was searching the empty carriages of the train. Then she turned to the girl. 'My name is Miriam, and my husband is Cyril. What would you have us call you – Susie or Susan?'

'I like Susan.'

'If you prefer Susan, then so be it. Cyril has left the car out front. My brother Percy let us borrow it – so much more convenient than catching the tube.' She didn't wait for a reply. 'Ah, there you are, lovey. Please take Susan's suitcase to the car. Now, where was I? Oh, yes, the reason we are a bit late. The weather, my dear, has been dreadful. I can't remember when it has rained so much. Buckets and buckets we've had!'

Susan wondered if Cyril ever got a word in, but Miriam was so very homely and bubbly she found it hard not to like her. If she had to describe what a mother should be like, she would pick cheerful, chatty Miriam.

Later when she was alone in her room she gazed out across London from the small attic window, and reflected upon the most exciting day of her life: her first train journey, meeting the tall and charming Harry, her first car ride, sharing a light supper with a clean tablecloth and beautiful china, and tasting one of Miriam's famous fruit tarts. And changing her name. Miriam called her husband 'lovey' and Cyril called his wife 'deary.' It pleased Susan to see them enjoying themselves and making little jokes to each other. They were well matched, and so happy that it made Susan feel all warm and fuzzy. She wondered if one day she would meet a gentleman like Cyril.

Miriam had also given her the grand tour, both upstairs and downstairs. Susan tried to remember all she had seen. On the ground floor was the shop, with a glass counter and a large display window. Next door was the shop kitchen and two of the largest ovens Susan had ever seen, while out back was a small paved yard, which contained a lavatory, a clothesline and a storage shed. Above the cake shop Miriam and Cyril had their private rooms: a sitting room, a kitchenette, a small bathroom and the main bedroom.

Susan was given the attic at the top of the building. She looked around the room at the pretty floral wallpaper. A single bed with a cream bedspread and matching curtains blended well with the dark furniture. A table with a mirror and a wardrobe were the only other pieces in the room. A picture graced either side of a small fireplace. One was of Miriam's birthplace, Aylesbury in Buckinghamshire, where the Blore family came from, and the other was of Shoreham-by-Sea, where Cyril had been born. Miriam had explained every detail, including the paintings.

The Blores seemed to be well off. They had a farm in Aylesbury, three butchers' shops, a small hotel and a very popular cake shop in London, all owned by one brother and two younger sisters.

Percy Blore and his wife, Tess, had two sons. Michael managed one of the shops, while Malcolm was still at school. Percy's sister, Grace, owned the Carrington Hotel with her husband, Donald Meadows. June, their sixteen year-old daughter, attended secretarial college. Susan had learned all this from Miriam within a few hours of arriving.

Miriam also informed Susan that she would meet the entire family on Sunday at the Carrington, as the family were getting together to celebrate Michael Blore's coming of age. It was so thrilling to be included in the family celebration: she could hardly contain herself. Perhaps her lifelong dream of belonging to a nice family was finally coming true.

On the Sunday just as dawn was breaking Susan leapt out of bed, too excited to sleep any longer. Quickly making her bed, she hurried to the bathroom to clean her teeth and wash herself, as Mrs Elliot had instructed. Opening a jar of face cream she had been given as a farewell gift, she gently rubbed some into her face, neck and hands and crept back to her room, hoping she hadn't disturbed Miriam and Cyril, whose bedroom was next to the bathroom.

Wanting to look her best, she took a red and black checked dress and a black cardigan from the wardrobe and spread them on her bed. They had been Mrs Elliot's, but once they got busy with a needle and thread they fitted, although the woollen cardigan still hung a little loose on her, even with a few tucks here and there. Mrs Elliot told her that in a few months she would fill out and the clothes would look much better.

With a new hairbrush – also a parting gift – Susan brushed her locks twenty times, as Mrs Elliot had instructed. It would make her hair shiny; it also caused it to curl riotously. Not to be deterred, she took a piece of black ribbon, pulled her curls back from her face and tied them into a big bow at the nape of her neck. Looking at her reflection in the small mirror, she was quite pleased with what she saw.

Sitting on the bed quietly reading a book, she waited until Miriam called her for breakfast, although she didn't know how on earth she was going to eat anything, as butterflies filled her stomach. She just couldn't wait to meet all the family and see inside a hotel.

She was not disappointed when, along with Miriam and Cyril, they arrived at the Carrington and were shown upstairs to Grace and Donald's private rooms. The carpeted staircase was very grand indeed and reinforced Susan's notion that the Blore family were richer than Mrs Elliott. A long polished table with silver cutlery and glistening glassware occupied the centre of the room. A bowl of spiky yellow chrysanthemums sat in the middle of the table and matched the embroidered cotton napkins which decorated each place setting. Susan had first discovered table napkins at Mrs Elliott's, then at Miriam and Cyril's, and now at Grace and Donald's. Well-off people, she decided, must always use napkins.

'Percy and Tess haven't arrived yet,' Grace informed Miriam and Cyril. 'I expect they're having trouble getting Michael out of bed. He went up the West End last night with his mates celebrating and most likely didn't get home till the wee small hours.'

'This is Susan Cadiz' Miriam cut in, 'a friend of Margaret Elliott. You remember Margaret, don't you? I went to school with her.' After introductions had been made, Donald departed, taking Cyril with him to have a beer in the bar downstairs and leaving the women to 'chinwag', as Donald called it.

'June has gone to the pony club' Grace continued. 'She'll be back in time to join in the celebrations. Did you bring the birthday cake?'

Miriam nodded. 'The hotel seemed very busy as we came upstairs.'

While the two women were chatting, Susan perched on a chair nearby, gazing around the room and barely listening. The highly-polished furniture and patterned floor rugs blended well with the fringed reading lamps. Delicate ornaments and family photographs were displayed on a shiny side table near a beautiful piano, which stood along the far wall. Miriam had told Susan that the family gathered around it on special occasions to sing songs. It was the loveliest room she had ever seen, and much larger than Miriam's dining room above the shop. She would like to belong to this happy family and join them at their gatherings with lively singalongs around the piano. It was obvious to Susan that this family enjoyed each other's company.

Voices on the stairs interrupted her thoughts, making her aware that the rest of the family had arrived. Tess came into the room first, followed by a spotty boy who could not have been more than thirteen. June, the sixteen-year-old daughter of Grace and Donald, was the last to enter and the first to speak.

'I met Aunt Tess getting out of a taxi. Daddy, Uncle Percy and Uncle Cyril are giving the birthday boy a tot of whisky in the bar, they'll join us shortly.' June gave Susan a questioning look and then threw herself into one of the armchairs, dangling a booted leg over the armrest. 'I'm starving, what's for lunch?' she asked.

'We are having roast beef and Yorkshire pudding, and we'll be sitting down to eat as soon as the men can tear themselves from the bar,' Grace informed her daughter.

'Now, I do think you ought to change out of those riding clothes.'

Giving a heavy sigh, June ignored her mother and turned to Susan. 'So, you're the girl employed to work in Aunt Mim's shop, are you?'

'Yes, I am,' she answered timidly.

'Have you been up the West End to see a show yet?' June didn't wait for an answer. 'There's lots to see and do. I have an idea, let's both go and see a musical. I'll ask Daddy to get tickets. Now, what show would you most like to see?'

'Shakespeare's Twelfth Night show, please.'

June laughed. 'Twelfth Night is not a musical!' she said. 'It's a boring old play. Where did you hear about Shakespearean musicals?'

'Someone on the train to London told me,' she ventured, sucking her bottom lip.

'Well, they were either pulling your leg, or maybe they're as dumb as you.'

Before Susan could answer, Grace intervened.

'June, mind your manners. And for the last time, go and change from those riding clothes.'

'I wasn't doing anything,' June protested.

'Yeah, she wasn't.' Malcolm, the spotty boy, defended his cousin. 'Do you think Dad will help me with my crystal radio set?'

'June, go and change immediately. As for you, Malcolm, why don't you go downstairs and ask your father about your radio? And while you're there, find out how much longer the men are going to be.' Grace rolled her eyes as June and Malcolm slouched out of the room.

Unclenching her teeth, Susan eased the pressure in her mouth, wondering how often she would have to meet these two. She turned to study the women as they resumed their conversation. Tess Blore looked to be in her mid-forties. Her dark hair was sprinkled with strands of silver-grey, highlighting her smooth olive complexion and dark brown eyes. She was a heavily-built woman, a perfect example of a butcher's wife. In contrast, Grace was slim and petite, with thick blond hair tied in a bun. She was the exact double of her older sister Miriam, except that Grace couldn't cook at all and relied on the staff she employed in the hotel to do all the cooking while her brother, Percy, ordered the supplies. The Carrington also served afternoon tea in the hotel dining room and sold Miriam's delicious cakes and tarts. It really was a family affair.

'I think those Germans are up to something,' Percy addressed his brothers-in-law. 'Why, only the other day I was speaking to a carrier from Smithfield market and he was telling me that the Germans have marched into the demilitarised zone that was set up at Versallys after the war to end all wars.'

'Dad, it's called Versailles, not Versallys' said his son Malcolm.

'I can't pronounce those French words, but you know what I mean, Donald. Don't you?'

'It's just sabre rattling, Percy,' Donald replied after

swallowing some wine and placing his glass back on the table. 'We gave them what for in the Great War, and they won't tangle with us again.'

'I agree,' Cyril added, supporting Donald.

Percy shook his head and methodically cut a piece of beef, which he placed at the side of his plate. He prepared a small slice of potato, a little serving of vegetables, a piece of Yorkshire pudding, some gravy and a dip of horseradish sauce. Then he gathered his selection onto his fork and popped it into his mouth. Resting his knife and fork on his plate, he sat back in his chair, relishing the food.

Susan watched him, mesmerised. This man turned eating into an art form as he slowly savoured each and every mouthful. Everyone she knew up north gulped his or her food – everyone, that is, except Mrs Elliott.

'It's not the Germans I'm worried about,' Tess chimed in, 'but that awful American, Mrs Simpson, who wants to marry our king.'

The conversation stopped and everyone looked at Tess. Then Malcolm asked, 'Why can't the King marry who he wants?'

'Well, lad, she's been married before, and neither the church nor the government will tolerate a divorced woman on the throne,' Percy informed his son.

'So,' June cut in, 'the poor King can't marry the one he loves, and he has to please the government and the church. It's unfair. I wouldn't do it, and neither should the King have to.'

'Yes, we all know what you'd do, June, but you're not a

royal, and if you were, you'd have to do what you were damn well told.'

'Percy, no swearing in front of the children, please,' Tess admonished her husband.

'If we don't have to worry about Hitler, Uncle Cyril, can we fight Mussolini instead?' Malcolm asked.

'Perhaps.'

'Cor, wouldn't that be great! Will you go and fight, Michael?'

'The only fighting I'll be doing, little brother, is scrapping with June for another slice of roast beef.'

'The cook has left the beef and gravy keeping warm in the oven. Please help yourselves,' Grace instructed with a smile. She was delighted; the birthday party was turning out just as she had planned.

June stood up first and raced towards the kitchen at the end of the hallway. 'You won't beat me, cousin.'

Susan had only been half-listening to the conversation around the table, as she was preoccupied in observing the birthday boy. At twenty-one, he was most attractive, with hazel eyes and sandy hair parted on the left and brushed to one side, and a pencil-thin moustache which added to his good looks. He wore a magnificent jacket of houndstooth check and a dark-green cravat.

When he caught her studying him, she quickly looked away. Suddenly, he stood up, collected his plate and followed June. A few minutes later, Susan excused herself and headed for the bathroom, but she pulled up short when she heard her name coming from the kitchen.

'What do think of Susan?' a female voice questioned.

'She looks like a skinny little scarecrow,' came the reply, and loud female giggles followed. 'And she's as dumb as anything – Shakespearean musicals, I ask you! And her hair, Michael, tied back with that awful ribbon and those clothes. Did you get a look at her clothes? She really needs to learn how to dress properly. Then she just might find a boyfriend.'

'No man in his right mind would want her.'

More giggles followed. Then June asked, 'What kind of name is Cadiz?'

'I dunno.' Michael said. 'The only Cadiz I've heard of is a sleazy little town somewhere in Spain. Let's face it, I don't think my Hollywood idol Susan Hayward has anything to worry about from Susan Cadiz. There's just no comparison.' More laughter followed.

Susan had heard enough. She hurried into the bathroom to take a long look at herself in the mirror. She pulled the ribbon from her hair and stuffed it into her cardigan pocket. With a deep frown, she clenched her teeth until her jaws ached and vowed that one day they would swallow their hateful words. In fact, the whole Blore family needed to learn some manners. Even Percy Blore, head of the family, had only acknowledged her with a mere nod of his head when Miriam made the introductions. Then he had totally ignored her throughout the meal. June was a horror, the youngest son, Malcolm, was rude, and no words could describe the birthday boy. Only Miriam and Cyril had showed any kindness towards her.

This had been the first and the worst birthday party she had ever been to. Tossing her hair back, she determined that no one would see just how unhappy she was. With a thin smile on her face, she endured the rest of the birthday celebrations, refusing a small glass of champàgne to toast Michael and only nibbling at a slice of birthday cake placed in front of her. She did not congratulate the birthday boy on reaching his maturity, nor did she join in the singing around the piano. She sat there meek and mute, watching this rich family enjoying their rich lifestyle.

Chapter Three

Susan hummed softly as she eagerly decorated cakes and placed them on tiered stands, ready for display in the shop window. It had been more than two years since she had arrived in London. Not only did she serve customers, she now decorated cakes and tarts. The deportment academy Mrs Elliot had suggested was now in the hands of Mrs Firbank's daughter, Louisa. When Susan was not working in the shop or at the academy, she was in the library or walking around the streets of London, gazing longingly in shop windows in Bond and Regent Street. She loved the tiny lanes and alleys, which hid quaint shops, old taverns and London's marketplaces which blended in well with the modern buildings. Susan was slowly falling in love with this city. She was also becoming very friendly with Louisa and some of the girls enrolled in the class, occasionally joining them on outings to the theatre or spending evenings with Louisa talking about beauty and fashion.

Susan flatly refused every invitation to accompany Miriam and Cyril to Blore family gatherings. She could not forget how unfriendly and unwelcoming the family had been, especially Michael and June, who had gossiped so spitefully about her. In fact, the whole family had paid her scant regard, all except Miriam and Cyril, who always treated her as part of their family. She loved them both dearly.

Under Louisa Firbank's guidance, Susan had blossomed into a smartly-dressed young woman. Her mentor had bought her a book called *Hygiene and Beauty* as a birthday gift and even found a retired dressmaker who made copies of dress designs from *Woman's Illustrated* magazines. Every penny she earned was spent on quality materials from a warehouse near Southwark Docks, and shoes, gloves, hats and handbags from another. Susan guessed that some of the goods were being sold illegally, but when she had enquired she had been informed by Miss Firbank that what she didn't know wouldn't hurt her. Louisa was not only her mentor but her dearest friend. Susan adored her.

With the cake shop closed half a day each Tuesday, Susan would write to Mrs Elliott or stay at the academy and study with Louisa. She even spent Christmas with Louisa while Cyril and Miriam joined the Blore family.

Miriam noticed that Susan's manner was changing and that she was losing her northern brogue and speaking in a softer, well-modulated tone. That's not all Miriam noticed. Apart from the regulars, the shop was being invaded by young boys from sixteen to eighteen years old who came into the shop and waited until Susan was free to serve them. Even Cyril noticed that the sales of custard tarts had increased, and when he asked his wife she nodded in Susan's direction. At seventeen, Susan was turning into a very attractive young woman.

There was an unpleasant task she had to perform when Miriam returned from her weekly afternoon tea with her sister; Susan desperately hoped that her news would not upset Miriam or Cyril too much. Louisa had found a position for Susan in women's fashion at Swan and Edgars in Piccadilly, at twelve shillings a week, and was urging her to take it and leave the cake shop.

'My dear, think of your skin and hair with all that flour floating around' she said. 'What about your fingernails? Clipping them short to bake cakes is definitely unladylike. And what of your beauty sleep when you rise at an ungodly hour to light the ovens?' Eventually, Louisa had won, and Susan agreed to talk to Miriam and ask her to look for another young girl to replace her.

She was just practising what she would say when the bell above the shop door sounded, breaking her concentration. Wiping her hands and with a smile on her face she walked into the shop from the kitchen, expecting to see Miriam. Instead, a policeman stood there, removing his helmet. For a fleeting moment, Susan thought that she would not be able to buy cheap material from the docks any more.

'Good afternoon, does Mrs Carter live here?' he asked.

'Yes, she does live here.'

'May I have a word with her?'

'I'm afraid she is out at present. Can I help?'

The policeman eyed the smartly-dressed young girl in her red gingham apron and matching hat. She was quite pretty, as well as polite.

'Are you a relative, miss?' he enquired.

'Niece, sir.' If there was any unpleasantness to be faced, she could cope much better than Miriam or even Cyril. Miriam was a bit squeamish and easily agitated. Cyril was a worrier.

'It's concerning her husband, Mr Cyril Carter. He was involved in an accident earlier today. It's bad news, I'm afraid, miss.'

'How bad? He's all right, isn't he?'

'No, miss. Mr Carter is now deceased.'

The colour drained from Susan's face. She held onto the edge of the counter. 'What happened? I mean, how did he die?'

'Some scaffolding from an adjacent building fell while Mr Carter was leaving the Pearl Insurance office. He was badly crushed and died shortly after. He never regained consciousness.'

Putting her hand to her forehead, Susan tried to think clearly. How was she to explain this to Miriam? News of her beloved Cyril's death would destroy her. What should she do? How could she tell Miriam and remain calm? She needed help.

'Are you all right miss?'

'Yes, yes, thank you. I have to contact other family members. Can you look after the shop while I run to the phone box on the corner?'

'Begging your pardon, miss, wouldn't it be more prudent if you closed the shop before telephoning your family?'

'Yes of course. Please excuse me. I'm not thinking too clearly. Thank you for your help. You've been wonderful.'

He smiled and held the shop door ajar, watching her remove her apron and hat, put on her coat, and drop the shop keys into her pocket. He had never been called wonderful before and felt pleased with himself. His wife called him everything under the sun, but never wonderful.

'If you need any further assistance, miss, you'll find me at Fulham police station. Constable Newman.' After escorting Susan to the telephone box he left.

She picked up the telephone. 'Am I speaking to Percy Blore of Blore's Butchers?' she began.

'Yes, this is he.'

'This is Susan Cadiz. I work in Miriam's shop. Can you please come to the shop immediately? Something awful has happened to Cyril. Miriam is visiting Grace and you must hurry. I...'

'Hang on; let's take this a bit slower. What's happened? Is Cyril sick?'

'Worse. A policeman has just called at the shop. Cyril is...' Tears filled her eyes and she sobbed, 'He's dead.'

She heard the receiver being slammed down at the other end. Leaving the telephone box, she hurried back to the shop. Several people were waiting outside when she arrived.

'I've never known Miriam to close the shop so early. Is everything all right, my dear?' a regular customer asked.

Feeling too emotional to speak, Susan dashed away her tears with the back of her hand and gave a weak smile, but she did not reply as she reopened the shop. When the final customer had left she put the closed sign up, locked the doors and went to her room to lie down.

Louisa had cautioned her to keep her emotions in check and not cry, but she wanted to bawl like a baby. She was devastated and confused at the news of Cyril and of Miriam's reaction when she was told. Dear Cyril, he had been such a sweet man. He had put up several shelves in her room for her hairbrushes and make-up and fixed a table lamp next to her bed to allow her to read in the evenings. Just three weeks before Cyril and Miriam had taken her out for her seventeenth birthday to Lyons Tea House and presented her with a pair of gold earrings in a red velvet box. Life around here would never be the same, and Susan felt tears well up in her eyes again. He had been like a father to her – the only father she had ever known.

Towards dusk she was still lying there thinking about Cyril when her bedroom door flew open, startling her into a sitting position. In the doorway was Michael Blore. He stared at her for some minutes before turning to shout, 'I've found her, Dad, and she's all right.'

Coming further into the room, he perched on the end of the bed, pulled a handkerchief from his jacket pocket and gave it to her.

'Thank you,' she murmured, drying her eyes.

'We've come, Dad and me, to take you back to our house' he said. Never had Michael seen a girl more lovely

than the one before him. She was perfect in every way −
of medium height, with beautiful shoulder-length tresses,
pink cheeks and a full mouth − and those shapely legs gave
her an animal grace. Even her violet eyes, now glistening
with tears, took his breath away.

'No, I can't go. I have to wait for Miriam' she said.

'Aunt Mim is at our house with Grace and Mum. She
needs you. She gave us the keys to the shop so that we
could come and fetch you. She's worried that you're on
your own, and Dad and I are not leaving without you.' He
stood up, shaking his head when she offered to give him
back his handkerchief. 'Can you pack a few things for Aunt
Mim and yourself? Dad and I will wait downstairs.'

Michael returned downstairs to find his father putting
the shutters up on the shop windows. 'I've put all the
pastries in the icebox' he said. 'My God, son, you look
pale, almost as if you've lost a pound and found a shilling.'

'That can't be the skinny scarecrow that came to my
twenty-first birthday.'

Percy Blore rolled his eyes. 'I wish you'd forget about
women for a moment. I dunno, thinking about crumpet
at a time like this.'

'Dad, honestly, she's beautiful, and speaks like an
angel.'

'I don't care to hear any more. Is she packing a few
things, is more to the point. I can't hang around here all
night.'

'I am sorry to keep you waiting, Mr Blore' Susan
apologised as she set her portmanteau on the floor.
'Miriam's suitcase is upstairs. I couldn't carry both.'

The gooseberry tart Percy Blore was eating almost choked him as he beheld the stunning young woman in a navy dress and coat. Perched on her head was a matching velvet hat with a cute fawn feather at her right ear. He wondered if the gold earrings were genuine. They certainly looked it.

'You're right, son. She's a cracker,' Percy whispered to Michael as he passed him on his way to fetch Miriam's case.

'Have you eaten?' Michael asked her.'

'Um, no,' she said shaking her head.

'When we drop Dad off at our house, how would you like to go out for something to eat?'

'I don't think that's a very good idea in the light of what's happened.'

'They're all closeted with Aunt Mim, crying their eyes out. I know it's a sad time, I think you and I should get away for a while and find some breathing space. What do you say?'

'Only if Miriam agrees.'

'All right,' he said giving her a wide smile. After picking up her case, he took her hand and led the way to the car.

Michael drove her to a restaurant in Piccadilly called the Blue Lantern, which had pristine tablecloths and flickering candles. He asked her if she wanted a cocktail before ordering the meal, but flashes of her drunken mother popped into her mind and she shook her head. He suggested fruit juice, as he said she could not sit at the table without sipping something, and she agreed.

Leaning over the table after the dishes had been removed, he reached across, covered her hand with his and stared at her. 'I'm going to marry you one day' He murmured.

She smiled a little shyly, unsure of what to say. He couldn't possibly be serious. Perhaps the wine he had drunk with his meal had affected his thinking. Her mother used to babble on ridiculously when she had had a few drinks.

He was of average height, good-looking and seemed very likeable, but she doubted he was in love with her, any more than she was with him. Besides, she had no idea what love was. Susan was flattered by his attention and decided to play along.

'Why are you so keen to marry? And why me, Michael?'

He smiled. 'Call it love at first sight.'

'Hardly. I met you at your coming-of-age celebration and you barely noticed me.'

'You've changed, and so have I.'

'Yes, I've grown up. But I'd like to get to know you a lot more, before considering marriage. Besides, I'm too young to get married.'

'What would you like to know about me? I don't snore.'

She laughed. 'I don't want to know your bad habits, although, on second thoughts maybe I do.' He started laughing and she joined in. 'I mean, we should get to know each other better.'

'All right,' he replied, 'I will get to know you and vice versa, over the next weeks and months.'

Dessert arrived and she changed the subject. 'I'm worried about Miriam. She'll be lost without Cyril.' As she remembered all the happy times she had spent with Miriam and Cyril, her sadness deepened, tears filled her eyes and she started to sob out loud. 'It's all so unfair. So well suited, and so in love. Why, Michael? Why? Please can you tell me why?'

A middle-aged woman who had been dining at the next table suddenly appeared before them. 'Young man, you should marry this sweet girl.' Then she turned and walked briskly out of the restaurant.

Michael and Susan stared at each other and burst out laughing, 'The old girl must have thought I was giving you the brush-off,' Michael said between bouts of laughter.

A few days later a solemn group stood around the graveside as the vicar led the funeral service. Miriam was draped in a heavy black veil and held Susan's hand throughout the ceremony. Each female in the family, including Susan, held a white lily and stepped forward to throw it onto the lowering coffin. Miriam was weeping quietly, and a teary Susan cradled her in her arms. Michael, watching them, detached himself from the other family members, walked over to the two grieving women and wrapped his arms around both of them.

'My two favourite girls in the world,' he whispered, hugging them closely.

Everyone was invited for afternoon tea at the Carrington. Grace poured the men a glass of Scotch and the ladies a sherry, to drink to the memory of Cyril, and Percy gave a moving speech. His distraught sister had retired to a bedroom to grieve, accompanied by Susan. 'What am I to do? How shall I live without him? He was the love of my life!' Sobbed Miriam.

'I know he was, Miriam dearest. We have to take each day as it comes, and we will cope. I know we will.'

'What about the shop? Oh, Susan, what am I to do?'

'We can run it together and ask Michael or Mr Blore to help out, just until I get my full driving licence. Then I'll be able to do deliveries and pick up supplies. We'll manage, you'll see. Please don't cry any more, dearest. You'll make yourself ill.'

'You are a sweet girl. My Cyril thought the world of you. Do you really think we'll be all right?'

'Of course! Please, don't worry.'

Just at that moment, Tess popped her head around the door and asked if they wanted a cup of tea. A little while later, Susan left both women sipping tea and went downstairs to the sitting room. Michael was talking to June, both of them sitting with their backs to her, huddled together in conversation.

'We said some beastly things about Susan at your birthday. Do you remember, Michael?' June asked her cousin.

'I'm ashamed to say I do.'

'Thankfully, Susan didn't hear. Daddy always makes the remark that people who listen at keyholes never hear anything good about themselves.'

'Don't remind me.'

'You're sweet on her, aren't you Michael?'

'How old are you now, June?'

'Almost nineteen. Why?'

'Then act your age and mind your own business.'

She was a bit miffed at his words and decided to create a little mischief.

'Lillian in our office told me she saw you and Susan going into a swanky West End restaurant. Lillian's been sweet on you for months. Remember, Michael, you didn't get that from me.'

'My glass is empty. Excuse me.' Michael marched off towards the makeshift bar that Grace had set up in the dining room. Yes, he was sweet on Susan. In fact, it was more than sweet. Her womanly curves drove him to improper thoughts. She was everything he wanted in a woman.

A gentle tap on his shoulder announced the arrival of the object of his desire.

'Miriam would like to go back to Fulham' whispered Susan. 'She'd like to leave quietly with no fuss. Can you help?'

A quick nod answered her question. 'I'll bring Dad's car to the rear entrance. You and Aunt Mim can slip out down the back stairs. I'll drive you both back to Fulham.'

When they parted, Susan made her way towards Grace and Donald, who were standing talking to Percy. It sounded as if the conversation was becoming heated.

'I tell you, Donald, those Germans have marched into Austria and taken the Sudetenland from Czechoslovakia, all with our Prime Minister's blessing.'

'It's German anyway, Percy. What's all the fuss about?'

'Well, I'll tell you, if you will listen. The only thing Mr Chamberlain brought back from the Munich conference was a worthless piece of paper saying 'peace in our time'. He waved it about at Croydon Aerodrome as if it was an answer to a prayer. Like Mr Churchill, I don't trust the Germans. While we sit back and enjoy 'peace in our time', those blasted Germans are getting stronger and stronger, and are probably going to swallow up more countries. We should be re-arming, mark my words.'

Susan signalled to Grace, who followed her to the bedroom. With Tess helping they managed to get a sleepy Miriam downstairs and into the waiting car. Before Susan climbed into the car, Tess pulled her to one side.

'I've given Miriam a sedative the doctor prescribed' she said, giving the remainder of the pills to Susan. 'Hopefully, it should allow her to sleep most of the night.'

'What kept you?' Michael whispered after noticing his aunt fast asleep on the back seat of the car, wrapped in a thick woollen blanket. He was pleased that Susan would be sitting in front with him as they drove off through London's rain-soaked streets.

'Your father and Donald were arguing again about Germany. That's why it took so long.'

Michael laughed. 'Dad calls Uncle Donald a conscientious objector, and Uncle Donald calls Dad a warmonger. Uncle Donald never talks about it, but I believe he had a bad time in the trenches in the Great War and he's against killing anyone for a bit of dirt. Dad was a tail-gunner in the Royal Naval Air Service and he came through the war with barely a scratch. He thinks the Germans have expansionist ideas and he wants to stop them now.'

'Do you think your father is right when he says the Germans want to fight us?'

'No, I don't. They haven't the nerve. Don't listen to Dad. He always looks on the black side.' He smiled at Susan, hoping to chase away her troubled frown. 'What are your plans now? Are you going to stay with Aunt Mim or take the job you were telling me about?'

She was surprised at his question. Didn't he know that she loved both Cyril and Miriam and would never desert them?

'I'm staying. Miriam needs me more than ever, and as for the position at Swan and Edgar's, I have no intention of taking it now.'

'I'm glad. Aunt Mim thinks the world of you, and so does the rest of the family. If there is anything I can do to help, you only have to name it.'

'I do need a favour.'

'Ask away,' he said, glancing at her with a lopsided grin.

'Will you help me to pass the driving competency test? I have an examination to get through. Cyril was going to…' she hesitated and tried again. 'You see, it would help Miriam and the shop. It would also help me.' She sighed. 'My dream is to have a car of my own one day.'

He was only too willing to do anything to keep this lovely girl with eyes that shone like amethysts and her hair the colour of the midnight sky, by his side. What a stroke of luck, Uncle Cyril turning up his toes when he did.

'I'll take you out every Sunday, and you can practise in this,' he replied, nodding at the steering wheel. 'It won't take you long, and I'll help you every step of the way. As for buying your own motorcar, they're not cheap. Dad paid over two hundred quid for this Crossly two years ago.'

'Thank you for your kind offer Michael. I shall look forward to a driving lesson whenever possible.'

When the car came to a stop outside the shop he leaned over to kiss Susan, but she turned her face aside and he ended up just brushing his lips against her cheek. 'Can you please help me to get Miriam upstairs?' she asked. He nodded and gathered a sleepy Miriam in his arms and carried her to her bedroom. 'Goodnight, Michael' was all Susan said as she closed the shop door.

Within a few days, Susan opened the shop and began operating with limited stock while Miriam was bedridden and dosed up with sedatives prescribed by the doctor, who was a regular visitor. Michael too called in most days, always with a bunch of flowers, and talked constantly about marriage. Susan appreciated his help doing errands and deliveries and assisting behind the counter when the shop was busy.

Six weeks later Susan began examining her feelings for Michael. Deep in thought, she climbed the stairs to check on Miriam, before continuing to her own room. He had taken her out driving every Sunday as promised, but tonight had been different. After the driving lesson he had taken her to dinner, kissed her in the car and asked her to marry him. While she was fond of him, she did not love him, but she had enjoyed her first kiss. She was not eighteen yet, although she told everyone she was. Nevertheless, she felt she was too young to marry. Her ambition to find a better life was never far from her mind.

Suddenly a thought germinated and took hold. Michael's family were well off, and as the eldest son he would inherit the farm, the butchers' shops and the elegant Victorian house in Queens Road. Miriam had told her that Percy had money invested in both a construction business and a local bus company. If she married Michael, she would never have to work again. Michael had told her that he did not want his wife working; he believed a woman's place was in the home. As his wife she would be able to buy all the beautiful things that she could not afford on her small wage. The thought of regularly visiting a beauty shop and weekly visits to the hairdresser sounded heavenly. She had almost persuaded herself to accept his proposal when she fell asleep dreaming of a beautiful white wedding dress with six bridesmaids.

When the housekeeper of a big house in Eaton Square sent a message to the shop for a large order, Miriam finally roused herself from her grief, and the two women began to work long hours. Finally, the boxes of cakes and tarts were packed and delivered by Michael in Percy's car. Tired and worn out, Miriam slowly went into the shop kitchen. Susan heard her groan and rushed to her side.

'Two large boxes with the special miniature fruit tarts have been left behind. Oh, dear,' Miriam wailed, 'they were ordered as a table decoration. What shall we do?'

'Is that all? I thought for a moment you had fallen over. Give me the address. I'll deliver them.'

When Susan arrived at the large red-brick Georgian house, she went to the basement entrance as instructed by Miriam. A maid in a white apron and bob cap opened the door, invited Susan in and went to fetch the housekeeper. After placing the two boxes on a large deal table in the middle of the kitchen, Susan wandered to the other side looking at all the shiny copper saucepans hung in rows above a huge cooking range. Milk pitchers of various sizes stood in neat little rows like soldiers on parade. A huge pantry stood opposite the ovens, and beneath the window were three deep sinks – for washing dishes and cleaning vegetables, she guessed.

So preoccupied was she in inspecting the kitchen that she did not hear the door open.

'Jessie, help a poor fellow and make a sandwich. I'm starved. I haven't...' The speaker stopped in his tracks.

Susan swung around and stared at the man who had entered. He was tall, with thick curly bronzed hair and slate-grey eyes. It was the colour of his eyes that told her who he was.

'Good morning. It's Harry Fortescue, isn't it?'

The man nodded curtly. 'Who, may I ask, are you?' he asked.

'Susan Cadiz. We met on a train journey to London a few years ago.'

Suddenly, a beaming smile covered his face, and within two strides he was at her side. He lifted her off her feet and swung her into the air.

'Susan, you *have* changed! You're positively lovely. Where do you live? What are you doing here? Do you work? Tell me all.' He had not changed much except that he was taller and more muscular, but he was still firing questions at her like darts.

'I work in a cake shop on Fulham Road and I came to deliver these,' she responded, pointing to the boxes on the table. 'They were left off the main delivery.'

'It's really good to see you again,' he said, completely ignoring the boxes. Harry could see that the naïve girl with huge violet eyes and rough northern brogue he had met on the train had vanished, to be replaced by a modishly-attired young woman who spoke English faultlessly. The smart belted coat and brimmed hat in a camel colour were very becoming, too.

The young maid returning to the kitchen interrupted his thoughts. After reporting that the housekeeper was having a nap, she bobbed a small curtsy to Master Harry, picked up the boxes and disappeared into the pantry. Harry called her back and ordered some tea for his guest. The maid gave Harry a curious glance. It was most odd; the family and their guests always had tea in the drawing room. She gave the girl from the cake shop a puzzled look and left to obey, returning a short time later to put the tea things on the table and pour tea into china cups. Bobbing again, she left, noting that Master Harry was unaware that tea had been served. He was too busy gazing at the pretty young thing sitting opposite him.

'So, now that Miriam's husband has died and Miriam

is unwell, you operate the shop on your own. I can see that you're a woman of many talents. Do you have any gentlemen friends?'

'I'm thinking of getting married.'

'Congratulations. Who's the lucky chap?'

'Actually, it's Miriam's nephew, Michael Blore.'

'Do you love him?'

'I don't know.'

Harry threw back his head and laughed uproariously. 'Susie, you are a scamp! When will you know?'

'Harry Fortescue, are you making fun of me?'

'I apologise,' he said.

'What are you doing now?' she asked, turning the conversation around.

'I'm at Sandhurst. I expect with all the rumours about war that the regiment will probably go abroad soon, and I will join them at the end of training.'

'Why is it that everyone I meet is talking about war?'

His grey pensive eyes looked away. 'It's a possibility.'

She quickly changed the subject again. She had heard enough from the Blores about war. 'How is your mother? Does she still do charity work?'

'Indeed, she is on various committees of worthwhile causes, and still finds time to help at St John's and the Red Cross. I hardly ever see her or my sister these days.'

'And your father?'

'He's at the FO.'

'The FO?'

'The Foreign Office.'

'As you can see, I'm still a dumb country bumpkin, but no longer a pipsqueak – your words, if my memory serves me correct.'

He started laughing, and she joined in.

'You're neither of those things, and I apologise for the ramblings of a pompous schoolboy' he laughed.

When she had finished her tea she stood up, saying, 'Harry, it was lovely meeting you again,' and smiled. 'I wish you well, and I hope there isn't a war.' She reached for her coat and hat.

'You're leaving so soon?' He looked a little disappointed.

'I'm afraid so. Miriam is alone and I have to get back to the shop. Good luck at Sandhurst.' She leaned over the table to give him a peck on the cheek and then turned and walked towards the kitchen door.

'Wait!' he called, and hurriedly scribbled his Army address on the back of the housekeeper's notepad. 'Let's keep in touch,' he suggested, tearing the page out and handing it to her. She dictated the shop address and then gave him a beaming smile before taking her leave.

With arms folded, Harry leaned against the deal table, staring at the door long after she had gone, thinking that the ungainly, ungraceful and under-fed girl he had met on the train had blossomed into a lovely and enchanting young woman. The man she was planning to marry was a lucky chap, and he hoped she would find happiness with him. It was obvious to Harry that she saw him only as a friend and not a suitor. That was just as well. From his family's point of view, that was all he could ever be. A girl from a working-class background, no matter how well-spoken or refined, would not do. Harry heaved a sigh, wishing it wasn't so. He knew he would have to follow the dictates of his parents and not his heart.

Walking away, Susan turned for a last look at Harry's family home. It was an impressive building, and although she had only seen the kitchen, she could well imagine the rest of the rooms. She remembered him saying on the train that his father worked for the government, and made a mental note to ask Louisa what kind of work was done at the FO.

Harry was very sweet and she liked him very much, and although they came from vastly different backgrounds they enjoyed each other's company. If he was going abroad with the Army and she was thinking of getting married, it was very unlikely that they would ever meet again. However, now that she had his address she would try to keep in touch with an occasional letter.

Chapter Four

When Susan arrived home from Firbank Academy, she saw immediately that something was wrong. The shutters which covered the shop windows had been put up, the 'closed' sign was displayed and the shop door was locked.

Taking her keys from her handbag, she let herself in and saw a note on the counter in Miriam's handwriting. The note told her not to go into the shop kitchen under any circumstances, but to telephone her brother, Percy.

Ignoring Miriam's request, she went straight towards the door and tried to open it, but it was firmly closed. It felt as if something was blocking it. Putting her shoulder to the door, Susan heaved a few times against the panelling before it gave way. She almost tripped on several towels rolled up behind the door.

Then she screamed. Gas! The terrible smell sent her reeling back into the shop, coughing and choking. Grabbing an apron from beneath the counter and covering her nose and mouth, she rushed back into the kitchen and headed for the backyard door. When she reached it, she flung the bolt back, threw it open and then ran to the windows, opening them wide. Her eyes were watering so much that she could barely see.

That was when she nearly tripped over something on the ground; the inert form of Miriam. Leaning across her, she turned off the gas, retching and vomiting all over her coat. Wiping her mouth on her sleeve, she stumbled back into the front of the shop and threw the door open, sucking in great lungfulls of air. Her fearful eyes darted up and down the street for help. Spying a boy playing with a ball, she called to him.

'Hello? Over here!' she cried between coughing bouts. 'I need an ambulance and police, urgently. Hurry, please hurry!' Then she dissolved in tears.

The boy, after seeing the mess on her coat and hearing the urgency in her voice, replied, 'Righto, miss,' and ran off, leaving his ball lying in the gutter.

Going back into the shop, she tentatively sniffed the air. The smell was still overpowering, but it was clearing. Dropping to her knees, she lifted Miriam's head and shoulders out of the oven and gently moved her away from the stove, pillowing her head in her lap. Miriam's eyes were half-open, she had a faint smile on her lips, and her body was still warm. With tears streaming down her cheeks, Susan prodded Miriam's face and called her name, but it was hopeless.

The police constable found Susan on the floor, cradling Miriam in her arms and sobbing bitterly. After asking a few questions, he disappeared. Two other policemen arrived to keep the crowd that was forming away from the shop. Next to arrive was the ambulance, followed by a deathly-pale Percy Blore and his sister Grace, whose eyes were red and puffy. The ambulance left within minutes with Miriam's body and a doctor arrived to examine Susan, who was inconsolable and in a state of complete shock. Eventually, after being examined and given sedatives, she was taken to the Carrington Hotel to stay with Grace and Donald.

Miriam's death left the Blore family stunned. Six months after Cyril's tragic death they were now mourning their beloved sister. The Coroner's verdict was death by suicide, and Miriam's body was released later that week for burial. Susan begged Grace to contact Mrs Elliot, and when she did, back came more bad news. Mrs Elliot was bedridden with pleurisy and unable to attend her friend's funeral, but she sent some money to buy a wreath.

A few days later, Percy Blore gave Susan a sealed envelope, which contained thirty pounds and a note from Miriam. She had written that the money would buy a lovely wedding dress and hoped that Susan and Michael would be as happy as she and Cyril had been. She went on to say that she could not live without her beloved husband and had gone to join him. All her assets were left to the Blore family. Nobody in the family could make pastries and cakes like Miriam, so Percy reluctantly put the business up for sale.

Although staying at the Carrington was comfortable, Susan knew it was only temporary. With no job and no home, now that Percy Blore was selling the cake shop, the shock of losing the two people she loved prompted Susan to accept Michael's proposal of marriage. Within two months all the arrangements were set in place. Instead of the lavish white wedding she had dreamed of, the celebrations were very low key, as a mark of respect for both Miriam and Cyril.

Percy paid for and organised the wedding, and even fixed up the problem of Susan's missing birth certificate after obtaining a copy from Somerset House. Percy had Susan's name legally changed from Caddy to Cadiz to save any awkward questions from family and friends, who had been calling her Susan Cadiz since her arrival in London. He handed it to her without a word; she knew instinctively he had read it. All this time she had been telling everyone her father was an officer in the Spanish Navy, when in fact the birth certificate showed that the father's name had not been recorded. 'Non Marital Child' had been written on the document. Only her mother's name was lodged, revealing that Susan was indeed illegitimate. Ethel had repeatedly told her daughter that she was not a bastard.

Susan wanted to cry; she had believed her mother, and Ethel had not told the truth. She was grateful that Percy had changed her name to Cadiz.

In any event, the wedding went ahead as planned. As bridesmaid, June dressed in lavender, while Louisa Firbank looked cool and attractive in pale blue. Even Tess was elegant in pearl-grey *crêpe de chine*, while a morning suit of striped trousers, black coat and grey top hat was a perfect fit for Percy. The groom's family and friends filled the pews on the right hand side of the church, whereas on the left only Louisa and a few of the students from the academy were seated. Susan was delighted that her Mrs Elliot had been able to travel to London to attend the wedding, and presented Susan and Michael with a magnificent canteen of cutlery as a wedding gift. However, Susan was disappointed that Mrs Elliot could only stay for a few days due to teaching commitments.

With a happy smile, Susan walked down the aisle on Donald's arm to Mendelssohn's *Wedding March* in a cream dress of wild silk, wearing a small hat of the same colour and carrying a spray of red roses interlaced with dark green fern. Michael looked magnificent in a grey morning suit with a matching cravat, carrying a top hat and gloves and with a red rose in his lapel. Within half an hour of entering the church, Miss Susan Cadiz had become Mrs Susan Blore.

The wedding celebrations were in full swing at the Carrington when Michael came up behind his wife, put his arms around her waist and whispered, 'You are the loveliest girl in this room and I'm a very lucky man. Are you looking forward to our honeymoon in Scotland, sweetheart?'

'Oh indeed. It will be good to get away from all the sadness.'

Michael frowned. That was not what he meant at all. His poor wife had been through a lot lately, what with Miriam's funeral closely followed by wedding preparations, and he put her behaviour down to nerves. Once they were in the Highlands everything would be different.

'Sweetheart, my father wants to discuss some business with me. After that I see no reason why we shouldn't push off and catch our train.' Michael gave his wife a gentle kiss and went to join his father.

Percy Blore was waiting in Grace's private kitchen, upstairs. He was pacing up and down clutching a glass of Scotch when his eldest son arrived.

'Come in and close the door' he said. 'I've a few things I'd like to get off my chest and I don't want anyone eavesdropping.'

Obeying his father, Michael pushed the door closed and leaned against it. 'What's all this about, Dad?'

Percy tossed the Scotch down his throat, placed the glass in the kitchen sink and looked at his son.

'Now that you're married I want you to stop fornicating with other women. Susan is a beautiful girl, if a bit naïve. Your mother and I want you to do the right thing by her. We...'

'Aw, Dad,' Michael moaned, hating the way his father criticised him.

'Don't 'Aw, Dad' me! I'm telling you to settle down, and no more womanising. And another thing, I want you to buck up your ideas at the Camden Town shop. I gave you the manager's job because you said you'd make a go of it. Well, sales are down, and if you can't do any better than that, I'll find a manager who can. Now what's it to be?'

'I know I've been slacking off a bit, but I have a wife and responsibilities now. I will do my utmost to run the shop better, honestly.'

'Remember, Michael, you can't toss your wife away as easily as you do with your fancy women.'

'I haven't got any fancy women, as you call them.'

Percy gave his son a shrewd look. 'Donald and Grace saw you two weeks ago in Leicester Square with a blond woman. She works in June's office, as I understand.'

'I only met her to tell her that I was getting married and I couldn't see her any more.'

'Well, see that you don't. Your mother and I are very pleased with your marriage. Susan's a nice girl. We wish you both every happiness. We've bought you a small house in Camden Town as a wedding gift. It's near the shop so you won't be late for work. Here are the keys.'

Michael ignored his father's jibe about being late for work. 'Gosh, Dad, thanks a lot.' A smile creased his whole face. 'I don't know what to say.'

'I'll give you three months to prove you can run the shop to my satisfaction. Otherwise…' He didn't finish the sentence, but just shrugged. 'Oh, and another thing, don't run up any more bills in Jermyn Street for handmade shoes. I'm not paying for your little luxuries any longer. Just who the hell do you think you are? The Aga Khan?'

It hadn't escaped Percy's notice either that his son was wearing a solid gold ring on his little finger. Money always burned a hole in Michael's pocket, and he knew that his son couldn't afford a nugget that size. Tess indulged both of her sons, but Michael was the favourite. Percy would lay odds that his wife had given Michael the money to buy the ring.

The guests tossed rice and children threw flower petals at the happy couple.

A chorus of oohs and aahs greeted Susan as she came downstairs in a soft pink and pearl-grey dress and jacket with matching hat, shoes and bag. Susan and Michael smiled, and waved goodbye to the, guests. She was holding her bouquet in her hand, as she planned to place it on Miriam's grave as they passed the cemetery on their way to the station.

Susan was feeling melancholy when she returned from Scotland two weeks later. The honeymoon hadn't been all she had hoped it would be. The first week she had taken her monthly cycle and could not perform her wifely duties. The second week had been even worse. He had pounced on her and brutally torn at her nightgown, covering her mouth with his, then thrust himself between her thighs and satisfied himself. Then he had rolled off to the other side of the bed and fallen asleep. The next day they had had their first row when she had told him she didn't care for sex and he had responded, 'This is a fine bloody time to tell me. Well, you'll just have to get used to it, because I'm no eunuch.'

Susan had tried to reason with him, but it was useless. He stormed out of the hotel room and returned some hours later drunk, tossing insults at her and adding to her fears. When he had fallen asleep and slid off the chair onto the floor she had helped him into bed. After that Susan tolerated the nightly couplings in silence, willing herself to respond to him, but she had neither the skill nor the stomach for his kind of animal lust. Each time, she lay there with tears running down her face, wishing it would soon be over.

Memories of her childhood surfaced from the recesses of her mind where she had buried them and she heard again the nightly creaking of the bed springs and the grunts, groans and filthy language coming from her mother's bedroom. Through the paper-thin walls of the hovel where she had been brought up she had been able to hear everything, and now she blamed her mother for her dislike of sex. Susan had naively hoped that being married would ease her anxiety, and that her husband would be patient and show regard for her feelings, teaching her how to love him and how to enjoy lovemaking. She was sadly disappointed. Affection didn't seem to play any part in Michael's lovemaking. No tenderness or gentleness was shown during or after sex. Susan merely accepted it. What else could she do?

She assumed her husband was behaving in the same manner as every other man. At least, that's what she had gleaned from overhearing some of the female customers telling Miriam about their husbands. During the day, Michael was kind and caring towards her and she enjoyed his kisses and cuddles, but at night he was like a rutting bull.

By and large, the rest of their life together was happy and she had little to complain of except the unpleasant interludes in the bedroom. She blamed herself for creating fear of the marriage bed, and suspected that the mauling she had suffered years ago had affected her deeply and caused her to loathe being touched between her legs. All this she kept to herself, convinced that Michael had no idea how she really felt; or if he did, that he didn't care. Did other young brides in London have such a horrible introduction to the marriage bed?

However, all her despair vanished when she saw the house Percy and Tess had bought them as a wedding gift. The small semi-detached with green painted window boxes, where nasturtiums of red and gold bloomed, was delightful. Michael opened the garden gate and stood aside to allow his wife to walk up the pathway first.

'Michael, isn't it beautiful?' she cooed excitedly as she stepped up to the front door.

'Wait,' he said. 'It's a man's duty to carry his bride across the threshold.' Unlocking the door, he pushed it open. Sweeping Susan into his arms, he carried her into their new home. Slowing releasing her, he gave her a long gentle kiss and murmured, 'Welcome home, wife.'

Towards the end of summer, Susan had her first real home completely furnished. The sitting room held two armchairs and a sofa in a biscuit brocade, and a mahogany dining table with four chairs sat in the bay window. A glass china cabinet, which held a dinner-set that Grace and Donald had bought as a wedding gift, stood along the wall near the fireplace. In the corner of the kitchen a wooden spiral staircase led to the bedrooms. The front bedroom overlooked the street, and Susan decorated it with a double bed, dressing table and wardrobe. Chintz curtains and bowls of fresh flowers were arranged during the day in every room, even the spare bedroom they used as a storeroom. A tiny bathroom held a small bath and an even smaller wash basin. A clothesline, washhouse and outside lavatory were along one wall in a tiny paved yard. It was small but comfortable, and her first real home. She had spent all she had saved, including the small legacy from Miriam's will. Michael had borrowed some cash from his father to pay for the rest of the furnishings.

Susan hummed to herself as she stripped the bed. Since enrolling at Firbank Academy she had developed a fetish about cleanliness, so much so that she couldn't bear to go to bed without having a bath. As she did not like sleeping in sheets for more than one night, she changed the bed linen daily. The laundry bill was creeping up and was becoming rather noticeable. Even Michael mentioned it, but when she explained that she loved sleeping in freshly clean bed linen he indulged her.

One afternoon an unexpected knock had Susan hurrying to open the door. June stood on the doorstep with a smile, clutching a large bunch of chrysanthemums. Since the wedding June had become a frequent visitor. They were not bosom pals, but they were becoming closer.

'Thought you might like these,' she said, pressing the

flowers into Susan's arms. 'They're lovely, thank-you. I've just put the kettle on to make tea. Would you like some?'

'Rather,' June responded and followed her friend into the kitchen. She watched Susan arrange the flowers in a tall vase before reaching for teapot, cups and saucers as the kettle came to the boil. 'I've come to give you some news.'

'Oh?' replied Susan picking up the tea tray and heading for the sitting room.

'I've joined the WAAF,' June said, trailing behind with a plate of biscuits.

'What's that?'

'It's the Women's Auxiliary Air Force.'

'What on earth for? I mean, you have a good job in the law office in town and haven't you just been promoted to senior secretary?'

'That's just it. I can put my office skills to use in the Air Force. Besides,' she grinned, 'I like the uniform.'

'What will your parents say?'

'I haven't told them yet, but I expect they'll read the Riot Act – spending their hard-earned cash to send their 'one and only' to secretarial college and this is how she repays us. You know, the usual stuff parents gripe about.'

'I have some news, too. I'm going to have a baby.'

June leapt out of her seat and hugged Susan.

'This is wonderful news, blossom. What did Michael say?'

'Well, he's been so busy at the shop I didn't want to worry him.'

'If I know Michael, he'll be over the moon. You'll have to tell him.'

'We're invited to his parents for lunch on Sunday. I'll announce it then.'

'A word of caution, blossom,' June said. 'Tell him before you announce it to the family, or he may get annoyed. The husband should always be the first to know.'

'When do you leave to join the Air Force?' Susan changed the subject. She liked June very much, but resented anyone, no matter how good his or her intentions, butting into her marriage.

'Next week I leave for basic training at West Drayton and after that I'll be posted to a unit.'

'I wish you well, June. Although I can't understand why you're joining the WAAF.'

June heaved a sigh. 'Susan, I know you're wrapped up nice and cosy in your lovely new home but there is a whole world beyond these walls. There's going to be a war. Everyone's talking about it.'

'When?' she gasped.

'Don't you read the papers? Listen to the wireless?'

'Not since I married. I haven't had time.'

'Really, you should keep up to date with world events,' June said, placing her empty teacup and saucer back on the tray.

Susan calmly responded, 'I have a husband to cook for, a home to look after, and in six months a baby to care for. World events will have to take a back seat for now.'

Laughing, June stood up to leave. 'Susan, you really are

funny. Europe is practically on the brink of war, and all you're thinking about is cooking and cleaning.'

'What would you have me do, June? Join the Air Force? Will that prove that I'm abreast of the times?'

'They don't take pregnant women.'

They both burst out laughing and hugged each other goodbye.

Chapter Five

The following Sunday Percy, Tess, Donald and Michael were all playing cards in the sitting-room while Susan and Grace were in the kitchen putting final touches to the trifle that would follow the Sunday roast.

'Where's June?' Susan asked.

'She and Malcolm have gone to the pony club, something about a dressage competition. I told them we couldn't wait lunch but I'll keep theirs warm in the oven till they get back. What do you think of June joining up?'

Susan aimed for diplomacy, well aware that Grace and Donald were not very pleased with their daughter.

'I was surprised, but June is very determined and she'll make a good service woman.'

'I'll say. It's unheard of – girls joining the services. Well, in the Blore family it is. I was told that the women who join up are only groundsheets for the fighting forces.'

'I'm sure that's not true, Grace. Besides, she'll be in some nice cosy office doing shorthand and typing. Which is no different to what she's used to, except that she'll be wearing a uniform.'

Percy's voice yelling down the hallway had both Grace and Susan covering the trifle with a clean tea towel, popping it in the icebox and hurrying to the sitting room.

'Who's winning?' Grace asked as they walked in.

'Dad's been cheating again,' groaned Michael.

'Hush,' said Percy putting his forefinger to his mouth and at the same time turning up the volume on the wireless.

'We interrupt this broadcast…'

Then they heard the solemn voice of the Prime Minister, Mr Chamberlain.

'I am speaking from the Cabinet Room of 10 Downing Street. This morning the British Ambassador in Berlin handed the German government a final note stating that unless we heard from them by eleven o'clock that they were prepared at once to withdraw their troops from Poland, a state of war would exist between us. I have to tell you now that no such undertaking has been received, and that consequently this country is at war with Germany.'

Tess started crying. Susan picked up the sherry glass lying on the card table and gave it to her.

'Here, have this. Don't cry.'

Susan felt like crying too. She was expecting a baby – she should be happy – but this news of war was frightening. She was scared for everyone in Britain, especially her unborn child. Thinking to cheer everyone up, including herself, and taking everyone's mind off the terrible news, Susan announced that she was going to have a baby. The radio was quickly turned off, and everyone in the room was suddenly smiling and congratulating her and Michael.

Percy walked over to the card table, turned his cards over and spread them out. Four beautiful aces were staring at him. 'I've won,' he announced, scooping up the money piled in the middle of the table amid howls of protest from the other card players. He went towards his daughter-in-law and put the money in her hand. 'This is for my first grandchild's piggy bank' he said, and kissed Susan on the cheek.

Later that evening after arriving home, Susan murmured goodnight to Michael and made her way upstairs. After locking the front door, her husband came striding after her, seized her wrist, and dragged her down the three steps she had ascended and swung her around to face him.

'Why didn't you tell me you were pregnant before you announced it to the world? I felt like a complete idiot. Well, why didn't you tell me?'

'I didn't think...'

'You didn't think! What gives you the right to think anything? You're my wife and you'll do what I tell you. Now get upstairs. I'll show you who's boss!'

The steely edge to his voice cut the air like a knife, and a dangerous glint smoked in his hazel eyes. She stared at him for a few seconds before turning and hurrying upstairs. These temper tantrums were a new side to the man she had married, and she did not know how to handle him. She was in two minds whether to do as he had ordered or run to the spare bedroom and lock herself in and escape from him and his physical needs. She wanted to choose the latter, but meekly submitted. She cried during the whole ugly encounter, realising for the first time that she was beginning to loathe her husband.

To the rest of the Blore family, the newlyweds were a happy loving couple awaiting the birth of their first baby, but it was a facade. As the months passed, Susan kept her opinions to herself and her mouth firmly shut whenever she was in her husband's company. Luckily for her, that didn't occur often, as she was increasing in size and Michael was spending more and more time away from home. They seldom had a meal together, since he had started having dinner out. Their marriage was crumbling and there was nothing she could do to save it, even for the baby's sake. Her unborn child compounded the misery of her unhappy marriage. She refused to give way to tears of remorse and tried to be pragmatic about the turn of events in her life.

At the beginning of November Michael came home early one evening and said he wanted to talk to her. He told her how sorry he was that their marriage was floundering and begged for the sake of their unborn child to put the unfortunate events behind them and try again. He was quite willing to do anything she wanted to save their relationship.

'You can't know how sorry I am about our marriage, nor can I put into words how thrilled I am about the baby' he said.

'I feel the same,' Susan whispered, 'and I'll try if you will.'

Then he dropped two bombshells: his father had sacked him because the shop wasn't making any money, and he had joined the Middlesex Rifle Corps and had to go to Ireland for training.

'I suggested to Dad that as I'm going into the Army you should move to Queens Road with them while I'm away. We can have the second floor, and Mum and Dad will occupy the ground level.'

'What about our beautiful house and furniture?'

'Dad will rent the house, and we can store or sell the furniture and keep any bits and pieces in the cellar at Queens Road. Susan, I don't want you living here alone. The newspapers are saying that this war may take a year or more before it's over, and you would be much more comfortable with my parents. They'll be there to help when the baby comes.'

'When do you go to Ireland?'

'In two weeks, and I would like you settled at my parents' house before I leave. Now, you sit there and I'll go and make some tea for us.'

Surprised by his offer of tea, she sat back in her chair; her baby was growing, and she moved her body to find a more comfortable position. She smiled to herself, glad that her marriage was back to normal and all the recent unpleasantness was a thing of the past. They had made up and forgiven each other. She was sad to be leaving her home, even sadder to be selling the furniture, and hoped they could store it for a year or so until this stupid war was over

Susan loved the house at Queens Road. One part of the cellar was used to store foodstuffs and wines, and above the cellar were three stories of elegant Victorian high-ceilinged living areas with beautiful sash windows. There were two bathrooms, one with an inside WC, a huge kitchen with an icebox, and an inside laundry area. There was even a telephone in the hallway. Outside was a lovely garden with flowers and fruit trees, a place to sit in the spring sunshine while she awaited the birth of her infant. Tess employed a cleaning lady, and that would leave her time to play a nanny role when the baby arrived, allowing Susan to go out and look for work to support herself and the baby.

That December was one of the worst ever recorded, if the newspapers were to be believed, with snowdrifts, icy roads and freezing conditions. Everyone's windows in Queens Road were coated in a dull opaque frost that was almost impenetrable, and rows of misty icicles hung down like delicate necklaces along the eaves of the houses. The water pipes in the street were frozen solid in almost every house, with the exception of number twenty-one. Percy had had the water pipes lagged months before. His neighbours had neglected to do so, and he allowed them to draw buckets of water, especially over Christmas.

Neither the weather nor a war could ruin the Blore's Christmas family gathering. Michael was home on leave, looking handsome in his uniform, and June looked chic with her blond locks cut into a short bob, her Air Force hat sitting at a trim angle nestling amongst the curls. Both Michael and June were the embodiment of young Britishers enlisting to save their country. Susan was proud of them.

Percy had brought home a turkey from the shop. It was the biggest Susan had ever seen. While the turkey was being cooked everyone exchanged small gifts of gloves or colourful scarves for the women and thick woollen socks and cigars for the men. Donald opened a bottle of champagne and when every glass was charged he gave a toast to the King, the government and the armed forces, wishing they would be victorious against Herr Hitler. Eventually, everyone sat down to enjoy a magnificent meal followed by plum pudding and brandy custard.

The conversation around the table inevitably led to the war news. Susan wished she had a penny for every time the word 'war' was mentioned at a Blore family get-together. She dearly hoped the German Army would go back home and the British Army would return from France. She wanted to have her baby in peace and quiet without everyone talking incessantly about *war, war, war.*

While everyone at the table discussed the superiority of the Royal Navy, Susan noticed that Percy was not only lighting up another cigar but pouring himself another Scotch; unless she was mistaken, that was his fifth. She wondered if he was worried about his business, or perhaps because it was Christmas he had decided to let his hair down and get tipsy. She hoped Percy wouldn't get too drunk. People who had too much alcohol frightened her

– a legacy from her childhood. Susan was beginning to like her father-in-law because he always took her side, whether it was choosing the colour of the cot for her baby or a new hat. He was much nicer to her now than when she had first met him. She wondered if she should ask Tess or Michael about Percy's drinking habit, but memories of Michael's temper when she made any comment about his family caused her to keep her lips sealed. Tess was a dutiful wife who agreed with everything Percy uttered. Susan would get nothing from her except trouble.

'You're very quiet. Dreaming of your little baby, no doubt.'

'Actually, June, I was thinking how lovely it would be to get out of these pregnancy smocks.'

'Not long now, blossom. I suppose you and Michael have a name picked out.' She gave a quick nod and changed the subject.

'Tell me about your unit.'

'Well, it's all rather hush-hush, you know. I work in the RAF office, taking dictation from an officer who's got the longest handlebar moustache you have ever seen – and it's carrot-red, too.'

Laughing, Susan's eyes roamed the room and saw Percy filling his glass again. She dropped her eyes quickly when he caught her looking at him.

'He's been giving the bottle a nudge tonight,' June whispered after catching Susan watching him.

'Would you join me in the kitchen while I make some tea?'

June nodded, and the two women left the table and went down the long hallway that led to the kitchen.

'The thing is, June, Percy isn't normally a heavy drinker. Do you think he's got some business worries?'

'I wouldn't have a clue, but Uncle Percy is a wheeler-dealer. So who knows? Why do you ask?'

'About two weeks ago he asked me to drive with him to Aylesbury. We had a lovely time stopping off at an old country pub for lunch, around a very cosy fire. I could have stayed there all day. Later at the farm, I was inside taking tea with the farm manager's wife while the men were inspecting the piggery. When Percy said he was ready to drive back to London I saw that under my seat was a dead animal wrapped in a hessian bag. To cut a long story short, I think he's selling meat on the black market.'

'Hell! The authorities will lock him up and throw away the key if they find out.'

'I only suspect, June. I don't know for sure. We'd best keep it from the family.'

'But why, Susan, would he invite you to go to Aylesbury?'

'If Percy had been stopped by the police, they wouldn't ask a heavily pregnant woman to get out of the car, now, would they?'

'Elementary, my dear Watson! And to think I once accused you of not being 'in the know'. You'll keep me posted on future developments, won't you?'

'Of course, but you must promise not to say a word. Percy is not unpatriotic, only a little shady in his dealings with the government. He's not a bad man.'

June put her right hand over her heart and whispered, 'I swear not to tell a soul. I have to push off now. I have a heavy date in town.'

'Oh, who's the new man in your life?'

'He's a pilot, just finished training – very cute, but shy.'

'Just your type?' June's only answer was a cheeky grin.

After June finally bade a fond farewell to her family who were sitting around the table still discussing the war, Susan went with her into the hallway and watched her friend wrap up against the blizzard outside. Pressing her nose to the glass as she closed the front door, she heaved a deep sigh, wishing for the umpteenth time that she had not married so hastily. Then perhaps she would be going out and having some fun just like June.

Chapter Six

Winter was slowly giving way to spring, and with the sun shining brightly for the first time in months Susan decided to cut some of the early daffodils that lined the garden wall. While bending low over a cluster of golden blooms she doubled over in pain, dropping the garden shears. No, it couldn't be! The baby wasn't due for another four weeks, according to her doctor. He had advised that because of the war she should consider going to a nursing home in the country for her confinement but she had ignored his advice, preferring to remain in London.

Another spasm doubled her up and she shuddered, clutching herself. She tried to call Tess, who was indoors baking a pie for dinner, but the pain robbed her of speech, and all she could do was moan helplessly.

At that moment Tess, who was standing at the kitchen sink, glanced out of the window to see Susan on her knees obviously in pain. She rushed outside to help.

'It's too soon, too soon!' Susan cried as Tess wrapped her arm around her daughter-in-law and half-carried, half-dragged her into the house. Slowly but surely, Tess led Susan into a downstairs bedroom, knowing that climbing the stairs was out of the question. After seeing her daughter-in-law safely on the bed, Tess dashed into the hallway to telephone the doctor. Then she rang Percy, who came speeding home.

Midway through the afternoon the baby still had not been delivered. Susan was weakening and wanted nothing more than to be rid of the excruciating pain.

'Save my baby!' she pleaded with Doctor Kaye, who calmed her by gently patting her hand and speaking softly. Susan was worn out and did not have the strength to follow the doctor's directions.

Finally the baby came into the world with the aid of forceps. Leaning on her elbows Susan lifted her head from the bed and cried, 'Is my baby all right?' A tiny cry gave her the answer and she slumped back against the pillows, exhausted and relieved. Why, oh why, hadn't anyone told her about the awful pain and the complete lack of modesty when giving birth? She fell asleep with that thought.

Dr Kaye took Percy to one side and told him that the infant was very small and they would need to employ a professional nurse to nurture it over the next critical days. He recommended a retired nurse he knew who would fit the requirements. Percy nodded and urged the doctor to send for her.

It was a few weeks before Susan actually held her daughter in her arms, as the tiny creature had been so weak. Over the following days the nurse showed Susan how to handle the small infant and encouraged the young mother to do some exercises to regain her figure. The baby thrived, and it was the nurse who finally gave the infant a name. 'With her bright sandy hair she looks like a shiny new penny,' she said as she bathed the child.

'Then I shall call her Penny, Penny Blore,' Susan said, smiling at the nurse.

Congratulatory cards and letters arrived from Michael, June and Louisa Firbank. Susan had kept in touch with Louisa and had visited her during her pregnancy. Louisa had sent the most adorable pink and white baby dress and bonnet with matching booties for Penny to wear when the warmer weather arrived. Percy and Tess purchased a navy blue Silver Cross baby carriage with a fringed canopy to be attached in the summertime, for their first grandchild. Percy paid for the private nurse, and when Susan thanked him he just smiled and dismissed her gratitude with a carefree tilt of his hand.

Michael had written a note to Susan and sent a photograph of himself in uniform to her daughter. He asked Susan to pin it above his daughter's cot so she would know what her father looked like. Furthermore, he wrote, he did not like the name his wife had given his daughter. On his next leave, he was going to rename his daughter Tess after his mother. She shrugged off his scornful comments. As usual, whenever she made a decision he took umbrage. Well, Michael could go to blazes as far as she was concerned.

The christening of her daughter was in two weeks.

Michael could not get leave as his regiment had returned to Ireland for further training, so Percy was standing in for him. June had managed to get some leave to be at the christening. June and sixteen-year-old Malcolm were godparents.

'Our lads are stuck on the beaches at Dunkirk and the ruddy Jerries are going to drive them into the sea' Percy raged. 'Wars are not won by retreating. Heads should roll in Westminster for this!'

'Who told you our soldiers are stuck on the beach, Dad?' Malcolm queried.

'A mate of mine has a fishing boat at Southend and he was telling me that the Royal Navy was commandeering every small boat around the coast for a rescue mission from Dunkirk. He has it on good authority that the Navy is going to take the Army off and bring them home.'

'I haven't read any of this in the papers.' Donald's face expressed the doubt he was feeling.

'The government are trying to keep a lid on it so the British people don't panic. I mean, can you imagine the outcry if it got out that the bloody Germans are driving our boys into the sea?'

'Hope it's not a lost cause and we've had it.'

'Donald, we have not had it, not by a long chalk, and we're not going to throw the bloody towel in, either.'

'Percy, mind your language,' Tess interrupted.

'Aw, Percy, come on. I didn't say that,' Donald said.

'It was implied' Percy muttered.

'We have to regroup,' was Donald's rebuttal. 'I just wish

the Jerries would go back to Germany and leave us alone.'

'I agree with Donald,' Susan smiled as she joined the men. 'I hate to break up this war council, but my daughter needs her grandfather and grandmother for some official christening photographs.'

'Stop the war, Donald. The Blore women have a bigger crisis that can't wait.' Smiling, Percy followed in Susan's wake.

The beginning of summer was glorious, with long hot days followed by warm balmy evenings. Percy kept saying he could not remember a summer so hot. Tess continually complained that the heat was causing her to lose her appetite – much to Susan's amusement, as her mother-in-law was grossly overweight.

One lovely day in early June, Tess came hurrying towards Susan, who was sitting in the garden on a blanket dangling a soft toy above her child's head.

'France!' she panted. 'France has fallen! They'll be coming after us now, won't they?' She was close to tears. 'Doris, my cleaning lady, heard it on the wireless and came to tell me. She said the Germans will kill us all. I'm scared, really scared, honestly I am.'

Jumping to her feet, Susan cradled her mother-in-law in her arms.

'Don't upset yourself. Everything will be fine; you'll see.' Susan had calmed Tess' fears, but she could not calm her own. The Germans had conquered the Low Countries and now France. Every night on the wireless there were reports of merchant vessels and Royal Navy ships being sunk with amazing regularity, frightening the British people. The German war machine, as Percy called it, seemed unstoppable, and everyone worried what would happen next. There were rumours that the Germans would soon occupy the Channel Islands, and if this happened, surely it was only a question of time before they arrived in London. It was unthinkable that the German Army could invade Britain, but the French must have had similar thoughts about their fate, she reflected. Gossip about citizens from conquered countries being arrested and imprisoned or executed abounded in London, and fear was spreading like wildfire. Would the Nazis imprison the King and his family? Or would they escape to Canada or even Australia? Everyone said that Churchill and the entire British government would be shot, and that all male children would be killed and female children brought up to be loyal Germans and breed for the Reich.

Susan gazed at her daughter lying on the blanket playing with a cuddly toy. Would her child grow up to breed for the Reich? It didn't bear thinking about.

Susan shuddered and her eyes filled with tears. She had told Tess not to listen to gossip, but she had not taken her own advice as she, too, had been listening to the talk on the streets and in the shops. She must do something to help her country. Then she remembered the posters on the underground station asking for volunteers. She bent over and picked up her baby.

'Let's go inside and have a nice cup of tea. Tomorrow,

would you be a dear and look after Penny for me? I'm going to register as a volunteer.'

Tess stopped walking and gaped in surprise. 'What can you do?'

'Well, I expect they'll find something for me, even if it's only making the tea. I certainly can't sit here without offering to help, can I?'

'What will Michael say?'

'He can't say much if he isn't here, can he?'

She didn't care what her husband's reaction would be; what he didn't know wouldn't hurt him. When she saw the frown on her mother-in-law's face she didn't voice these feelings, but said, 'I'll write and tell him what I'm going to do. He won't mind.'

Returning downstairs after putting Penny down for her afternoon nap, Susan heard the door-knocker and called out to Tess that she would answer it. If it were the cleaning lady, she would give Doris a piece of her mind for scaring Tess so much. When she opened the door a young girl was standing there holding a small suitcase.

'Can I help you?'

'Would this be the home of Corporal Michael Blore, now?' She was of medium height with flaming red hair, beautiful green eyes and a thick Irish brogue.

Her curiosity aroused, Susan invited the girl inside, explaining to Tess that the young woman was looking for Michael. All the Blore's had been curious as to where Michael had been posted after he had left Ireland, but he could not tell them because he did not know, and it became a topic of conversation whenever the family got together. Malcolm had suggested that his brother's regiment had been sent to Brighton on the south coast to stop any German invasion, and June's guess was that they were in Malta to protect British interests there, but Percy said that in his opinion the only place where there was any action was in Egypt, so they all believed that Michael's regiment was in the desert. The Blore family, mindful of the government posters, which said, 'Loose lips sink ships', kept their opinions within the family circle.

'I'm afraid my son is abroad with the Army' Tess said. 'Why do you want him?'

'I was always knowing he was shipping out – he told me – but, y'see, he forgot to give me his address. So his friend Joe Tocker, who's after breaking his leg and couldn't travel with the regiment, as he is still in hospital in Belfast, he gave me this address. I s'pose I should tell you. Me, name's Katherine O'Donnell, everyone calls me Katie and me and Michael, we're walking out together and we're planning on getting hitched. Well, truth to tell, I'm pregnant, and me Ma thought if I come to London and wait until his next leave we can get married.'

The silence was deafening, and Katie thought the older woman was going to faint. The younger girl had paled. 'Oh, bejasus, he's not dead now, is he?' Katie asked, tearing her gaze from the two women and looking around the room. Michael had told her that his family was very rich, and from the quality of the furnishings he had not lied. 'He's not dead is he?' Katie repeated, as she looked again at the two shocked, silent women standing side by side.

'He will be when his father gets hold of him,' Tess muttered under her breath.

'Shush!' Susan whispered as she tried to recover from the shock. The wicked scoundrel! How could he do this to her, his new baby and his parents? Katie broke in on her thoughts by asking to use the lavatory. Susan was grateful for the interruption, as it would give her time to collect herself. She showed the girl to the outside toilet. When she returned indoors, Susan found Tess wringing her hands and muttering as her eyes filled with tears. Hurrying to the drinks cabinet, Susan poured a glass of sherry; her mother-in-law looked as if she was ready to fall in a heap.

'Percy warned him about this,' Tess said sipping her sherry. This information stopped Susan in her tracks.

'Has he done this before?' she exclaimed.

'Michael had many girlfriends, but when he married you he said he was going to turn over a new leaf. Like a couple of fools, Percy and I believed him.'

'How could you and Percy allow me to marry your son, knowing he was a womaniser?' gasped Susan. 'How could you? What a naïve little idiot I am! Just how many illegitimate offspring does your son have?'

Tess did not answer, but burst into a flood of tears.

Susan paced up and down from one edge of the Axminster rug to another. It was all becoming clear now: all those weeks he had been working late at the shop and not coming home for dinner, he had been out with his fancy woman – or should it be women? What an evil snake he was! What a deceitful dog! Susan couldn't think of words bad enough to call him. She had trusted him and made a nice home for both of them and their unborn child, while he was playing around. He wanted to have his cake and eat it, too. Well, he couldn't. How could Percy and Tess have allowed her to be led up the aisle like a lamb to the slaughter? She wanted to cry, not for her wrecked marriage, but because she had been deceived by the Blore family.

Susan decided she had to somehow get out of this mess with some dignity. Swallowing her feelings of revulsion for the Blore's, she turned to Tess, saying she was going to see where the Irish girl was, and made a quick exit.

Susan was glad Penny was upstairs asleep. She had only just put her down for an afternoon nap five minutes before the Irish girl arrived. Thank God she had!

She found Katie in the garden.

'You found the lavatory?'

The girl nodded. 'What a lovely garden this is. It'll be just grand for me to sit out here waiting for me bub to be born.'

'I'm afraid you cannot stay. There is no room here, and besides, Michael's mother is quite upset with what you have just told her.'

'And who are you to be telling me what to do? His Ma isn't the only one that's upset. Me ma is, too, and she told me to get meself over here and get a ring on me finger. Who are you anyway, his sister?'

Susan didn't trust herself to answer and shook her head. She would divorce that rotten rat. This girl was welcome to him. She even considered warning the Irish girl about the kind of life she could expect married to that animal.

'Well, what are ye, then? Me darlin' Michael told me he had a cousin. Is that you?'

Susan gave a quick nod. 'Would you like some tea and something to eat before you leave?' She had already decided against warning Katie.

'I'm no eejit. I didn't want to share Michael's bed. He had to coax me, and when he offered to marry me, well, I let him have his wicked way. Even if I wanted to go back to Ireland, I've no money.'

'I'll give you five pounds.'

'Are you trying to buy me off? Well, it won't work. I love him and he loves me. It wasn't my idea to wed. It was his. I just wish he was back from wherever they've sent him.'

She sniffed. 'I hope he doesn't go and get himself killed now.'

Susan wished him in hell, but she didn't say so. 'Why don't you come inside and rest a while?" she said. "Then I'll call for a taxi to take you back to the station. I'll give you his Army address, and you can write to him. When he gets leave you can marry him. Now, you must be hungry. Let's go inside.'

'To be sure, I could manage a cuppa and sometin' to eat before I go. I'm eating for two now, ye know.'

Tess, who had been listening from behind the open door, scooted into the kitchen to put the kettle on and prepare some pressed tongue and pickle sandwiches. She wanted the girl out of the house before Percy came home, for there would be hell to pay. He would probably disown Michael into the bargain. Tess loved her son no matter what he'd done, and she wanted to protect him from Percy's wrath. Michael was very naughty, getting that Irish girl in the family way, but boys will be boys.

Later that evening, when Percy had calmed down, he wearily climbed the stairs and knocked on Susan's bedroom door, only entering when she called for him to do so. She was standing at the window gazing out into the darkness.

'Can I please talk to you for a moment?' he said.

She turned around to face her father-in-law with swollen eyes. 'I can't stop crying,' she said.

'Dig your fingernails into the palm of your hands as hard as you can. If your nails are short, use anything sharp and press it into your palm. Works every time.'

She tried his suggestion and felt better; the harder she pressed her fingernails, the less the tears came. Susan looked towards him. He looked very tired and weary, as if he had all the problems of the world upon his shoulders, but she felt no pity for him after the mind-numbing events of the past few hours.

'Firstly, Susan, I would like to say thank you for handling a difficult situation today. I wish you had telephoned me at the shop. Tess tells me you were magnificent, you even gave the girl some money for her fare home to Ireland.'

'I took the money from your petty cash tin in the bureau.'

'I'm glad you did. You can use the petty cash any time, and for anything you want.' Percy cleared his throat. 'I know how you must be feeling, and I would like to explain. Michael told us he was in love with you, and that all he wanted was you by his side. Both Tess and I believed him. We thought that once he was married he would settle down and be happy and content. We were wrong. I would like to apologise for not making you aware of Michael's shortcomings. Tess and I feel you are like our daughter, and we love our sweet granddaughter. Please don't leave us.'

'I am going to divorce your son.'

'I'm glad you're getting rid of the wretch. I'll pay for the divorce.' Then he sighed heavily. 'I can't put into words, Susan, how much of a disappointment he is to his mother and me. I don't want him in my house ever again. I've hired a locksmith to fit new locks on the front and back doors next week. So his blasted key won't work, if he ever shows up here.'

Susan knew quite well that Percy would never stop his son from entering the family home, nor would Tess allow Percy to disown him. But he had tried to reassure her, and she was grateful.

'Thank you' she said. 'I feel a little better, but to be honest I am so confused, I really don't know where to go or what to do.'

'Please stay with us. Tess will look after Penny and you can become a volunteer. Sorry, Tess told me what you are planning,' he said by way of explanation. 'I was talking to a chap the other day who's in charge of the Air Raid

Protection at St John's depot. I hear they're looking for volunteer drivers for ambulance crews, and you're a better driver than me and that's the truth. Another thing, Susan. Why don't you get out of the house with June now and again, enjoy yourself and put this whole nasty business behind you?'

'May I ask some questions?' she said. He nodded. 'When Michael told me he was working late to lift the profits, he wasn't at the shop, was he? In fact, he was rarely at the shop. That's why you sacked him, wasn't it? And was it your suggestion that I move in with you and Tess?'

Percy gave a brief nod. He didn't want to upset her more than he had to; the poor girl had been through enough. Susan hadn't told the Irish girl that she was Michael's wife when she gave the girl his Army address. Then she had given the girl five pounds and called a taxi to take her back to the station and home to Ireland.

Percy was proud of his daughter-in-law. She had courage and kept a cool head in a crisis; he respected her for that. Tess, on the other hand, had gone to pieces, and so it was left to Susan to handle it. And handle it she had, with grace and dignity. Percy hoped she would not leave.

Chapter Seven

A screaming siren suddenly pierced the air. It was a most terrifying sound, and one Londoners had come to hate. Susan was heading home after her night shift duty, but she quickly changed direction when the siren sounded and hurried towards one of the many underground stations to escape the air raid. She fervently hoped Tess had taken Penny into the Anderson shelter Percy had erected some weeks before.

Joining the queue shuffling down the stairs towards the underground platform, Susan saw children crying with fear. Some people were pushing and shoving to find a space. There were a few disagreements, but most families huddled together, quietly awaiting the 'All clear' so that they could emerge from the tunnel and get on with their lives. Several women fell to their knees praying, some were cursing the Germans, while still others were knitting, sewing, playing card games or reading the newspaper, as if the danger overhead could not disrupt their normal activities.

She marvelled at the stamina of the Londoners. They seemed to take everything in their stride. Nothing rattled these people, and she was glad she was one of them. It was widely accepted that if London could hold out against the Luftwaffe, the rest of Britain would too.

Her mind wandered back over the last three days. She had been called out during a night raid to pick up injured survivors from bombed buildings. The Air Raid Protection and rescue squads dug through the debris to find those who had perished and those who were alive but injured.

Susan took the badly wounded to the nearest hospital and the injured to the nearest first aid centre, and if that was too busy she drove around until she found one that was not. It had been a long, arduous shift, and she was ready for a break when 'Moaning Minnie' went off again, sending everyone scurrying below ground like moles. Daytime raids were worse than night raids. The streets were crowded with people going about their business, and many were caught without protection, whereas at night Londoners remained at home under a table or staircase or in Government-issue shelters.

After a daytime bombing raid two days before, an urgent call had come in for ambulances to go to St Andrew's school. Susan and her team were one of the first to arrive. The firemen were still battling the flames at the rear of the school, and rescue teams were entering the smoky ruins at the front to search for anyone, dead or alive. The school playground was completely waterlogged from the firemen's hoses, and everything and everybody was soaked. The terrible smell of burning flesh and the screams of the dying and injured were heart-wrenching. It was well known among the volunteer ambulance teams that many children had died from injuries or illnesses due to the lack of doctors. Most doctors had been called up to treat the men in the armed forces, leaving only trainee medical students and doctors who had come out of retirement to care for the people of London.

Teams from the rescue squads were laying the dead children in rows and covering the bodies with canvas tarpaulins on the far side of the playground away from the prying eyes of passers-by while they waited for trucks to take the bodies to the mortuary. Small sandalled feet were sticking out from beneath the tarpaulins, while crying mothers roamed the playground searching for their children.

The sight of dead and dying children with their clothing blown from their small bodies had Susan gulping back tears as she worked tirelessly to save those who were still breathing. Her insides were shaking as she looked at the small, still forms, and she found it hard to concentrate on her work. She tried sucking in deep lungfulls of air to steady her nerves, but the air was so full of acrid smoke that it made her vomit. Controlling herself, she managed to overcome her discomfort and focus on helping the children. She was there to do a job.

A small boy with a severe head wound and a glazed look in his eyes staggered towards her, crying for his mother, who he said worked in the school canteen. Susan gently picked him up and carried him to her ambulance, all the while talking to the boy, who said his name was Ronnie, and answered questions about his family. Although she drove the ambulance as fast as she dared through the chaos of the bomb-damaged streets, when they arrived at St Bart's the boy was dead. Later, back at the depot, she learned that the boy's mother had run straight into the burning school calling his name.

The horror of bombs being dropped on schoolchildren made her more determined than ever to carry on with her volunteer work. However gruesome it was, and despite the long hours, she would continue. A few weeks before she had been ready to throw in the towel and look for some other kind of volunteer war work, as the grisly sights she witnessed left her emotionally drained and at times unable to cope. Then one day she saw a sign that changed her mind: it was a sign outside a bombed-out shop which said, 'Business as usual'.

When she joined the volunteer ambulance service, she had to take a special driving test and have some of knowledge of first aid. As an ambulance driver, not only did she have to save lives; she was also responsible for checking that her vehicle's tyres, battery and radiator were in good working order and making sure that the back of the ambulance was clean before they left the depot. The ambulance volunteers were mainly women and were a good bunch to work with. Pamela Nelson was the new Officer-in-Charge, the previous officer having been killed in a raid two weeks before. The women worked in shifts and had one weekend off in three.

Death was a constant companion in the volunteer ambulance service. Everyone was aware that the war was turning the living into selfish individuals, hoping that the badly injured would die quickly without a fuss. It was all so terrible.

The noise of the 'All clear' signal cut across her thoughts as she emerged from the underground and looked around the damaged city she had come to love. London resembled a colossal building site, with sandbags towering like giant sentinels, guarding doorways to prevent damage from bomb blasts. Scaffolding and hoardings enclosed precious statues, making London look like a ghost city. Craters in roads were becoming familiar too, some of them deep enough to accommodate a car, a van or even a bus. Entire streets were oceans of bricks, dust and stone. The whole city looked like a sea of rubble, and many of the buildings that remained were mere skeletal frames. To add to the eeriness, giant cylindrical barrage balloons hovered above the city like something out of a horror film.

She took her last look at the gloomy city as she hurried to the bus stop. Halfway there, she saw a bus and sprinted to catch it. Susan never ceased to be amazed that amongst all the carnage, death and destruction trains and buses still operated, the postman still managed to deliver the mail and Londoners went off to work each day. How brave the people were.

Entering the house, Susan bumped into Malcolm, who was just leaving. She glanced at his suitcase, but before she could utter a word he said, 'I've joined up, and the oldies are hopping mad'.

'But you're only sixteen!'

'According to the Navy I'm eighteen.' He looked at Susan sheepishly. 'I lied about my age.'

She could sympathise with him, as she had often lied about her own age. 'Oh, Malcolm!'

'Please don't,' he said. 'It's something I want to do, but if you can pacify the oldies, especially Mum, I would appreciate it. Look, I've gotta rush. Bye!' he ran down the steps.

Tess was in tears when Susan walked into the sitting room. She always seemed to be crying these days. It was almost a daily occurrence to hear of a neighbour who had lost a family member or even their home, casualties of this awful war.

'His ship will sink, I just know it will,' Tess wailed as she blew her nose and dabbed her eyes. 'Why can't they send somebody else's son? Why do they have to pick on me all the time? I tell you, it's just not fair.' Then she burst into another round of tears and nose-blowing.

Susan had heard enough. It was always the same, returning home each day to find Tess in tears, carrying on about some catastrophe, real or imagined. Susan would listen in silence and then go to the drinks cabinet and pour a soothing sherry for her mother-in-law.

'Is Penny sleeping?' she asked, striving for a little sanity.

'The little lamb went off to sleep after her meal,' Tess sniffed. 'She is the sweetest child, but I do have to watch her, especially when she's in the kitchen. She heads straight for the open door, and I do so worry about the steps that lead into the garden. I must ask Percy to have a small wooden gate made to put across the back door when it is open.'

Heaving a sigh of relief that Tess had lost her black mood with the help of the sherry, Susan went into the kitchen to make some tea. Tess followed glass in hand, chatting non-stop about the endless queues at the shops. Susan paid scant regard. The silly woman never had to wait in line for anything, as Percy bought all they needed through the black market, which was rife in London. He spoiled his wife just as he had spoiled his sons. Tess went everywhere in a taxi. In fact, Susan couldn't remember the last time Tess had been on a bus.

'What time are you meeting June?' Tess asked.

'She's calling around sevenish.' Susan had changed her mind and decided to go out tonight. She needed to be in the company of normal people for a change, especially after what she had witnessed at St Andrews school. She wanted to dress up and enjoy herself for a while and put this terrible war out of her mind, if only for a few brief hours. Some weeks before Louisa had given Susan a few yards of sheer silk georgette, almost the same colour as her violet eyes. She had it made into a calf-length cocktail dress which floated out whenever she walked, and she was just longing to wear it.

'Where's the party being held?' Susan asked as they were driving towards the city.

'The Savoy' June replied with a chuckle.

Susan had never been to the Savoy but she knew it was exclusive. She had been out a few times with the crowd June mixed with. They were carefree and fun to be with, and she was looking forward to escaping from the war tonight.

With a sidelong look towards her friend, Susan remembered how good June had been when she had found out about Michael's pregnant Irish girl. She had marched Susan off to an old colleague of hers who was a lawyer in the office where she had worked before the war. It was explained to Susan that there were sufficient grounds of adultery to divorce Michael Blore. However, nothing could be done until he returned home, probably after the war came to an end. June had consoled her by saying 'Not all marriages are made in heaven,' and now she had become one of Susan's closest friends, so much so that the two of them went out frequently together.

For June, joining the WAAF had not only been for King and Country; she was rather partial to men in uniforms and would swoon if the uniform had a pilot in it. Each time she had weekend leave, she would meet some RAF friends in the West End. If Susan was free, June always invited her to join them.

'Who have you blackmailed to get the keys for this?' Susan asked, looking at the plush interior of the car.

'Actually, it was given to me to look after.'

'I don't believe you. C'mon, June, what else are you looking after?'

'Well, the pilot I used to dream about has gone and got

himself married, and while he's on his honeymoon I've got his stupid dog.'

'And the car?' Susan asked, trying to hide a smile.

'He would have taken that, too, if there had been enough petrol in the tank to drive his bride to Wales.'

This time Susan laughed. 'Oh, June, perhaps one day you'll find the right man.'

'I hope so, blossom. I do hope so.'

The entrance to the Savoy was covered in sandbags which some patriotic bright spark had painted red, white and blue. The music, the laughter and the buzz of happy voices filled Susan's ears as she entered the foyer. After checking their coats and giving the name of their table, the *Maître d'* led them in to the supper club just as the orchestra began to play a foxtrot. Three men, all in Air Force uniforms, stood up while an elegantly-dressed woman remained seated. June made the introductions before they claimed their seats. These men weren't June's usual crowd, and Susan didn't know them. They were dressed in officer uniforms, and one of them had so many pips on his shoulder Susan thought he must be very high-ranking indeed.

'Champagne, ladies?' one of the men offered, reaching for a bottle nestled in an ice bucket after they were all seated.

'Do try the pâté,' the other said, pushing forward a dish of what looked like meat paste disguised as pâté, surrounded by delicate triangles of toasted bread. Food supplies were in short supply even for the Savoy, Susan guessed.

Her mind wandered back to when they had been driving towards the Savoy. Susan had noticed it was a clear night, often called a 'bomber's moon'. Knowing the Germans never missed an opportunity, she wondered if they would raid London tonight. She had been called out countless times when off duty and hoped there would be no air-raid warning tonight as she would have to leave early and report for duty.

Her musings were interrupted when one of the men asked her to dance. She responded with a smile of acceptance, and he led her to the floor.

A group of officers at a table close to the dance floor were talking and eating – all except one. He was watching a woman in a violet dress circling the floor in the arms of a British airman.

'What a beautiful woman' he said.

At his words, the other three officers followed his eyes. One of them squinted through the smoke-filled room. Suddenly his eyes widened with surprise, and he stood up just as the dance finished. It was Captain Harry Fortescue,

'Excuse me, gentlemen.' He walked towards Susan with a dazzling smile on his face. She was breathtakingly beautifully, even more so than when he had last seen her in the kitchen at his parents' London home. 'We meet again,' he said as they came face to face.

Susan excused herself from the Air Force officer, and when he departed she turned.

'Oh, Harry, how wonderful to see you,' she beamed, her eyes taking in his uniform and his dapper Mayfair moustache. 'You look very dashing. Have you graduated from Sandhurst?'

He gave a swift nod and a big smile. 'You're enchanting.' The orchestra struck up *A Nightingale Sang in Berkeley Square*, and Harry asked, 'Shall we?'

She stepped willingly into his waiting arms. As they started dancing, he inquired, 'Why didn't you write?'

'Miriam died, the cake shop was sold, and during the move I lost your address. Allow me to apologise.'

'I wrote several letters to the shop and all were returned.'

'If you are trying to make me feel guilty, you are succeeding.'

He laughed and then changed the subject. 'Did you eventually wed that lucky chap?'

She shook her head. 'Terrible mistake.'

'Oh, he wasn't the love of your life, then?'

'Please, Harry. Let's not talk about him. What rank are you now?'

'I'm a Captain in the Royal North Devon Hussars.'

'The family regiment?'

'Great-grandfather, Grandfather and Father all served in the Hussars. What are you doing now?'

Susan told him about her volunteer work as an ambulance driver. However, she did not mention her child, or that she was still living with Michael's family.

'What are you doing in London, Harry?'

'I've been seconded to escort a group of Americans around.' He withheld the fact that the Americans were setting up headquarters for General Eisenhower's arrival and that he was to act as liaison officer between the British and American personnel. When the dance ended he took her arm and said, 'Come and meet some Americans. They're new in town and would like to meet a lovely English girl.'

When they arrived at the table the men stood up, and Harry made the introductions, starting with the highest-ranking.

'This is Major Patrick Carlon. Sir, may I introduce Susan Cadiz, an old friend of mine.'

The Major reached out and took her hand in his. Her fingers quivered, and he tightened his grip and looked down into her eyes with a grin.

'Call me Rick' he said.

His handshake was gentle but firm, and Susan found herself gazing into a pair of dark, shrewd, intelligent eyes. Rick arched an eyebrow, wondering if she was going to reply. Suddenly, realising they were still holding hands, she quickly retrieved her hand and said, 'Call me Susan.'

Smiling, he invited her to sit down. Susan returned his smile, but before she could take her seat, Harry introduced the other officers. Bringing her attention back to the Major as he spoke to Harry, she noticed that his accent wasn't a rough Yankee twang but polite and polished. However, it was his attractive dark eyes, perfectly-shaped eyebrows and fine chiselled features that made his profile so handsome. He was quite striking, a little in the Clark Gable mould, and she found it difficult to avert her eyes.

'Would you like to dance?' he asked with a broad grin.

Aware she was staring at him, Susan blushed, trying to collect her thoughts. She wanted to apologise for staring, but could not form the words. He held out his hand and smiled.

Getting to his feet, he took her hand, placed his other hand in the small of her back and led her onto the dance floor. His touch caused butterflies to dart around inside her. She hoped she wouldn't miss a step and tread on his highly-polished shoes, which were so shiny they looked like mirrors. The orchestra started to play 'Moonlight Serenade' as he took her into his arms. She closed her eyes and lost herself in the music.

'You're the most beautiful woman I've seen since arriving in England,' he murmured close to her ear.

She wanted to tell him he was beautiful, too, but was afraid that it would either embarrass him or make him feel big-headed. So she kept silent. He was probably married with several children in America, or he was the secret dream of dozens of girlfriends.

When the music stopped, and with his arm still around her waist, he stared at her as if transfixed. She felt the attraction immediately. Inside, Susan was shaking, but she was hoping she looked cool and calm on the outside, just like him. They both stood on the dance floor smiling at each other until June interrupted and broke the spell.

'Pardon me, Susan. We are thinking of going on to the Carlisle Club for a nightcap. Are you coming?' It was a downright lie, but June had to think of some way to get her out of this American's arms and back to the Air Force officers' table. She had raved to her boss about Susan's good looks, so much so that he had asked June to invite the young lady to his birthday celebration. He was a bit peeved when Susan had deserted the group so soon and had asked June to find her. When she first spied Susan, she had been dancing with a British officer, and now she was with an American – and a Major at that, she noticed, glancing at his military insignia.

Susan was forming the words of reply, but before she could speak, Rick, without taking his eyes from Susan, answered, 'Susan is staying right here. Miss?'

'Meadows. June Meadows.'

'Don't worry, Miss Meadows. I'll see the lady home safely.' The music started again, and Rick, completely ignoring June, swept Susan away and began circling the floor. 'I've just found you and I don't want to lose you. Hope I didn't speak out of turn just now.'

'I didn't want to go to the club anyway.'

'So you're not offended?'

She smiled. 'Not at all.'

'You're the first English woman I've met and I'd like to get to know you some more.'

When the music finally died away he held her at arm's length. 'Shall we go for a walk?'

'What about Harry and the others?'

'I'll pull rank,' he chuckled. 'I'll wait in the bar while you collect your coat.'

Later, while walking towards the embankment, he told her that his father owned a horse stud in Virginia, which had been in his family since early last century. He was the only son and had one sister. The stud had thirty horses, mostly brood mares, and his father was constantly trying to improve bloodlines. Rick did not elaborate about breeding techniques, as he thought it inappropriate and might make her blush. He knew, rather than being told, that she was a little naïve.

Susan was spellbound listening to his description of the stud and his home. He had graduated from West Point, just like his old man, who, he explained, had been a cavalry officer in the Great War and wanted his son to follow in his footsteps. Rick's interests were horses and the breeding of top-class stock, but he had put this on hold until the war with Germany and Japan ended.

'Would you like to go horse-riding if I can arrange it?' he asked.

'I have never been on a horse.'

'Then I will teach you. OK?'

'Thank you.'

'You haven't told me anything about yourself.'

'There's not much to tell. I live with relatives, and I'm a volunteer ambulance driver.'

She was desperate not to lie to him, so she refrained from telling him too much. Whenever he asked a personal question about her family she avoided it by changing the subject. He lit a cigarette and offered her one, but she refused. Several weeks before June had coaxed her to try a cigarette; she had ended up being sick and her face had taken on a green tinge. Susan had neither the funds nor the desire to smoke cigarettes.

'All I know so far is you don't smoke, you only drink tea, you live with relatives and you drive an ambulance.' Rick would bet his last dollar that there was a lot more, but she was not about to tell him – not tonight, anyway.

Glancing at the sky, Susan was surprised to discover that it was almost dawn, and they had been walking and talking for hours, with Rick doing most of the talking. He was such an interesting man that she wished this night would never end. Earlier, he had spied a small café which was still open and they had enjoyed coffee together. He told her that the coffee in England tasted like muddy water; in contrast, the women in England were like golden champagne. He had bought her a posy of violets from a flower seller, saying they matched her eyes. Susan was overwhelmed.

'Your folks live in London?' he asked, interrupting her thoughts

'No' she answered succinctly.

He blew the smoke from his cigarette into the night air and regarded her thoughtfully. 'You're difficult to figure out. Quite an enigma. Or perhaps I'm too inquisitive.' Tossing his cigarette into the gutter, he hailed a taxi, and when they arrived at Queens Road he asked the taxi driver to wait at the corner. Hand in hand, they walked down the road to number twenty-one, but before she could speak he pulled her into his arms and gave her a gentle kiss. Then he turned on his heel and headed back to the waiting taxi.

Rick leaned back against the leather upholstery as the vehicle sped through the pre-dawn streets. He had wanted to hold her in his arms and kiss her long and deep, but was unsure how she would react. As a staff officer he did his job efficiently with tact and diplomacy, and these qualities had rarely deserted him – until tonight. When Harry had introduced this stunning woman, Rick felt as if he had been hit in the guts with a baseball bat. He could not wait to hold her in his arms and had asked her to dance only seconds after she had taken a seat at the table. His training made him an expert at getting information for his commanding officer, but the only information he had gained about her was her telephone number, and this he had obtained from her friend June at the bar.

What on earth had driven him to invite her to go riding? Only last week he had purchased four mounts at Tattersall bloodstock sales and shipped them down to General Eisenhower's country retreat. The General was still in Washington, and with a bit of luck Rick could arrange to take this beautiful woman riding before Ike stepped off the plane in England.

He slid further down into the seat. He was well aware of the directive issued by the previous commander to all American personnel serving in the United Kingdom, a directive, which, in part, forbade all fraternising with British women. He wondered how the hell that could be enforced, as a quarter of the men stationed near London had already shacked up with women. General Eisenhower and his father, Abe Carlon, had been friends since their West Point days, and Rick knew he would have to watch his step. He had sworn an oath before he left the States not to get involved with any woman while over here. The

United States forces were here to beat the Nazis and return home, and that's what Rick intended to do. Duty would be his only mistress.

He ran a hand along the back of his neck and sighed. Tonight he had been seduced by three things: a pair of eyes that reminded him of the wild violets that grew in the forest near his home; the fine line of two perfect eyebrows which lifted in surprise when he suggested horse-riding; and the music of soft laughter. He knew true beauty when he saw it, and she had enough to melt a man's heart and put paid to any oath. He hoped that when General Eisenhower arrived in London he would rescind the fraternising order. If not, Rick would have to deny himself the company of the prettiest girl in London, and that was something he did not plan on doing.

Susan closed the front door and leaned against it. His kiss had tasted of tobacco and Scotch, and there was a musk fragrance about him, too. His mouth was warm and inviting. Susan was intoxicated at the taste, feel and smell of him. This was a new discovery for her, and she longed for more, but he had quickly lifted his lips from hers and departed. She was confused as to why he had left so abruptly and wondered if it was because she had refused to tell him about her family. If she had, would he have bolted like one of his stallions?

She did not understand men, nor was she an expert at kissing, but she was learning. In the taxi earlier, he had been the perfect gentleman; he had not forced himself on her or tried to paw her, as June said some Americans did.

Instead, he had arranged to meet her for dinner at the Dorchester Hotel in two days' time. From the way he talked and smiled at her and kept her out until almost dawn, she just knew the attraction was mutual – or at least she hoped it was.

Upon entering her bedroom, Susan slipped off her coat and shoes and picked up her dictionary. He had used a word tonight she had not fully understood.

Chapter Eight

Knowing she wasn't on the roster for two whole days, Susan lay in bed day-dreaming about Rick Carlon. For the first time in her life, she was completely happy, and she was convinced she was falling in love. He made her feel all shaky inside when he looked at her with such admiration in his eyes, and when he smiled at her, it was as if she was floating on clouds. Lately she had lost her appetite, which Louisa had told her was a definite sign of being in love. She wondered if the Blore family or her friends at the depot had noticed a change in her.

There was only one thing spoiling her happiness: Tess had informed her that June was gleefully telling everybody about the American. Gossip soon spread, and several friends and neighbours were making jokes about the Clark Gable lookalike. Susan was determined to face June to put a stop to the gossip, and she arranged to meet her at Lyons tearooms.

'This nonsense has to stop, June" she told her. "If Rick finds out, he may well be angry at having all and sundry gossiping and giggling about him. Besides, Rick does not have a moustache. He's clean-shaven and his eyes…'

'…Are dark as jet, and the actor's are grey. I know,' June interrupted. 'It was only a bit of harmless fun. Anyway, Rick is terribly dishy.'

'I thought you only liked Air Force types,' Susan snapped.

'A girl can change, can't she?' June replied.

The resentment Susan felt towards June was overpowering. She had never experienced jealousy in her life before and quickly swallowed the words that were threatening to spill out and ruin their friendship. Instead, she gave June a look that said, 'Enough is enough,' and then changed the subject.

'I have been invited horse-riding next week and I need some advice about what and what, not to do. You know all about horses. Can you help?'

'Well, you'll need an outfit, jodhpurs, boots and…'

'Jodhpurs?'

'Riding pants, tight fitting from knee to ankle, wide-hipped with a snug bottom.' At Susan's raised eyebrows, June added, 'I'm afraid you cannot go riding in a dress and high heels, blossom. I've got a spare pair of jodhpurs you can borrow and some boots as well. If, as you say, dreamboat has stables in Virginia, he will be an expert horseman. So copy everything he does.'

'His father owns a horse stud.'

'It's the same thing' June sighed, wishing she had met Dreamboat before Susan had. When he had cornered her in the bar at the Savoy, June had used all her feminine wiles to attract him, but the only address or telephone number he had wanted was Susan's.

Her friend's voice brought her back to the present.

'Is there anything else I should know?'

'When you're mounted, wrap your legs around the animal's flanks and squeeze firmly. Then gather the reins and hold tight, just as if it were Dreamboat between your legs.'

Susan blushed. 'We haven't. He never…'

'He will, he will,' June said with a wicked smile. 'By the way, have you heard they're selling a new style of knickers in Selfridges? One Yank and they're off.' June gave a loud belly laugh, which echoed around the tearooms. Susan picked up the menu to try and hide. Sometimes June went too far. Susan guessed she was picking up all this loose talk from the WAAF.

The following week, Rick picked her up in an Army Jeep. It was a beautiful fresh morning as they motored down the picturesque country roads of Surrey. The fields were bathed in speckled sunlight, creating shifting patterns on wild meadow flowers. It was so peaceful and perfect. Even the Nazis, Susan reasoned, could not destroy the beauty of the English countryside.

Eventually, Rick turned off the country road and their journey was over. Susan wished the drive could have lasted longer, as she loved being close to him. Continuing along a shaded driveway, she could see only chimney pots. As they got closer a large grey-stone house emerged from the greenery, with ivy creepers curled around one side of the building, giving it a quaint country look. Rick brought the vehicle to a halt on a small gravelled quadrangle and asked her to wait for him. Susan waited patiently, but she was not alone for long as two officers came out of the main entrance and walked towards her, followed seconds later by another two from a side door.

'Howdy Ma'am' said the first. 'My name's Matt Kelly. This is my buddy, Montgomery, but we call him Monty after your General. Nice touch, hey?'

Without waiting for her to reply, he went on to introduce the others. 'Say, have you any sisters? This sure is a cold country, so different from Texas. Have you been Stateside, ma'am?'

The men had encircled the vehicle and were bending down resting their elbows on the Jeep. They were crowding her, not even waiting for her answer. The one named Matt was doing all the talking, while the others were just staring at her as if she were some kind of museum specimen. Susan was feeling decidedly uncomfortable and wondering where Rick had disappeared to, when she heard his voice.

'OK, you guys.' He had rounded the corner to see his fellow officers hanging over the Jeep like bees round a honey pot. Susan looked uneasy. Rick was annoyed.

'Only keeping the lady company, sir,' Matt offered the only explanation.

When Rick gave an imperceptible jerk of his head, the men took the hint, stepped away from Rick and the vehicle and headed back indoors. Susan, who was watching the men disappear inside, now turned her attention to Rick. He had changed from his uniform into riding clothes, and looked even more attractive. His jacket of forest green perfectly blended with buff-coloured riding breeches, black knee-high boots and turtleneck sweater.

'Sorry about the audience,' he said. He opened the door of the Jeep, helped her step down from the vehicle and led her to where the horses waited.

'Are you ready?'

She sucked her bottom lip, drew a deep breath and nodded, hoping to hide her nervousness. He seemed to sense she was uneasy and helped her into the saddle, adjusted the stirrups, showed her how to set her feet and instructed her how to take hold of the reins.

'You don't think I'll fall off?'

'Don't worry. I'll catch you,' he answered with a grin.

Astride her mount, Susan watched him leap with ease into the saddle of a large chestnut stallion. With a firm grip on the reins, Rick checked the spirited horse and gentled it by patting its neck and whispering to the animal. The material of his riding pants stretched firmly across his thighs and disappeared into knee-high boots. Susan experienced a strange feeling of desire sweeping over her.

'Are you OK?' Rick asked. 'You look uneasy.' He leaned over to seize the bridle of her mount.

'Yes, yes, I'm all right,' her normally soft-spoken voice squeaked. 'I must have been sitting awkwardly,' she lied. She would rather be strung up by her toenails than tell him the truth.

'OK, let's go.' Rick wheeled his horse and fell in beside her as their mounts walked slowly down the driveway and turned onto the parkland. As they went he explained how to hold the reins and how to use her heels. When he thought she had mastered the walk, he began a slow trot, heading towards a small stand of trees in the distance. He kept the horses riding close to each other, the chestnut and the bay moving effortlessly across the turf. He would have liked nothing more than to give the chestnut his head in a brisk gallop, but that would have to wait for another time. He wanted Susan to gain some confidence and conquer her fear.

Glancing over to check whether she was coping, he noticed that her grip on the reins was very taut and her knuckles were almost white; she was pulling the reins too tightly. He called to her to ease off, but she didn't hear him, or was concentrating so hard that she was oblivious to everything except staying on the animal.

Without warning, a stiff breeze swept over the parkland and with no hat, her dark hair began to fly out behind her. His eyes locked onto the column of her neck and further down, the outline of her breasts, clearly visible as the wind whipped her blouse firmly against her body. She looked sensational.

Suddenly, she flew into the air like a trapeze artist. She landed on her bottom, while the horse bolted. After checking she wasn't hurt, he took off after the frightened animal and eased it to a stop. Talking softly to calm the mare, he led it back to where she was sitting.

'Oh, Rick, that was wonderful,' she said, standing up and rubbing her bottom. 'Can I try again?'

'Sure, only this time slacken your grip on the reins, and try a rising trot. That means lifting your butt out of the saddle,' he explained when he saw her questioning look.

She blushed and nodded. Walking up to her mount, Susan gently rubbed its muzzle.

'I didn't mean to scare you. I'm only a beginner,' she murmured to the bay, and then leaned forward to kiss the animal.

As he watched, Rick was both surprised and pleased. She seemed unafraid around horses. With a bit of practice she might become a competent horse-rider.

They took off again. This time she was more relaxed, and so was the horse. They were going so well that Rick increased the pace from a rising trot to a canter and was delighted to see that she was able to keep up with him. Feeling more confident, Susan relaxed and gazed ahead at the small copse they were heading for. Tall silver birch trees stretched gracefully skywards, and beneath the shaded canopy she could see emerald grasses dotted with clumps of bluebells.

Taking her eyes from the scene before her, she turned to Rick and called out, 'I think I'm getting used to it now.' No sooner had the words left her lips than she left the saddle again. Flying through the air, she tumbled to the ground and landed on her back. She lay there slightly winded, but not in pain. The scent of grass and flowers filled her nostrils, and the animal's hooves striking the ground filled her ears as Rick chased after her horse. She lay there, taking in short shallow breaths and hoping that Rick wouldn't think her a complete idiot, when she heard his voice.

'Are you hurt?' he asked, his expression full of concern.

She tried to laugh, but couldn't. When she tried to sit up she suddenly became dizzy. He picked her up, carried her beneath the trees, and hurried to get a flask from his riding jacket, which he had tossed across his saddle.

'Sit up in a crouching position to relax the muscles,' he suggested. After ten minutes she started to breathe normally, and the dizziness passed. 'Sip this slowly,' he commanded.

Gulping it down, she burst into a fit of coughing. 'I thought it was water.'

'That is the best bourbon in the States.'

'Rick,' she said, coughing, 'I don't drink alcohol.'

'Honey, I did say to sip it. Bourbon's the best thing for shock after a fall.' She found that piece of information hard to believe and ignored it.

'Tell me, what did I do wrong this time?'

'Nothing. A bird spooked the mare, she kicked her back legs and off you came,' he replied with a gentle smile. He did not add that an experienced rider would have checked the animal and stayed in the saddle.

Rick examined her legs, arms, spine and shoulders, and was convinced she had no broken bones. Eventually the dizziness passed. Riding was so exhilarating that she was eager to have another go.

'Shall I try again?'

'I think you've had enough for one day. Monty informs me that there are riding stables close to headquarters. So I'll organise something for next week.'

As Susan lay in the grass, Rick noticed some of the buttons of her blouse were undone, revealing a lacy camisole. With her shiny dark hair tangled in the bluebells, she was like a gift he could not wait to unwrap. Lowering himself towards her, he kissed her gently. At first, she was shy to respond, but then a spark between them ignited. As he deepened the kiss, his hands moved rapidly over her body, unfastening the blouse, lifting up the edge of her camisole and covering one of her breasts with his right hand. Seizing both of her hands in his left grip, he stretched them above her head and started kissing and licking her nipples.

Susan felt light-headed and shaky. Her pulse was racing and her stomach was doing somersaults. This feeling had nothing to do with her recent fall and everything to do with the man fondling her.

The sound of voices close by startled Susan and she tore her lips from his.

'Rick, please stop!'

He recoiled at her words, cursed under his breath and got to his feet. Retreating a few paces, he saw some school kids with fishing rods slung over their shoulders, Just as well she had stopped him.

Fastening the lacy material with shaky fingers, she buttoned her blouse, tucking it into the waistband of the jodhpurs and shaking out her shoulder-length tresses. Rick came over to join her and started plucking bluebells from her hair.

'If I can arrange it, will you spend a weekend with me?' he asked.

She looked into his eyes and saw naked desire. It made her heart skip a beat. It told her everything she needed to know.

'Yes' she whispered.

Rick stared at her. The silence punctuated the air with a faint rustle of the wind through the trees. No 'ifs', no 'buts', no silly modesty. She had just said yes.

This woman, who could take his breath away with a smile, was not only beautiful; she made him feel like the most important person in the world. Whenever he was speaking, she gave him her full attention. Her eyes were on him and only him, never glancing around the room as some women did.

'Are you sure?' he asked in a low voice.

'Yes,' she answered. She had never wanted a man to touch her intimately until now, but all that changed when she met Rick. The raw ache inside convinced her, as nothing else could, that she was in love with him.

The next day, Rick and Harry met for a drink at the Connaught Hotel. After discussing details of Eisenhower's headquarters, Rick told Harry about the riding lesson.

'Are you and Susan going out together?' Harry asked.

'Yeah, I guess.'

'That doesn't sound very convincing. What's the matter, old boy?'

Something about Susan bothered Rick. It was like an itch he could not scratch.

'I have a hunch she's holding out on me.' Rick raked his fingers through his hair. 'I just know there's something she's not telling me. Whenever I ask a personal question she dodges the subject or changes the conversation around.'

'Why don't you come right out and ask her, old boy?'

'Jolly tricky, old boy,' Rick said, mimicking Harry's accent.

'I'll tell you what I know. She was orphaned as a baby and brought up by a schoolteacher aunt. Then she came to London to help in a family cake shop. I heard the owner of the cake shop died tragically, and Susan went to live with the shop owner's brother and his family.'

Harry did not tell Rick that she had been married, as he felt that was none of his business. Besides, it was up to Susan to tell Rick about her failed marriage.

'Thanks for the low-down.'

'Are you serious about Susan?'

'Yeah.' Rick did not add that he wanted to marry her. He had already written to his folks. They were always at him about getting married and settling down, but he had told them he was waiting until he found the perfect woman. He had posted a letter and included a picture of him and Susan taken at Tower Bridge, with the words, 'I have found her'.

'To repeat an ancient quote, 'Faint heart never won fair lady'.'

'Thanks, Harry.'

'Susan's a beautiful woman and she's warm-hearted. What more do you want?'

'I know so little about her. For instance, is she British, with a name like Cadiz? It doesn't sound like it. And if she isn't, where does she come from?'

'I always thought you Americans didn't care about breeding.'

'Don't you believe it. My father is a horse breeder. He sets great store by bloodlines.'

'So you want to know if Susan comes from good stock? I believe her father was an officer in the Spanish Navy, and as a horse breeder you know the Spanish are responsible for breeding those aristocratic Lipizzaners. They're really proud of them.'

'To interrupt, Harry, I think you'll find the Spanish Andalusian and Iberian breeds were responsible for the Lipizzaners.'

'I stand corrected. Nevertheless, you have to agree, a Spanish father, an English mother – not a bad combination. Moreover, to prove it, Susan is incredibly attractive and is bound to produce perfect offspring. Doesn't it rather depend who's in the saddle, old boy?' he ventured, before picking up his drink and clinking it against Rick's glass.

'You're outta line, Harry, and you goddamn know it.'

'You're right. Please accept my apologies for conduct unbecoming.' Signalling the barman, he ordered the same again. 'Have you heard the latest rumour circulating headquarters?' Harry continued without waiting for a reply. 'Apparently, during an air raid the other night de Gaulle hid in a filing cabinet and got stuck. When the all clear sounded, one of the rescue boys had to free him. How terribly uncomfortable and embarrassing for Le General!'

When their laughter died away Rick changed the subject.

'Now that Roosevelt has re-equipped the British with Sherman tanks, how do think Monty's Eighth Army will go against the Afrika Korps? Hopefully, not another snafu.'

'Let's hope not. Churchill has replaced so many battle commanders that I think he'll swallow his double corona if Monty isn't victorious.'

Both men grinned. Rick tossed the drink down the back of his throat and said he had to leave, as Ike was flying in from the States.

Leaning on the bar, Harry watched him go. Rick knew nothing of Harry's feelings for Susan – and neither did she, come to that. Harry was a man in love with a woman who barely knew he was alive. Susan treated him more like an older brother than a potential lover, and if she and Rick wed, he would be the first to offer them his best wishes. Harry drained his glass, wondering how many more men he would envy and congratulate.

Lying in bed at the Pier Hotel, Susan lazily stretched her limbs and yawned, relaxed and happy. She felt like a complete woman for the first time in her life. A sense of relief washed over her. She was not the piece of ice that Michael Blore had once called her, but a loving woman who had responded with eagerness to a man – the right man.

She was deeply in love. Susan now knew that it was impossible to separate love and desire. Both feelings were always present whenever she looked at Rick. Last night she had shared many tender moments with him. His mere touch had caused every nerve in her body to fire up, until suddenly their foreplay had become a whirlwind of passion. He was gentle, sensual and loving. He knew the geography of her body better than she did, and introduced her to his. With practised skill, he showed her how and where to touch him to heighten his pleasure. At last, Susan had found a man to love.

Listening to his even breathing, she knew he was still sleeping. She did not want to disturb him, so she just lay there, marvelling at the wonderful night they spent together and all the things he had whispered to her.

His voice interrupted her daydreaming.

'I'm not the first, am I? Do you want to tell me about him?'

Although he was not angry with her, he was jealous as hell, and wanted to know who she had been with.

She was stunned. Being in love for the first time, Susan did not want anything to come between them to ruin their romance. She had not mentioned anything about her marriage, or given any thought to what his reaction might be if she told him.

Feeling embarrassed and lost for words, she started to rise from the bed. Quick as a flash he was on her, pinning her to the mattress with his body, capturing her eyes with his.

'Leave me alone, please, Rick.' His cold dark eyes looked so different now.

'I want you to be honest with me.' The silence lengthened as they stared at each other. 'Tell me, damn it!'

She squirmed, shying away from his prying eyes. She had found love one day, only to lose it the next.

'You'll hate me.'

'I love you, and I want to know everything about you. Now tell me.'

'When Miriam died – I told you about Miriam?' He gave a nod and she continued. 'I had nowhere to live, no work and no money. A nephew called Michael Blore proposed to me. I was barely eighteen and frightened, and I accepted.'

'You loved him?'

'No, I didn't know what love was. The marriage was over when I discovered he was a womaniser.'

'If you didn't love him, why marry the guy?'

A slight tremble coursed through her. She had been afraid to tell him the truth for fear of losing him, but now Rick wanted answers. From the look on his face, he wasn't going to let her off the bed until she told him.

'He, or rather his family, had money. I was desperate, I was alone, and I was broke. So I married him.'

'My family have a lotta dough. Would you pull the same trick on me?'

Susan flinched. To her mind, it was a man's world, and women had to survive as best they could. Without family connections, influence or money, it was next to impossible for any woman to get by without a man. She had never loved anyone except this man who was pinning her to the bed right now. Susan's reply, when it came, was a whisper.

'I wouldn't care if you were the poorest man in the world. I would still love you.'

Rick was satisfied that she had finally come clean and told him the truth, and was relieved that she hadn't loved this Blore guy, who sounded like a real louse. Watching her toy with the hairs on his chest, his loins began to ache. If she only knew what a poor dope he would be without her. Dropping his head lower, he kissed her. She was better each time he tasted her, he just could not get enough. Over the years he had bedded a few women, but this beautiful creature excited him like no other. She was like a drug he just had to have. He would make enquiries about renting a place, and she could move in with him. Then he would have her all to himself.

Within a month, Susan had moved in with Rick. She had tried to avoid leaving Queens Road, but Rick had insisted. She loved him so much she did not resist or object to any of his plans. Percy and Tess had begged her to leave Penny with them, as Tess was so attached to the two-year-old and could not bear being parted from her. Not telling Rick about her daughter put Susan in a difficult position. She felt she could not turn up on his doorstep with a suitcase and a child in tow, so she convinced herself that Penny was better off with Grandpa and Grandma for the time being.

She let herself in with the latchkey he had given her and found some flowers with a note attached.

Hi, Beautiful
Welcome to our love nest. Home late. Big meeting. Love you
Rick

If Susan thought the house in Queens Road was elegant, Rick's domicile in Kenton Mews, Chelsea was more so, with thick red rugs and large club chairs. A dark maple dining table surrounded by four matching chairs occupied an alcove. There were rows and rows of books along one wall, with a gramophone and several Glenn Miller records sitting on an oak table next to a drinks tray. The red theme carried throughout the rooms. Susan wondered briefly who it belonged to and how Rick had managed to find it. Influence, she supposed. After all, he was on General Eisenhower's staff.

After wandering around, Susan went upstairs and came to a halt in a large bedroom. Silver-backed hairbrushes with his initials engraved upon them and bottles of cologne and hair oil sat on a small dressing table. Picking up one of the bottles, she read the label. It was unfamiliar. 'He didn't buy these in England,' she muttered to herself. A huge bed with a scarlet quilt dominated the room. It even dwarfed the tall wardrobe – or closet, as she had recently started calling it.

After hanging up her clothes, she climbed into the bath with the regulation six inches of water – one of the wartime regulations she loathed. With a towel coiled around her hair she put on a lavender nightgown and went into the kitchen to make a hot drink. She was disappointed to find there was no tea. Reading the label on the coffee tin she had picked up, she smiled. His parents must have sent it; he said he was going to write and ask them to send some decent coffee.

Before reaching to take a cup from the Welsh dresser, she remembered another annoying regulation and walked over to the window to close the blackout curtains. Then, turning to the small enamel stove, she put some water on to boil. She opened most of the cupboards to check the groceries. She found a teaspoon in the dresser drawer, finally made a cup of weak coffee and took it into the sitting room.

When she switched on the wireless, a voice announced that the music of Carroll Gibbons and his Savoy Hotel Orpheans was being broadcast throughout London. Susan curled up in one of the deep chairs and thumbed through some American horse magazines, humming softly to the orchestra playing *That Old Black Magic*. The magazine showed pictures of Virginia, and Susan spent some time reading the articles and gazing at the pictures of the beautiful countryside. The advertisement at the front of the publication boldly stated that Virginia was the home of thoroughbred horses, and, from what Rick had told her, she could well believe it. At eleven thirty she went to bed, leaving a small lamp on in the sitting room for Rick. He had requested that she sleep in the raw, as he put it. Susan tossed her nightgown on the chair and fell asleep dreaming of him.

The dream was in such detail. He was kissing her neck and stroking her breasts, making her moan with pleasure.

She could even smell after-shave lotion and a faint odour of tobacco. The dream was so clear he even whispered to her, 'C'mon, honey, open those beautiful eyes for me.'

'I love you,' she whispered dreamily.

'And I love you,' he kissed her. 'I want what I've been thinking about all day. C'mon honey, wake up.'

She didn't want the dream to end. 'Mmmm, leave me.'

He kissed her again, this time more passionately, and her eyelids fluttered open. 'Rick, you're here,' she said through a sleepy haze.

He was lying next to her. Slowly running a hand over his chest and down further, she discovered he was as naked as she was.

'How was the meeting?'

'OK, but right now, I have a different kind of meeting in mind.' Nibbling the shell of her ear he continued, 'I have to leave London in a few days and I need you, now,' he whispered, gently stroking her naked body.

Now she was fully awake, he had her full attention and she turned to him. 'First, can't you tell me why you're leaving London?'

'Beware the fury of an impatient man,' he growled and pulled her beneath him. 'We'll talk in the morning. Tonight is for love.'

Chapter Nine

It was Harry who explained to Susan that General Eisenhower had taken command of Allied troops in French North Africa, and because of Rick's fluency in French, he was included in the team.

'I shouldn't be telling you any of this and I want you to keep it to yourself' he said. 'You've seen the posters scattered around the country telling us 'Careless talk costs lives'.'

'Harry dear, thank you. Rick wouldn't tell me anything, and I needed to know. That's why I telephoned, although I didn't expect you to take me to the Ritz for afternoon tea.'

He smiled. 'I aim to please, sweet Susie.'

He had not seen her for some weeks, so when he had received the message she had left for him at the military club, he had thought it a good idea for them to meet. He suggested the Ritz and turned up early, ordered a Scotch from the bar and waited. He knew, without being told, that she had arrived when he saw dozens of male heads swing around to admire her as she walked towards him in a navy and tan outfit. She seemed oblivious to the admiring eyes and even some envious ones from a small group of women.

'It never ceases to amaze me, sweet Susie, how you manage to look more elegant each time I see you' He said. He had recently started calling her 'sweet Susie', and she reciprocated with 'Harry dear'. He was the only one she allowed to call her Susie.

'I have friends in high places' she said jokingly.

'Churchill, I suppose.'

She laughed merrily, 'Whenever I'm with you, Harry dear, you always make me laugh.'

'I hope you'll always laugh when you're with me.' And only me, he wanted to add but didn't. She was Rick's woman.

'I will,' she replied absently while glancing at dainty sandwiches and sweet pastries, delicately arranged on tiered cake stands, served at the next table. 'I thought there was a war on and food was rationed?'

'If you have money you can buy almost anything, even in wartime. Will you take China or India tea?'

Harry signalled the waiter, and an elderly man in a morning coat approached the table, gave a polite nod to Harry and muttered, 'Milord?'

'The lady would like India tea and I will have China tea, and perhaps some tipsy cake.'

'What on earth is tipsy cake?' Susan asked after the waiter had gone.

'It's an almond creation with lashings of cream. Our cook makes it, and it happens to be one of my favourites. I thought you would like to try it. I daresay the cream may be a bit sparse or perhaps missing altogether, with the wretched rationing.'

'I'm sure I shall enjoy it. Harry dear, have you noticed the waiters are all old?' she whispered, feeling sorry for the elderly men, laden with trays, shuffling about on the polished floor.

'I would hazard a guess that they've been lured out of retirement, with all the young men being called up for military service, and with women taking over traditional male occupations in factories, farms, and transport drivers, London restaurants and clubs are short of staff. I believe the salary in the restaurant industry compares favourably.'

'The waiter called you 'Milord' and all this time I thought you were a captain,' she said with refreshing simplicity.

Harry laughed out loud at her candour, although he was sure it was contrived for the sole purpose of making him laugh.

'You cheer me up. I should invite you to tea more often' he added.

Susan smiled at Harry before turning to chat to the waiter who had arrived at their table with their tea and cake. Harry was staring at the wall behind her. From a report he had read at headquarters, the war was going badly for the Allies, and optimism in Britain was waning. One could see it on people's faces – the terrible feeling that Britain could be defeated persisted amongst the populace – yet no matter how bleak things became, he fervently hoped that Susan would stay alive.

His eyes fell upon her and he saw that she was cradling her chin with her hands, watching him.

'I apologise. I was thinking of something else.'

'I know, I was watching you. Now, you were going to tell me about Milord and the Ritz.'

He smiled. 'My father and I used to come here frequently before the war. The waiter thinks I'm him.'

'Your father has a title?'

'A very minor one.'

Harry was surprised at himself, feeling the need to make light of his father's position. Perhaps after the war titles wouldn't mean much. Harry thought the whole world would be different when the war finally ended. Right now, though, he had an irritating problem to deal with. He was being pressured by his parents into proposing marriage to the tiresome Charlotte Cardwell, the daughter of Lord and Lady Cardwell, and therefore in his parents' eyes eminently suitable. He had told his parents that he would not consider taking a wife while the war was still raging. He had hoped this excuse would work, but it hadn't. He was astute enough to realise that he was being manoeuvred into marriage. He would have to outflank his parents and put himself in the position of being able to make his own choice and not marry someone of his parents' choosing. They needed an heir to the title in the event that their only son was killed in action.

'You look troubled, Harry dear.'

Suddenly, his eyes lit up and a smile crept across his face, showing even, white teeth.

'I have an invitation to a Noel Coward show at the Duchess Theatre next week and I don't have a lady to escort.'

'If that is all that is troubling you, I will accompany you, if you want me too.'

Want her to? He would walk over hot coals to be with her. With Rick in North Africa Harry had been trying to pluck up the courage to invite her but had not known how to bring the subject up. His fears, however, were short-lived, as it had turned out to be quite easy.

A week later, Harry arrived at Kenton Mews looking splendid in his formal dress uniform of black-braided jacket with red facings. The performance was especially for officers and their ladies, and Susan wanted to look her best. With Louisa's help and Percy Blore's money, she was dressed in a black strapless evening gown piped with white satin. From June she borrowed black suede peep-toe shoes and silver combs for her upswept hair. The long white gloves, short black bolero and evening purse were Louisa's. For the first time in her life, she wore a full-length dress and she felt like a lady. She smiled to herself; with barely a pound in her purse she was dressed as if she had a million.

She greeted Harry at the door and gave him a light peck on the cheek. He could feel her moist lips on his skin and her hand lightly resting on the sleeve of his uniform. Harry stared at her for a long time; she was so achingly attractive, more so tonight than he had ever seen her. Presenting her with a small gift, Harry smiled when he saw surprise on her face as she discovered 'Je Reviens' from Worth.

'Are you not going to splash some on?' he asked smiling, as she stared at the elegant glass bottle.

Returning his smile, Susan excused herself and disappeared into the bedroom to dab some perfume behind her ears and on her wrists before leaving the mews.

As the taxi motored through London's streets, Susan sighed inwardly. What a surreal life she was living, from being surrounded by death and destruction as an ambulance driver to dressing in the finest, being wined and dined and escorted by a handsome officer to a West End show. This terrible war demanded that one lived for the moment, as death was a frequent visitor to London.

When the taxi came to a stop, so did her unruly thoughts. Harry stepped onto to the pavement before the theatre entrance, paid the driver and turned to assist Susan.

At the interval an officer on General Eisenhower's staff came towards Susan. 'Say, Miss Cadiz, do you remember me?'

Puzzled, Susan shook her head. 'I'm sorry.'

'I'm Lieutenant Montgomery. The guys at headquarters call me Monty. I come from Cadiz, ma'am – Cadiz in Harrison County, Ohio. I met you some time back when Major Carlon took you horse-riding.'

Her heart leapt. She had always thought there was only one Cadiz, and that was in Spain, the only place her father could have come from. Now it seems there was a Cadiz in Ohio. Perhaps her father was American. With her hair colouring she seriously doubted it, but anything was possible. Susan gathered her wits and smiled at Monty.

'Pleased, to meet you again, Lieutenant. Harry, have you met...?' Harry cut in, 'We have. How are you, Monty?'

'Swell.' He turned to Susan again. 'I have to say, ma'am, you look very chic.'

'Thank-you please call me Susan,' she invited with a beaming smile. 'Where is your partner, Lieutenant?'

'Powdering her nose. If I'm to call you Susan, ma'am, then you must call me Monty.'

Smiling, she refused his offer of a drink. Monty turned to Harry 'Drink, sir?' At Harry's nod, Monty turned on his heel and went to the bar.

'Powdering her nose?' Susan asked.

'Ladies' room,' Harry whispered.

Susan chuckled. 'I can't keep up with all these quaint American sayings. Rick's been trying to teach me.'

'Wanna cawffee?' Harry said, mimicking an American accent and sending Susan into peals of laughter.

'You should hear Rick imitating an English gentleman's accent. It's as funny as your American drawl.'

After leaving the theatre, Harry was having trouble finding a taxi and decided to walk up the side of the market. He took Susan's hand to assist her as they stepped over squashed cabbage leaves, carrot tops and crushed apples that had fallen from hand-carts being unloaded by hawkers, barrow boys and lorry drivers.

'Loverly night for it, guv,' a barrow boy called.

'Oi likes the frock, ducks!' another yelled, followed by a wolf whistle. 'Ow much for the bag o' fruit, guv?' came another bellow. 'Cor, them's loverly peaches, luv. Don't get many o' them to a pound!'

Susan couldn't stop chuckling, and Harry was having

trouble controlling his amusement. Eventually they found a vacant taxi and climbed inside, leaving the market and the joking workers behind.

'It's sad that Covent Garden is only a fraction of the size it used to be. This blasted war has changed London,' Harry complained.

'Have you seen Hyde Park? It looks like a battlefield, with trenches and anti-aircraft guns. Rumour has it that the government are going to dig up all the flower gardens to plant cabbages, carrot and potatoes.'

'Let's forget the war. How about a nightcap?'

'Where?'

'Fortescue House. Father has moved to the country to rest after a recent fall, Mother is in Scotland for the duration of the war, and my sister is in Plymouth with the Red Cross. The house is empty and I use it from time to time. Oh, Jenkins, my batman, will be there,' he added, when he saw the look of indecision on her face. 'I fear the house won't remain vacant for long. The military want to commandeer it to billet officers when they are in London.'

Before opening the main door, Harry lit a single candle and handed it to her. 'I'm afraid there's no electricity. Father had it switched off. We shall have to survive with candles and oil lamps.'

Standing in the marble entrance hall, holding the candle up above her head Susan was surprised at the size and style of the house, although right at this moment it looked anything but elegant. In the centre of the hexagonal foyer stood a dusty table, which held an even dustier Greek urn. She imagined that before the war the table would have been highly polished and the urn brimming with seasonal flowers. There were several doors leading to other parts of the house, and straight ahead, a sweeping staircase, which seemed to disappear into the darkness.

Harry called for his batman, and then threw open a door. 'Shall we wait in the library until he decides to join us?'

Three sides of the library were filled from floor to ceiling with books, while on the other side full-length windows were completely covered, with batten shutters. Before sitting down behind a mahogany desk, Harry lit an oil lamp. He placed it on the desk near a chair and invited Susan to be seated.

'What would you like to drink? I know you seldom take anything stronger than tea, but I have an excellent oloroso sherry from Spain. It is older than we are, and I invite you to try a little.'

She smiled at his funny remark. 'Just a tiny drop, please,' she said, holding up her thumb and forefinger to show him just how small she meant, while wondering what oloroso sherry would taste like.

Susan watched agog as he pulled a handle forward and part of the bookcase disappeared to reveal a drinks cabinet.

'Is this the same house where I delivered the cakes and we bumped into each other in the kitchen?'

'The very same.'

'Can I ask a favour, Harry dear?'

'Anything, sweet Susie.'

'Will you please show me over the house before I leave?'

She almost shot out of her seat, and nearly dropped the glass Harry had just given her, when she heard a voice behind them.

'You called, sir?'

'Jenkins, would you bring a branch of candles? I want to look over the house. By the way, Susan, this is Jenkins, my batman.'

'Pleased to meet you, Jenkins.'

'Likewise, miss. If you'll excuse me, I'll see to the candles.'

Jenkins hurried away, thinking that Captain Fortescue had never brought a female to the house before so the young lady must be special, and such an attractive thing she was. He hoped the captain had met his ladylove at last. That would keep the Earl off his back.

'I'm afraid we'll have to view the house by candlelight.' Harry stood up, gently took hold of Susan's forearm and followed Jenkins, who was holding the candles aloft. 'These are the reception rooms. In the old days they held formal balls and supper parties here.'

Susan gazed up at the chandeliers enclosed with dustsheets. The room was magnificent, with delicate slipper chairs arranged around the ballroom. Most of them wore dust covers.

'Did anyone famous come here?'

'I have it on good authority that the Prince Regent dined here once. As to dancing, I think he was a bit overweight, and no lady could fit in his arms because of his huge girth.'

Susan chuckled at his description. 'How wonderful it must have been to dance in such elegant surroundings.'

Taking the candles from Jenkins, Harry quietly dismissed him and turned to her. 'Your wish is my command, sweet Susie' he said. Then, placing the candelabrum in the middle of the floor, he stepped up to her, gave a low bow and held out his hand. 'Would you do me the honour of dancing this waltz with me, my lady?'

Susan laughed. He couldn't possibly be serious! But one look at his face told her he was. 'What do I say?'

'Curtsy gracefully, and accept graciously.'

She held her skirts, just as she had been taught at Firbank Academy, and made an elegant curtsy.

'I would be delighted, sir.'

'Excellent. Now place your hand on my sleeve, and I will lead you onto the ballroom floor and we can begin to dance.' Taking her in his arms, he started to hum a Strauss waltz before calling out, 'Help me sweet Susie. I can't remember the tune.'

Susan joined in, and soon both of them were humming and travelling across the floor in sweeping circles. Suddenly, she was in another century. Dancing in the shadow of the flickering candles made it all so romantic. Bending his head, Harry gave her an irresistible smile, with his copper curls glinting in the candlelight reminding her of a courtly gallant with a bronze halo. She was so intent on looking at Harry that she missed a step. She would have fallen, had he not caught her.

He gazed into her eyes as he supported her in his arms.

Beneath her self-confidence he detected a vulnerability that appealed to his chivalrous nature. A fierce desire to protect her from the evils of this world swept over him. She had never been this close to him before. He did what he had been aching to do and pressed his lips to hers. Susan responded, and he seized the opportunity and gathered her closer, with his lips firmly locked on hers. This was not what she had expected, but she clung to him, unable or unwilling to break the spell.

Harry lifted his mouth from hers and whispered, 'Marry me.'

She came back to the twentieth century with a thump and struggled to free herself from his embrace. This was insane. Harry was her friend, nothing more. She blamed herself for being swept along, dancing in the candlelit ballroom.

'Harry, please.'

He steadied her on her feet and then released her from his embrace. 'Are you all right?'

'That should never have happened, Harry. I blame myself. I'm sorry but I got caught up in the dance in this beautiful room.' She was staring at the floor, too embarrassed to meet his eyes.

'Allow me to apologise.' But he was far from feeling apologetic. She had returned his kiss, and now he knew that she was not indifferent to him.

'Harry, I have betrayed Rick, and he will never forgive me. I love him. If I hadn't had that glass of oloroso, if I hadn't danced by candlelight, if...'

'Sweet Susie!' he interrupted. 'I will not listen to these self-recriminations any longer; you have betrayed no one. It was a kiss, a simple kiss. May I add that he doesn't own you or you, him? I assure you he will never find out from me, if that's what is worrying you.'

'Harry, can you get a taxi for me?'

'I will take you home.'

'No, please.'

'Sweet Susie, it was nothing but a moment of madness, that's all. I am your friend and I must see you safely home. Are we still friends?'

She looked up at him and smiled. 'Of course.'

The next day on her way to the ambulance depot, she remembered the dance and the kiss in the ballroom with Harry and shook her head at her silliness. It was the wine, perhaps, or the magic of the dance, the candles and the ballroom that had transported her to another world. For a moment she had become Lady Susan, dancing with a handsome aristocrat, instead of Susan the ambulance driver. Harry had been drinking wine earlier that evening at the theatre, and she was sure he had been a little tipsy when he had kissed her. She was convinced he would not remember a thing this morning and dismissed the evening from her mind.

A quick glance at the roster in the depot told her that she was on duty in the East End, standing in for someone who was injured or ill or perhaps had found a paying job. The roster changed with swift regularity as some of the women went to work in munitions factories for big money, joined the Land Army, the Women's Royal Navy Service, the Women's Army or, like June, the Women's Auxiliary Air Force. Those who remained were constantly moved around from one depot to another, or wherever they were most needed. The uniform, a white Viyella blouse with navy skirt and jacket was ill fitting and along with a cumbersome tin hat, looked ridiculous on just about everyone, including Susan. Dark hose and black brogues completed the outfit, and although Susan hated the uniform, she had to swallow her dislike and wear it. Rules were rules.

Stowing her gas mask under the driver's seat, she set off after receiving the petrol allowed for emergency vehicles. She had only gone a short distance when the air raid warning sounded. Ignoring it, she kept going until several streets later a policeman halted the vehicle.

'Can't go any further, miss,' he said, giving her a stern look. 'Park the vehicle down that side street and take cover over there.' He pointed to a shelter used by the general public and watched her go, shaking his head. A mere slip of a girl! Ignoring the warning like that, she was in danger of getting her head blown off.

'Oh, bother,' she muttered to herself as she climbed out of the driver's seat. Suddenly, the ambulance bell started clanging, and before she could turn around and retrace her steps the policeman shouted at her, 'Turn that off!'

'Blast!' she muttered. She must have accidentally hit the switch while reaching for her gas mask. She hurried quickly to open the driver's door and silence the bell.

'There's one born every minute,' Susan overheard the policeman say to an air raid warden as she hurried past them into the shelter.

'Wanna cuppa char, ducks?' a cheery Cockney woman asked, holding up a Thermos flask. Susan smilingly declined.

She had barely entered the shelter when a huge blast rent the air. She was thrown to the other side of the shelter, and dirt and dust from falling masonry and the smell of gunpowder overwhelmed her. She lay on the ground for a few minutes, gathering her senses. Then, shocked and scared, she slowly picked herself up and checked to see if she was still in one piece. Her dark hose were in shreds, her uniform was torn, both legs were bleeding and she was only wearing one shoe. Otherwise, she seemed all right.

Stumbling forward and flicking on a small torch she found in her jacket pocket, she searched for others in the shelter. There were mangled bodies all around her. Some were moaning, and others lay motionless and wide-eyed; Susan knew they were dead. She saw a hand still clasping a misshapen Thermos and stuffed a fist in her mouth to stop herself from screaming. The body the hand belonged to had been torn apart.

Grief, anger and sheer hopelessness raged within her. Still shaking, she stared at the dead and wounded with despair. Would this cold, bloody murder never end?

'Blimey, that's close to a direct hit,' an old man said as he sat cradling his head in his hands.

Susan suddenly stopped as great clouds of dust fell on

her shoulders like flour. Brushing off the dirt, she began clambering over the rubble to see who needed assistance. She forced herself to speak as calmly as she could but could not get rid of the lump in her throat. Looking around at the carnage, her training came to the fore. Then, she spoke.

'Please, can I have your attention? My name is Susan and I'm an ambulance driver with first aid experience. We need to separate the injured from those who've died. Can you please call out if you are not badly hurt and are willing to help?'

A young lad limped forward. His face was smeared with black dust and grime and he had a nasty gash on his chin. He stepped on someone's leg and nearly fell.

'I'll 'elp.'

'Gerrof!' yelled a woman, rubbing her leg. The young boy turned to Susan after helping the woman to her feet.

'What do you want me to do, miss?'

'Let me bandage your head. Then you can help me to move the injured over near that wall.'

'Oi can help as well. Nuffin' much wrong wiv me, ducks,' an old man shouted, ambling towards her.

'Me neither.'

Before long Susan had a small group of willing workers. It took some time to get things organised. Nevertheless, they persisted with the grisly job in silence. Some of the wounded were traumatised and wept openly, while others, some with gruesome injuries, lay quietly.

'When will they dig us out of this hellhole?' wailed a

young woman who had three fingers missing. Susan had torn off her own under-slip and bound the woman's hand as best she could. Other dressings had been taken from the dead: a piece of scarf, lining from a torn coat, singlets and handkerchiefs.

'I'm sure they know that we're down here and as soon as the 'All clear' goes they will come looking for us.' At least Susan hoped so. Without water, food or medicines, they would all die.

'Lunnon is sure coppin' it, eh, miss?'

Susan only nodded at the man, fearing that if she spoke she would start crying.

It was several hours before the last survivor was hauled out of the bombed shelter. Two more had died awaiting rescue. When Susan finally emerged into what was once the street, she could see fires burning all around the city. Some flames were so intense it looked as if the fires were out of control, with thick rising smoke as far as the eye could see. Several animals lay dead in the rubble, and fat rats were feeding on a dog's lifeless body. Water ran down the cratered streets like rivers, filling up the holes and forming deep pools as firemen battled the blazing inferno. The whole of London seemed to be engulfed in a huge fireball. It looked like hell on earth.

A young woman emerging from the shelter stared at the fires and started screaming hysterically. One of the rescue workers took hold of her and slapped her across the face. The poor creature sucked in her breath and began to weep quietly. Susan's eyes filled with tears as she watched the dead being brought out from the shelter. Those unfortunate people had been struggling to survive, and now they were gone, snuffed out like candles. She took a deep breath and gazed up through the smoking ruins to see a full moon shining like a beacon. Even the moon was against them, guiding German bombers to the city she loved.

When everyone had been brought out of the air raid shelter, Susan began trudging back to the depot to report that her ambulance was under a pile of rubble. She wanted to rush to Queens Road and hug her daughter, but as there were no transport systems working, she had no idea how she was going to manage it. Luckily Pam, the Officer-in-Charge at the centre, who was making hot cocoa for some tired volunteers who had just finished their shift, introduced Susan to her son. He had recently finished basic training and was due to join his regiment. He smiled at Susan and offered her a lift on his motorbike.

'Let's clean you up first and find you another uniform,' Pam said. 'We can't have you going home looking like that, now, can we?'

Susan gave her a weak smile. Pam was talking as if Susan had been out gardening instead of being caught in the middle of a bombing raid. It seemed that everyone these days tried to make light of the terrible conditions and ignored the desolation all around them. She vowed that if she lived through all this, she would never take anything for granted again.

Before she went out to the locker room to wash and change, she turned to Pam and asked about the roster.

'We needed you back here later tonight, but after what you've just been through you can have the night off. We'll see you in the morning.'

Twenty minutes later she was thanking Pam's son for the lift before racing up the stairs at Queens Road to be met by Tess at the front door. 'The little darling's asleep,' Tess informed her. 'I've made some tea. Would you like some?'

'Thank you. I'll just run upstairs, check on Penny and change out of these clothes. Then I'll join you.'

A few minutes later, Susan was pouring herself another cup and offering a refill for Tess. 'Where's Percy tonight?' she asked.

'Well, Grace telephoned a while back. She was in a terrible state. It seems Donald fell down the cellar steps and hurt his back. Percy went dashing round there to help, but he shouldn't be long. Grace won't reopen the bar tonight, not after the raid.' Tess stopped long enough to take a breath before continuing, 'I hear the East End took a battering tonight.'

'Yes, I was there. The whole area was ablaze and a lot of people were killed.'

'God love us and save us,' Tess said, cupping her face with her hands. 'I knew they were coming tonight. I was listening to that awful Lord Haw-Haw on the radio and he said the Luftwaffe had a nice present for London. Please don't tell Percy I switched on 'Germany Calling'. He gets so angry if I listen in but, as I say, as least if we tune in, we know when they're coming, because that terrible man is never wrong.'

Susan stared at Tess. The woman couldn't stand the sight of blood but she could listen to some crazed idiot telling her that the whole of London would be reduced to ashes and Londoners blown to smithereens. It was no wonder Percy got angry with her.

Susan wondered what Tess would say if she told her what Pam said regarding the latest Nazi tricks. Apparently, they had started targeting historic landmarks and buildings, bombing them to demoralise the people of Britain. And to top it off, the Nazis were using a pre-war tourist book called the Baedeker tourist guide. How could anyone sink so low as to destroy a country's history? Tess was fiercely patriotic. Susan decided not to tell her and upset her further.

Chapter Ten

Two months later, Susan was informed she had to attend a training session concerning new ambulances arriving from America and was released from the duty roster for a day. Seizing the opportunity, she decided to visit her daughter and take the new winter coat she had bought for her.

When Susan arrived at Queens Road the place was in uproar. Doris, the cleaner, was trying to calm a screaming Tess and a sobbing Penny.

'What on earth has happened?'

Doris shook her head in despair. 'Oh, Susan, I'm real glad to see you. I need your help!' Springing into action, Susan calmed her daughter with a dummy dipped in home-made blackberry jam and placed her in a playpen with toys. Next she poured a sherry for a weeping Tess, wishing that just once the bottle might be empty, but it wasn't. The sherry soon worked, and eventually Tess was given a Beecham's Powder and put to bed.

Only when peace and quiet had been restored did Susan get an explanation from Doris.

'Tess heard on the wireless that Malcolm's ship has

been torpedoed. The Germans are claiming to have sunk it with the whole crew. Tess got hysterical, and then Penny started crying too. I was cleaning the upstairs bedrooms, as I do every week, and was almost finished when the screaming started and I rushed downstairs. Well, I didn't know whether to call a doctor or telephone Mr Blore at the shop, and then you arrived.'

Much later, as Susan was finishing preparing the evening meal, Tess wandered into the kitchen.

'Did you manage to sleep at all, dear?' Susan could not ignore the red-rimmed eyes of her mother-in-law and felt sorry for her.

'I did, a little,' she said, still rather teary. 'What will I do if Malcolm is…'?

'Tess!' Susan interrupted. 'Please don't. You'll make yourself ill. Don't you think the Admiralty would have informed you if Malcolm's ship had been sunk? I think that until you hear officially, Malcolm is still alive. Now, how about a nice cup of tea?'

Drying her eyes, Tess replied with a feeble smile. 'I'd love some. By the way, where's Penny?'

'I bathed and fed her and put her down. I've decided to sleep here tonight, Tess, so that I can spend some time with Penny in the morning before I go to the training centre. Will that be all right with you and Percy?'

'Your room is just how you left it, Susan. You're welcome here any time, but I don't have to tell you that. You're not going to take Penny away from me, are you? I couldn't live without my little cherub. She calls me Nana now.'

Suffering pangs of guilt because she had not told Rick about her daughter, Susan sat resting her elbows on the table deep in thought. Somehow she had missed the opportunity to tell him before his departure to North Africa, and it was not something she could tell him in a letter. Besides, why would she burden the man she loved with that kind of news when he could be in danger? Susan's, private thoughts were interrupted by Tess.

'I'm terribly sorry for my outburst earlier. It was such a shock to hear that my youngest son may have been killed. Susan, you are very sensible, and I agree with what you said about the Navy informing me. Please don't worry. I'm not going to cry again.'

Tess lied. How could a mother not cry for her son? But she would not do so in front of Susan again, or she might take Penny away.

'I'm going to wash my face and tidy my hair and pop down the road to see Doris' she said. I owe her some cleaning money, and I think I'd better apologise for my outburst earlier. I won't be long. Will you be all right, dear?'

'Why yes, of course.' Susan went back to thinking about Rick. She hoped he was not in any danger. She had read in the *Daily Express* that there had been a terrible battle at a place called Kasserina, and the loss of American GIs had been high. The newspaper did not release the numbers of killed or injured, only saying that losses had been heavy and things were looking bleak. Susan sucked her bottom lip, hoping and praying that Rick was safe. She was getting as bad as Tess, she thought, as tears began to form they always did whenever she thought about him.

A noise in the hallway had her wiping her eyes and hurrying to see who was there. 'This is a nice surprise,' Percy said.

Smiling, Susan reached up and kissed him on the cheek. 'How are you, Percy?' She had a fondness for this man that did not extend to his wife.

'Who do you think I met on the front doorstep?' he said. Standing aside, he announced, 'The Navy's here,' and stepped back to reveal Malcolm and two other fellows. They all wore double-breasted Royal Navy jackets with brass buttons, their peaked caps at a jaunty angle. A huge grin covered her brother-in-law's face.

'Malcolm!' she cried out and rushed to give him a hug. The callow youth she remembered from a few years ago had grown into a handsome young man. Not only had he lost the acne that had plagued him, he had lost that boyishness, and now looked confident and mature.

Susan led the way to the sitting-room. After introductions to his shipmates, Paul and Roger, had been made and handshakes exchanged, Percy poured beer for the young men. A little impatient, Susan just had to ask if the news about *HMS Hawke* being torpedoed was true.

'We were sent to Whale Island for a gunnery course a couple of weeks ago and now we have been given leave' said Malcolm. 'I know the Jerries are claiming to have sunk the *Hawke*, but she's only slightly damaged and we'll rejoin her when she's completed repairs.'

'Your mother will be relieved. She heard the news on the wireless and has been terribly upset ever since.' Susan didn't mention Tess' hysterics, as she knew it would upset both Percy and Malcolm.

'I should have let her know I wasn't on board during the attack, but how was I to know the Germans would claim to have sunk her, or that Mother would hear about it?'

Malcolm quickly changed the subject and went on to tell Susan and his father that he loved the Navy. He explained that as Ordnance Artificer he worked on the ship's guns, adding that Roger and Paul were Electrical Artificers.

'When this blasted war's over, I think I'll make the Navy my career and become a Chief Petty Officer with a nice pension at the end of thirty years of service' he said.

Everyone talked about 'when the war is over', but to Susan there seemed to be no end in sight. As far as she could see, the Nazis still controlled Europe.

'Do you have the same plan as Malcolm?' Susan asked the other two handsome artificers. The young EA called Roger had a sunny disposition, whereas Paul seemed reserved and reticent.

'I think the Navy is smashing, and like Malcolm I plan to remain in the service after the war. EAs are the unsung heroes of the Navy,' Roger added.

Coughing loudly, Malcolm interrupted, 'Unsung! Roger, that's debatable.' 'When the war is over', Paul cut in, 'my feet will stay on terra firma.'

While Susan was talking with Roger and Paul, Malcolm studied her. She was an attractive woman and any man would be proud to have her as his wife, but not his numskull brother. Michael was a spoiled brat who was easily bored. He was a philanderer who flitted from one woman to another. He had lost Susan for good, and since the episode with the pregnant Irish girl the folks rarely talked about him, especially if Susan was around. He had received one letter from his brother asking why he had not heard from Susan, and Malcolm took great delight in telling him. The laughter in the room arrested his attention.

'I will be happier when this war is finished. I really don't enjoy the Navy' said Paul.

'Tell Susan and Dad why you don't like the Navy, Paul.'

'Aw c'mon,' Paul pleaded, 'don't tell the whole world.'

'It's only between us,' Malcolm said grinning. 'Paul's not scared of U-boats, but he's terrified of the Medical Officer's needle and faints each time we have to line up for a jab. Isn't that so, Roger?'

'Spot on, Malcolm. What is it they're always telling us? Ah, yes. 'If you want to see your next of kin, don't put your daily tablet in the bin'.'

When the laughter had died down, Percy winked at the others and then turned to Malcolm.

'I remember a young lad of fourteen whose knees were knocking when he had to ask a young girl to go to the school dance. Do you recall that, son?'

'C'mon Dad. Don't tell the world.'

'It's only between us,' chimed Paul and Roger in unison.

As for Paul's plans to leave the service,' Roger

continued, 'well, I think he's daft, and has probably forgotten the mess motto 'To strive, to seek, to find and not to yield'. I have it on...'

Roger was unexpectedly interrupted. 'Percy, Percy!' Tess yelled out as she came hurrying down the hallway into the sitting room, panting with exertion. 'There is a man who's been after me since I left Doris' house.'

Everyone was stunned into silence, which was eventually broken by Percy. 'That is wishful thinking, Tess dear.'

Susan covered her mouth with the palm of her hand, shaking with suppressed laughter, and headed to the drinks cabinet to pour a sherry to calm the excitable Tess. One look at Malcolm and his shipmates told her that they were having the same trouble, while Percy exhibited a satisfied smirk. Her husband's remark was completely ignored by Tess.

'Malcolm, my dear boy, I heard your ship sank,' she cried out, with tears tumbling down her cheeks. She clamped her youngest son to her ample bosom.

Eventually, Roger and Paul left to go to the Carrington Hotel, where Malcolm had arranged a couple of free rooms from his Aunt Grace. Tess went to bed, leaving Percy and Malcolm talking. Susan sat quietly listening. She could not believe that two brothers could be so different. Malcolm was so attentive, caring and considerate – attributes his elder brother did not possess.

Her brother-in-law's voice broke into her thoughts.

'A few weeks ago whilst on convoy duty in the Med –

sorry, Susan, Jackspeak, or I should say Navy jargon; I meant Mediterranean,' he explained when he saw her puzzled look.

'One of the merchant ships was hit, and it just folded in two and sank in a matter of minutes. The poor fellows who survived the blast and jumped overboard were wishing they hadn't, as the sea was burning with oil.'

'Did you pick up any survivors?' Percy asked.

'Couldn't. There were too many U-boats in the area and they were picking us off like ducks in a shooting gallery. They hunt in packs, those U-boats. Some go after the Navy escorts, while the others wait to torpedo the poorly-armed merchant ships. We threw up a screen of shells and we were spreading depth charges as thick as marmalade on toast. Eventually, one of our ships managed to hit one of the bastards. Sorry, Susan, 'scuse my French.'

'I've told you, son, say 'bar-stools' when in the company of ladies.'

Percy's words made Susan smile. If he only knew what was said at the depot. These days, women were not protected from bad language.

'To get back to my story,' Malcolm said impatiently, 'a few minutes later we got one, and the other U-boats broke off the engagement and sneaked away. We heard no more from them that night. The ship's crew were cheering when the captain gave a 'well done' Tannoy announcement.

'What is a tannoy?'

'It is a loud speaker used on the ships.'

'I am glad you're home in one piece, Malcolm. It's

wonderful to see you again safe and sound.' Susan smiled at him and then made her excuses to go upstairs.

'A moment Susan, before you leave. Could you do me a favour?'

'Yes of course Malcolm. What is it?'

'There's a dance next Friday for the crew of the *Hawke,* and I was wondering if you would be my partner.' He hoped she would agree, as he couldn't wait to see the looks on his shipmates' faces when he walked in with Susan on his arm – especially the sub-lieutenant from New Zealand who thought he was God's gift to women.

Susan had no plans for next Friday and she was not on duty at the depot, but neither did she want to go out. But Malcolm seemed tense and appeared to hold his breath waiting for her reply. No matter how tired she was she just could not disappoint him

'Yes, I'd love to go with you.'

'Great! I'll meet you here at seven.'

'There, I told you she'd say yes,' Percy said with a satisfied look on his face, giving two of his two favourite people a big smile.

Climbing the stairs, Susan wondered if perhaps her only contribution in this war was partnering servicemen to functions. Two weeks before she had joined Matt and Monty at an American Army dance. Then there was a lunchtime recital with Harry, and a week later June had coaxed her into going out with some of her RAF friends.

Susan sighed and went into her daughter's room. Penny looked exactly like Michael, with the same sandy hair and strong cheekbones. She hoped her little angel would not grow up to be a spoiled devil like her father.

Leaning over the cot, she bent to kiss her daughter, smiling at Penny's eyes, which were tightly closed. She wore a dreamy expression upon her face. Susan thought the world of her daughter and hoped Penny could come and live with her and Rick soon.

Chapter Eleven

There was a chill in the air as winter nipped at the heels of these autumn nights. Susan curled up on the sofa, drawing the woollen shawl around her shoulders. It was almost the end of the old year and the beginning of a new one, and everybody desperately hoped it would signal the end of the war.

During a visit to Queens Road she told both Percy and Tess of her plan to take Penny to live with her in Chelsea. She was planning to tell Rick about her daughter when he returned from North Africa, and ask him if Penny could live with them.

Percy Blore persuaded Susan to leave her daughter with him and Tess, as the child was happy with her grandparents. He feared that if Penny were taken away, it would shatter Tess and leave her with nothing to occupy her time, except to annoy him. He pointed out that if Penny lived with her in Chelsea, Susan would not be able to continue with her voluntary work and still go out with June and her other friends. His argument left Susan in no doubt that he was well aware she was with Rick and would not allow his grand-daughter to live there. However, if she remarried or bought a place of her own, then he would reconsider allowing Penny to live with her mother.

Percy knew everything about his family − or if he didn't, he soon found out. He neither condoned nor condemned her actions, but asked her to trust him. Eventually, she agreed. He treated her more like his own daughter than his son's estranged wife. Anything she needed he provided, especially when it came to money. When she told him that Louisa's school had closed after being badly damaged in an air-raid, Percy had gone to see for himself. He began giving Louisa extra food rations now and again to help her endure the deprivations of war.

Rick was never far from her thoughts. A horrible empty feeling never left her. It had started the day he went to North Africa. She missed him terribly and longed for his return.

Writing to him was difficult, as there was no certainty that mail would reach him, and letters were censored. She had only received one reply from Rick to her many air-grams but she cherished it and read it over and over again. Each night she listened to the wireless, and whenever American losses or gains were mentioned in the news she held her breath, fearing the worst but always hoping for the best.

She had just recently posted another letter to Rick and one to Margaret Elliot, from whom she had not heard for weeks. Susan was concerned about her schoolteacher, who suffered dreadfully from time to time with pleurisy.

A sudden noise had the hairs ruffling on the back of

her neck. She rose from the sofa and hurried to the door. Standing on the threshold, she saw Rick leaning against the door-jamb. Her beaming smile quickly died as she saw his gaunt face and sagging shoulders. He was blinking at her as if she were an apparition. He swayed unsteadily on his feet.

'Darling,' she cried and rushed toward him. He slumped almost to the floor, but Susan caught him against her body, saving him from collapsing. He was so heavy, but she managed to keep him upright. Susan took control, the only time she had done so since meeting him.

'Can you move, my love? Can you?' She saw him nod and she began to shuffle her feet forward. He copied her, moving one foot in front of the other. It was slow going, but with her patience and gentle encouragement they finally arrived in the bedroom. Exhausted, Susan pushed him none too gently onto the bed. Quickly undressing him, she sponged his face and the rest of his body before placing a quilt over him, and went to the kitchen to prepare some food. Her mind was numb and she couldn't think properly. Like an automaton, she moved around the kitchen, reaching for some powdered egg and cheese to make an omelette. With a full tray, she returned to the bedroom. Plumping up the pillows, she put a glass of water to his lips. He sucked at the rim, allowing the water to trickle down his throat. He pushed the water away.

His eyes were closed but his lips were moving. She bent closer and heard, 'Helluva trip.'

'I'm sorry you're ill, but you are home now. I'll look

after you. Please, eat something, darling.' She did little to hide her concern for him and with tears in her eyes she tried to tempt him with a piece of omelette.

His eyes flicked open. 'I can do that,' he growled, brushing her hand away.

She knew his grumpy manner was merely a symptom of his exhaustion.

Placing, the tray on the bed where he could easily reach it, Susan replied, 'I want you to eat it all, and that's an order, Major Carlon, not a request.' Men were always difficult patients, as she had discovered when ferrying them to hospital in her ambulance.

Leaving Rick to feed himself, she went to have a bath. When she returned to the bedroom some time later he was fast asleep and the food lay untouched.

He slept for almost two days, recovering from the hazardous journey from North Africa.

Rick rolled over in bed and winced as painful memories of the bloody battle at Kasserine Pass surfaced. French infantry, as well as German Afrika Corps, had been killing American GIs, and losses were staggering. Quite simply, it was clear the French had no orders about whom they should be fighting. Rick was ordered to try to make contact with the French on behalf of General Eisenhower and broker a ceasefire. The American landings had been a foul-up from the start, with Rommel taking advantage of the extended American battle-lines. The French were shooting anything that moved, and the Germans were hell-bent on mass slaughter.

The American GIs learned the hard way and slowly began to claw their way back, mastering the basics of desert warfare and eventually taking Tunis. On Rick's return to Britain the ship he was travelling in had been torpedoed, and he and several others from the General's staff had been fished out of the drink by a Royal Navy frigate. They had been put ashore along the south coast of Britain and had to make their own way back to London.

A week after his return from North Africa, Susan was happy to feel him next to her, and lay quietly as she did not want to disturb him. Eventually, when she tried to sneak out of bed a heavy arm tightened about her and she heard his husky voice.

'Stay. Don't leave me.'

'Darling, you're awake. I thought I would creep out of bed without disturbing you.'

'Mmm, I want you to disturb me,' he said, nuzzling her ear and tightening his grip to prevent her from leaving.

'I'm so glad you're home. I cannot find the words to tell you how happy I am.'

'Oh, you've never had that kinda trouble before.'

'Rick, don't tease. Please allow me to get up so I can cook breakfast.'

'Why?'

'You must be hungry.'

'I am, but not for food.'

She gently nudged him. Susan dreaded the thought of him going away again and wondered how other women coped when their men left them. Her eyes became misty with tears. Rick, upon hearing a sniffling sound, propped himself, up on one arm to examine her closely.

'Hey, honey, what is it?'

'Do you think we will win this dreadful war?' she tearfully whispered.

'Sure we will.'

'Promise me you won't go away again.'

'I will do my best not to leave you. I promise. Now give me a smile,' he commanded as he kissed her tears away.

Later, when Susan was cooking breakfast Rick came into the kitchen, folded his arms across his chest, and leaned against the wall, watching her. Although he looked much better than he had a few days ago, clean-shaven and in a smart new uniform, she couldn't help noticing how much leaner he was in the face than before North Africa. She guessed he had been through hell.

'Darling, how brown you are. Can you tell me where they sent you?'

'Nope.'

She knew precisely where he'd been, but she didn't want to betray Harry. 'Did you have a difficult time getting back?'

'Nope.'

'Was your assignment a success?'

'Hey, I'm taking more flak than our airmen over Berlin.'

'Rick, you're trying my patience. Won't you tell me anything?'

'OK. I love you.'

She rushed into his arms and kissed him. She didn't care if he wanted to keep his military secrets. He loved her, and that was all that mattered to Susan.

He gazed at her for some time before continuing. 'Look, I've got a great idea. Let's go out to eat and take in a movie tonight. The guys at headquarters tell me there's a good one playing in Leicester Square.'

Rick remembered Monty telling him that *Gone with the Wind* was the best romantic movie he had ever seen, but then again Monty was a sucker for a sob story and had been in raptures about the star. 'For an English broad, Vivien Leigh plays a beautiful Southern belle,' he had raved.

Rick wasn't crazy about romantic movies. He would much prefer to see a good Western or a detective drama, but it was widely accepted that women liked love stories. He guessed Susan was no exception, and he was willing to do anything to make her happy.

Leaving the cinema later that evening, Rick stared into the foggy night, looking a little bewildered, as the whole place was covered in thick fog hanging in the air like a steamy grey blanket.

'What in hell is this?'

'It's fog, a London pea-souper,' Susan informed him, and pointed to a bus clippie walking in front of a bus with a small torch, guiding the driver. People without a light were walking into lampposts, bumping into each other and getting lost down side streets. Rick flicked his Zippo lighter on to light their way. Linking arms, they set off, keeping as near as possible to the white line on the edge of the pavement, their breath fogging the air as they walked.

'I think Rhett Butler was mean to leave Scarlett, don't you?'

'I guess, but if she's any kinda woman, she'll get him back.'

During the film he had watched Susan from time to time, her rapt attention plainly obvious. 'What did you think of Clark Gable?' he asked, giving her a sidelong look when she laughed. 'OK, what's so funny? C'mon, out with it.'

'June once compared you to Clark Gable.'

He grinned, suddenly stopped walking and turned to face her. 'All I can say is, I don't give a damn what June says. Darling, you're ten times prettier than Scarlett.' Then he flicked the lighter off and kissed her long and deep, until a dog walked between them and brushed them apart. 'Damn dog,' Rick muttered. He gave the animal a swift kick it yelped and dashed out of the way, to be swallowed up in the dense fog.

''Ere mister, what's your game?' came an angry young voice. 'That's my Alfie you've just booted up the arse, and now he's scarpered up the frog and toad.'

Rick flicked the lighter on again to see a young boy not more than eight years old, with a taper and a box of Swan Vestas matches in his hand. He had a mass of tangled curls and a cheeky face streaked with dirt and grime, and he constantly wiped his nose on the sleeve of his jerkin.

'Is this kid speaking English?' he asked Susan.

'Cockney,' she replied with a smile. 'Frog and toad' is road.' Then she turned to the boy. 'We're sorry about your dog.'

The boy held the taper higher, looked at Rick's uniform and then gasped.

'Cor blimey, you a general or somefink? Them real medals? 'Ave you killed a lot of Jerries?'

Rick seemed highly amused both with the questions and the boy's accent. He was slowly coming to grips with what the kid was saying.

'In answer to your first question, no, to the second, yes and to the third, some. As the lady said, we're sorry about your dog and I think you should take off after it.'

'Oh gawd, a Yank. Got any gum, chum?'

It was payback time, and Rick used the thickest southern drawl he could muster.

'Jeez, shucks, buddy, ain't chawed gum since I was knee high to a grasshopper. You git my drift?'

'What's he bleedin' sayin'?' The boy had turned to Susan, pointing his thumb over his shoulder at Rick.

Wiping the grin from his face, Rick said sharply, 'How about you apologise to the lady for cussing?'

'But, General, sir, she's your wife, ain't she?'

Grabbing the kid by the collar, while trying to stifle a smile, Rick said, 'Say sorry or cop a beating. Your choice.'

'I done nuffin', guv' protested the boy, but then Rick tightened his grip. 'All right, General, you win.' A cheeky smile showed the many gaps in his teeth. 'I'm sorry, Missus General. I didn't mean no 'arm.'

Fishing in his pocket, Rick tossed the kid a sixpence. 'Buy your own gum, chum. Now skedaddle.'

'Cor! A tanner! Fanks a lot, General.'

Resuming their journey at a steady but slow pace, Susan commented, 'The boy wasn't the only one who had trouble understanding what you were saying. I did, too.'

He laughed. 'It was pure gobbledegook, but perhaps it taught him a lesson. I had a hunch that he was laying the Cockney lingo on a mite thick for my benefit.'

'He probably was. Do people really talk like that in Virginia?'

'Some, but folks in the Deep South sure do.'

'I expect you're missing your family and your mother's home cooking.'

'Mother doesn't cook now, too busy selling war bonds, Mazy handles the cooking. Her husband, Jed, is the stable foreman; been with us for years. Real nice folks. They have a son in the Navy serving in the Pacific and one in the Marines.'

'Are your parents Southerners?' Susan asked.

'My mother's family came to Virginia from Quebec a couple of generations ago. When she isn't selling bonds she's either out riding or sitting on the porch, swinging from sunup to sundown, answering her mail.'

'Does everybody in your family ride?'

'Sure, that's why I want you to master the basics before I take you to meet them. Can't have the neighbours saying, 'Abe Carlon's son has a girl who doesn't know a muzzle from a fetlock'.'

'Please, tell me about your family?' She said hurriedly changing the subject.

'Well, there's my sister, Judy. Somehow I don't think

she'll ever marry. She prefers horses to husbands. Little Danny, he's just a kid. His mother, Pa's sister, died when he was born and he came to live with us. Then there's my father. He lives and breathes horses. In fact, so does everyone on the stud. There's not a lot to tell about my father. He is a quiet-living man. My great-great-grandfather came from Ireland. Now, there was a Rhett Butler type. He used to ride the Mississippi steamers, cavorting with Southern belles and losing his shirt in crooked card games.'

'I'm glad you're not like him.'

'Mother tells me I take after her family – quiet, God-fearing, law-abiding citizens. They sure sound a boring bunch.'

'Give me the boring bunch every time.' Susan laughed, and he joined in.

Rick suddenly spotted a cab crawling along at snail's pace and hailed it. 'C'mon, honey. I have had enough of this damn fog.'

Chapter Twelve

The next day Susan paid her fortnightly visit to Louisa, who produced a length of silk she had been hoarding and spread it over the table.

'Percy Blore sees to it that I have enough to eat and this is my way of saying thank you. This pale peach silk would make a beautiful gown if and when the Major takes you somewhere special. Are you still seeing him?'

'Oh yes,' Susan said dreamily.

Louisa shook her head. A tender look always came into Susan's eyes whenever the American was mentioned, and Louisa felt compelled to warn her.

'When this miserable war is over he'll go back home, and you'll be left behind in England. Modesty prevents me from spelling it out, but you are being careful, aren't you?' A nod was the only answer Louisa received as she looked across the table to see Susan's crimson face. Despite having been married and given birth, Susan was blushing like a schoolgirl. She was indeed an unusual woman, and Louisa liked her more than she cared to admit.

Now in her mid-thirties, Louisa Firbank had once been a house model for Debenham and Freebody, but a boating accident on the Thames had left her with a twisted foot, a walking stick and no job. She found employment in her mother's flourishing business, The London Beauty School. Eventually, Louisa took over the enterprise when her mother died and renamed it Firbank Academy. At first, Louisa was very successful and business was quite rewarding, until war was declared. Most of her students left London to join the military services, and when a bomb damaged the top floor of the academy she had to close the business.

Reaching for her walking stick, she limped over to an old chest, took out a piece of fine lace and put it on the table next to the satin.

'The peach material looks beautiful, Louisa.'

'Yes. It will look exquisite when it is made up. The peach skirt and coffee-coloured lace bodice will be just perfect.'

'The colours are wonderful together, how did you manage it?'

'I dyed the lace,' she explained, in answer to Susan's questioning look.

'Gosh, Louisa, it's stunning! Thank you.' Susan was in raptures and gave her a peck on the cheek. Taking hold of her friend's hands, Louisa said 'Susan, when men are a long way from home they get lonely for female company, and I don't want to see you getting hurt. So please remember what I told you about taking care of yourself.

There are too many unwanted babies being born, and heaven help the poor little blighters when this war is over.'

'Yes of course. Now, I really must dash.' Giving Louisa a quick hug, Susan hurried out of the sewing room.

When the door closed, Louisa felt something in one of the pockets of her cardigan and pulled out a pound note. The dear girl must have put it there when she threw her arms around her for a goodbye hug. She was always doing little things like that. Louisa had long suspected that it was because of Susan that Percy Blore had called to see her and started giving her food to help out. Percy told Louisa to dress Susan in the best, and he would pay for it. She suddenly decided to make the dress herself as a surprise for Susan.

It did not take long for Percy and Louisa to become very close. According to Percy, his wife did not want him in her bed any more, and as he was still a virile man he had turned to Louisa. Men were fickle lovers. It was the woman who suffered the consequences of a romantic dalliance. She fervently hoped that the young man from across the Atlantic loved Susan and would not hurt her. The Major, if he had any sense at all, would know that Susan was madly in love with him and this was not a casual affair on her part. Men are complicated creatures – always exact and difficult to understand, she sighed.

The next morning Percy Blore's voice came down the telephone line.

'Susan, I have a rather bulky envelope addressed to you,

from a legal firm in the north. It came two days ago and I took the liberty of opening it. Hope you don't mind.'

'No, not at all. What did it say?'

'It's sad news, I'm afraid. Margaret Elliot has died. She has left you some money in her will. There is also a set of house keys with the documents.'

Susan was shocked and deeply saddened at the news. 'I've just written to her. I hadn't heard from her for several weeks. How did she die? Was it an air raid?'

'No, it was pneumonia.'

'When is the funeral?' Susan did not want to go back to the town she had left years ago, but out of love for her schoolteacher she felt she must.

'A week Thursday. There are some papers you must sign at a firm of solicitors. Do you want me to drop the letter off, or will you come round and pick it up?'

'Thank you Percy. I'll call in.' She replaced the receiver and walked into the bedroom, where Rick was getting dressed.

'Hey, why the long face?' He asked.

'A dear friend of mine has just died.'

'I'm real sorry, darling.'

'I will have to go up north next week.'

'For the funeral?'

'Yes, I hope it will only take a day or two.'

'I don't have to say that I'll miss you. You know darn well I will. You won't forget Ike's birthday bash,' he added, and taking her in his arms he kissed her tenderly.

The railway station was a sea of uniforms – it seemed as if the whole country was in service uniform – and looking at the crowded platform Susan doubted if she would be able to board the train, never mind find a seat. The train was smoke-filled and crowded with service men of all descriptions – hardly any civilians. Susan's carriage was crowded, with soldiers in khaki playing cards. Two women in wren uniforms were talking quietly and there were three Scotsmen, complete with kilts and sporrans. Other service personnel lined the corridor, laughing and smoking. Susan guessed they were telling jokes. One soldier had a harmonica, and as the impromptu tune 'Run Rabbit Run' filled the carriages, voices joined in singing, whistling or humming along. The train was vastly over-crowded but no one seemed to mind. Susan wondered if they were all going off to war or on leave.

An hour after leaving the station the train came to an abrupt halt, sending suitcases and military kit bags toppling to the floor and tossing passengers about like leaves on a windy day. Susan ended up in the lap of a Scotsman. A train guard came hurrying along the passageway, stepping over sprawling bodies and calling for people to don their tin helmets as an air raid was in progress.

'Here, have mine, hen,' the Scotsman said, offering his helmet. 'But what about you?'

'He's got a thick heid, lassie. He'll no be needing it,' the other said, chuckling.

She felt guilty, but at the insistence of the smiling men she put the helmet on. Then someone shouted, 'Hit the deck!' An explosion rocked the train. One of the Scotsmen threw Susan to the floor and covered her body with his own. He was no lightweight, and Susan was finding it difficult to breath with his chest pressed against her back. Luckily, it wasn't much of a raid, just Jerry ditching the last of his load before returning to base, the Scotsman told her. He was probably right, as it seemed only minutes before the train was allowed to proceed. Everyone in her compartment was of the opinion that there could not have been any damage or they would have been held up for hours.

'Och, dinna worry hen. You keep that yin. I've got anither at the barracks,' the soldier told Susan as she tried to return his helmet, which was almost as big as a fruit bowl and sported a tartan chinstrap.

Some hours later she smiled again, saying goodbye to the Scotsmen and wishing them good luck. She left the train and went in search of the taxi to take her into town. On this bitterly cold afternoon, she was dressed in a chocolate brown skirt and jacket with a stylish fawn hat and gloves. Everything about her spelled quality and quiet confidence.

It was late when she left Mrs Elliott's doctor, who had explained the circumstances of Margaret's death. She then went to a stonemason, where she ordered a plaque for her friend's grave. Arriving at the hotel, she left her small suitcase with the porter to take it to her room, and went straight into the restaurant. She was famished. The menu was rather limited but Susan finally chose the fish stew, served in a small oval dish with chunky bread. There were more vegetables than cod in the stew. She knew that fish was in short supply due to German activity in both the Atlantic and the North Sea. Smiling at the waiter, she politely refused the cottage pudding served with custard, as she knew it would have been made with powdered egg, which she didn't like.

Hoar frost lay thick on the ground and crackled underfoot as Susan walked towards the rugged-up vicar, the dismal grey morning reflecting her feelings. Shivering, she pulled the collar of her black coat securely about her neck and glanced around at the poor showing for Margaret Elliot's burial. Apart from the doctor, there was a young woman in flashy clothes which were not suitable for a funeral or the freezing conditions. She was standing a few yards away, shuffling from one foot to the other in the highest heels Susan had ever seen. She wore a headscarf over her hair, and a cigarette burned between her fingers. Two gravediggers nearby, leaning upon shovels, were the only other people in attendance.

'I am the resurrection and the life...' The vicar started the service without ceremony. Susan guessed that the cold weather had something to do with his haste. 'We therefore commit her body to the ground,' he droned on.

She paid scant regard to his words, as she had never been very religious, and could not pretend to be now. Instead, she spent the time reminiscing about her wonderful teacher and the happy times spent together. Susan loved Margaret for giving her the opportunity to go to London, and if it had not been for Mrs Elliot she would never had met Rick. He had offered to accompany her to the funeral. Susan finally dissuaded him. She did not want him to see the shoddy slums where she had been born.

A tearful Susan gently placed a bunch of flowers on Margaret's coffin after the service and whispered a final farewell. She wanted to get away from this sad, cold place as soon as possible. It seemed the vicar was in the same frame of mind. After a few brief words of condolence to Susan and a short verbal exchange with the doctor, he hurried away.

She quickened her pace and was almost at the churchyard gates when a voice stopped her. It was the flashily-dressed girl she had seen earlier.

'Do ye not know me, Susie Caddy?'

The girl's marked Sunderland accent, a sound Susan hadn't heard for years, sounded strange. 'I do not. Are you a friend of Margaret Elliot?'

'Aw, aren't we posh? I'm Janet Bell. We were in the same class at school. You've come up in the world. Made a fortune, did ye? Where did ye get them fancy clothes? Lying on yer back, like yer ma?'

Shocked and stunned, Susan just stared at her. Suddenly, she remembered Janet Bell, who had been a horror at school, encouraging girls in the class to call Susan a whore. As she appraised her, Susan noticed that the scarf had slipped off and her hair was redder than she remembered. She had used some sort of dye, probably henna, her eyelids were grotesquely lined with a black pencil, and a thick red slash across her mouth reminded Susan of girls prowling the streets in Piccadilly for customers.

'I'm in a hurry. Excuse me.'

'Don't ya want tae know how yer bruvver is?' she asked, lighting another Woodbine cigarette.

Susan stopped, turned and faced the girl.

'You know Erik?' she was shocked, not only at the hostility in Janet Bell's voice but also at the hatred in her eyes.

'Aye, he's in the merchant navy now and when his ship's in, he comes round for a quick shag in the back yard behind the lavvy. He's awful 'andsome, and 'im and me, we might get wed. Wouldn't that be funny? You an' me sisters, eh?' She cackled out loud and nearly choked on the cigarette.

'Erik is too young to be in the Navy and much too young to get married.'

'He's old 'nuff tae shag me. And if I gets a bun in me oven he'll have tae wed me.' She spluttered and hacked out another choking cough.

Susan hurried away, the laughter still ringing in her ears as she climbed into the waiting taxi that she had asked the hotel to arrange.

Arriving in the town centre, she quickly found the solicitor's office and entered. The receptionist held out her hands and offered to assist in removing her coat. Susan's mind was still on Margaret's funeral and her encounter with Janet Bell, and she allowed the office girl to take her coat and hang it up before being shown into the inner sanctum of the solicitor's office. A mouldy smell overwhelmed her, probably emanating from dusty books and papers piled high on shelves. Quickly reaching for a handkerchief from her handbag, she held it to her nose.

A shabby Dickensian figure dressed in black with thinning white hair and a pince-nez perched on the end of his nose sat behind a desk strewn with documents and books. She had no idea how he ever found anything in that untidy heap. Memories of Ebenezer Scrooge and 'A Christmas Carol' reminded her of the Dickens' novels that she and Mrs Elliot had read aloud together. She wouldn't have been at all surprised if he had muttered, 'Bah, humbug!'

Rising from a worn leather chair, Claude Peel admired the pretty peacock before him, with her slim white hands, delicate pink fingernails and luscious red lips. But it was the neckline of her dress that arrested his attention, and he could not take his eyes off her charming breasts. He was however an expert at concealing his feelings, and cloaked his appreciation of the woman standing before him. With a hand gesture, he invited her to be seated.

'Pardon me,' he said, sniffing, while reclaiming his chair. 'I neglected a cold and this is the state in which you now find me.' Focusing his eyes on the documents in front of him, he continued. 'Ahem, the late Mrs Elliot was a client of my partner, now sadly bedridden. Rich man's disease'. When Susan gave him a questioning look he added 'Gout. Therefore, I am now acting for the estate of Mrs Elliot. Upon your instructions we will sell the residence and furnishings of the deceased and will place the monies at your disposal. Of course, any keepsakes or memorabilia, with which you may have a certain attachment, will become your property upon execution of the last will and testament of the late Mrs Margaret Smith Elliot. Ahem, Mrs Blore, will you please sign the documents where I have indicated?'

Susan had not understood one word of what he had said, except that he had a cold and the senior partner had gout. His monotonous speech punctuated with tiresome 'ahems' and the sidelong looks he gave her made her feel very uneasy. However, in order to get out of there quickly, she picked up the legal document he had pushed across his desk, gave it a cursory glance, took the fountain pen he offered, signed and passed the papers back to him. She observed the bespectacled man with owl-like eyes and spidery blue-veined hands as he added his signature. His jacket was crumpled – it looked as if he had slept in it – and there was a gravy stain on his necktie as if he had rushed his meal.

'Ahem, are you are staying overnight, Mrs Blore?'

'No, I am returning to London immediately.' Susan had never told Mrs Elliot about her troubles with Michael Blore, or that she had reverted to her single name. Susan's name would remain Blore until she could obtain a divorce, and that would not happen until Michael returned from the war.

'How unfortunate, how very unfortunate,' he repeated, wringing his hands in the manner of Uriah Heep, while continuing to stare at her breasts. 'I was going to propose a meeting with you this evening to discuss investing your legacy.'

For the first time since entering his office, Susan became aware that his eyes were riveted on the neckline of her dress, and she was angry with herself for allowing the receptionist to remove her coat. She had not been concentrating and had completely forgotten that she had changed into a low-cut dress to wear for dinner with Rick upon her return to London.

Susan shuddered inwardly and ignored his comment. The mere thought of meeting this repulsive little man with leering eyes made her feel quite ill. His demeanour frightened her, and his conversation confused her.

'Thank you for offering to invest my legacy, but my bank manager in London will help me with any investments,' she lied. Never in her life had she had any money to invest, but she was sure that Claude Peel would be the last person she would choose to help her.

He coughed again as he extended one of his hands in a gesture of farewell. Susan started to turn away, and quickly withdrew her hand as his blue veined hand brushed hers, but he had taken a firm hold of her wrist and would not let go.

'Mr Peel, please release my arm.' He did so and she swiftly hurried to the door only to be halted by his voice.

'I may need to see you again, and I would be obliged if you would leave your current address with my secretary if, as you say, you are no longer residing in Queens Road. Good day, Mrs Blore.'

'If you wish to see me again regarding Mrs Elliot's will, my husband will accompany me,' she lied again. If she had to come to his office for a further visit she would ask Rick, or failing that she would bring some kind of protection from this strange little man who had continuously ogled her when he thought she hadn't noticed.

Susan fled into the outer office and almost tore her coat from the peg in her haste to leave. She buttoned the coat up to her neck, pulled on her gloves and without a backward glance hurried away to catch her train.

Travelling back to London, Susan chose first class, hoping for a quiet, more peaceful journey than the one she had experienced the day before. Leaning back against the headrest as the train gathered speed, she tried to put the face of Janet Bell out of her mind, but could not. She had to admit that the girl could have been attractive, with auburn hair and green eyes - a touch of the Celtic, she guessed – but her appearance, language and behaviour were disgusting. Her clothing and that awful thick make-up were downright hideous.

She wondered briefly if she would have ended up like Janet Bell if dear Mrs Elliot had not helped her to escape. Susan wished her schoolteacher was still alive. She would miss Mrs Elliot, and the many letters they exchanged over the years. Having the keys to Margaret's house, Susan had spent some time going through her schoolteacher's things and had kept a few of Margaret's keepsakes, such as her collection of Dickens novels and the lovely brooch that Mr Elliot had given to his wife before he left for France in

1916. In her mad dash to leave the solicitor's office, she had forgotten to leave the house keys with the receptionist, but nothing would induce her to return the keys in person. She would send them back by post.

Closing her eyes, she tried to sleep, but the vision of Claude Peel appeared before her. She just could not believe how careless she had been. Percy had once told her she was a woman of the world and she had been flattered, but perhaps she needed a few more lessons regarding dirty old men.

Turning her thoughts to more pleasant things, Susan decided she would ask Louisa to make her a dress for General Eisenhower's birthday party. She should feel guilty about the money Percy paid for her clothes, especially as materials were scarce, but justified it whenever she remembered how badly his son had treated her.

She was somewhat nervous about attending the General's birthday celebrations. He was, after all, the most important man in Britain, apart from the King and Mr Churchill. Rick had advised that she should just be herself and everything would be swell. She hoped he was right.

When the train pulled into Kings Cross Station she was delighted to see Rick waiting at the barrier. Having difficulty carrying the case and the bulky hat and wanting to have some fun, she placed the hat on her head as she hurried towards him. The first thing she noticed was that he was not wearing his service uniform. Instead, he wore a dark sports jacket and a pair of grey pants and a matching shirt. He looked magnificent, but then to her, he always would.

He saw her and gave a wave, and she rushed to greet him. Giving her a gentle kiss on the lips, he said, 'Never kissed a girl in a tin hat. Now, honey, don't tell me you've enlisted!' He chuckled.

Removing the hat, she stretched up high on her toes and kissed him longingly. 'Mmmm,' she murmured.

Reluctantly, he lifted his lips from hers, and whispered, I've missed you.'

Rick picked up her small suitcase and with his arm around her waist they walked out of the station, Susan telling him about the air raid on the journey north and how she had acquired the helmet. He laughed out loud when she told him it would make an excellent flowerpot.

'Darling, why are you in civilian clothes?' she asked.

'I have a weekend furlough and I've booked a small hotel in the country, near a riding stable. Let's get away from uniforms, bombed buildings and the war for a few days, huh?'

'Pam gave me whatever time off I needed for the funeral and said to contact her when I arrived back.'

'Then let's go.' He took her to a black Humber Snipe, and it was her turn to raise her eyebrows. 'I requisitioned this,' he said by way of explanation. 'What do you think?'

'Rick, it's beautiful. Where's the Jeep you usually drive?' He walked around and opened the passenger door for her.

'That belongs to the Army. This belongs to us. Now jump in. I thought we'd eat in town, and then stop in

Chelsea to pick up a few things before heading into the country.'

'Sounds wonderful.'

'We're going to a little place in the Strand Monty told me about.'

When they were shown to a table Rick removed her coat and gave it to the waiter. He made no comment about the low-cut neckline of her dress, but she caught him looking at her cleavage from time to time as they waited for the menu to arrive.

'Tell me, how did it go with the attorney?'

She gave an involuntary shiver. 'Oh, Rick, he was awful – a thin, odious man with beady eyes who kept leering at me over the top of his spectacles. I think he was mentally undressing me. If I have to go there again can I take your revolver with me?'

Rick tossed his head back and roared with laughter. 'You're aiming to shoot the poor guy? Honey, you don't even know how to use a gun.'

'I know that, and so do you, but he doesn't. An empty gun will do the trick. I just want to scare the pants off him.'

He roared with laughter again. 'Honey, I thought the whole idea was to get him to keep his pants on.'

'Oh, Rick, please be serious.'

'I'm trying, darling. If you wore that dress, no wonder he was leering at you. You probably fogged up the old guy's lenses. I'm having trouble keeping my eyes off your beautiful breasts myself.'

'Rick, I wish you would try to understand how

uncomfortable I was sitting in that dingy little office with that awful man telling me he wanted to see me again. Then he took my hand and wouldn't let go.' She shuddered at the memory.

'OK, I get the picture. The next time you go there, I'm coming with you, and if we see the gallant Scotsman you can return his damn tin hat. I don't want you keeping another man's possessions, nor do I want you taking anything from any guy except me.'

'If that's how you feel, I'll throw the silly helmet away.' She smiled at him, slipping off a shoe and gently pressing her toes against his trouser leg.

'I'm only human, honey, and with your breasts teasing me, your foot rubbing against my leg and your dewy eyes telling me you want me, I am almost at breaking point. You're in grave danger of being tossed onto this table and ravished.'

It was true she wanted him, and he knew it. She had been constantly leaning over the table to give him a better view of her cleavage, and it wasn't only her eyes that were moist. She had never craved a man before, but she wanted this man. She was aching for him to make love to her, and from the way he was looking at her, he felt the same way. They would both have to curb their impatience until later.

Rick ordered wine for himself and a glass of tonic water for Susan to accompany their meal. They were talking quietly when three Navy sub-lieutenants arrived. They were very noisy, and Susan wondered if they had been drinking elsewhere. One of the men recognised her, and as Rick glanced up he caught the man waving at her.

'You know him?' He asked.

'No, yes, er, no.'

'Susan, I need a straight answer.' He waited a few minutes and then said, 'Tell me.'

'When you were in North Africa Malcolm Blore, who's only eighteen and like a brother to me, invited me to a Navy dance. I didn't really want to go but I felt sorry for him, just arriving home after a dreadful sea battle. At the dance was the sub-lieutenant you saw waving at me. He asked me to dance, and knowing he was drunk I refused, but he was persistent. Eventually, after several attempts to get rid of him, Malcolm told him to get lost, and the sub-lieutenant punched him in the face. Roger and Paul came to the rescue, and while Paul kept the sub-lieutenant away from Malcolm, Roger hailed a taxi and helped me to assist Malcolm with his blood-soaked mouth into the taxi. It sped away to the hospital. I thought his jaw was broken.'

'This guy, Malcolm, what rank does he hold?'

'He's an ordinance artificer. He's only been in the service since the war started.'

'So a sub slugs a junior rating and nothing's done about it?'

'I don't know the rules or regulations. I was only concerned about Malcolm's injury.'

While they were talking the sub-lieutenant sauntered up to the table and slurred, 'Well, my little beauty, you wanna dance tonight?'

Rick rose to his feet. 'No, I will. Outside, OK?' Rick glared so fiercely that even Susan flinched.

'Well now, here's a civvy who wants to dance. After you,' the sub-lieutenant offered, making way for Rick to precede him. Then he turned to Susan. 'I'll be back for you later.'

Sucking her bottom lip, she wondered whether she should go after Rick, or call the police or the restaurant manager. She was unsure what to do and was worried. Rick had only recently returned from North Africa, and she guessed he might not be a hundred per cent fit. They had gone outside either to argue or to exchange blows. Susan desperately hoped that only heated words would pass between them.

It was quite late and the place was almost empty. The other two officers remained seated. One was quietly eating, and the other had his head resting on the table and appeared to be asleep. Perhaps they hadn't seen what had happened or were too drunk; she couldn't tell.

Susan had just pushed her chair from the table and was rising when Rick appeared. There were no visible signs of a scuffle. In fact, he looked the same as when he had walked out of the restaurant, with the troublesome lieutenant. Giving a sigh of relief she sat down as Rick claimed his chair.

'Would you like me to order some tea?' he asked, picking up the bottle and filling his wine glass.

'Rick, please, tell me what happened.'

'Nothing much,' he smiled, flexing his right hand.

'You hit him?'

'Only once, and then I put him into a cab and told the

driver to take him to the railway station and put him on a train to Portsmouth.'

'What did the sub-lieutenant say?'

'He kinda wasn't awake at the time, but the cab driver assured me he would deliver him.'

'Did you pay the taxi fare?'

'No, the sub-lieutenant had plenty of dough. I checked his pockets and gave his wallet to the cab driver.'

'Rick, you knocked him out? But you are a senior officer.'

'I know that, and you know that, but he doesn't,' he replied.

She bubbled over, and it was only when the tea arrived that she stopped laughing. The sub-lieutenant had got what he deserved, and she was glad.

'You and I have to have a discussion, honey. I don't mind you going out in a group, but I sure as hell don't want you to go anywhere with a kid still wet behind the ears. There's a big bad world out there, and some guys are unscrupulous with women. There are all types of military personnel from other countries loafing around London on furlough, and most of them are ready to exploit anyone. Now take that jackass attorney. Old as he is, he probably thought you were a cute little thing ready for anything. I guess what I'm saying is, you need to be on guard at all times. Don't put yourself at risk, especially if I'm not with you.'

'Darling, you are my knight in shining armour,' she said, taking hold of his hand.

'Is that how you see me?

'Yes, Sir Knight, I do.'

'Then, Milady let me find my trusty steed and I'll whisk you off to my castle.' He called for the bill, helped her on with her coat, and arm in arm they left the restaurant. Leaving Chelsea after collecting riding clothes and footwear they drove north into Buckinghamshire and booked into a quaint Jacobean hotel with a riding stables not too far away.

Chapter Thirteen

Alvamoor House was a palatial mansion of gigantic proportions. Susan couldn't believe her eyes as she walked between the Corinthian pillars into the foyer. The birthday party for General Eisenhower was in full swing, with an American Army band providing the music. There was so much gold braid and so many military medals and gilded decorations on display. Susan blinked at their brilliance.

She recognised the General immediately. He was in conversation with a group of officers, laughing and talking. He was a well-built man, with fine hair, blue eyes, healthy complexion and an easy grin. Charm radiated from him. One of the General's hobbies was horse-riding, so Rick and Susan had purchased a leather riding-crop, with his initials carved on it, as a birthday gift.

Removing her wrap, Rick handed it to a waiting orderly and placing his hand beneath her elbow, led her into the main reception room. The skirt of the gown swished around her ankles as she walked. The lace bodice and sleeves of the dress were elegant. Her hair was gathered at the crown with a golden barrette to hold her hair in place and allow the dark curls to cascade riotously down her back.

They had only just enter the reception room when an orderly bearing a tray came towards them, offering Scotch, wine or non-alcoholic punch. Susan selected the punch and Rick a Scotch.

Harry was standing on the far side of the room with several American staff officers, who noticed Susan and Rick's entrance. They were an extremely handsome couple, Harry thought. Susan outclassed nearly every woman in the room, and he wasn't the only one who thought so. Many heads turned to look at her as she swept into the room. He smiled to himself; men, whether sixteen or sixty, always admire a beautiful woman.

Dancing had commenced in the ballroom, and many couples were leaving the reception area to dance or listen to the music. One American officer was giving a lively demonstration of the jitterbug, swinging his partner around at a furious pace. Harry was on the point of wandering over to ask Susan to dance when he saw the General approach the handsome couple.

'Rick, how you doin'?'

'Okay, sir. May I present Miss Susan Cadiz?'

'I would be disappointed if you didn't.' Then he turned to Susan. 'Delighted to make your acquaintance. Are you enjoying the party, Susan?'

With her knees knocking and her stomach churning, she was amazed that she managed to smile. She had never been invited to the birthday party of such an important person and she wanted to make a good impression.

'I, I'm pleased to meet you, General, sir.' Heavens! She had stuttered and mixed up his title. What must he think of her?

'Susan has a gift for you, sir.' Rick flashed her a look, and she held out the brightly-wrapped package.

'Happy birthday, General Eisenhower,' she said, placing the gift in his hand.

'Say, this is very kind,' he answered with an irresistible grin, his blue eyes lighting up when he saw the riding crop. 'It would appear Rick has being filling you in on one of my favourite pastimes. '

'Actually, Rick, I mean Major Carlon, showed me the horses at your country retreat.' Susan held her breath. Had he told the General they had used his horses? She squirmed inwardly, hoping she had not put her foot in it, especially if Rick had not been given permission to use the horses.

A broad grin put her mind at rest. 'I sometimes ride at Bushy Park. Feel free to join me whenever time permits.'

'Thank you, sir.' Susan did not add that she had spent more time on the ground than in the saddle, but with Rick's expert coaching she was slowly coming to grips with equestrian skills.

'As a rule I don't dance, but a pretty girl is always the exception. Would you like to dance, Susan?'

Too dumbstruck to answer, she flashed him a brilliant smile, taking his proffered arm. He handed his birthday gift to Rick saying, 'Look after this.'

Rick watched them go. He was bursting with pride. He had the loveliest woman at the party, and she had eyes only for him.

Seeing Harry, he headed over to him. Monty had told him that Harry had partnered Susan to some forces show while he was in North Africa, and he wanted to warn the Englishman to lay off. Never before had Rick experienced jealousy of this magnitude. When he had finally dragged the story out of Monty, white-hot rage exploded inside him, and he couldn't wait to get his hands on that British sonofabitch.

The dancers moved aside to allow the General room to manoeuvre with his partner. Susan noticed that while some of the women were in long gowns, the majority were in uniform, and she wished she had a nice smart uniform to wear instead of her old serge one.

'Do you know Rick's family, General Eisenhower?'

'I remember his father from my West Point days. Abe runs a fine stable in Virginia.'

'Do you live in Virginia too, General Eisenhower?'

He gave her a wide grin. 'My name and rank are a bit of a mouthful. So how about you stick to Ike? I'm from Abilene, Kansas. Nice town, friendly folks.'

Susan smiled, studying him closely. Rick had told her that the General had an unenviable job. Apart from planning war strategies and being continually busy with the organisation of thousands of American troops arriving in Britain, there was also the daunting task of constantly keeping the British and American top brass from disagreeing with each other, as well as placating the feisty General de Gaulle, who disagreed with everybody. Rick had told her that Ike often joked that it was probably easier fighting the Nazis.

'Are you and Major Carlon mere acquaintances, or is it more serious?' he asked.

She was embarrassed and chose her words carefully. 'We have known each other for several months, and enjoy each other's company.'

'It's reassuring to know that our military personnel are welcomed by the British people.' She smiled sweetly at his tact and changed the subject.

'You're a very good dancer, sir.'

'And you are a very charming young lady. Most of the women I've met in London are.' He answered her smile with one of his own, and when the music stopped, took her back to Rick. 'I'll take the riding crop and give Susan back to you, Rick. You sure gotten the best outta the deal.'

Hardly had the General departed than another officer claimed her for a dance and twirled her around the floor. When the music stopped she hurried over to Monty.

'Have you seen Rick?'

'I saw him go outside with Harry a while back.'

When she arrived at the main door there was nobody there apart from several military policemen on guard duty, and she had no idea where to look for him. Taking a chance, she headed for the conservatory to the left-hand side of the building. As she got closer she heard Rick's voice.

'I want you to stop issuing invitations to Susan' he was saying.

'For heaven's sake, we only went to a show.'

'I don't mind Susan going out in a group, and she knows that, but damn it, I will not have these little intimate tête-à-têtes.'

'We've been friends for years, and there is nothing between us except friendship. I might add that you're making a mountain out of a molehill.'

'Stuff your molehills. If I catch you going out with her alone again, I won't answer for my actions.'

'Threatening a subordinate officer, Major Carlon?'

'OK, Captain Fortescue, I'm ordering you to stay away from Susan. If you don't, I'll have you tossed out of headquarters so quick your damn feet won't touch the ground, Churchill or no Churchill. Understand?'

'Yes, *sir.*'

Concealed behind a thick shrub, Susan had heard enough. She quickly retraced her steps, found Monty and asked him to follow her. When she found an empty alcove, she stopped and took hold of Monty's hand and pulled him behind a large ornamental plant and started questioning him.

'What did you tell Rick? It was you who told him I went to the theatre with Harry, wasn't it?'

'Sheesh, I just happened to mention that I'd seen you and Harry. Then he went nuts and wanted to know every damn thing. You don't know the Major when he gets the bit between his teeth. He's as feisty as those horses in the General's stable.'

She didn't have to be told how ruthless Rick could be when he wanted information as she had ample knowledge of that.

'You have caused a rift between two friends, and they are arguing with each other outside the conservatory.'

'Shucks, ma'am, what can I do?'

'You can go out there and tell Rick and Harry that the General requests their presence.'

'Gee, ma'am, are you asking me to lie? I'll be in trouble with the Major if I say that and it ain't true.'

'You will be in trouble with me if you don't,' she threatened sweetly. 'Now, will you please be a dear and help me?'

'I'll try, ma'am.' Monty watched her walk away. Susan was a persuasive woman when she wanted something. Rick was a swell guy, and he would follow him to hell if the Major asked him, but boy oh boy, did he have a temper. What a couple they made.

Following Susan's directions, he rounded several bushes and heard raucous laughing, the kind of laughter men indulge in when in the company of other men and there are no women around. Monty saw the Major sitting on the grass and the Captain with a leather flask to his lips. After a swig, he passed it to the Major, both of them laughing their heads off.

'Excuse me sir, I've been sent to look for you,' he said. 'General Eisenhower...' was all he got out as the two men came to their feet, brushing the grass off their uniforms.

'Carry on, Lieutenant. We're right behind you,' Major Carlon snapped.

With her hands clenched tightly to stop herself from trembling, Susan had kept her eye on the entrance, praying for Monty to appear. Finally, when he did materialise, he gave her a wink, a broad smile and a thumbs-up sign.

Delighted, she returned his signal with a beaming smile and even blew him a kiss. It felt like hours had passed as she waited impatiently, even refusing a few requests to dance. Seated on a blue velvet slipper chair, she tapped her foot anxiously, gazing occasionally at the dancing couples, but always with one eye on the entrance.

At last she saw them in the foyer together. Talking and smiling, Rick slapped Harry on the back and walked off towards the General. She held her breath, hoping she had not caused Monty any trouble. How could two officers behave so childishly? One minute they were arguing and threatening, the next laughing and slapping each other on the back. Susan sighed. She would never understand men.

Without warning the lights dimmed, there was a drum roll and two men carried in a large cake with one candle. Everybody started singing as the General was presented with a sword to cut the birthday cake. He seemed bashful, making jokes about his age, his weight and the English weather.

As soon as the sponge cake, thick with cream, had been carved up and handed around on small serving plates with cake forks, the dancing resumed. Susan had not danced with Rick all evening, and as her eyes searched around the room she was disappointed to see him escorting a woman in a smart uniform of the United States Army Corps onto the floor. His head was bent towards the woman, and suddenly he tossed his head back laughing. Susan was both annoyed and miserable as she watched them. Why hadn't he come over to her when he returned from the conservatory? Why was he dancing with her, and who was she? Questions whirled around in her mind like streak lightning. The woman was most attractive, and Susan was sure she had not seen her before.

She was just about to flounce off to the ladies' room when a voice said, 'A penny for them.'

Susan turned to find Harry at her elbow. 'You startled me.'

'I apologise, sweet Suzy. Would you like to dance?'

'I think not.'

'What the deuce are you saying?'

'I was in the garden, Harry. I heard most of what was said.'

'Oh, that! Rick was over-reacting, as usual.'

'Perhaps, but we shouldn't see each other again, unless we're in a group. Don't you agree?'

'No. It's utterly ridiculous.'

'Harry, I don't want to be responsible for two grown men almost coming to blows because of me. Honestly, you would think that in the middle of a war there was enough conflict without friends and allies fighting each other.'

He smiled. 'My sweet Suzy, men have been coming to blows over women for centuries, and I daresay it's not going to change now, or in the foreseeable future.'

'What a smooth tongue you have, Captain Fortescue.'

'And you, sweet Suzy, are gullible.' He was annoyed that Rick was going to stop her from seeing any male friends at all. Rick was eaten up with jealousy and would love to lock Susan away. To Harry's mind, his attitude was totally unreasonable.

'I know, and I know you are a little annoyed with me, but I love Rick. Can't you understand, and help me to keep him happy?'

'Do not give it another thought.' Harry would do anything to please her. Unlike Rick, he could not hurt her; nor could he impose strict rules. For the umpteenth time he was sorry he had introduced them. Had he known how it was going to turn out, he would have swept her into a taxi and taken her home from the Savoy the night she met Rick.

'In that case, Harry dear, I won't.' She was relieved that they had agreed to meet only in the company of others in the future. Changing the subject, she asked, 'Who is that woman dancing with Rick?'

'That's the General's driver,' he replied, following her eyes.

'She's very attractive' Susan grudgingly conceded.

'Jealous?'

'Not in the least.'

'Then dance with me, sweet Suzy. We are in the company of others,' he coaxed, eyeing the crowded dance floor.

'With pleasure, Harry dear,' she replied and took his arm as he led her to the floor.

Sweeping her around the dance floor, he gave a deep sigh and murmured, 'Now this is better than standing on the sidelines of the ballroom floor being tense, isn't it?'

'How did you know I was tense?'

He smiled at her. 'I know when you're happy and I know when you're not. Call it instinct.' He twirled her around. Over the top of Susan's head, Harry shot a glance at Rick circling the floor with his partner. He didn't look happy. Serve the Major right for acting like a lovesick schoolboy and threatening to have him kicked out of headquarters. Besides, he and Susan were obeying the rules; they were, to all intents and purposes, in a group. Harry quietly chuckled to himself and thanked providence that he did not have a jealous bone in his body. It must be hell trying to keep that kind of emotion under control.

The music stopped, and he led Susan from the floor. Harry decided to have some fun.

'Perhaps we can meet for lunch next week. I'll invite half a dozen officers from the Mess to join our group,' he suggested, emphasising the last word. She smiled, knowing he was teasing her.

'Actually, I would love to join you and the officers for lunch. Perhaps I could invite some of the volunteers from the depot to come along.'

'That's a wonderful idea. I hope you can afford to pay the bill for the group.'

'Me pay, I'm flabbergasted!'

His lips twitched. He was enjoying this silly bantering. 'I can see that. I expect your flabber has never been so gasted.'

'Well, of all the…' suddenly she burst out laughing, and so did Harry.

'My sweet Suzy, I have a better idea. We could meet in a restaurant, by chance, and if all the tables are full, technically we'll be in a group.' Smiling, they both left the floor. Rick and his partner were heading towards them.

Susan braced herself and fixed a smile on her face. Ever since Rick had taken the woman onto the dance floor, Susan had wanted to meet her.

'Kay, this is Susan Cadiz. Darling, this is Kay Summersby.'

After the introductions had been made, Kay said with a beaming smile, 'Rick is a fine horseman. He has been giving me a few tips.' She turned to Harry. 'Oh, Captain Fortescue, it's been such a long time. How about we circle the dance floor together?'

With Harry's murmured assent they left, leaving Rick with a satisfied grin on his face.

Rick calling her darling in front of Kay and Harry was a pleasant surprise for Susan. Had he done it because Harry was present or to reassure her? Kay Summersby was an attractive and accomplished woman in her thirties and was so much at ease and confident with everybody. It was rumoured that Kay and Ike were very close, but Susan didn't care how close they were, as long as she had Rick.

'The next dance is mine, darling. Say, are you OK?'

'I feel wonderful, honestly.' She gave a beaming smile to dispel the look of concern in his eyes. 'I felt a little off-colour a while ago, but it's gone now.' It wasn't a complete lie. She had felt unhappy when Rick had been arguing with Harry and she had been tense while he was dancing with Kay.

The band started playing *Moonlight Serenade*, and Rick swept her into his arms. 'Our music,' he whispered against her cheek.

'Did you organise it?' she murmured.

'Uh huh.'

Susan sighed. It was heavenly being in his arms as they moved together in silence, hardly taking any steps at all, their bodies just swaying to the music. All the while Rick was pressing his lips against the side of her forehead. Susan felt as if she were floating on clouds.

'You fire my heart and fill my soul with love,' he said in a husky voice, barely audible above the music. 'I want to marry you.'

His words were music to her ears. She loved him so much and wanted to be married to him but had feared he would never ask her. Rick was smart, witty and charming and came from a respected family. She was none of these things. On the outside she was *à la mode*, while inside she felt she was still a girl from the slums. If she told him the truth about her dreadful past, would he still love her?

Then Rick arrived home, yelling 'The Allies have taken Normandy and are moving inland! With a bit of luck, Paris will be next. Ike wants new headquarters set up over the Channel. I'll be leaving in the morning, with my team.' Laughing, Rick picked her up and spun her around. 'Don't you see, honey? The war will soon be over and we can go Stateside and get married.'

Susan hugged him and laughed, delighted with the news as much as he was. They danced around, hugging and kissing, unmindful of the dinner burning on the stovetop.

'Let's go out and eat.'

'But darling, what about the meal I've prepared?'

'I think,' he said sniffing the air, 'it is now a burnt offering.'

'Oh, blast!' she cried. She flew into the kitchen to turn off the gas and then hurried upstairs to change.

'Don't be too long, honey. I'm starving,' he called as he went to answer the front door.

'Does Miss Cadiz live here?' said a male voice.

'Susan? Yeah, sure.'

'I'm her brother. Is she in? I'd like to talk to her.'

Rick stared at the tall blond youth with a puzzled frown. Hadn't Susan told him she had no family? He shrugged his shoulders and opened the door wider. 'Step inside and I'll get her' he said, Rick entered the bedroom, pulling on his ear lobe. 'There's a young guy downstairs says he's your brother. He wants to talk to you.'

She paled and placed both hands on each side of her face. Rick saw stark fear in her eyes, not unlike the terror he had witnessed in some soldiers when they were embarking for the D-Day landings.

'Please, Rick, tell him to go.'

'Why? What in hell's going on?' He stood there, hands on hips, regarding her in angry silence, waiting for her to reply.

'Please, please tell him to go!' she begged, tears filling her eyes.

'Hang on' he snapped and disappeared.

She could hear the voices of two men talking, and then the door closed. She collapsed on the bed, shaking and weeping into the pillow.

'I want the truth, Susan. Is that guy really your brother?' He stood over the bed his black brows knitted together, demanding answers. She could not or would not tell him, and this only increased his anger. Taking hold of her shoulders, he drew her towards him.

'How come you told me you had no family, and then your brother turns up? Didn't we agree to be truthful with each other?'

Although she was sobbing loudly, she heard him. She had wanted to forget the terrible life she had escaped from, but it seemed she could not. Most of all, she had wanted to shield her shameful past from Rick, but even in that she had failed. How had Erik found her? It must have been through Janet Bell or Claudius Peel. Susan never wanted to see anyone from Sunderland again, including Erik.

Many weeks ago Louisa had cautioned her not to count on a wartime romance. Susan had ignored that advice, convinced that the love she shared with Rick would overcome any barrier, but would it survive her terrible past? It seemed love's sweetness also had its bitterness. She did not want to divulge her past life to anyone, especially to the man she loved. She had to distract him, and drying her eyes with the back of her hand, she tried a different tack.

'Darling, you're going away tomorrow. Please don't let this spoil our evening,' she said, brushing away her tears.

'This is too important to leave. Hell, I don't know how long I'll be in France, and I need to know now. Don't you trust me?'

'Of course I do.'

'Susan, tell me.' His words were spoken softly but firmly.

However distasteful this was going to be, it seemed there was no way out, and she would have to tell him everything. Standing up, she walked to the dressing table, flicked her shoulder-length tresses behind her ears, and turned to face him. Digging her fingernails firmly into her palms to force back the tears, she tried to speak calmly.

'Before I tell you,' she said in a shaky voice, 'I want you to know that I love you. I just wanted to protect you from my sordid past.' She swallowed, feeling her throat constrict, threatening to bring back tears. She hesitated, dug her nails deeper into the palm of her hands her hands and started to speak, watching him closely for his reaction. 'My mother slept with men for money and my Spanish father was one of her customers. My half-brother Erik who you just met was the result of a liaison with a Swedish sailor. I hated my mother and I loathe the place where I was born.'

She stopped speaking and took another deep breath. 'I know that a girl with my background could never hope to marry a man like you. That is not the reason I kept it from you; I kept it from you with good intentions.'

'Sometimes intentions, even the best, lead to disappointment. Is that everything?'

'No,' she blinked away the tears that still threatened. 'One of my mother's regulars tried to rape me when I was fourteen, and with the help of a friend I ran away to London.'

Combing his hair with his fingers, Rick paced from the bed to the door as if his anger would not allow him to remain in one place for any length of time. Suddenly, he punched the wall with his fist, making her jump. If only she knew what he was thinking! As the silence lengthened, Susan was convinced he was having difficulty accepting the truth. She had gambled and lost.

Then she heard him speak.

'Does Harry know any of this?'

'No. Only you.'

The pacing and the silence resumed, only this time he was rubbing his chin with his hand. Minutes seemed like hours, and with a feeling of rejection Susan silently made plans to pack a suitcase and leave. She would have to stay with the Blores until she found her own place, if they would have her. She just couldn't face Louisa, as she would be sure to say 'I told you so.' Louisa had told her many times to be wary of any man in uniform, as they seduced young girls and satisfied lonely married women. Susan had not believed or listened to Louisa, and now she was going to lose the man she loved because her mother was a whore and she was illegitimate. Life was unfair. So horribly unfair!

It was up to her to make the first move. She knew she must say something to put an end to this protracted silence.

'Rick, I think it best if I leave. I hope things go well for you in France.'

Rick's expression was unreadable. 'When I get back from France I'll hunt down the bastard who tried to rape you, and if he is still alive he'll wish he wasn't.' Then he pulled her into his arms and gave her a fierce hug. Not another word was spoken as he comforted her. In all the time she had known him she had never heard him use bad language.

'Rick, please don't. It would be impossible to find him.'

'My love, anything in this world is possible. Your mother will give me the information I need and I'll find him. How about the baby?'

'What baby?' she blurted out aghast.

'Our baby.'

'I was, I...' she stammered. 'How do you know?'

'Since falling in love with you, I have learned to keep one step ahead. You're far too secretive, darling. If you really must know, I heard you being sick in the bathroom a few mornings and put two and two together. I was waiting for you to say something.'

'I meant to tell you tonight, during dinner, but my past reared its ugly head and all my carefully laid plans went amiss.'

'Susan, your past is not important to me. I love you. Just as you tried to shield me from knowing about your life, I will protect you with mine.'

She hugged him and stretching up on her toes, kissed him. 'Darling, I love you so much, but please tell me that you are not marrying me just because of our child.'

He tried to keep a straight face. 'Not this one,' he said giving her a wicked grin. 'I happen to want more than one.'

A miracle had happened: he was hers, and she belonged to him. She was overjoyed that he loved her, despite her disgusting past. Louisa had been wrong, so wrong.

'Do you still want to go out and eat?'

For her, hunger had vanished and she wanted nothing except to remain in his arms. 'Are you hungry, darling?'

He shook his head, looking at her in that old familiar way, and in a flash had scooped her up into his arms and lowered her onto the bed. Then he lay down next to her.

'When the baby arrives, shall I send a photograph to you in France?'

'Whoa, I'll be back in a few months and hopefully will be here for the birth, unless Ike changes his plans.' He turned to her and kissed her waiting lips.

Later they discussed her divorce. 'You can get a quick one from that Blore character in Reno' he said. 'Then we can marry immediately.' He gave her the address of Carlon Stud and asked her to write to his parents and tell them about their upcoming marriage and the new addition to the family. He told her he had put in for furlough and it had been granted for Christmas. They would fly courtesy of the United States Army to Washington and then travel on to Virginia and Reno. He explained that he would have to return to headquarters in France after his furlough, but she and the baby would remain with his folks, as it was safer. Hitler's buzz bombs were systematically destroying London, and he wanted her out of harm's way.

Early the next morning, Rick took her in his arms. 'Be seeing you, darling,' he whispered, wiping her tears. He hugged her one last time, then headed for the door. Rick forbade her to wave him off, as he hated goodbyes.

Still crying, she pulled the curtain aside and looked through the window in time to see the staff car drive off. She had turned and headed for the kitchen when a sudden thought made her stop in her tracks. She had forgotten to tell him about Penny! Through all the tension, tears and confessions of last night, her daughter had completely slipped from her mind. She now wanted Rick to know everything. Susan decided that the first thing she would do when he returned from France would be to take him to Queens Road to meet Penny.

Women who were pregnant were excused from any war work, and she planned to call into the depot and tell Pam of her condition. While standing in front of the dressing table combing her hair, she saw a dollar bill on her pillow, reflected in the mirror. Picking it up, she read the words, 'Yours forever, Rick'. After kissing the bill, she folded it into a tiny square and put it in a locket he had bought for her in Bond Street three weeks ago. Fastening the chain around her neck, she finished dressing. Susan planned to go to the ambulance depot to speak with Pamela, visit her daughter, and later meet June to have lunch at the Orchid Café.

June was sitting at her favourite table near the window with a view of a small garden when Susan arrived. 'Have you been waiting long?' she asked.

'A few minutes,' June replied succinctly, and immediately started telling Susan all about the latest lover in her life. June was in and out of love at the drop of a hat. With the war, June thought life was so uncertain; she did not expect to survive and was grabbing all the good times she could. London was full of uniformed men of different nationalities, and they all seemed to drift in and out of June's life like flotsam and jetsam. Last week, she had been gooey-eyed about a French Lieutenant, the week before it had been a Polish airman and now she had just met a Canadian pilot.

'I know I'm very naughty hopping into bed with them, but what the hell. We might all be dead next week. I went out with an American flyer last week, and he was teaching me a new song. You know how we sing 'Overpaid, oversexed, over here'? Well, he sang, 'Underpaid, underfed, under me'. I didn't like him or his song, but he was wonderful in bed. Last night my Canadian pilot whispered in my ear. 'A woman should be treated like an aeroplane: get inside her three times a week and take her up to heaven.'

This horrible war, Susan decided, was turning women into promiscuous strumpets and men into randy lechers. It was awful and she wished the war would end.

At five the following evening she was making some tea when the doorbell rang. It was Harry. He had an oddly serious look on his face.

'Harry dear, what a nice surprise. Do come in. Would you like some tea, or something stronger?'

'Thank you. I wouldn't say no to a Scotch.'

Thinking this was the first time he had not greeted her with his usual 'sweet Suzy', she poured him a drink.

'I'm sure Rick won't mind if you have a glass of his single malt. Do you know he prefers it to bourbon now?

I'm amazed at all the luxury items that are unobtainable to most people in London, but Headquarters seems to have no difficulty acquiring them.' She handed him the glass and was surprised to see him toss the liquid down his throat in one gulp. Then he clutched the empty glass tightly in his hand and gave her a strange look.

'It was decided that I should be the one to tell you.'

'Tell me what, Harry?' she asked with a smile. Rick was probably returning sooner and he had sent Harry to tell her.

'I'm so sorry, Susan. The aircraft Rick was travelling in never arrived in France. I'm afraid he has been posted missing.'

He didn't add, 'Presumed dead'. No need for that, not just yet.

She stared at Harry, not wanting to believe what he had just said. A lump as big as an apple stuck in her throat, preventing her from speaking. She felt nothing, nothing but horror and fear, and she started shaking. Her head was spinning and her legs were weak, causing her to sway. Colour suddenly drained from her face, and she collapsed in a dead faint at Harry's feet.

Picking her up, he placed her on the sofa and trickled some Scotch into her mouth. He had not wanted to deliver this ghastly message, but he had been told at headquarters that it was best coming from a trusted friend. He knew as soon as she opened the front door that her radiant smile would be wiped from her face when he passed on the dreadful news.

Someone so young and beautiful should not have to

cope with this. 'Missing, presumed dead' was worse than 'Killed in action'. It created a forlorn hope in loved ones, and hope was always the last thing to die.

He gently patted her face, calling her name. She coughed and spluttered as the Scotch took effect. When her eyes opened, Harry saw nothing but emptiness in them. Her face was devoid of colour, and she began to cry.

'I am aching all over as if I have been crushed by a buzz bomb,' she sobbed. 'I cannot live without him. Please tell me it's not true.' She tearfully whispered.

'My sweet Suzy, it will take time, a long time, but you will survive. I know you will. Now I'll go and make you some tea.'

She grabbed both his hands. 'Harry dear, don't leave me. You know I was never truly religious, but I will pray each and every day, if God will bring him back to me. That's not too much to ask, is it?' She dissolved into tears again.

He calmed her down and went to make the tea. An Army doctor had given him a sedative, and as she was so overwrought, he was going to put it in her tea. Knowing her as he did, she would refuse the medicine if he offered it.

There was another delicate problem he had to handle. The mews dwelling that Rick had occupied was to be handed over in a few days to some colonel from Washington. Accommodation was at a premium in London; with all the top brass arriving from the States, private residences were like hens' teeth. Harry had already decided to take Susan to the family estate in Kent. There was a small lodge within the grounds, and he planned to let her stay there so that she could recuperate from this terrible tragedy. Four weeks before his father had suffered a stroke and was now confined to a wheelchair, unable to walk. So he would get no argument from him. His mother and sister were not in residence, and to all intents and purposes Harry was now master of Hayward Hall. The old retainer, Tom Marsh, who managed the estate, had told him about the empty lodge some time back, and Harry intended to put it to good use.

General Eisenhower was writing to inform Rick's parents, and it was his request that Harry should be the one to tell Susan. Ike's wishes or whims were treated as commands. The General was greatly admired and respected by all his men, including Harry. Since being assigned as liaison officer between the British and Americans, Harry had got to know him and thought he was the best man to bring victory to the Allies. Ike was a master at smoothing the ruffled feathers that often cropped up between the top brass on both sides. The General had been devastated at the loss of Rick and the team who had accompanied him. Although the Allies controlled Normandy, the Luftwaffe were still shooting down Allied aircraft. Flying was an extremely dangerous occupation in wartime, and there were many aircraft losses. The King's youngest brother had met a similar fate.

When at last Susan fell into a deep sleep, Harry sprang into action. He packed all her clothes and personal belongings and loaded them into the staff car he had borrowed. Finally Harry wrapped his charge in a blanket and carried her to the vehicle. Laying her on the back seat, he locked the door of the mews and sped off into the night. Harry knew that packers and cleaners were due at Kenton Mews in two days to gather all Rick's personal belongings and deliver them to headquarters where they would eventually be shipped to his family in Virginia.

Chapter Fourteen

Gazing over the fields as she walked towards the village, Susan reflected upon the past agonising months. Harry had been right: she had survived, but only just. Not long before, whenever she heard music playing on the wireless, which she and Rick had danced to, she would break down and cry. Once, when eating breakfast and their favourite tune had begun to play, she had picked up the plate and thrown it at the window, cursing God for killing Rick. She blamed the war for his death and she also blamed the Army and the Nazis. She couldn't imagine life without him. She didn't know if she had a future or, if she wanted one.

She was plagued with recollections: his wonderful sense of humour and his lopsided grin when he teased her; those dark wondrous eyes that crinkled with amusement but could change just as rapidly to scowl in anger or blaze with passion.

He used to laugh at her when she accused him of telling lies. He would arch his eyebrows and say, 'Men don't tell lies. They just alter the facts.' Pictures of him haunted her:

a fancy dress party the officers gave, when he dressed up as a wolf and laughed at her Red Riding Hood costume; making love under the stars when they had been riding at dusk; murmuring that he would love her forever. Susan cherished these memories. However, some nights she would wake up in a cold sweat to feel the touch of his lips on hers and would call out his name, begging him to hold her in his arms, and with a sudden jolt she would realise she had been dreaming again. These tormented nights always ended in tears.

She missed him terribly and would have done anything to see him again or hear his voice, just for an instant, but all she had left was emptiness and a persistent, tight knot in her chest. For weeks she had hoped that he would come walking through the door, but in her heart of hearts she knew he wasn't coming back to her. Eventually, through not eating, she became quite ill and ended up in the cottage hospital in the village of Birchwood, two miles from the Hall.

In the months after returning from hospital, she wandered about aimlessly, unable to care or even think about anything, including the child she was carrying. She knew that thousands of wives, mothers, and sweethearts carried grief as great as or even greater than her own, but at this moment she could not spare a thought for anyone else. She was eaten up with her own grief.

As the weeks turned to months her sadness did not fade. Lying in bed she would whisper to him. 'I love you

Rick because you are witty, intelligent and romantic.' At this point tears would flow and she would cry into the pillow and eventually fall asleep.

But slowly, very slowly, the pain began to ease, and she started to accept that Rick was never coming back and there would be no marriage.

During this time Harry was her only visitor. The doctor paid a visit from time to time, and a young scullery maid delivered cooked meals from the kitchen at the Hall. Harry had arranged this when he discovered Susan was starving herself and was very weak. He would try to cheer her, talking about Rick, and she knew only too well he was doing it just to help her.

'Did you know Rick was one of the youngest staff officers at headquarters?'

'Harry, I don't want this baby.'

He was both surprised and shocked to discover that she didn't want the child of the man she loved. Harry silently vowed to stand by her and give whatever assistance he could.

'Sweet Susie, this baby is part of you and Rick. Come, be brave. He would be disappointed to see you like this. Let's go for a stroll around the grounds. I don't believe you've left the Lodge in weeks, and the doctor advised that a walk outside in the fresh air would lift your spirits and put some colour in your cheeks.'

She smiled at her good friend, Harry dear. What would I do without you? It's wonderful of you motoring down here from headquarters so often. I really don't know how to thank you. Shall we go for that walk?'

'Yes, get your coat. I'll wait here.'

A moment later he heard an agonised moan. Taking the stairs two at a time, he found her crumpled at the top of the stairway, and he bent down to cradle her in his arms.

'Is this it?' he asked. Her answer was a quick nod before another spasm hit her, doubling her over. He quickly and carefully carried her to the car. 'Off to hospital with you, my girl.'

Marching up and down the waiting room of the maternity wing at the hospital, Harry thought he could do with a Scotch or two to quell his nerves. Instead, he downed the cocoa the hospital tea lady had given him on her rounds. He was just about to look for her and request another when a nurse popped her head around the door.

'You have a beautiful baby boy. I'll take you along to see your wife now. Please follow me. Oh, by the way, I have some of your wife's personal belongings. Can you please take them with you when you leave?'

If only he really was the husband and father, he mused. For the umpteenth time he wished the regiment had not been ordered to India. He had been informed that it was shipping out in a month to relieve war-weary British troops in India. Harry had been ordered to rejoin his regiment. It was anyone's guess how long he would remain. If Gandhi's 'non-cooperation with British rule' campaign intensified, the regiment could be away for years.

The doctor's voice cut across his thoughts and stopped him before entering Susan's room. 'I'm afraid she doesn't want the child' he was saying. 'She won't even look at it. In my opinion, she is suffering from acute melancholia and needs time, a great deal of time, for this depression to ease. Perhaps, Captain Fortescue, you could talk to her?'

She was lying in bed, her dark hair splashed across pristine white pillows; even after all she had just been through, she looked radiant. He had no idea how to broach the subject but he had to try.

'How are you feeling, sweet Susie?'

'Harry, I don't want the baby. Please help me. I can't cope,' she wailed, dissolving into bitter tears.

When Harry returned to the Lodge he unpacked Susan's personal items that the hospital had given him. Among the jewellery he found a gold locket and inside, an American dollar bill with the words. *Yours forever, Rick*. He parcelled the items up and placed them in Susan's dressing-table draw.

When Susan left hospital ten days later to take up residence at the Lodge, her son had been given to a childless couple on the Haywood estate. John and Rose Miller had been heartbroken after losing lost their six-month-old baby with whooping cough, and agreed to take care of Susan's child, who had been named Edward, until she was well enough to have him back. The child's mother was welcome to visit her son at any time. The doctor was of the opinion that the baby would help the Millers recover from their tragedy and give Susan time to come to terms with the loss of the baby's father. At the doctor's insistence Harry, arranged it. He also told the estate manager to send all the bills concerning the child to him, as he did not want to burden the Millers, and he knew Susan could not afford it.

After he had registered the birth of Susan's son, he placed the certificate in a leather pouch and left it on a shelf in the book room at the lodge.

Before leaving for India, Harry paid one last visit to Susan. He didn't tell her about registering her son's birth; it would only end in tears, and he wanted her to get well. He did say that while she was more than welcome to remain at the Lodge, as she could not shut the world out forever; nor could she hide in Kent for the rest of her life.

'Two things that make life meaningless are regret and illness,' he said. 'Now start living.' He embraced her and wished her well, telling her that he was shipping out to India in a matter of days but would keep in touch.

As the weeks turned to months and winter became spring, Susan slowly began to feel better. The desolation and disbelief that had followed Rick's passing were healing. She seldom cried now and had stopped punishing herself. The pills the doctor prescribed calmed her whenever she felt like screaming, but she still wasn't strong enough to cope with a baby. Harry had told her the child was the image of Rick, and she could not bring herself to accept the fact that the baby had lived and Rick had died – at least, not yet.

To occupy her time, she went for long walks and frequently saddled up one of the horses from the stable. Susan was a competent horsewoman now. Rick would have been so proud of her. Dragging strands of hair from across her face and tucking them behind an ear, she raced across the landscape. Rabbits darted across the fields, popping their heads up from beneath grassy knolls, several pheasants and reddish-brown partridges pecked at anything on the ground. Early springtime blooms were sprouting up everywhere. It was exhilarating to breathe fresh air, and she urged the horse onwards.

Harry had been right: she was hiding at Haywood Hall. She had wanted to die and join Rick when she first came to the Lodge, but now she wanted to live and put all the misery behind her. Rick would always be close to her heart and his locket even closer around her neck. She hardly ever took it off.

Two days before, she had picked up a Bible from the small book-room in the Lodge, thumbed through it and stopped at Ecclesiastes: 'A time to love and a time to hate, a time for war and a time for peace'. Having had times of love, hate and war, she now desperately hoped that this was her time for peace, especially in her heart.

On VE Day she put the wireless on and listened to the celebrations. Mr Churchill gave a patriotic speech, and then the King spoke. Everywhere, people were rejoicing that the war with the Nazis was over and they were dancing and singing in the streets. Bonfires were lit across the length and breadth of Britain, and everywhere there was a feeling of hope for the future. She would have liked to be in London right now, but she knew she wasn't well enough to cope with the crowds and sat in the Lodge listening to the celebrations.

The previous day she had written to Louisa. Susan felt guilty about ignoring her friend and apologised. Then she went on to explain that she had suffered from a long illness and was staying with some friends in the country. She wrote that she was planning a trip to London and would catch up with Louisa soon. Susan didn't mention Rick's death, the baby's birth or her depressed mental state. She also penned a few lines to Harry, thanking him for helping her and telling him she was feeling better and looking forward to her first walk to the village post office.

Birchwood had not changed since the Victorian age of cobbled streets, hitching posts and water troughs. In the middle of the village, a duck pond and a bench seat encircled a large birch tree. Waddling ducks, swooping birds and happy children catching tadpoles in old jam jars had Susan smiling at the picturesque scene.

Turning around, she admired the lovely quaint cottages, with neat window boxes filled with colourful springtime blooms. The post office, the corner store and chemist were all in a row. A quaint old tea-shop with a bay window looked inviting. On the other side of the duck pond was an old tavern, named the Birchwood Arms, with a thatched roof, gabled windows and tubs of flowers lining the whitewashed walls. She smiled, inwardly trying to imagine the village years ago. Horses tied to the post would be drinking cool water while their owners went about their business. She imagined village girls in sweet dimity dresses with straw bonnets, squires in britches and topcoats with smart waistcoats, and children dressed in anything from knickerbockers to pinafores with frilled pantalets. Susan hugged herself, thankful to be alive.

After months of confinement, it felt wonderful to be out and about, thinking of more pleasant things. As summer started to arrive, she went riding every morning and began to feel like her old self again. She was surprised to discover she was enjoying galloping over hills and dales for the first time in months.

On her way back to the stables after a morning ride, her eyes were drawn to a black Daimler coming up the drive. When it came to a halt, two classically-dressed women emerged from the shiny vehicle. They barely glanced at her before disappearing under the portico leading to the entrance of the Hall. Susan shrugged and rode on, dismissing them.

A week later, while she was washing her hair, the doorknocker sounded. Quickly wrapping a towel around her head, she hastened to answer it. On the doorstep was a young woman in her thirties. She wore a tweed dress belted at the waist, a string of pearls, matching earrings, and sensible walking shoes. Her copper-coloured hair was scraped back in a bun, making her features look sharp.

'Can I help you?' Susan asked, tucking strands of curls beneath the towelling material.

'I am Elizabeth Fortescue and my family own this Lodge. More to the point, who are you?'

Susan immediately recognized Harry's surname. This must be his sister. 'I am Susan Cadiz. Would you like to come in?'

'No thank you. I would like to know who gave you permission to take up residence here.'

'Your brother.'

'Are you Harry's mistress?' Her speech was both demanding and rude.

'No, I am not,' Susan answered firmly. Taking a deep breath, she added, 'I was unwell, and Harry kindly suggested I leave London and stay here until I recovered.'

'How very convenient.'

'It's the truth. You can write to him in India and verify it, if you like.'

'Well, you will have to vacate the Lodge, as my aunt is coming to take up residence.'

'Harry never told me of his aunt.'

'Aunt Alice is Mummy's sister. I do not know why I have to explain my family history to you.'

'You don't, but thank you for telling me. I will leave at the end of the week, if that is convenient. I was really sorry to hear about your father being so ill, and I am equally sorry Harry did not tell you I was living here.'

'The end of the week will suit. I believe my aunt is planning to spruce up the Lodge before moving in. How long have you been here?'

'Almost twelve months.'

'You must have been very ill, but you have recovered, I see. Was that you I saw mounted on one of our horses when we arrived?'

'Yes, Harry said I could make use of the stable when I was feeling better. He is such a dear friend.'

'You obviously don't know my brother very well. I have never known Harry to have a female friend. He usually desires them, beds them, and discards them. Friendship? Absolutely not.' With this parting shot, Elizabeth Fortescue turned on her heel and left.

What a rude woman she was, and so unlike Harry in looks and manners. Susan had wanted to give Miss Toffee-Nose Fortescue a piece of her mind, but she held back, fearing she might stir up trouble for Harry. Watching her visitor walk briskly towards the Hall, Susan closed the door and leaned against it, drying her hair. Elizabeth Fortescue was wrong about her brother. How could any male in his right mind desire a skinny, naïve waif with a heavy northern brogue, no manners, limited education, whom he had met fleetingly on a train bound for London? Why, he had even called her a pipsqueak, which she now understood to mean small and insignificant. Later, when they had met again, Harry had told her that all he wanted was to be good friends, and that's exactly what they were. Elizabeth did not know her brother very well at all.

Susan would have to move, but where could she go? One thing she must do before making plans was to visit the Millers to enquire about her son and notify them that she was leaving the Lodge.

'We are so proud of Edward' said Rose Miller when Susan arrived. 'He never cries and sleeps right through the night, such a good boy. John just adores him. Actually, you just missed John. He's working over the other side of the estate this morning. Listen to me prattling on!' Suddenly she stopped, and her eyes filled with tears. 'You've come to take Edward, haven't you?'

'Only for a walk, if I may. Rose, please let me explain. I cannot possibly take my son with me permanently as I haven't any money or work and I don't have anywhere to live as yet. Could you please take care of him for me until I am able to?'

Rose nodded, her face wreathed in smiles. 'John and I will take good care of your son. You can leave him with us for as long as you want. We love him so much.'

'Yes, I can see that. And thank you both for everything.'

Susan set off, pushing her son in the walker, and as soon as she was out of sight of the Millers' cottage she just had to stop and look closely at her son, who was playing with a soft toy. She had been on tenterhooks at the thought of seeing Edward up close for the first time. Harry was right: Her son was the image of Rick. Even his frown was the same. She felt guilty at not being in a position to care for him and hoped that in the future he would understand and not blame her for leaving him. John and Rose Miller were a wonderful couple and loved him as if he were their own. She knew instinctively he would not be treated unkindly. Nevertheless, she could not hold back her tears when she left him with Rose. As soon as she was settled she would visit him regularly and make sure he had everything he needed.

The next day she received a letter from Louisa inviting her to stay with her, and she rushed off a quick reply. After posting it in Birchwood village she paid Tom Marsh, the estate manager, a visit.

'Well, miss, Master Harry told me to leave you alone until you contacted me. I expected a visit from you, now that the Countess and her daughter have returned home. Do you want me to look around here for lodgings for you?'

'Thank you, no. I plan to go to London. I called in and have given Mr and Mrs Miller my forwarding address, and whenever time allows I will come and visit you all.'

'Edward is a healthy boy, don't worry about him. The Millers are great people and will treat him like their own. Now, don't feel guilty about leaving him, either. You have brought happiness into the Millers' life. Looking after your boy is the finest thing that could happen to them, believe me.' He stood up and took her hand in his. 'I'm sure everything will go well for you in London.'

She smiled at him. He was a kind man, and she hoped his parting words would come true.

Chapter Fifteen

Arriving tired and drenched, having waited over twenty minutes for a bus in a summer downpour, Susan was met at the door by Louisa. 'My dear girl, you look exhausted. And just look at your skin! I'll have to make up one of my famous beauty packs and cover you from head to toe.'

Susan smiled; some things never changed. Louisa's welcome was like slipping into a pair of favourite slippers – familiar, warm and cosy. This woman had been her friend and mentor for more years than she could remember. Susan hugged her warmly after removing her wet coat and shoes and drying her hair with a soft towel supplied by Louisa.

Between chatting about the rebuilding of London since the end of the war and catching up with local gossip, they managed to eat a lunch of cold roast beef and a salad of lettuce, cucumber, radish and tomatoes, with apple pie and custard for dessert.

'I'm so lucky that Percy provides me with a few luxuries now and again' said Louisa. 'If it weren't for his generosity, I wouldn't have survived the war. You know, Susan, he was quite worried when you left London without a word. He made several enquiries, but no one seemed to know where you had gone. Did the American officer go home and leave you?'

'He died on his way to France.' Her voice trembled a little. 'I went to stay with some friends in the country.'

Louisa came around the table and embraced her. 'My dear, how you must have suffered. You should have come to me. I would have looked after you.'

'I had a good doctor who helped me a great deal.' She didn't want to dwell on the past twelve months. 'What news of the Blores?'

'The eldest son Michael came home from the war, but Malcolm is still in the Navy. Percy wouldn't allow Michael to remain at Queens Road. So now he has a flat and a fancy piece living with him. Percy gave him a job in one of the shops, only to please Tess.'

'Oh, is Michael's new girlfriend Irish?'

'I don't know. Never met her. According to Percy, she's a dyed blonde with big tits. Works at the George. A 'ruddy barmaid', he called her,' Louisa said, mimicking Percy's accent.

Susan smiled at Louisa's attempt to copy Percy. Then her thoughts flew to Michael Blore. Unless the Irish girl had dramatically changed her appearance, it didn't sound as if Michael was living with the girl he had left in the family way in Ireland.

'I didn't want to visit the Blores and have to explain about Rick's death and why I left London so suddenly.'

'Percy is coming round tomorrow. Why don't I tell him the American chap went home? You were a bit upset and visited friends in the country. He'll tell the family, and you don't have to explain anything. I'll keep your secret, upon my word I will.'

'You are sweet, Louisa. Thank you. Why is Percy coming here tomorrow?'

Susan watched her friend's face take on a slight tinge of pink and wondered why she was looking all coy and embarrassed.

'Well, I shouldn't tell you, but as we are sharing secrets I will. Percy and I have an understanding. Tess has gone to fat since the end of the war and still likes a sherry. She dotes on Penny and ignores Percy completely. Why, she even sleeps in the same room as your daughter. I felt so sorry for him and decided to give him what he was not getting at home. To put it plainly, we are lovers.'

Susan was mildly amused rather than shocked. Louisa was good-looking, and her twisted foot was hardly noticeable. She carried herself so elegantly, even with her carved walking stick. On the other hand, Tess was her own worst enemy and had only herself to blame. However, knowing Percy, he would never replace his wife with Louisa. Perhaps Tess knew this and was not too concerned where her husband was getting his creature comforts.

She smiled at her friend. 'Percy always had an eye for an attractive woman, so I'm not surprised.'

'You're not shocked about Percy and me being lovers?' Louisa said in a shaky voice.

'Good Lord, no. I am very happy for you both. Tomorrow, before he arrives, I will make myself scarce and go out to do some window-shopping in the West End.' She had no intention of staying here while the two lovers disappeared upstairs. She couldn't tolerate listening to bed-springs twanging, reminding her of her childhood. Susan guessed Percy would not like her living here, and made plans to move out of Louisa's house as soon as possible.

'Please stay and talk to Percy before you go out' said Louisa. 'He's been so worried, and if he can just see you for a minute or two that will be enough.'

'All right Louisa. I'll wait.'

Susan spent a restless night tossing and turning and trying to make plans for the future – but how could she make plans without money? The threat of poverty was never far from her mind. She would have to find employment very soon, as the little money she had left was meagre to say the least.

Roused from her thoughts by a noise outside her bedroom door, followed by a sharp knock. Susan scrambled to pull the quilt up and cover herself when Louisa came walking in with Percy close at her heels.

'Good-morning, dearest. Percy couldn't wait to see you. I hope you don't mind us barging in like this.'

Before she could answer, Percy side-stepped around Louisa, put the tea tray he was carrying on the side table, leaned over the bed and seized Susan in a bear hug, saying, 'How's my favourite girl?'

'I thought we'd all have a nice cuppa and a chat.' Louisa smiled, and poured the tea.

'How is London, Percy?' Susan asked.

'Grey as ever. Maybe a bit greyer, but now you're back in London things may get better. Perhaps even the weather will cheer up.'

When they had finished laughing Percy said, 'Louisa told me you've been ill. Are you in the mood to hear some good news and some bad? Or should I wait until you're feeling better?' Susan smiled and nodded for him to continue. 'I have a cheque from the solicitors in Sunderland from Margaret Elliot's estate, and an invitation for you from the Volunteer Ambulance Service. Apparently, volunteers from all over London have been invited to attend a garden party at Buckingham Palace, given by the King and Queen. Oh, and before I forget, just wait till you see little Penny. She's as pretty as a picture and goes to school now. She's a little madam and bosses us all.' He stopped talking suddenly.

'And the bad news, Percy?'

He cleared his throat. 'The Carrington Hotel took a direct hit from one of Hitler's buzz bombs. Both Grace and Donald were killed, along with customers and staff. June took it very badly. With the lump sum she received, she bought herself a small semi-detached in Brent. She is now working as a secretary for some medical establishment that has just been opened by the government. She hates being alone and would like you to go and share with her. What do you think?'

'Does June know I'm here?'

'I'm to blame,' Louisa butted in. 'Last night after you went to bed I sneaked out to the local pub and telephoned Percy and told him the news and…'

'I told June,' Percy interrupted. 'When you went missing, June was very upset, like the rest of us. We made enquiries at your depot and even at Eisenhower's headquarters, but we drew a blank. We contacted every hospital we could think of in London, without success. After searching bombed buildings, we finally came to the conclusion that you had been killed in an air raid and buried under a mountain of rubble. They've been flattening bombsites and filling them in, bodies and all. A whole street in Camden Town took a direct hit and killed most of the people living there. It was covered over with sand and soil – those poor souls were buried under that lot.'

'Didn't you get my letter?' Susan interrupted. She had seen and heard enough gruesome sights during the war. 'I wrote to let you know I wanted to get away from London and went to work on a farm.' The lie had been dreamed up during the night.

He did not believe for a moment that she had been anywhere near a farm. To Percy, it was of no consequence where she had been, as long as she survived the war.

'The letter must have gone astray during an air raid. It happened all the time, you know.' Changing the subject, he said, 'I can't tell you how glad I was when Louisa phoned to give me the good news, and this morning I went around to June's and told her. She begged me to ask you if you would consider moving in with her.'

'Poor June, she must be devastated about her parents. I'll go and see her today. If I'm asked, I will move to Brent.'

Percy looked delighted that she had agreed to share with June. Susan's guess was right: he didn't want her living with Louisa and playing gooseberry with the two lovers. Her main concern now was that she needed a job. She did not want to spend the small legacy Margaret Elliot had left her and hoped to build on it for the future.

The weather for the garden party at Buckingham Palace was warm and sunny, with just a light breeze – a perfect English summer day. Dozens of liveried footmen were on duty at each marquee, and beneath each domed canopy, tables with oval plates of wafer-thin sandwiches and tiered stands displayed an assortment of cakes and pastries. Silver bowls brimming with roses decorated the tables, perfuming the air. Footmen poured soft drinks of lemonade and iced water from crystal jugs, while tea and coffee were served from gleaming samovars. In every marquee, smaller tables and chairs had been arranged for guests to sit and take refreshments in comfort, while an Army band in Guards uniform played popular airs.

Pamela, the senior officer who had been in charge at St John's depot, had attended an earlier meeting with an equerry regarding the etiquette expected from invited guests. In turn, they had instructed their teams.

'It isn't very difficult, small curtsies, from the women, and a bow from the men. Please remember to address them as Your Majesty first, and then Sir or Ma'am, but only if they speak to you.'

Susan was amazed that she had been invited, as she had stopped working as a volunteer twelve months before the end of the war. She had no idea what had happened to her uniform, but Pam came to the rescue and gave her one to wear for the day. As her eyes travelled around the crowds of assembled guests, all in uniform, Susan smothered a laugh: the garden party resembled a military parade, with almost everyone in some kind of uniform. Guardsmen were positioned all around the garden to assist guests and to make sure that everybody behaved and did not monopolise the King and Queen's time.

Suddenly, voices quietened and a hushed silence came over the crowd. Everyone looked towards the full-length glass doors on the terrace, as they swung open. Out stepped the King and Queen. The band instantly struck up the National Anthem, and the guests stood to attention.

The King was dressed in a naval uniform, with more gold braid than Susan had ever seen. The Queen looked elegant in powder-blue with a wide-brimmed hat decorated with darker blue flowers. Her jewellery of pearls with sapphire clasps was stunning. She was the epitome of an English lady.

The Queen worked her way down one side of a long line of densely packed guests and the King the other, stopping intermittently to meet and greet as they went. As the King made his way down the line, Pam whispered to Susan that he was getting closer and closer to their group. This information did not help Susan's nerves one bit, and she steeled herself as the King stopped right in front of her. The president of the London Volunteers held a clipboard.

Pam stepped forward and pointed to Susan's name, and the president made the introductions. 'Miss Susan Cadiz.'

King George VI stretched out his hand and said, 'How do you do?'

Susan curtsied, extended her hand and smiled at him, silently cursing for not having put her gloves on as instructed, but he didn't seem to mind as he took her hand in a gentle hold. His hand was cool to the touch, his fingers long and tapered, his nails beautifully manicured. A brown nicotine stain on his index finger was the only thing that marred his perfection.

Giving another curtsy she replied, 'I would like to apologise for not wearing gloves, sir.'

'Such pretty hands do not need covering,' the King smiled. 'You have an unusual name. Spanish, is it not? '

'My father's Spanish, sir.'

'You are British?'

'Indeed, Sir.'

He smiled, inclined his head and moved on, leaving Susan with wobbly legs and a queasy stomach. Before leaving home that morning, Susan was far too excited to eat breakfast, and now she was glad she hadn't, as she would probably have heaved all over the Buckingham Palace lawns. She hurried to the nearest marquee for a glass of water for her parched throat and her queasiness. When she arrived she halted mid-stride, standing at one side of the entrance in a Red Cross uniform holding a cup and saucer was Elizabeth Fortescue.

'Well, if it isn't Harry's woman. Hardly recognised you without a towel on your head. I have been informed that you left a little bastard on our estate and my brother is the father. Didn't marry you, then, did he? Went off to India. That's men for you.'

Too horrified to answer, Susan spun around and quickly went towards one of the guardsmen. She told him she was unwell and asked him if she could leave the palace. He escorted her to a small ante-chamber with a nurse in attendance. After some tea and an aspirin, Susan closed her eyes and rested. She would have much preferred to go home and forget the despicable things Harry's sister had said. Susan felt a little guilty for taking up the time of the guardsman and the nurse. When the garden party had ended and the King and Queen had departed, Pamela Nelson arrived and offered to take Susan home.

A few weeks later, Susan was still talking about her day at Buckingham Palace. She did not mention Harry's sister and the insulting remarks she had levelled at Susan.

'June, the King was so easy to talk to and he didn't seem to mind I wasn't wearing gloves. They were still in my handbag in the cloakroom. What a twit I was, forgetting to say 'Your Majesty' as we were told. He probably thinks all his subjects are impolite, nervous Nellies.'

'I shouldn't worry too much, the Royals must be used to all that with the amount of hand-shaking they do.'

Then she noticed June had a writing pad before her at the dining table. 'I'm sorry, did I interrupt you?' she said, eyeing the writing materials.

'No, you didn't, not at all. Do you remember that suave Canadian pilot I was sweet on? Well, we've been exchanging letters ever since he went home.'

'Are you friends, or is it more serious?'

'It started off quite friendly, but just recently he's been hinting at romance.'

Susan barely listened to June chatting happily about her Canadian. Over the years she had heard enough about June's lovers, so she switched off and turned her thoughts to her own plans. Since moving to Brent she had opened her first bank account and deposited the small legacy Margaret Elliot had left her. With June's help she had found a job at the medical research centre. At first she was serving lunches in the staff dining room. Then a vacancy came up in the supply department ordering supplies, everything from writing materials to medical supplies, in fact, anything the research doctors requested. She wore a white button-through uniform similar to the laboratory coats the doctors wore and carried a clipboard wherever she went in the Georgian red brick building.

The research doctors worked in the laboratory and came from countries all around the world. Susan didn't care where they were from; her only concern that she had a future and was working again.

Her divorce from Michael Blore had been granted, but only after several blazing arguments about their daughter.

Michael had finally agreed not to contest the divorce, but insisted that Penny remain with her grandparents. He engaged a clever legal representative, who threatened to tell the court that Susan had deserted Penny to live in sin with her American lover. Michael wanted his daughter and was using her for the divorce he knew Susan so desperately wanted. Eventually, her lawyer advised her to accept, with a proviso that she could see her daughter during school holidays. She now had a decree absolute.

Every Saturday morning Susan baked cakes, and she had just put a fruit slice in the oven when the doorbell sounded. Opening the door, she found a young lieutenant standing there in a smart uniform. His name, he told her, was Mark Sanders and he was on compassionate leave from India, as his father had died rather suddenly. Harry had asked him to deliver a gift to Susan. Inviting him into the sitting room, she served tea and slices of Madeira cake that she had baked earlier.

'I'm most dreadfully sorry about your father' she said.

'Thank you, ma'am.'

'How is Captain Fortescue? Does he like India?'

'He is Major Fortescue now, and he's doing well in India, in more ways than one.'

'Oh,' she smiled sweetly, filling his teacup.

The fresh-faced young lieutenant had no qualms about discussing his commanding officer's personal life with Miss Cadiz. He had been led to believe by Jenkins, the Major's batman, that the woman seated before him and the Major were practically related.

'You'll be happy to know that he is walking out with the Colonel's daughter, Miss Helena Carruthers, and quite a beauty she is too.' He smiled openly. 'The officers are all making wagers that she'll not be a miss much longer.' He chuckled.

She was not happy to hear this news; in fact, she was piqued and felt like throwing the fine Indian silk shawl that Harry had sent her at the laughing lieutenant. No wonder he had replied with only one letter to her three; he was too busy with the lovely Miss Carruthers. She tried to hide her displeasure, but knew she had failed when she heard the young man's voice.

'I say, I hope I didn't speak out of turn.' The code of an officer and a gentleman prevented him from telling her about the Major's gorgeous Indian mistress, but he had thought she would be pleased to hear that one of her relatives had found his lady love at last.

When Lieutenant Sanders left, Susan was still smarting about the news of Harry's impending marriage. She sat down to write a very cool letter, saying that she hoped he would be very happy and spitefully adding that she had met a rather nice man and was head over heels in love. She thanked him for his generosity in sending the fine shawl and told him that she would use it on her honeymoon when she married the new man in her life. Susan was angry with Harry and justified the lies she told him.

However, when she was walking home after hurrying to catch the post, she felt perhaps she had gone too far. He was a friend, a very dear friend, and was entitled to marry whomever he pleased. She had written lies and vindictive drivel: there was no man in her life, nor was she intending to marry again. What had compelled her to act this way? She could not retrieve the letter, and all she could hope for was that he would dismiss it as gibberish and destroy it.

Harry stood on a rocky outcrop and squinted at the sun's hot rays, watching his men climb down from the armoured personnel carriers for their brew-up. They were to proceed into the Punjab region and link up with elements of the brigade, where trouble between the Muslims and the Hindus had flared again. He took off his hat and wiped the sweat from his brow.

India was as vast as it was crowded, as luxurious as it was squalid and as cruel as it was kind. From the featureless plains to the giant Himalayas, nothing – absolutely nothing – was quite what one expected. The parched barren plains were dry and dusty, and everything was seen though a dun haze. Sudden dust storms turned day into night in an instant, and there was always the heat, the relentless heat. British soldiers, and even the locals, went a bit crazy with the heat, causing tempers to flare for the most trivial of reasons. The hot weather was responsible for many suicides, murders and robberies. Major Fortescue had not been surprised that this reconnaissance had been ordered.

Harry's batman had placed some mail in his hand as they were leaving the barracks, and Harry had not found time to read it until now. Taking a cheroot from between his teeth, he blew the smoke into the air, before sitting down on a boulder. With his boots at ten to two and his arms resting on his knees, he opened the first letter, which was from his sister, Elizabeth.

Quickly scanning the pages, he read that she categorically refused to do what Harry had requested. Furthermore, she was not sorry that she had evicted the Cadiz woman from the Lodge; nor would she apologise or make amends. She stated that only when Papa died and Harry became lord and master of the estate could he then arrange things to his own liking.

'Bitch!' Harry tossed the curse into the air. He did not read any further and stuffed the crumpled letter back into his tunic pocket. He recognised Susan's dainty hand immediately and tore open the other envelope. Another curse flew into the air: she was congratulating him upon his forthcoming marriage to Helena Carruthers. He had no such plans, even if Helena and her mother desired it. He would tear a strip off young Sanders when he returned from England. He swore a third time when he read that she was planning her own wedding, and then again when he read that she would wear his gift on her damned honeymoon.

'To blazes with you and your blasted husband!' he grunted. He tore her letter into pieces and crushed them beneath his boot, followed by his cheroot. He would find solace in the arms of his mistress, who never let him down and always comforted him. The Sergeant's voice cooled his anger.

'Ready to move, sir.'

'Very good, carry on.' Harry threw his shoulders back and lengthened his stride to follow the Sergeant, thinking he may as well wed the chit Helena. As the only son, he would need an heir to carry on the family name when his father was finally laid to rest.

Chapter Sixteen

The annual dinner dance at the Medical Research Centre was held in May. Both Susan and June had received invitations and sought Louisa's assistance with their gowns. She advised June to wear a lavender dress with silver buttons dotted along the long sleeves and down the back of the gown. A few weeks later, when June finally saw the completed gown, she went into raptures. For Susan, the suggestion was red velvet and matching ribbons threaded through her upswept hair, and a pair of gold earrings to match the locket she always wore. Louisa had asked her to wear a crystal pendant with matching earrings, but she refused to take off the locket.

The orchestra was playing a foxtrot as the two well-dressed ladies entered the ballroom and proceeded to join one of the tables reserved for administration staff. June knew the entire group at the table, whereas Susan barely knew any of them, as she did not work in administration. She only knew the staff that wore white laboratory coats.

Susan had just taken her seat at the table when she was

asked to dance, first with a clerical officer, then with an accounts manager, and she partnered a young research doctor whom she knew quite well. He had invited her to the cinema a couple of times, but she had politely refused. Since arriving, she had been dancing non-stop and was longing to sit down, when June, who was dancing with her boss, signalled that dinner was being served. The meal placed before her looked overcooked. Consequently, Susan only ate the salad and had one glass of wine.

'Do you see that tallish blond fellow over there at the bar?' June asked Susan. 'Well, he's been staring at you for some time.'

Looking in the direction June indicated, Susan saw an attractive man in a dark suit casually leaning against the bar.

'I've never seen him before. Who is he?'

'That is Doctor Bernhard Roehder, ladies.' Tony, one of the administration officers who had been listening to their conversation, had joined in. 'I understand he is involved in several research projects – anything from debilitating diseases and chronic disorders to cancer leukaemia and, would you believe it, the common cold.'

Just for fun, several office staff who had been listening started sneezing, coughing and laughing. Tony waited until the clowning around had ceased before continuing. 'He speaks five languages. They say he has an ear for it. Apparently, after a few weeks in Greece he was speaking like a native. Oh, I forgot to mention, he's German.'

'German!' June shrieked aghast. 'What's he doing in England?'

'Rumour has it that he volunteered to remain behind in the field hospital when the Eighth Army overran the Germans in Egypt. His knowledge of desert diseases is invaluable, so he was put to work with our army doctors. Later, he was shipped to England as a prisoner of war and given medical duties in a London hospital. Eventually, he ended up here.'

'Why did he stay here after the war ended?'

'I don't know, June. You'll have to ask him.'

'Which department is he in?' Susan just had to ask, for she knew most of the medical staff, but had never seen him before.

'The overseas section. He travels quite often to Europe lectures, meetings and conferences, and gives talks on desert diseases. From his wartime experience.'

'Shh! He's coming over,' June whispered.

'I would like to invite you to dance,' said Dr Roehder, with an unmistakable German accent. His piercing blue eyes looked straight at Susan.

'Take a Luger with you,' June whispered to Susan as she rose from her chair to take the doctor's outstretched hand.

'My name is Bernhard Roehder. Your name?' he said as they started to circle the floor in time to the music. His eyes slowly travelled over her, studying every detail.

'Susan Cadiz, and I think your English is better than my German.'

His eyebrows shot up as he started to speak. 'Warum, kannst du Deutsch sprechen?'

'Doctor Roehder, please forgive me it was silly a joke.

I don't speak German at all. I was merely praising your knowledge of English.'

He laughed; it was a warm, attractive sound.

'English gives me problems, but perhaps you can teach me to speak as well as you do.'

She smiled. 'Do you really speak five languages?'

He looked at her narrowly. 'How do you know this?'

'A fellow at our table told me. He also said you helped British doctors in Egypt. Is that true?'

'Yes it is. I became a prisoner of war, and as I could speak English, French, Italian, a little Spanish and some Arabic, I assisted in many field hospitals.' His eyes quickly scanned the table. 'I would like to say that I do not know any people at your table.'

"The man who told me doesn't know you personally, he knows of your reputation.'

'Ah, now I understand.'

As they were gliding around the dance floor, Bernhard thought she had the most arresting smile, the perfect accessory for a woman, and he drew her closer to towards him as they circled the floor once more before the music stopped.

Glancing at his watch he said, 'I have to leave after the next dance, but I should like to invite to lunch tomorrow. Can you meet me at the Dorchester at one o'clock?'

Susan fondly remembered dining with Rick at the Dorchester. She had not been there since, as it was very expensive. She eagerly accepted his invitation.

'Thank you, I shall look forward to it.'

'Has anyone told you that you have beautiful eyes?'

'Only men, never women.'

He burst forth with another attractive laugh. 'I can see that a lot of fun could be had tomorrow' he said. When the music died away, he asked 'Will you come outside and say goodbye?'

She accepted with a smile and followed him. A London taxi driver seated behind the wheel greeted them with a nod. Bernhard open the door, turned and taking her right hand in his raised it to his lips. He released her hand and stepped towards the taxi saying, 'Until tomorrow'.

Climbing into the back seat he muttered something to the driver and the vehicle sped off.

Susan strolled back into the ballroom and went towards her table. What had possessed her to go outside at a man's invitation? June always said it was the oldest trick in the book to take a woman outside to steal a kiss or two. But he had been different. He had taken her hand and gently pressed it to his lips. Susan sighed. Most romantic!

'I saw you going outside with Herman the German. Did he kiss you and have a grope?'

'Honestly, June, I wish you wouldn't be so rude.'

'Why? Men say much worse than that. Well, what happened?'

'If you must know, he invited me to the Dorchester for lunch tomorrow.'

June whistled, 'Classy eatery! Are you going?

'Yes, yes I am,'

'He's good-looking for a Jerry.'

'Yes he is, but his English needs some attention. All words beginning with a 'W' he pronounces with a 'V'

'With a bit of luck he may not talk at all when you're in his bed, and if he does you can stuff a sock in his mouth. Is he married?'

It was impossible trying to get June to change. Ever since her time in the Air Force her language had become embarrassingly crude. But some of June's sayings were funny, and Susan had to stifle a smile as she pictured the German doctor in bed with a sock stuffed between his teeth.

'I don't know if he is married. I will find out tomorrow.'

'Shall ve join in ze conga and forget about Herman ze German?'

'Let's' Susan replied, rising from her seat.

Leaning back in the taxi, Bernhard wished he didn't have to leave the lovely woman he had just met to attend a dinner in Belgravia with Dr Ross Chisholm, the Director of the Medical Research Centre who had recommended him for a place on the team. Unbidden, his conversation with Susan had brought back memories of his life in Germany at the start of the war.

Bernhard was the eldest son and heir to Roehder Textiles, and in 1939 he had been studying medicine at Göttingen University. It was his final year, and he was eager to finish so that he could apply to the Schweitzer clinic in equatorial Africa. He had already made some enquiries by letter.

The sound of loud voices filled his ears and echoed around the high, vaulted ceilings of the Roehder family home. Bernhard hurried towards his father's study at the rear of the building, but before he could reach for the handle of the door it swung open and his mother flew past him in tears. Bernhard knew this was serious and squared his shoulders before entering, but the scene that met his eyes was both comic and chaotic. His father was standing in the middle of the room, which was strewn with shredded newspaper cuttings, while his younger brother, Hans, strutted around in the uniform of the Hitler Youth, a dagger engraved with a swastika hanging from his waist. Neither father nor brother registered Bernhard's presence; nor could he make himself heard above the yelling voices. After several attempts to gain their attention, he opened the office door and slammed it shut.

'The kitchen staff are shaking in their shoes, the dogs are cowering under the stairs and Mutti has just sped past as if all the demons of hell are after her. Now, will someone please, tell me what is going on?'

'Ah, my eldest, do come in. Now, here are two sons any man would be proud of. On the one hand I have a son who wants to conquer the world, and on the other I have a son who wants to cure it.' Both offspring watched their father brush a hand through his thinning hair as he moved to lean against his desk.

'Now, I'll tell you what I want. Firstly, Hans, go upstairs and take that ridiculous uniform off and get rid of that silly book – and these,' he said, kicking the newspaper cuttings nearest to him. 'Bernhard,' he said turning to his eldest son, 'whilst I continue to pay for your medical studies I do not want to hear any more talk of Africa. With scores of young men volunteering for the military, I need you both to help in the factory. Is that clear?'

'Father, why won't you listen to reason? I cannot resign from the Hitler Youth and I will not throw the Chancellor's *Mein Kampf* away, either. If you would only read it you would feel the same as I do.'

'I do not read trash, nor will I have it under my roof. Get rid of it.'

'How dare you, Father? The Chancellor was imprisoned and endured untold hardship to write down his plan for us. Germany will become the greatest nation in the world.' Turning to his brother he asked, 'Have you read *Mein Kampf*, Bernhard?'

'No, I haven't.'

'I shouldn't have asked. You only read books about curing the incurable,' Hans scoffed.

Ignoring his brother's remark, Bernhard faced his father. 'Sir, about Africa.'

'Enough!' his father roared. 'I give the two of you fair warning: if you do not obey my wishes, then you will not live in this house. Is that clear?' Herr Roehder walked over to a small table that held a drinks tray, poured himself a large cognac and slumped into a leather chair. 'Where did I go wrong raising you two? Both of you should be helping me in the business, especially now. Bernhard, I'll be damned before I allow you to devote your life to philanthropic work in Africa, or let you, Hans, join a set of jumped-up plebeians masquerading as elitist snobs and calling themselves the Nazi Party. Now leave me!'

Entering the house after a stroll around the garden to clear his mind, Bernhard found his mother in the salon, comforting his younger brother. Mutti, at forty-five, was still an attractive woman. Her beautiful blond hair, which she wore in a bun, blended well with a creamy complexion and eyes as blue as a summer sky. His mother was an only child and had one cousin who owned an office stationery business in the capital. Uncle Helmut had never married and lived the high life in Berlin society, according to family gossip.

'My dear, please come and join us and have some coffee.'

'Thanks, but I am not in the mood for anything,' he replied, lowering himself into one of the fireside chairs.

'Please put Africa to the back of your mind until you get your degree. Your father will come round. Just give him time.' Then she turned to her youngest. 'Hans, please don't talk about your Hitler Youth platoon or bring newspaper cuttings and political books about the Nazi Party into the house. You know your father is old-fashioned, but if we work together we will change his mind. If you want my opinion, I think Chancellor Hitler is very kind building houses for the poor, and I'm proud of you, Hans.'

'Mutti, you are a gem,' Hans said, giving her a bear hug.

She smiled. 'One of our kitchen girls has joined the League of German Maidens. They practise athletics, and in the future they will produce healthy children for Germany. Now what do you think of that?'

'Mutti, it's the League of German Girls, and they not only do athletics. They are taught domestic science, housewifery and motherhood. Our Commandant gave a speech to our platoon. He told us to marry tall healthy maidens with blonde hair and breed strong children for the Nazi Party to make Germany the greatest nation in the world.'

'My dear, Germany has always been great,' Mutti added.

'You can't wed at sixteen, bonehead!' Bernhard laughed, chiding his brother.

'When I'm eighteen. I will have dozens of sons for Germany. Just wait, you can deliver them all, Herr Doctor, providing you're not up to your armpits in African bugs. Personally, I think you are a traitor going to Africa when the Vaterland needs good doctors.'

'What about that nice English medical student we met a few years ago during our skiing holiday in Switzerland? Do you know, I cannot remember his name now,' Mutti butted in, determined to change the subject.

'Ross Chisholm,' Bernhard replied. 'His father has a practice in Harley Street in London. The last letter I had from him, which was months ago, said he was going to specialise in haematology. He wrote that if I ever managed to get to England I should contact him. If I get the chance I would like to spend a few months with him in London before I embark for Africa. '

'Hemo what?' Hans interrupted.

Bernhard gave his brother a tired look. 'Haematology, the study of blood diseases.'

'My dear brother, you will find out there's more to life than speaking foreign languages and poking around inside people's bodies. As for Englanders and their stuck-up attitude, they make me sick. I'd rather go to hell than go to England,' Hans said with a contemptuous sneer. 'Now, now my dear boys, that's quite enough. Please don't talk in this manner. I must say, it's been lovely chatting to you both, but I have some letters to write.' The two sons rose from the chairs. Hans motioned to his brother to remain, and as Mutti left the room they reclaimed their seats.

'By the way, Ingrid the kitchenmaid, the girl you were taking your pleasure with in the loft during summer recess, was fretting for you when you went back to medical school. So I took your place. Although she says I'm a bit rougher than you, she likes it.'

'You are only sixteen and she is twenty-five!' Bernhard said, outraged.

'I'm almost seventeen, and the size of a man's dick has nothing to do with age, dear brother,' Hans sniggered wickedly.

'You are stupid and naïve. What the hell will you do if she gets pregnant?'

'No, you're the one who's naïve. A few of the local lads have dipped their wicks into Ingrid's honeypot. So how can she blame Hans Roehder, a mere schoolboy? If you want her brother, you can have her. In fact, I have an idea we can both have her, as she never tires of it.' He let out a laugh and Bernhard threw a cushion at him.

It was ten months later that Bernhard's world fell apart. He was sitting in the student recreation room sipping coffee with Manfred, a fellow student, and talking about the changes in the New Reich. The Anschluss with Austria, the ceding of the Sudetenland and the occupation of Czechoslovakia did not really interest Bernhard. However, the disappearance of German dissenters, Jews, gypsies and the mentally incapacitated did.

'Have you heard?' Manfred whispered. 'Professor Obertz has been arrested.' 'Why, for heaven's sake?'

'For being Jewish.'

'Professor Obertz is the best medical lecturer they have here.'

'Shhh, keep your voice down, Bernhard. The walls have ears, and if some big mouth reports you to the Gestapo then you will disappear.'

'Who would have thought we would end up living in a damn police state?' Bernhard said angrily. 'Well, they can all go to hell. I only want my medical degree. Then I'm off to Africa.'

'Heil Hitler!' The crisp voice from behind Bernhard's chair made him flinch, but it was only one of the first-year students the teaching staff used as messengers. 'Herr Roehder, I have been looking everywhere for you. You are to report to the Dean's office immediately.' Then he clicked his heels together and punched the air with a rigid arm before leaving.

Bernhard did not reply but quietly finished his coffee before picking up his leather notecase and making his way to the Dean's office, his mind on the final examination results due out that day. Tapping on the walnut door complete with gold cipher, he waited a few moments and then entered. The look on the Dean's face convinced him that he had failed the examination. Bernhard slowly approached and waited; he would not sit down until invited to do so.

The Dean eyed him over the top of his horn-rimmed spectacles and cleared his throat. 'I have some bad news' he said. 'Firstly, I received a most damning communiqué from the regional Gestapo office.' He cleared his throat again before continuing. 'I have to inform you that your father, Herr Roehder, has been arrested for crimes against the Reich, and therefore you are dismissed from this university.'

At the Dean's words, Bernhard's face crumpled and his shoulders sagged. Stunned, he stood there staring at the walnut panelling above the Dean's head. His father had been a war hero, decorated by the Kaiser in 1917. A traitor! It was unbelievable. Thank God his mother was visiting her parents in Switzerland.

'Be seated, my boy. The last time I spoke to your father I told him to be careful about speaking out against the Reich, but you know how stubborn he is. I have to tell you that the factory, the house and land titles are probably being seized as we speak. Where is your mother?'

'Visiting her family in Zürich.'

'Good. She must remain there. I will send her a message to that effect. What of your brother, Hans?'

'When Mother left, Father sent him to Uncle Helmut in Berlin.'

'Excellent. Now we must plan what you should do.'

'What do you mean?'

'Now listen, Bernhard. I joined the Party last year and I do know what I'm talking about. You must join the Wehrmacht, my boy, and you should do so without delay. Then you will be safe. Otherwise, you'll end up like your father. Now here is some good news. You have passed your final examinations with honours. With your degree and my letter of recommendation, they will put you in the Medical Corps. Make up some plausible excuse to your fellow students why you will not be at the graduation ceremony with the others. By the way, have any other members of your family joined the Party?'

'Not that I know of.'

'Pity. Are you aware that we have lost a quarter of the teaching staff due to Nazi Party edicts?' He sighed heavily. 'What cannot be cured must be endured.'

The Dean stood up, placing a small box in Bernhard's hand. 'Some time ago your father left this with me to give to you. I understand it's a family heirloom.' He indicated that the discussion was over. Bernhard got to his feet and slipped his father's ring on his finger, placing the box on the Dean's desk. Bernhard stretched out his hand and bid him farewell. At the door he turned and asked, 'What will be my father's punishment?'

'Shall I be blunt?'

'Yes.'

'Execution.'

'Thanks for telling me,' he replied, closing the door while fighting down a lump in his throat as he walked back to the recreation room.

'Christ, Bernhard! You look as if you've seen a ghost. What's up?'

'I've been dismissed; that's what's up.'

'What the hell for?'

Unable to bring himself to talk about his father for fear of crying like a child, he replied, 'The lecture is about to start, you'd better not be late.'

'Where are you going?' Manfred asked, watching Bernhard slipping into his overcoat. 'The recruiting, office. Where else?' he responded, leaving his friend gaping.

Withdrawing the syringe from the soldier's arm, Bernhard turned away in disgust. The poor bastard would be dead by dawn; yet another casualty sent from a field hospital. Bernhard had been in this Army hospital for three years. As a medical trainee straight from university, he did all the dirty work, but he didn't mind. What irritated him was the constant snapping to attention and saluting of those smart-arse surgeons who insisted on their rank being acknowledged. He hadn't been in the Wehrmacht very long, but he knew a smart salute when he saw one, and the sloppy attempt these senior doctors demonstrated was laughable.

He was going off duty in half an hour to meet his brother at the Hotel Adlon in the Pariser Platz. Pulling Hans' letter from his jacket pocket as he boarded the tramcar, he read it again. He hadn't set eyes on his brother for a few years and during that time he had only received two letters, including this one. His mother corresponded with him regularly from Zürich, although she had made no mention of his father in any of her letters.

Standing in the hotel lobby looking for his brother, he was surprised to see so many officers with attractive woman at their sides.

'Don't stand their skulking like a dirty Jew,' Hans said before giving him a fierce hug. Surprised and a little embarrassed, Bernhard quickly freed himself from his brother's embrace. Smiling, Hans clicked his thumb and middle finger, and a waiter materialised instantly.

'Willie, be a good fellow and see if my table is ready' he said.

'All is in readiness, Untersturmführer.'

'Good, lead the way.'

Bernhard was agog at the change in his brother. Hans had grown tall, and his close-cropped blond curls did not even reach the collar of his smart black uniform with silver epaulets and shoulder flashes. Tight-fitting breeches disappeared into shiny black knee-high boots. A black belt and holster that housed an engraved service Luger, a black cap with a silver death's head insignia and black leather gloves completed the picture. Bernhard recognised the uniform immediately as that of the Waffen-SS, the élite combat troops who had the reputation of being fanatical fighters. Hans' poise and style spelt success, along with his breezy confident manner, stopping occasionally at tables to greet others in black uniforms. Having changed into civilian clothes, Bernhard felt awkward and shabby by comparison.

'Here's to us, brother,' Hans toasted as he lifted a glass of Schnapps. 'I was glad to hear you joined up. But the Medical Corps – what a waste!'

'I wanted to continue my career and…'

'So, you're one of those damn pansies who can't salute to save themselves and run around in white coats in foul, smelly field hospitals.'

'I'm still a trainee.'

'For fuck's sake, Bernhard, are you joking? You're not trying to tell me that you empty shitty bedpans?'

'No, the ward orderlies and some nurses have that honour. I do mundane things like yanking out bullets, setting broken limbs, stitching and bandaging wounds and retrieving pieces of shrapnel from festering flesh. I also prepare patients for operations and assist in the theatre when they are busy or if the senior surgeon is in a rush to keep a dinner engagement with some tart. I have even administered last rites to those who are not going to make it. So to answer your question: yes, I am a doctor, but in reality a very junior one.'

'That's fucking terrible.'

'Yes, isn't it? My job is to try and save the poor bastards from God and guns.'

'Come on, Bernhard. Cheer up, for Christ's sake.'

'You're right,' he replied, giving the ghost of a smile. 'Tell me, what are you doing in Berlin?'

'I was awarded the Iron Cross, second class, for courage and devotion to duty. I'm in Berlin to receive my award from the great man personally – our beloved Führer.'

'And what heroic deed did you accomplish to receive such an honour?'

'Our unit was posted to Poland. We raced across the border like hounds to the hunt, cut through the mounted cavalry units like a knife through butter, and swept the Polish Army aside.'

Bernhard grimaced. 'You like being an officer in the Waffen-SS?'

'It's the best. They gave us leave after Poland, but having no home to go to, I remained in Berlin.'

'Speaking of home, do you hear from Mutti?'

'She writes me sheets and sheets, but we are always on the move and it takes time for her letters to reach me. Does she write to you?'

'Frequently. She never mentions father and it...'

'Don't speak of him,' Hans interrupted. 'He was a traitor. So let's leave it at that. By the way, Uncle Helmut is giving a cocktail party tomorrow night. Lots of girls have been invited and they are more than willing to keep us soldiers happy.' Hans gave a hearty chuckle. 'How about joining us?'

'Thanks for the invitation, Hans. The meal was superb. It was great to meet again even briefly. The Fifty-first Regiment is mobilising for an overseas posting, a fully-equipped field hospital is going and I'm included along with a Lieutenant-General called Rommel. This is why I will be unable to attend the party. Give my regards to Uncle Helmut.'

'Where are they sending you?'

'North Africa.'

Hans laughed out loud. 'Your dream of going to Africa is coming true. The only difference is, you will serve Rommel instead of Schweitzer.'

The taxi came to a sudden halt in Belgravia, and so did Bernhard's thoughts. After paying the driver, he mounted the steps and grasped the shiny brass doorknocker.

Chapter Seventeen

Puffing and panting, Susan reached the entrance of the Dorchester and the concierge swung the door wide to allow her to enter the hotel lobby. Moving further into the foyer, she stopped beside a tall plant with large green foliage and tried to catch her breath. It was then she spied Bernhard near the entrance to the restaurant, arms folded and tapping his right foot. He looked impatient or irritable; she couldn't decide which. Regaining her breath, she walked towards him.

'I'm sorry to have kept you waiting. The bus was late.'

He gave her a smile and told her he accepted her apology. Bernhard escorted her to the entrance of the restaurant, extending his arm and saying 'After you.'

While waiting to be seated, her eyes travelled around the room to the other guests who were wining and dining. There were men in tweed jackets and cravats, others in dark business suits, and even the occasional military uniform. Men always looked smart in uniform. The ladies, by contrast, looked glamorous in colourful street-length dresses and two-piece suits, some with fox fur draped around their shoulders and the most wonderful feather creations on their heads.

The decor of the room was a statement of style and sophistication, with elaborate gilded cornices and amber walls. It looked to Susan as if it had been recently refurbished, because everything looked so new and fresh. The table linen was of palest oyster with a crystal bowl of colourful begonias. The silver cutlery and glassware glistened under subdued lighting. His voice brought her observations to a close.

'Shall I order for you?'

'Yes, please, with one exception: I do not eat chicken.'

'Nor do I.'

When he had finished ordering from the menu, a glass of wine arrived for him, along with the small glass of oloroso Susan had requested. When he picked up his wineglass, she noticed a gold band on his left hand.

'Are you married?' she blurted out.

'No, in Germany the wedding ring is worn on the right hand. Are you married?' 'I was.'

'Your husband: a casualty of war?'

'No, I'm afraid not. He came home in one piece.'

'You're refreshingly honest. Do you have any children?'

She was still bitter about the divorce settlement. 'A daughter, who lives with my ex-husband' she said, and then changed the subject. 'It was dreadful in London during the war. We had to learn to run and duck rather quickly. Do your parents still live in Germany?'

'My father is dead. This is his ring I am wearing. He was arrested when he refused to join the Nazi Party. Our family home, business and lands were seized. Mutti – sorry, I mean Mother – went to live with her parents in Switzerland. I had just completed medical studies at university. My younger brother, Hans, liked playing boy soldiers. Eventually, both of us ended up in the military, I to Egypt with the Afrika Korps, and he to Russia. Hans was killed near Moscow.'

As he spoke she studied him. He was quite tall with a strong, attractive features and hair the colour of ripened corn, neatly swept back from his forehead. His eyes were the bluest she had ever seen, and with his straight white teeth and warm smile, he seemed almost perfect. She remembered the propaganda films she had watched during the war, and he seemed to be the essence of what the Nazis called the Aryan race, bred to win the war for Germany. The meal arrived, and she was relieved to find that he had ordered fish and not beef, as fish was one of her favourite meals.

'Tell me, your family?'

To Susan, every question he asked sounded like an order. It was his clumsy use of English, she decided, and she ignored it.

'I was an orphan. My parents died soon after I was born, and my schoolteacher aunt looked after me. I was married for eighteen months and only recently divorced. During the war I worked as an ambulance driver. After the war, June, who is a good friend, helped me to get a position at the Medical Research Centre.'

'She is the woman who said you need a Luger? Did you bring one today?' He asked with a grin.

Susan was mortified that he had overheard June's remark at the dance the night before and flushed with embarrassment.

'I must apologise for June. She has a very strange sense of humour.'

'No matter,' he said with a wave of his hand. Smiling at her he continued, 'It is a long time since I have seen a pretty woman blush.'

With those piercing blue eyes riveted on hers, Susan's colour deepened, and along with his attractive smile her pulse began to race.

'The Olympic Games are being officially opened next month at the new Wembley Stadium near Brent where you live. Would you like to come with me and watch the ceremony?'

'Oh, yes, yes, I would love to go.' A few years before at the library she had read about the Olympic Games in ancient Greece, held on the plains of Olympia, but never in her wildest dreams did she think she would be given an opportunity to attend the Olympic Games in London. Tickets were expensive and hard to get, but she knew instinctively he would manage to get them. What was puzzling was that he knew the suburb where she lived.

'How did you know I live in Brent?'

'Like you finding out about me, I made some enquiries about you. Does this upset you?'

'Of, course not. I was merely surprised.'

'I suggest in the future when we want information we ask each other. Do you agree?'

Smiling, she replied, 'Yes, I do.'

Four weeks later at the Olympics, they found their seats among the array of tiered seating with the help of an attendant. The decorations in red, white and blue were wonderful. Flags from all the competing countries flew from the roof of the stadium, and garlands of flowers were draped everywhere around the arena. The official opening was being performed by the King and Queen. It was a brilliantly warm summer's day, made more so by the crowds of people attending the Games, the women dressed in colourful dresses with matching bonnets, the men in lightweight suits and panama hats.

While awaiting the arrival of the Royal Family, he leaned towards Susan, saying, 'In December I am going to St Moritz to spend Christmas with my mother. Would you like to join me?'

'St Moritz? They ski there, don't they?'

'Have you ever been skiing?'

'Never.'

'I'll teach you.'

'How much will it cost, and where will I stay?'

'There is a chalet my mother owns. As for cost, it is my treat.'

Overwhelmed at his invitation to go skiing at St Moritz, Susan was longing to accept. However, going away with a man she barely knew was not acceptable behaviour for any woman, and she should refuse. However, if his mother were there, too, surely everything would be above board. She made up her mind to go.

'I have never travelled abroad. Will I need a passport?'

'Most definitely, you will have enough time to arrange one.'

She nodded, making a mental note to ask June where the passport office was and what the requirements might be. June knew everything about those kinds of things.

Suddenly, a fanfare announced the King and Queen's arrival. Their car travelled around the arena and stopped at the Royal Box, where other members of the family waited. Susan was a few rows behind the Royal Box, but she had a splendid view of both the Royal Family and the stadium. At the conclusion of the National Anthem, the Greek athletes came marching from a dark tunnel into the bright sunshine with their country's flag billowing in the light breeze. The spectators erupted with cheers and applause. As the other athletes marched out under the flags of their respective countries, Susan was enthralled by the colourful spectacle of the uniforms and traditional costumes worn by Olympians. The biggest cheers were for the British team. They marched into the arena dressed in navy blue blazers, white flannels and red ties and plimsolls. The only difference was that women athletes wore white skirts. Everybody looked so relaxed and happy, waving and cheering, and Susan joined in.

'I think it is terrible that Germany and Japan were not invited to participate. I expect the Americans and the British, and possibly the French, will win all the medals.'

'That is a horrid thing to say. Are you suggesting they would cheat?'

He shrugged his shoulders. 'If the shoe fits, as you English say.' His rigid expression matched his words.

'I disagree. I'll have you know the Allies would never cheat, and I'm miffed that you would dare to suggest such a thing.'

'Miffed?'

'Offended.' Susan didn't wait for a reply. 'Apart from me, you owe the British, Americans and French an apology, Doctor Roehder.'

Susan was angry with him. Getting to her feet, she turned and said, 'Even you must admit your words were unwarranted.' Picking up her handbag and the souvenir program, she walked towards the exit. How could she have been so wrong about him?

She had not gone far when he seized her arm and turned her around to face him. 'You are right. I do owe you an apology for saying such things. Since meeting you, I don't want to go back to Germany, but I may have to, if the Foreign Office have their way. I was only giving voice to my anger. Susan, please accept my deepest sympathy for hurting you.' She smiled inwardly at his choice of words. 'If it will make you happy, I will drop to my knees and apologise to the British, Americans and the French.'

'That will not be necessary. I accept your apology. Why are you upset about the FO?'

'The FO?'

'The Foreign Office.'

'I'm not used to English slang. Perhaps I should learn. According to the FO,' he said with a bit of a grin, 'I may have to return to Germany, as I am here without the proper paperwork. I asked Ross Chisholm if he would make some enquiries on my behalf.'

'I didn't realise you were having difficulties with our government. Now it's my turn to apologise.' Ross Chisholm was head of the Research Centre, and if Bernhard had asked him for help it must be serious indeed.

Returning to their seats, they watched the opening ceremony, holding hands. At precisely half-past two, the King declared the Games open, and baskets full of white doves were released. The Olympic flag was raised and a twenty-one gun salute was sounded, just as a runner entered the arena carrying the Olympic Torch. Half-way around the stadium he climbed the steps to a huge cauldron. After saluting the crowd, he turned and lit the flame that would burn until the games ended.

At the conclusion of the Olympic Games opening ceremony, Bernhard took Susan to the Café Royal and ordered cream tea for her and a cheese platter and coffee for himself. Because of the earlier misunderstanding between them, Bernhard sat back and allowed her to do the talking. About everything, from the opening ceremony to the Christmas trip to St Moritz, he was content just to listen. When tea arrived he was surprised to see cream scones on a porcelain plate. He mistakenly thought the cream would be in the tea. He still had a lot to learn about this country.

Bernhard watched fascinated as Susan gently mixed, not stirred, the tea with a small silver spoon and placing it in the saucer. Picking up the teacup, with her thumb and forefinger at twelve and six and with her little finger delicately balancing the bottom of the cup, she took a sip. Her actions were so precise and perfect that Bernhard thought she must have been trained.

The next day Susan told June everything about the opening ceremony, the King and Queen, tea at the Café Royale, and Bernhard's invitation to go skiing. She swung around the room, ending with, 'Just think of it, St Moritz!'

'I hate to burst your bubble, blossom, but if you think he's taking you to Switzerland because he's just aching to teach you to ski, think again. He's aching all right, but for something other than skiing.'

'Oh, June, why do you have to spoil everything? This is my first trip out of England.'

June rolled her eyes skywards, wondering why her beautiful friend was so naïve, always looking at life through rose-coloured glasses.

'Susan, please listen. You may very well be skiing during the day, but at night you will be flat on your back staring at the damn ceiling, rewarding him for the holiday.'

'He's not like that. He's respectable. Anyway, his mother will be there.'

June heaved another sigh. 'They're all like that. And his mother won't be in your bed, he will.'

Looking thoughtfully at her friend, June remembered Uncle Percy telling her that he had no idea where the

American had gone, but Susan had fled to the country in tears. June would bet her life savings that the reason for Susan going to the country was that Rick had gone back to the States and left her. Susan was over the moon about Rick. It must have been devastating for her when he left. However, what June couldn't understand was why he would leave England without her. Rick seemed as wrapped up with her as she was with him, and she could not imagine him doing such a terrible thing to Susan. It was baffling. She could only conclude that there must have been a disagreement or a blazing row, and he had walked out, leaving her to pick up the pieces. No wonder it had taken months for her to recover. Every time she tried to get Susan to talk about Rick, Susan would clam up. Eventually, June gave up asking.

No matter how ill she had been, it did not show. June was certain that if Susan was laid low with the bubonic plague she would still look attractive. She used to be envious of the wolf whistles Susan received and the way men buzzed around her like flies round a cowpat whenever they went out together. Apart from her looks, she had a kind of femininity that radiated from her like a tempting fragrance, appealing to men. In every male, June decided, there lurked a demon, which drove them to the eventual conquest of a woman, and then they disappeared. At least, that was her experience of men.

June no longer envied Susan; instead, she felt sorry for her. She had loved and lost; not only Rick but her daughter, too. Michael, that louse of a husband, had taken

Penny from her in the divorce settlement. Why should she stand in Susan's way and warn her about going to Switzerland with a randy German? It was time Susan had some fun.

'I'm really glad you won't be in London at Christmas. That cute Canadian is coming to visit me and we want to be alone.'

'Oh June, how wonderful! Has he proposed?'

'Not yet, but I'm hoping he will. Anyway, that's enough about me. C'mon. I'll take you to the passport office, and later we can have tea and cakes at Joe Lyons.'

'Have you ever been skiing?' Susan asked June as she sipped her tea.

'Not actually skiing, but I've been tobogganing, which amounts to the same thing, except with skiing you're standing up, whereas with tobogganing you're sitting down.'

'Very, funny I'm quite sure there's more to it than that. I'll get a book from the library.'

'You do that. Unlike you, I've never been invited to go to the Alps skiing.'

Flinching, Susan said 'I'm sorry. I was only making small talk. I didn't mean to show off and upset you.'

'I've been in a bad mood all day.'

'Why? Is there something bothering you?'

'Well, if you must know I've been having an affair with a married man and I've missed a monthly. If I am pregnant I'm going to have to do something about it. I heard there is a doctor who was struck off the medical register. He performs abortions but he's always fully booked and very expensive. Failing that, I also have the address of a back-street woman who does it for thirty pounds. Honestly, men have all the damn pleasure and none of the pain.'

'Is there anything I can do to help?'

'I'm afraid there's nothing to do but wait. Perhaps you could ask Uncle Percy for some money. You know he'll give you anything, Susan. '

'I think it would be safer going to the doctor than to a back-street operator. I heard a story about a young girl who died after visiting a back-street abortionist.' When Susan saw her friend shudder, she added, 'don't worry, June. I'll get the money from Percy.'

'You are a good friend to me, blossom, and I have a confession to make. I was pea-green with envy and always hoped that you and Rick would split up and he would fall in love with me. Looking back now, I don't even think he knew I was alive. Shows you what a stupid woman I am.'

'Don't be so hard on yourself. Most women are silly about men.'

'You're not' June said.

'How do you know I'm not?'

'I've seen the way men look at you, all glassy-eyed.'

During the war it had been common knowledge amongst the Blore family that June was sweet on Rick. The more Susan tried to ignore the gossip, the more Tess was there to remind her. Susan had the distinct impression that Tess didn't like her and had never forgiven her for leaving Michael. In fact, Tess didn't like anyone, except for Percy and her two sons.

Feeling sorry for June, she said. 'What would you like me to bring you back from Switzerland? Please don't say a handsome Swiss skier. I won't have any room in my suitcase.' June laughed and Susan was glad; she wanted to steer the conversation away from the past. Susan was thrilled and excited about visiting her first foreign country and could not wait until Christmas.

Chapter Eighteen

Zürich was bathed in winter sunshine when they arrived at Kolton airport. Bernhard had booked seats on a train to Chur, where they would change to a steam train to St Moritz. Susan breathed in lungfulls of sweet fresh air and gazed at the towering snow-covered peaks. It was breathtakingly beautiful. Some of the mountain peaks had disappeared completely behind fluffy clouds that looked similar to the froth on Bernhard's beer stein that he had with lunch. The blue crystal-clear lakes, the majestic mountains and even the melodic clanging of cowbells in the alpine meadows below; it was so perfect, and just as she had imagined.

A few hours later, when the small train chugged into St Moritz station, it was snowing. Susan was pleased; even the weather was in keeping with what she had envisaged. A sleigh with a pony was waiting to take them to the chalet. Susan drew her red woollen hat down over her ears and shivered. Unexpectedly, an arm in a heavy alpine coat went around her waist and pulled her towards his body.

'Not long now,' Bernhard's clipped voice came from beneath a woollen muffler that covered his face to the bridge of his nose.

She was so close to him she could smell the fragrance of his cologne and the smell of hops from the beer still lingering on his breath. His body was snug and warm, and she snuggled closer and closer to keep out the cold. Tiny snowflakes clung to her eyelids, making it impossible to see. Covering her face with her scarf, she got even closer to him and closed her eyes.

He was a fascinating man, and Susan had been seeing him regularly for six months. Apart from being a little terse occasionally, his English was slowly improving. He liked tennis, golf, skiing and sailing, hobbies that had occupied his time before the war, and still did. His firm, athletic build attested to his devotion to sport.

He had told her that his family had lived outside Hanover and that his mother was Swiss-born, and his father had met her during a skiing holiday in St Moritz. His father had been firm but fair and wanted his sons to do well in commerce. One of his favourite maxims was, 'You cannot conduct business unless you speak the language of the client', and his two sons had to learn foreign languages, which their father considered essential in business. When he refused to join the Nazi Party and utilise slave labour in his business, he was arrested. The factory was seized, as was the family home.

Before his arrest, Bernhard's father had transferred money and assets into his wife's name and deposited them in a Swiss bank, hoping to retrieve them upon his release. But he had never returned. His wife remained in Zürich. She had no home to return to and no family, after her two sons were inducted into the military.

When Susan asked Bernhard how he came to be in England, he told her that Afrika Korps had been overrun by the British. He had been captured when he stayed behind with the wounded in the field hospital, while the remainder of the Afrika Korps had made a hasty retreat.

The sleigh suddenly halted, and so did her wandering thoughts.

'Welcome,' he said, with a broad smile, lifting her out of the sleigh.

Standing on a wooden step, Susan peeped out from beneath her red woollen beret to view the quaint wooden chalet, with green shutters and a large red door. The roofline extended low over the entrance. Susan loved it, as it reminded her of a Grimm's fairytale. The fairytale continued inside, with solid wooden furniture and hand-woven carpets and drapes in true alpine colours. She smiled when she saw a wooden rocking chair next to the fireplace; all that was needed now was a wicked witch. Would that be his mother? She hoped not.

Taking off his coat, hat and gloves, he told her to make herself comfortable while he attended to the fire. She watched him pick up a set of bellows, and in a short space of time the almost-dead fire sprang into life. When the wood was blazing, he tossed some more logs into the grate and the warmth soon began to radiate around the room.

She had expected that his mother would have kept the fire alight, or at least come out to greet them. Puzzled, she asked, 'Where is your mother?'

'She's in Zürich. We will join her for dinner on Christmas Eve,' came the answer from the kitchen area, which was separated from the main room by a wooden door that swung both ways. She could hear water running and guessed he was washing his hands.

'Then who lit the fire and switched the lamp on?'

'Oh,' he said joining her, 'one of the villagers attends to those things if you notify them of the time of your arrival.'

'Then are we alone here?'

'Yes.' Seeing the look of concern in her eyes, he added, 'Do not be afraid. There have not been any wolves in this area for centuries.'

She wasn't worried about the wolves outside, just the one inside. The kisses and cuddles they had exchanged in London were very different from spending the night together completely alone. He had an athletic build from all the sports he played, and she wouldn't stand a chance if he were determined to seduce her. Why hadn't she listened to June?

'We are dining at the Hotel Klum tonight. It is a special restaurant. You will like it. The manager, Max Hausmann, he is a friend to my mother.'

'I cannot go out for dinner dressed like this.'

He looked at her red slacks and fawn polo neck jumper. 'I do hope you have a dress in your suitcase.'

'Hmm.' She didn't know what to say. June had packed

her suitcase, and she hoped there was a dress in there somewhere.

'Can you tell me where my suitcase is? I'll check' she said. He probably thought she was a complete idiot for not knowing what was in her luggage, but she had been too busy. Susan had taken her son to see Father Christmas at the local toy store, and then rushed back to London to get tickets for a Christmas pantomime that Penny was longing to see, followed by hectic shopping trips for Christmas gifts. When June had offered to pack for her, she was most grateful.

Unlatching her case, she found a note:

Dear Susan

Merry Christmas. Have a good time, blossom. I packed that sexy black velvet dress with the long sleeves and plunging neckline. That should get him excited. By the way, I didn't put a nightgown in your suitcase as I thought you wouldn't be wearing one.

Hugs and kisses, June

Placing the black dress on the bed, Susan felt she would like to wring June's neck, and she probably would when she returned to London. How could she have been so silly as not to pack a nightgown or even pyjamas in these freezing conditions?

Suddenly there was a tap on the bedroom door, and in walked Bernhard with a box under his arm.

'Ah, you have a something to wear,' he said, eyeing the black dress. 'This I bought to give you on Christmas Eve at my mother's town house, but I think tonight you may need it. Open it, open it,' he encouraged as she stared at the satin ribbon that decorated the box.

Undoing the bow and removing several sheets of tissue paper, she found an exquisite grey fur coat with various shades of white markings through it. Too dumbstruck to speak, she picked it up and rubbed her face into the soft fur.

'It's a Siberian wildcat pelt. It will keep the cold out. You do not have any furs, I have noticed.'

'Oh, Bernhard, it's beautiful. I've never had such a lovely coat.' He was so kind to her, and after gently placing the coat back in the box, she reached up on her toes and gave him a sweet peck on the lips. But as she started to draw away, he pulled her more firmly into his arms and pressed his lips on hers. She responded out of sheer gratitude at first, and then from the fragrance of his cologne, and the gentle way he had of running his fingers through her hair, his firm body pressing against hers. Susan was caught up in the magic of the kiss

'*Liebling*,' he murmured against her ear.

'Thank you for the gift,' she whispered, 'but should we be changing for dinner?' He nodded, smiled, released her and left the room.

The restaurant was both hot and noisy, but Max found them a quiet table away from the boisterous crowd. He spoke German to Bernhard, who translated for Susan.

'Max has offered us a drink to warm us up. It is a famous drink in St Moritz called Kaffee Grischa, and to refuse would be considered an insult.'

The grey-haired Max placed a small wooden bowl in the centre of the table. Then, saying 'Prost!' with a big toothy grin, he left.

Susan had planned to keep her coat on throughout dinner, but there was a roaring fire in the restaurant and Bernhard smartly whipped the fur coat from her shoulders, completely upsetting her plans. Bernhard couldn't take his eyes off her dress, and once again, Susan silently cursed June.

After the meal had been ordered he picked up the wooden bowl and passed it to her. 'What is it?' she asked.

'Sip it and find out.'

'No thank you. It looks very potent. May I have a glass of fruit punch please?'

'How can you have an opinion about something you've never even tasted? Try it,' he ordered.

The drink was very sweet and warm, with a taste of cinnamon and herbs. It was so good that she took another sip and forgot about the punch. The bowl was passed back and forth until it was empty. Max loomed up with a smile, said something in German to Bernhard, and placed another bowl on the table.

'No more, please, Bernhard' she said. Leaving the bowl aside, he asked about her ambulance duties during the war, and she talked while he listened, inclining his head occasionally and smiling at the appropriate moment. She had the strangest feeling that his mind was somewhere else and that he had probably not heard a word.

'I don't think you're listening.'

'Always a difficult task for a man when he is looking at a beautiful woman.'

Flushing at his compliment, she smiled. He really was exceedingly charming. She liked him more and more each time they met. He looked particularly handsome tonight in a red polo neck sweater and a dark navy blue jacket. She had bought him some cufflinks for a Christmas gift, made of black onyx. She hoped he would like them.

'Would you like to live in France?'

France might as well have been on the moon for all the travelling she had done. 'Sounds wonderful' she replied.

The meal arrived. He did not answer but started to eat, and when he did speak he changed the subject to skiing. Now it was her turn not to listen; instead she wondered what tactics he would use to get her into bed. Would it be gentle persuasion or brute force? How could she fend him off?

'Will you marry me?' he asked, reaching across the table to take hold of her hand.

Stunned, she just stared at him. He had proposed in perfect English; the dear man must have been practising.

'Bernhard, we have only known each other for a short while. Isn't this rather hasty?'

'As a doctor, I am used to making snap decisions. So, you must tell me.'

'Yes, Bernhard, I must.'

He took her hand and pressed it to his lips.

'Darling, you've made me the happiest of men.' He signalled to Max, who told him he didn't have any French champagne left, only German Sekt. Bernhard thought Sekt was not special enough, and he would buy French champagne when he returned to London. In the meantime, his future wife had enjoyed the warm herb and cinnamon drink, and he ordered some more.

Dumbfounded, all Susan could do was stare at him. She had meant, 'Yes, she must give him an answer,' but he thought she had accepted his proposal. She did not love him but was attracted to him; perhaps love would develop when she knew him a little better. June was all set to marry her Canadian and probably leave England. Perhaps this was Susan's last chance for a better life, as her schoolteacher had once promised. She wanted to be alone and think this through more carefully.

'Please excuse me, Bernhard' she said. She rose at his nod, and left the table.

Needing some time to think, she walked out onto a balcony overlooking the snowfields. How bizarre it all seemed! Here she was in St Moritz contemplating marriage to a German, and he wanted an English woman. How she had loathed the Germans during the war – especially the bombers – and now she was considering marriage to one. She had to admit Bernhard was an attractive man and she was infatuated with him so much so that she was willing to accept his proposal, hoping that they would be happy. He was almost British, she reasoned. He preferred Harris Tweed jackets and smoked a Dunhill bent pipe – typically British habits. What a strange world this was.

Bernhard admired her shapely figure as he reclaimed his seat watching her walk outside onto the balcony. She had stood out from the rest of the women at the dinner dance in London. Her laughter and sense of fun delighted him, and she oozed femininity. When he first set eyes on her, he was determined to marry her, and whatever he wanted he usually got.

A few years before, all he had wanted was to finish his medical studies and go to Africa. Now he wanted this woman, and marrying her would also secure his British citizenship. That he desperately wanted, so he could work almost anywhere, including the United States.

During the war he had been assigned to a medical team attached to the Fifth Division of the Afrika Korps and the medical team was flown to Tripoli in Junkers aircraft along with the supplies. He had joined the Wehrmacht, not for combat but to amputate limbs, stitch up gaping machine-gun wounds and ease the dying as they passed from this world. His orders had been explicit: to patch up both officers and the poor foot-sloggers and return them to battle as soon as possible. There were a few shirkers, and these were usually suffering from venereal diseases picked up from brothels in Tripoli. The Korps had been fated as heroes when they pushed the British back to Tobruk. However, Bernhard had merely gazed over the desolate landscape dotted with furze and sandy scrub with little or no greenery and had thought to himself that the British could have it, for all he cared.

Bernhard was as different from his brother as night from

day. Hans used women, like a child with a toy discarding it when bored or suddenly discovering a new one. Bernhard had never forgotten their final meeting. They had met at the Adlon hotel on the Pariser Platz, the night before he left for Tripoli. His brother looked like a blond giant in his uniform, and Bernhard was proud of him. Now he lay buried in some frozen wasteland in Russia.

Bernhard hated the Nazis, who had robbed his country of its youth, along with millions of innocent people who had been put to death because of religion, race, colour, or physical and mental disabilities. He was proud to be German, but felt nothing but revulsion for the Nazis. He had seen people in Britain, recoil with loathing, when they found out he was German, and he could well understand their hatred. The British people had lost sons, husbands, fathers, and in some cases entire families during the blitz, just as families in almost every city in Germany had. It would take a long, long time to heal the mistrust and hatred on both sides.

His mother had urged him to make enquiries in Britain about Hans. However, neither the American nor the British authorities knew anything about the fate of thousands of German troops who had been captured or killed in Russia.

Susan's arrival at the table put paid to his thoughts.

'You asked me earlier if I would like to live in France. Can you please tell me why?'

'My contract in London is almost up. I have been offered a position at a medical research establishment outside Paris, and I wanted to know how you felt about living in France.'

'Will you be working for the French?'

He shook his head. 'The company is a French-American consortium. The head office is in New York. The team, however, is a mix of French, British, Italian and Spanish researchers. Even doctors from as far away as Australia and New Zealand have applied for positions. I have to bring the laboratory up to strength, with medical and administration personnel.'

'What will your position be?'

'I will be Directeur.'

Knowing how talented he was in his field she wasn't surprised at all he had been offered the position of Director, in charge of a huge laboratory with a team of doctors.

'Congratulations. You must be thrilled.'

'Tell June I adore the dress she selected and I'm happy she didn't pack a nightgown.' He had turned the conversation around, making her wonder if he was a little uneasy receiving compliments.

'Did you read June's note?'

'It was difficult not to. You left it in the kitchen.'

'Oh, I meant to ask you where to put the rubbish, but you were changing and I left it on the table inside the box. Are you angry?'

'No I am not. Shall we go back to the chalet and talk about our wedding arrangements and our honeymoon, darling?'

Susan gave him a beaming smile and a nod of agreement

Chapter Nineteen

'Please call me Mutti,' Bernhard's mother said, smiling at Susan after her son had made the introductions.

'Susan has consented to be my wife, and we plan to marry in London as soon as we can arrange it.'

'My dear, I'm so happy for you both. Congratulations,' she added, a little teary, embracing Bernhard and kissing him on both cheeks before turning to her future daughter-in-law. 'You will look after my son and make him happy?'

Susan thought Mutti looked anything but happy. Perhaps she was still grieving for her dead husband and younger son. Before the war they had been a close-knit family, but now only two of them remained. Susan knew the dear woman was not alone, for there were thousands of families just like hers.

'Yes, I promise to look after your son and make him happy.'

Mutti looked confused and Bernhard repeated Susan's words and turned to his future wife with an explanation. 'Without her hearing aid my mother is completely deaf.

You will have to speak, up or turn to her so she can read your lips. She hates wearing the device, especially when we have guests. I have told her many times that she must wear her hearing aid every minute of every day. Can you please speak in a loud voice when talking to my mother?'

Over the years Louisa had repeatedly told her that a lady does not yell, shout or speak in a loud voice. Susan had spent many hours developing a softer tone when speaking and did not know any other way. However, it was clear that he idolised his mother, and to please him she would try.

Bernhard was telling Mutti about the ski slopes, about how he had taught Susan to stay upright and balance correctly, and how she was more successful at cross-country than downhill skiing. Susan sat quietly while mother and son talked together after Bernhard had fitted Mutti's hearing device. On closer inspection, Susan noticed that Bernhard's mother was quite thin and had a rather sad face. Losing a husband and then a young son had taken its toll on the poor woman and perhaps was the reason she suffered from occasional bouts of loneliness. Her future mother-in-law's woollen dress of rich plum, with rose appliqué around the neckline and sleeves, was of the finest quality. Susan thought Mutti had good taste in clothes for a woman of her years.

Watching them so relaxed and happy in each other's company, she felt rather sorry for Mutti living so far from her only son. Susan suddenly realised that she was not only marrying the son but his mother too. Several months before, Bernhard had arranged for a local nurse to call once a week to attend to his mother. If her condition worsened, would Mutti have to move to France, and would it perhaps put a strain on their marriage? Susan hoped it would not.

Returning to the townhouse after a splendid dinner, Mutti went off to bed and Bernhard invited Susan onto the balcony and presented her with a beautiful solitaire diamond engagement ring. Then he took hold of the lapels of the fur coat he had given as a Christmas gift, pulled her towards him, bent his head and pressed his lips to hers. The ring was exquisite and must have cost a lot of money, and the only thing she had given him in return were onyx cufflinks and a silk scarf for his mother. There was nothing she could do to show him how much she appreciated his thoughtfulness, except to hold him close and surrender to his kiss with all the passion she could muster.

Later that night, she lay in bed with the keepsake locket around her neck and the diamond ring on her left hand, dreaming of her future in France. Suddenly, the bedclothes were thrown back and Bernhard climbed in beside her.

'Ah, no nightgown,' he whispered, as his hands caressed her naked body.

'Your mother, Bernhard!'

'You forget, darling, my mother is deaf. Can't the bridegroom sample his bride's charms before they wed?'

He had used similar words at the chalet when they lay on the rug before the fire. He had whispered love poems, then had quickly penetrated her.

'*Liebling*, you are the only gift I want,' he murmured, smothering any further protest with his lips. Later as they lay side by side he took her locket between his thumb and forefinger. 'You never take this off. Is it a family heirloom?'

'Yes, it is.' She could never tell him just how precious it was. That was her own private memory, and she wanted to keep it that way.

When they had finished making love, Susan turned on her side as memories of the night in the chalet flooded her mind. It was a night she could barely remember, but somehow could not forget. The snow was falling, the logs were blazing and Bernhard was making love to her on the rug in front of the fire whispering French and Italian love poems in her ear. Eventually, Susan fell asleep, on the floor.

Throughout the night in a kind of strange dream she could make out images of Bernhard heaving above her, taking his pleasure. His mouth seemed to cover hers, she moaned as he indulged himself with her time and time again while the winter storm raged outside the chalet.

The next morning they flew back to London on a British European Airways flight. Susan could hardly wait to tell June her news.

'June, oh, June, I'm to be married! We are honeymooning in Italy and going to live in France.'

'You're marrying Herman the German? Well I...'

'His name is Bernhard,' Susan interrupted. 'Please call him that.'

'Did he propose on the ski slopes? Now don't tell me;

I can picture the whole scene. You're lying half-buried in the snow with your legs in mid-air, while your skis fly down the slopes on their own with the poles in hot pursuit. He comes swishing up on his skis, digs you out of the snow and says, 'Will you be my Hausfrau?' How romantic!'

She let June have her fun. 'He's attractive, clever and kind, and his father has, or rather had, pots of money.'

'No woman could resist, but if I were you I'd marry the father.'

'Oh, June, do stop joking. His father is dead, and the Nazis took the family's home, lands and a large factory from them. I suppose they haven't got much now.'

'Do you love this man?' June eyed her suspiciously from the other side of the room.

'Why, yes, of course.'

'Are you serious about marrying someone you met only a few months ago?'

'Yes, I am. A wedding ring brings respectability. You should try it.'

Humming softly, Susan unpacked her suitcase, putting the beautiful grey and white fur coat in the wardrobe. The doctor had expensive taste, June reflected, if the fur coat and the diamond on Susan's finger was anything to go by. Had her friend only agreed to this marriage for money and security? Whatever the reason, June was sure that love had played no part in her decision. Nevertheless, she hoped Susan would be happy,

'I wish you all the happiness in the world. When is the wedding?'

'Next month, at Caxton Hall, and I would like you to be my bridesmaid.'

'I'd be honoured.'

'I have three questions that I want to ask. How did the pregnancy test go? Did your dashing Canadian arrive? And are you getting married, too?'

June shook her head. 'I've haven't got a bun in the oven. My charming Canadian breezed in here with a quick, 'Wham, bam, thank you ma'am.' He never mentioned marriage. Honestly, I don't seem to have your knack of getting a grown man on bended knee to ask for my hand. Perhaps you can give me lessons?' June didn't wait for a reply. 'My dashing Canadian is staying over in London for a while. So I expect we'll meet again. By the way, blossom, my house is up for sale. I've put a deposit on a small maisonette in Chelsea. So it's just as well you're moving out.'

A month later, a few special guests attended the wedding breakfast at the Dorchester: two of Bernhard's medical colleagues and their wives, including Bernhard's boss, Ross Chisholm, who was the best man. Bernhard's mother, who had taken to her bed with influenza, was too ill to attend. Instead, she sent a lovely wedding card and a cheque. For her wedding outfit, Susan chose a beige street-length dress and coat trimmed with dark brown fur at the collar and sleeves, and an elegant hat edged with the same fur. Bernhard wore an expensive lounge suit of dark grey with matching waistcoat and tie.

Getting to his feet, her husband gave a short speech thanking Ross and June for witnessing their marriage and the guests for their good wishes and attending the ceremony. Finally, he turned towards her and drank to the health of his new wife. Ross replied asking the guests to raise their glasses, brimming with champagne, to toast the newlyweds.

Everything that morning was so wonderful. Susan was bubbling over with excitement, and even more so when she arrived in Rome.

From the Roman Forum and Coliseum to St Peter's Basilica, Bernhard took her everywhere. There were dozens of restaurants on the Via Veneto, and the food was superb. It was her first experience of Italian food and she loved it, especially the coffee with a delicate froth on top. Rome was foreign but fun, and the city just buzzed with happy people strolling around the shops.

Bernhard thought the roads were too narrow to drive a car around so they walked, or hired a Vespa scooter with a rear pillion passenger seat and a small storage compartment. Susan bought a pair of slim-fitting pants and a matching sweater. With an Alice band securely fastened to stop the wind from blowing hair in her face and with her arms wrapped around Bernhard's waist, she felt comfortable. They went everywhere on the scooter, looking at the ancient ruins, statues and gardens, sometimes taking a picnic lunch or stopping to eat in a small family-owned trattoria. Bernhard opened not only his heart but his wallet, and bought her everything from

Italian clothes and leather goods to cameo jewellery and shoes. He treated her like a child in a toyshop, indulging her every whim. He was so patient and considerate, translating the language and encouraging her to try anything that caught her eye. With each passing day she was falling more and more in love with him.

On their last day in the ancient citadel they returned to the Fountain of Trevi. He told her that if she threw a coin into the water she would one day return to Rome. Bernhard laughed out loud when she said, 'Will I return to Rome sooner if I throw a handful of coins into the fountain?' It had been a wonderful honeymoon.

The move to France was hectic. Bernhard had to report for work immediately. They stayed in a hotel at the company's expense while looking for a place to live. Several estate agents accompanied Susan around the region, looking for a property that would please them both. On the third week she found a run-down, five-bedroom small château on the outskirts of Amboise. Within its grounds were a small orchard, a vegetable and herb garden, and overgrown flowerbeds surrounded by shrubs and trees.

The house desperately needed refurbishing, including plumbing, plastering and painting. It took six months before their home was ready, and they moved in on the day their packing cases arrived from storage in England. Bernhard loved the house and took her on a shopping spree to Paris, where they bought ornamental rugs for the marble floors, French renaissance furniture and one or two paintings Bernhard admired. The dining room led onto a terrace through French doors. The room was furnished with a beautiful dining table and sixteen chairs covered with lemon and gold striped brocade.

Bernhard's duties included entertaining visiting medical scientists and executives from head office. He employed Yvette, a mature woman, to cook and to help whenever they were entertaining, and Jacques, a gardener, to look after the grounds. He also employed a local girl, eighteen-year-old Brigitte, to do the laundry. She was very friendly and a bit of a chatterbox, often addressing her employer as Madame Susanne. This was the French way of saying the name, Brigitte told Susan when questioned.

Susan rather liked this French-sounding variation of her name. Over the ensuing weeks Bernhard began to use it too, until Susan started to adopt it herself. Within a few weeks everyone, including the baker who delivered everything from bread to baguettes, the friendly fishmonger who sold a variety of fish and seafood from Langoustine to 'le saumon', and the hawker with his fresh fruit piled high on his two-wheel barrow, all started to call her Madame Susanne.

Six months later Mutti unexpectedly arrived and suggested the three of them drive to the Côte d'Azur to a small place called Golfe-Juan. On account of his mother's persistence, neither Bernhard nor Susanne dared refuse her. After a delicious lunch on the seafront, she ask Bernhard to drive up a small road, and about half way along asked him to stop. Mutti leaned towards Bernhard and Susanne in the front of the car and held out a set of keys.

'This is my wedding gift to you both.'

Following Mutti's eyes, they both gasped. A picturesque villa, painted blue and white with a balcony stretching the length of the building, overlooked the sea. It was so beautiful Susanne fell in love with it on sight.

'Who owns all this furniture?' Bernhard asked as he strolled through the place.

'You do. I told the estate agent to buy it furnished.' His mother smiled as she looked at her son's expression.

Walking inside from the balcony with a smile from ear to ear, Susanne hugged her mother-in-law. 'Bernhard, please tell Mutti it's a beautiful gift.'

After conveying Susanne's appreciation for the wedding gift, he turned to her. 'Darling, I think I shall buy a small yacht and moor it in the harbour. Would you like that?'

'Oh, Bernhard, how wonderful!' She did not add that she had never been sailing, hoping he would teach her.

They stayed overnight and then had to leave early as Bernhard was due at a staff meeting later that day. He suggested that Susanne and Mutti return and stay for a week, and he would join them for the weekend. It was the best time the three of them ever spent together. Bernhard bought a small sailing yacht, and although his mother refused to climb onto the boat deck. Susanne was happy to and they went sailing almost every day. She loved it. The water was cool to touch as she lay in the boat, her outstretched hand skimming the waves as Bernhard piloted the craft. Adjusting her dark glasses, Susanne watched the sun glinting on the water, like a path of gold stretching out across the azure sea. They spent idyllic days sailing, swimming and relaxing in the sun. Sadly, all too soon it was over.

On their return to Amboise, Susanne resumed the conversational French class that Bernhard insisted she attend. Mutti stayed a few more days and then went home to Zürich.

Susanne loved France, but not all the people were friendly. Some of the locals were ill-mannered because she was English, and impolite to Bernhard when they found out he was German. He told her to ignore them, but he could not ignore the crisis that threatened his first Christmas in charge of the laboratory. Christmas Day fell on a Saturday, and the French doctors wanted to have an extra day's holiday. Bernhard was reluctant to seek advice from head office, feeling he should handle this problem himself. He called the grumbling doctors into his office and told them that the extra day off would not be allowed. The doctors stood firm and said they would take the time off anyway. It was common knowledge that experienced research doctors were hard to find, and they were trying to force Bernhard to agree to their demands. However, Bernhard was just as stubborn and told them that if they did not turn up for work on the designated day, he would sack them. They moaned and groaned and called him a mean Kraut – not to his face, of course. He came home one evening tired and worried, very worried. Susanne tried to cheer him up by pouring him a glass of his favourite wine, to no avail.

'I cannot afford to lose so many staff. We are working on an important project. They have a two-hour lunch every day, which none of the others have, and it is my responsibility to solve this crisis.'

'It wasn't your fault and maybe…'

'*Sei ruhig!*' he yelled, ordering her to be quiet.

He had never spoken to her like that before, and she hurried from the room, leaving him scowling on the sofa. Susanne went to her bedroom, picked up her French book and started to read. She heard him yelling at Yvette because the kitchen floor had not been waxed correctly. Susanne sighed; it was Brigitte who waxed the floors, not Yvette. He would have no staff at home, either, if he kept this up, she thought, and went into the bathroom to prepare for bed. Her first Christmas in France was turning into a disaster.

If that evening was bad, the next day was even worse. Bernhard cancelled lunch at their favourite restaurant and spent the entire day locked away in his study, accepting only a tray of food she left outside his door. Susanne was becoming quite concerned; tomorrow they were entertaining a group of doctors and their wives with a cocktail party.

Several telephone calls came in that evening from disgruntled doctors, saying that after thinking it over they would return to work as requested. All but three of them telephoned, cheering Bernhard up considerably. He wasn't worried at a mere three people leaving the company. They could manage the project without them. Besides, he had just hired some new staff. Bernhard left all employees, including the French doctors, in no doubt that in future no extra holidays would be granted, be it Christmas, Easter or Napoleon's birthday.

Head office applauded his efforts and sent him a memo, informing him he was scheduled to attend a conference in Washington the following June.

Ten days before they were due to fly to Washington, Mutti was knocked down getting off a bus, and Bernhard rushed to the hospital in Zürich. Later that evening he telephoned Susanne to tell her that Mutti had passed away. She immediately caught a train to join her husband for the funeral.

'If it had been any kind of disease I would have moved heaven and earth to save her, but a damn stupid car,' he said vehemently to Susanne when he picked her up at the station. 'I told her to wear her hearing aid whenever she went for a walk. Why did she ignore me?'

After the funeral they returned to Mutti's townhouse and Susanne could tell her husband was heart-broken. He had shed tears of sorrow at the graveside, but now he was angry. She knew only too well that this was all part of the grieving process. It takes time; she wanted to tell him, one miserable day at a time. He would heal, just as she had.

'Darling, would you like some coffee?'

He nodded. When she returned with the tray he looked at her with bleary eyes.

'I have to travel to Washington. I have several meetings before the conference. Will you take over here and join me when you have finished? Send all the family heirlooms to Amboise. I'll give you a list of what I want. Any jewellery you can keep or sell. Put the town house up for sale, but not the chalet. I hate to leave you with all this. Darling, can I rely on you?'

'Of course, I will do as you ask and meet you at the Statler in Washington as soon as I can get away. Do you want me to see your mother's solicitor regarding her will, or do you want to handle it?'

'I haven't time. You see to it. You'll find his address in her writing case. I have to race back to Paris to catch my flight tomorrow.' He scribbled something on a slip of paper and handed it to her. 'This will give you temporary Power of Attorney over my mother's affairs. If you have any trouble, ask them to contact me.'

Early the next morning, shortly after Bernhard had left, Susanne started going through his mother's papers and personal effects, making different piles of what she was keeping and what was rubbish. Discovering some photograph albums, she flicked through them and stared at the happy family snaps of smiling parents with a tall lanky boy no more than eight and a smaller one with thick, curly blond hair sitting on his father's shoulders. They were all dead now – except Bernhard. How quickly things change, she thought sadly.

Turning another page, she was shocked to see a photograph of her husband in a German military uniform. The picture was dated June 1940, and at that time the

Germans were bombing London with their blitzkrieg. She ripped the photograph from the album and tore it into sheds. She did not want to see any pictures of her husband in Nazi uniform. Besides, Bernhard had been a doctor during the war and more concerned with saving lives than destroying them.

The next page revealed a photograph of a younger man in a black uniform. On his hat badge was a silver skull. She shuddered as she gazed at the young face; she could not ignore the arrogance he projected or the proud stance he displayed. It was obvious for all to see. She threw all the military photographs in the rubbish, but kept the one of the smiling happy family taken before the war.

Within three days she had organised a removal company to pack and deliver the boxes to France and an auctioneer to sell the furniture, and had appointed an estate agent to sell the town house. Susanne was informed that Bernhard was the only beneficiary. It would not take long to process, and the solicitor assured her that he would keep in contact. Furthermore, he had said that there was a great deal of money tied up in shares in South Africa and asked if she wanted to sell these. Susanne told him that until he had heard from her husband, he should not sell them.

When Mutti's jewellery was valued, Susanne was astonished at the high price it fetched, and decided to keep one or two exquisite pieces and sold the rest. The last thing she did before leaving Zürich was to donate all her mother-in-law's clothes to a local charity, except for a beautiful silver fox fur that she just could not bear to part with.

Bernhard had asked her to telephone him when she was leaving for Washington, but Susanne had planned a stopover in London to visit her children, to catch up with June and Louisa and pick up a photograph she had left behind in London. She planned to telephone Bernhard from England before flying across the Atlantic to join him.

Chapter Twenty

Arriving in London a week before her flight to Washington, Susanne listened patiently while Louisa told her the bad news about Percy. It seemed he had been investigated by the Department of Inland Revenue for not paying tax and also charged with black marketing activities during the war years. The government had taken everything he owned, in a rather nasty court case. He had been made an example to other would-be tax dodgers and was extremely lucky not to have received a gaol sentence. According to Louisa, they had sold all his assets, including the pig farm, the shops and even his house in Queens Road, leaving Percy and Tess almost penniless. With nowhere to live, they had moved in with June. This was not at all acceptable to June, as she was not able to entertain 'Mister Right for Tonight' in her bedroom. Susanne thought that by relieving Percy and Tess' worries, she would be helping June too.

Climbing into a taxi, she went to Chelsea to talk with them. When she arrived, June and Tess were in the kitchen having words about whose turn it was to clean the kitchen floor, and Percy was reading the morning paper.

'This goes on all the time,' he groaned, nodding towards the kitchen.

With a big smile, Susanne shrugged her shoulders and walked towards Percy's chair. Some things never change; sometimes they get even worse, she thought.

'I hope you don't mind, the door was open,' she said, planting kisses on the left and right of his face, as is the French form of greeting.

'As usual, you look lovely my dear.' He said folding the *Daily Mail* and dropping it into the newspaper basket. 'I didn't know you were in London, what's the occasion?'

'Louisa told me about the court case. I thought you may need some help or a shoulder to cry on.'

'Thank you, my dear. You are the only one to walk through that door and offer me a kind word. All my so-called friends in the meat industry and even a cousin who owes me money have taken to the hills. I wasn't the only one in the black market racket, but I was the one who got caught. I helped a lot of families who were destitute during the war, but none of them showed up during the court case. Louisa gave me thirty pounds, her life savings. I was very grateful for that. The poor dear would like to leave London and go to live with her only relative, in Cornwall. I plan to pay her back when Malcolm sends me some money soon. His ship, *HMS Caledonia,* is currently in Hong Kong, but he promised to send me a few quid. Can you imagine me begging money from my own son?' Susanne shook her head as he continued. 'My eldest son gave his mother and me bloody nothing. Him and his dyed-blond wife are both working, and he couldn't even offer us a bed! Said he didn't have the room as Penny had moved in with them. We have since found out that the sofa in the lounge converts into a double bed; Penny told us. The tight-fisted bugger.'

'Percy, I'm dreadfully sorry to see you in this position. What will you do? How much do you need?'

'Both Tess and I want to leave London and retire near the coast. We saw a two-bedroom bungalow in Brighton for sale for two thousand five hundred pounds, and we wouldn't mind moving there. I have a little money but nowhere near that amount.'

'Get in touch with the estate agency and tell them you are going to purchase the place. I will give you the money you need, tomorrow after I have been to my bank.'

Percy's eyes misted over as he threw his arms around her and thanked her. 'Do you really have that sort of money? Where did you get it?'

'Now, Percy, a woman never reveals her secrets.'

'In other words, mind my own business.'

'Quite.'

'Blossom!' came a shriek from the kitchen door. Susanne turned as June ran towards her, and they hugged each other.

'What are you doing here, my dear?' Tess asked as they embraced.

'I am going into to Kent to visit some friends who were very kind to me when I was ill, before I leave for Washington.'

'I believe they call it Washington DC, blossom. Not to get mixed up with the other Washington.'

'You are absolutely right, June, thank you,' Susanne answered smoothly. June was always pointing out her shortcomings, just like Bernhard, but she took it with good grace.

'Can I announce that Tess and I are moving?' Percy asked Susanne with a raised eyebrow. A smiling nod gave him his answer, and he broke the happy news.

'How wonderful,' June said, and as an afterthought added, 'I'm sure you will both be comfortable in Brighton. I read somewhere that living by the sea is very therapeutic.'

'All our troubles started when peace broke out,' Tess muttered. Percy, June and Susanne just stared at her.

The journey into Kent by train was hot and sticky. It was one of the hottest summers in Great Britain since the war, according to the weatherman on the radio. Leaning back against the upholstery, she stared out of the window. She had given Louisa the thirty pounds Percy owed her. It would more than pay for her ticket to Cornwall. Susanne was happy to be in a position to repay the people who had helped her during the war years, especially Percy and Louisa. Susanne spent the money knowing it did not belong to her, it was Mutti's money, and she hoped Bernhard would never find out.

'How is Rose?' she asked John as they walked to where his Austin saloon was parked. Susanne really wanted to inquire about Edward, but out of good manners she asked about his wife.

'She's well, but in a bit of a panic about your visit. Would you mind if we stop in the village for a cup of tea and have a chat about Edward?'

The rest of the journey was in complete silence; a glance at John told her that he did not want to talk and was trying to work out what he was going to say to her. Susanne leaned back against the car seat, gazing out of the window from time to time, until the car came to a halt in Birchwood village. When the waitress had placed the tea things on the table, Susanne could wait no longer.

'What is it, John?'

'Rose is pregnant and frightened. To cut a long story short, she is worried that you will take Edward away. I thought it would be a good idea for us to discuss it without Rose present.'

'I see.' She knew both Rose and John idolised her son. Bernhard, on the other hand, had no time for children. He was too busy with his career and his lifestyle: travelling the world to meetings and conferences, wining and dining, enjoying the high life. Bernhard was a self-absorbed kind of person. He was constantly preoccupied with his own thoughts and quite often reminded Susanne of her good, but mainly bad qualities. He only talked to people who interested him and was easily bored. Practically all Susanne's time was taken up travelling with her husband, looking after him and accompanying him to social engagements and being hostess to their cocktail evenings. She mentioned to Bernhard that she would like to remain at home and was tired of constant travelling and living out of a suitcase. She had brought up the subject many times and his reply was always the same: 'The duty of a wife remains first and foremost with her husband.'

John interrupted her thoughts. 'Rose didn't want you to know about the pregnancy just yet.'

'Then I will not mention it. John, I have asked Edward many times to come and live in France, and he always refuses. When we have our weekly talk on the telephone he is always telling me how much he loves living in Kent, and especially, the horse-riding, hunting and fishing trips that you and the estate manager invite him on. I am well aware that you and Rose love Edward. He always tells me how good you both are. Does he enjoy boarding school? Whenever I ask him he is evasive.'

John smiled. 'Yes, he does, but he likes school holidays better. Fishing and hunting and horses have always been his favourite hobbies. You look after all his expenses, and we give him a happy, healthy lifestyle. I think he has the best of both worlds.'

Susanne returned his smile and added, 'We should go, John? My visit this time is only a short one. Edward wants to take me to the home farm to see a foal that he helped to bring into the world. Then I have to return to London to join my husband in America.'

Arriving at the Statler Hotel in Washington after an exhausting flight from London via New York, Susanne quickly paid the cab fare and was shown to her room. She showered and changed before ordering her favourite Earl Grey tea from room service.

'Darling, what have you done to your hair?'

Startled, Susanne almost dropped the teacup and turned to see Bernhard walking into their hotel suite with his arms open wide. She placed the cup and saucer on a sofa table, went into his embrace and stood locked in his arms while they kissed. He asked again about her hair. She knew he was not happy with her short bouffant style.

'I had it cut in Paris, my love. I just felt that long hair is for young girls, not a woman in her thirties. You don't mind?'

He ran a hand along his jaw line, a habit she was familiar with when he was displeased. 'Actually, I do. I just wish you had consulted me before having your beautiful tresses cut off. There's not much can be done about it now. However, it will grow again. Please fix me a martini while I shower and change. Oh,' he said, loosening his tie, and turning towards her at the bedroom door, 'there is a special evening being arranged tomorrow night to open the conference, and the guest of honour is the President of the United States.'

She let out a sigh as she walked to the drinks tray and started mixing gin and vermouth in a glass pitcher. Her husband was old-fashioned. He liked his women with curvy figures and long hair. He admired women who wore skirts or dresses, and not the new tailored pants that had become all the rage for women since the war. He did not believe women ever used logic and therefore dismissed anything a woman had to say unless she had a medical degree. Bernhard insisted his wife defer to him on just about everything, including cutting her hair, it seemed.

She had the distinct impression that he thought his wife was a nobody from nowhere, with limited education, and while not liking his attitude, she accepted it. Although there were lots of things she did not like about her marriage, she had to admit that her life with him, although busy, was a comfortable one.

Her conversational French was now passable and she had picked up a few German words; she was an avid reader and a quick learner. With the assistance of Yvette, the housekeeper, Jacques, the gardener, and Brigitte, the cleaner, she managed their large home in Amboise, leaving her time to raise funds for local charities, especially the Croix Rouge. Even with her busy lifestyle she still found time to make lightning trips to England to visit her daughter and her son. Her husband's voice interrupted her musings.

'Darling, I was expecting you to arrive earlier than a day before the conference opens. Did you have a lot of trouble organising things in Zürich?' he asked before taking a sip of his martini.

'I did, rather, and I apologise if my late arrival has spoiled your plans. I was held up with the lawyer. He is going to contact you concerning your mother's will – something about shares in a company in South Africa.'

'I will give you the shares for your birthday, darling. They are probably not worth a great deal. Mutti wasn't a shrewd investor. Now, if you will change into something more feminine,' he said, eyeing her tailored pants with some distaste, 'I will take you out for dinner.'

The next morning, Susanne woke up feeling happy, in

spite of Bernard's behaviour the previous night during dinner. He had found fault with almost everything, including the dress she was wearing. He really was irritable, and Susanne couldn't wait to return to her room and have an early night. Bernhard had other ideas, and she performed her wifely duties obediently.

Even her husband's mood could not dampen her enthusiasm as she made plans about how she was going to spend her day. Years before, when Rick had told her all about the capital city, she had listened intently as he had described the Smithsonian Institute and all the interesting things to see there, including George Washington's false teeth. She had accused Rick of telling lies and run off along a wooded pathway into the dense forest. He soon caught her and they both fell about, laughing. He told her that he would take her to the Smithsonian one day and show her the teeth.

Susanne set off after a light breakfast, intending only to spend an hour or two perusing the exhibits, and ended up several hours later still admiring each room she entered. Suddenly, she came to a halt at a glass case; sure enough, there were George Washington's teeth. Tears filled her eyes. Rick had been telling the truth all along.

Quickly drying her eyes after receiving a few odd looks from other visitors, she continued enjoying the many display cabinets with clever and unusual exhibits. Glancing at her watch she was surprised to see that it was almost five o'clock; the reception was starting at seven. Her plans to visit the Jefferson Memorial, Lincoln statue and the

Ford Theatre would have to wait until another day. She hurried back to the hotel to change for the medical conference cocktail party.

The opening of the conference was held in the Presidential Ballroom of the Statler. When Bernhard and Susanne arrived, they were greeted with waiters carrying trays of mouth-watering canapés, while others wove in and out amongst the guests offering drinks. Delegates from all over the world who were involved in medical research were present in business suits, while their wives wore cocktail dresses. Everyone was mingling and chatting before the guest of honour arrived.

When the President was announced, the National Anthem of the United States boomed out over the loudspeaker, bringing everyone to attention. He walked smartly to the dais and gave a speech of welcome in his usual clipped style, wishing the representatives well in their endeavours. The crowd separated and lined each side of the room as the President, flanked by two conference delegates, was introduced to doctors and medical scientists. Two bodyguards walked discreetly behind the presidential group, while the press, were at the rear of the procession.

Susanne watched President Eisenhower moving slowly down the line towards her. He had the same supreme confidence and easy grin and had not changed at all from when she had met him nine years before. Perhaps there were a few more lines on his face and a bit less hair, but the piercing blue eyes were still clear and bright.

Shaking Bernhard's hand, he murmured a cordial

greeting, and moved on to Susanne. Taking her hand, he smiled and passed on. She had not for one moment thought that he would remember her, for he must have met thousands of people during both his military and political career. But suddenly, he took a backward step and was before her once more.

'I never forget a face' he said.

'Neither do I, sir.'

He gave a hearty laugh. 'We met in London. You gave me a riding crop – a birthday gift, as I recall.'

She beamed at him with admiration. 'Yes, sir, I did,' she answered politely as the flashes from press cameras clicked in unison.

A meaningful look came into his eyes. He leaned closer, and for her ears only, said, 'Your riding instructor was a fine man. Do you know Carlon Stud is quite near here?' He smiled broadly, gave her hand a tender squeeze, and moved on.

Choked with emotion. She felt like crying. His look had told her that he remembered both her and Rick. She felt tears forming.

At that moment Bernhard was leaning closer and whispering in her ear, wanting to know what the President had said. She dug her long fingernails into her palms to steady herself and to stop the tears, silently chastising herself for calling him Sir instead of Mr President, but everyone called him Sir in London, and looking into his familiar face she had been swept back to the war years.

As soon as the President had departed the waiters

reappeared, and chattering voices echoed around the room again. Several inquisitive American doctors' wives approached Susanne, enquiring politely if she had met the President previously. For the first time since marrying Dr Bernhard Roehder, she was the centre of attention, not him.

Dr Douglas Weston, who was working on similar projects in Richmond to those Bernhard was working on in France, introduced his wife, Clare. They invited Susanne and Bernard to join them for dinner at a new Spanish restaurant which had just opened, complete with flamenco dancers. She was glad that Bernhard had agreed, as it gave her time to rein in her feelings and calm her nerves, giving her a few hours to invent a story that would satisfy him. Not for anything would she tell him about Rick. They were treasured memories, and she could not share them with anyone, not even her husband.

She could tell by the way Bernhard was looking at her that he was impressed that the President knew her. He was probably thinking she must have moved in very high circles during the war. She hoped his preconceived idea that she was nobody from nowhere would now be buried.

While the two men discussed the upcoming conference and swapped stories about their respective jobs, Clare turned to Susanne and told her that she was returning home. She invited Susanne to visit for a few days. The Westons' home was in Richmond. Bernhard had informed Susanne that there would be several day and night meetings and schedule conferences where dinner would be served during the discussions and he hoped that she would find something to occupy her time.

Clare was a pleasant, talkative woman with a beautiful smile and short bouncy curls. Susanne could not help but like her and accepted the invitation readily.

As they walked across the hotel lobby after their evening with the Westons, one of the conference delegates stopped Bernhard and asked for a few moments of his time. Susanne excused herself before the two men disappeared into the bar. Instead of going towards the elevator, she went to the front desk and asked the receptionist to order a hire car for nine thirty in the morning. She went up to their room, soaked herself in a warm bath and was fast asleep before Bernhard returned.

The telephone beeped at nine twenty to advise Susanne that the car was waiting out front, along with delivery driver. Bernhard had left earlier and Susanne who had just finished breakfast served in her room. Picked up her handbag she headed for the elevator.

' Good morning ma'am. Have you driven a Chevrolet, ma'am?'

She wondered why this young man from the auto company was questioning her. Susanne countered with a question of her own.

'I drove an American ambulance during the war. Does that count?'

'It sure does, ma'am.' He explained a few things about the vehicle and handed her the keys, adding as he opened the driver's door for her, 'Are you going far, ma'am?'

'As far as Richmond, goodbye and thank you.' She drove off.

Chapter Twenty One

After leaving Washington, Susanne headed for Richmond on the newly-constructed highway. She had been assured the journey would take just over two hours, depending on traffic. Today, Bernhard was busy with several meetings to attend and later had been invited to dinner. She told him she was spending two or three days sightseeing, staying with Clare in Richmond.

Two hours later she turned off the highway. Suddenly the road narrowed and became bumpy. Susanne was thinking that perhaps she might have taken the wrong exit, but she kept going anyway. The man at the gasoline station where she had stopped earlier had assured her that Carlon Stud was a few miles along this dusty road, but all Susanne could see were open range and mountains stretching into the distance. The morning was pleasant when she had set off, but now the temperature was rising. She was glad of the navy and white shirt- waister dress in cool cotton and a pair of open-toe sandals. Opening the window, she felt the air stir the hairs at the back of her neck and continued her journey with the window fully open.

As the car crested a steep rise she saw a large homestead nestled in a valley, with a long driveway and fields sectioned off with post and rail fencing. Horses cropped the grass while others cantered about with young foals following in their wake. Stopping the car, she got out, walked towards the fence and leaned against it, gazing into the distance.

The sun slanted across the entire valley, making the lush grass appear like an emerald sea and the homestead like a graceful ship anchored upon it. Majestic mountains and glistening rivers vied with patchwork fields and vast open spaces for sheer beauty. An aura of peace settled over her, and she felt refreshed and renewed just looking at the scenery, sensing she was closer to Rick than at any other time since his death. In her handbag lay a picture of him in a small frame. She intended to leave it at the homestead. In her mind she was bringing him home to a final resting place in the valley he had loved so much. Time seemed to stand still as memories of the man she had loved and lost filled her mind to the exclusion of all else.

Only the horn of a passing pick-up truck brought her back from the past. She had no idea how long she had been standing there.

Susanne's heart started pounding as she steered the car around a circular island in the middle of the driveway, displaying a statue of a horse. Several roads led off in different directions from the island. Susanne took the road that led to the front entrance of the house. Stepping out of the vehicle, she walked towards the porch. The first thing she saw was the swing Rick had told her about, where he sat in the evenings with his parents. Close to tears, she took a step backwards, thinking this was all a mistake and that she should not have come. Suddenly, the door opened and onto the porch stepped a middle-aged woman with familiar dark eyes and friendly smile.

'Hi, can I help you?'

The American accent sent her plummeting back in time, but she steeled herself to answer. 'Hello, my name is Susanne. I've come from Europe to look at some of your breeding stock. Is this the Carlon Stud?' She had debated whether to continue with the story she had concocted to mask the real reason for her visit, or to tell the truth. Her main objective was to see where Rick had lived and glimpse the stables he had described so vividly. If she could achieve that with a few white lies, so be it.

'Yes, it is. I'm Judy Carlon. Why don't you c'mon in and have a cool drink? It sure is hot out here.'

As she followed the woman down the hallway and into the sitting room, Susanne gazed around, transfixed. The hunting rifles above the big stone fireplace, the bookshelves lined with horse-breeding books, and the comfortable leather chairs were just as he had described them. She nearly faltered when she saw a picture of Rick in uniform displayed upon a fireside table.

'How did you hear of Carlon Stud?'

'I saw it advertised in a magazine,' she replied, dragging her eyes from the photograph.

The woman smiled. 'My father is always promoting the

stud since my brother convinced him to advertise to encourage new customers.'

There was an awkward silence, which was only broken when a woman appeared carrying a tray with glasses and a pitcher of iced tea with slices of lemon. Susanne guessed this was Mazy, the cook Rick had mentioned.

'This is a lovely room,' Susanne commented.

Judy was puzzled. While this woman was polite, she seemed a bit nervous; but more than that, she seemed familiar with the furnishings, even recognising paintings and photographs displayed around the room. Judy intended to find out who she was.

'Please sit down. How long is your visit to the States?'

'Two weeks,' Susanne answered before taking a seat on a leather sofa and sipping the iced tea. She knew the woman opposite was curious. Susanne wondered if she should tell her the real reason for her visit. She did not want to upset the family, and decided against it. 'My husband is in Washington on business, and as I am quite a keen horsewoman I fancied a trip to Carlon Stud after reading about it. I hired a car and here I am.'

When Mazy appeared and started to refill the glasses of iced tea Judy excused herself, and disappeared for a few moments and returned as Mazy went back to the kitchen.

'Did you have trouble finding our place?'

'No, I did not. I stopped for petrol, oops sorry, I mean gasoline, and the man who filled the car gave me directions. He told me he'd known Abe Carlon for years.'

'Abe is my father. He owns the stud and I help him manage it, as he is unable to look after the place on his own now. My brother used to help run the stud before the war.'

Susanne hesitated. 'Your brother?'

'Yes, Rick. He died in Europe. My mother passed away six months after we got the news. Rick was the apple of her eye, after his death she lost the will to live. Her death coming so quickly after Rick's near killed my father. He gets around in a wheelchair now, and I have taken over all the paperwork.'

Susanne was shocked to hear about Rick's mother and struggled to find the words to express her sorrow. 'I'm terribly sorry,' was all she could manage. Realising, tears were threatening, she stood up. 'I have to go.'

'Did you know Rick?'

Turning away from Judy and placing the glass on the coffee table, a silent nod was all she could manage.

'You're the English girl my brother fell in love with and wanted to bring back home. It's you, isn't it?'

Giving another small nod, Susanne fumbled in her handbag to find a handkerchief but Judy beat her, giving her a clean one of her own.

'My mother cried for days when he left for England.'

'My heart cries for him every day,' Susanne said, drying her eyes.

A tearful Judy threw her arms around her, and they both wept on each other's shoulder. 'I'm so glad you came to visit us. Rick would have liked that. Please don't leave.'

Judy dried her eyes and called for Mazy to bring some hot coffee.

'I'm the only daughter. Never married, and at forty not likely to, either. Why am I telling you this? Rick probably told you already.'

'Yes, he did.'

'Please stay for lunch and meet my father. He is lying down for his mid-morning nap, but he would be so happy to meet you.'

'How did you know about me, Judy?'

'At first it was a hunch. Then I remembered that Rick wrote to my folks and told them he had met the loveliest girl in London, with beautiful violet eyes.' She produced a photograph from her skirt pocket and handed it to Susanne. The picture was of Rick and her, taken near Tower Bridge. Tears were welling up again, and she quickly dabbed her eyes.

'I really shouldn't have come. I didn't mean to upset Rick's family.'

'Hush, now. At least I now know the kind of woman my brother wanted for a wife, and I like his choice.'

Embarrassed at Judy's compliment, she dropped her head to stare at the carpet. 'Do you still have Wildfire?' she asked, desperate to get out of the house and into the fresh air before she dissolved into uncontrollable tears.

'My brother's horse? Would you like to see him? I'll show you.'

'Could I go alone, Judy?'

'Sure, the stables are out back to the left. Keep going until you find them. Wildfire is in the first box.'

From Rick's description, Susanne recognised the

splendid roan with four cream-coloured socks as soon as she entered the stables. The horse whinnied at the stranger and ambled over to lean over the horse-box. She stroked his muzzle and kissed him, throwing her arms around the animal's neck and whispering to him that she had come a long way to meet him and that she loved his master, too. Taking the photograph of Rick she had brought from London, and entering the stall she placed it on a shelf at the back of Wildfire's box.

'I've brought him back to you,' she whispered to the horse, too choked with emotion to say any more.

Suddenly, she heard a sound behind her and turned round to see a young boy of about seventeen.

'I'm sorry to intrude, ma'am. Didn't know anyone was in here. My name's Daniel but everyone calls me Danny. My Uncle Abe owns this place.'

'Hello,' she said controlling herself and giving a faint smile. 'I was a friend of your cousin, Rick. We met in London. I was just passing and...'

'London? Is that London England? That's a long way off to be just passing through,' he interrupted. 'Your accent sure is cute.' He gave a cheeky grin.

Ignoring his jest, she responded 'I'm visiting Washington, and as I was so close I decided to visit Rick's family.'

He smiled and nodded. 'I was only a kid when Cousin Rick went off to war. My Pa lives in Kingston, upstate New York, but he doesn't visit here any more. Mom died when I was born. She was Uncle Abe's only sister.' Nodding towards the animal, he added, 'I see you have met Wildfire. He can be very stubborn sometimes. Only Rick was able to handle him.'

'I know. He told me how difficult Wildfire could be. Would it be all right if I rode him?'

'OK, but only if I come with you. He can be a bit flighty. There are some of cousin Judy's riding breeches, shirt and boots in the tack room. You wanna change in there?'

With the wind tearing at Susanne's hair and tears streaming down her cheeks, she urged Wildfire on, and he took off at a gallop, leaving Danny far behind. The horse seemed to know she wanted to be alone and raced into a belt of shadowy woodland where the ground was covered in violets. They slowed and eventually stopped. While Wildfire cropped at the grass, Susanne jumped down from the saddle and walked into the wood, picking the flowers, at peace with herself for the first time in years. With the reins slung over her arm, she led Wildfire deeper into the wood, both horse and woman breathing in the cool fragrant air. How she would have loved living here with Rick!

She heard Danny calling her name and leapt up into the saddle to join him.

'Were you lost?'

She had always felt lost without Rick, but since keeping the promise she had made to him to visit his home, she was content. Giving Danny a warm smile she replied, 'Not now.'

'I'll race you back to the stables,' he said, and they took off like the wind. 'I knew you would beat me,' she laughed when they arrived at the stables.

'Never give your opponent an even break' was Cousin Rick's favourite saying. That's what uncle Abe told me.'

While Mazy served lunch, Susanne was introduced to Abe, and out of the corner of her eye she observed him studying her instead of eating his food. Rick had more of a resemblance to his mother than his father, although he had had the same smile as Abe.

There was an uncomfortable silence around the table, and Susanne decided to try to lighten the atmosphere. She told them how Rick had taught her to ride and of the many times she had fallen off the horse, with Rick ordering her back in the saddle again. Then she went on to tell them about General Eisenhower's birthday party and about the rude naval sub-lieutenant Rick had put in a taxi. All her anecdotes had them laughing, and even Rick's father laughed heartily at her story.

'My dear lady, I've never enjoyed a meal as much as the one I had today, and it's because you are here. I can see from the sparkle in your eyes when you speak of Rick that you loved my son. It warms this old man's heart, I can tell you.'

'I loved all your stories, too,' Judy added with a grateful smile. 'Now, if you will excuse us, Danny and I have some work in the stables that needs attention.'

'Can I help, Judy?'

'No, please stay and have coffee with Pa. Back soon.'

'Would you like another coffee, Mr Carlon?' Susanne asked.

'Thanks. Let's talk about my son. And my name is Abe, OK?'

Smiling, she sat back in her chair and answered all his questions as honestly as she could.

'I sure wish you and Rick had married in London' he said. 'I could have had a grandson to leave the stud to. My sister's boy is going to get the place, and I hope the young rascal will manage it successfully.' He went on to tell her that his sister had died in childbirth, and young Danny had lived at the stud ever since. 'Danny's OK,' he continued, 'but it's not the same as a branch off my own tree.' He leaned over and whispered close to Susanne's ear for fear gossipy Mazy would be listening.

Feeling sorry for the old man, Susanne was tempted to tell him about her son in England, but that would be unfair to Danny as benefactor in Abe's will. Besides, she and Rick had not married, and she had no written proof that Rick was Edward's father. She hadn't even registered her son's birth. Informing the Carlons about Edward could tear the family apart, and she would be loathed for bringing an illegitimate son to their door. She knew that Rick would have told her to forget the whole thing and let sleeping dogs lie. That was precisely what she intended to do.

Stifling a yawn, Abe turned to Susanne. 'My dear lady, this old man has to retire for his afternoon nap. Please keep in touch with us, and whenever you come to the States pay us a visit. Say, why don't you stay over and we can talk some more, huh?'

Susanne leaned over the wheelchair to kiss Rick's father on the cheek. 'It was wonderful to meet you. Let's keep in touch.'

When Judy returned the two women talked over cups of coffee as if they were long-lost friends.

'I met President Eisenhower in Washington, some years ago' said Judy. My father and the President went to military school together. Pa was older than Dwight, but they remain friends to this day. However, now that he's President, he is far too busy, and with father in a wheelchair, they rarely meet. But they talk on the phone occasionally – Thanksgiving and Christmas.'

'Yes, I can imagine how busy he is. It was the same during the war. General Eisenhower shouldered all the problems. Rick told me that trying to get two countries on opposite sides of the Atlantic who share a common language to respect each other was a mammoth task, but it did not faze the General. He organised and hosted the British American Forces Dining Club. These dinners were successful in producing closer cooperation and greater understanding and mutual respect between the American and British top brass.'

Judy nodded. 'My father desperately wanted Rick to follow in his footsteps and encouraged him to apply for West Point. When the Japanese attacked the American fleet at Pearl Harbour, Rick had graduated from military school and was posted there. In 1942 he was promoted and went to London as part of General Eisenhower's staff. Father was so happy that Rick was a staff officer. Between you and me, I think Pa thought Rick wouldn't be in danger, but I believe no one is safe in war, not even civilians.'

'I agree. As an ambulance driver I saw schoolchildren,

women with babies and the elderly killed with bombs. I find it hard to forget, even now. The destruction of homes was terrible, and people were reduced to sleeping anywhere from scout halls to schools.'

'Did you lose any family?'

'No, but my friend June lost her parents. They were killed when a doodlebug crashed into their hotel and all the staff and customers were killed.'

'How terrible! Here on the mainland we didn't experience anything as bad as that, except for rationing gasoline and other products, but we got by.'

They drank more coffee, and Judy insisted Susanne stay overnight. However, as it was summertime it did not get dark until late, and she planned to be at Clare's place before nightfall.

Susanne was glad she had visited Rick's home. Now she could finally accept that while his death had shattered her, the grieving period was over. It had been hard to forget the man who had occupied her heart for so many years, but her visit to his birthplace had helped to make things clearer for her. Now she could move forward and stop living in the past, yearning for something she could never have.

Chapter Twenty Two

Six months after returning from Washington, Bernhard received a letter from the War Office in London informing him that the Soviet government had released some more German prisoners of war captured in Russia, and that his brother, Hans Roehder, was in a hospital in the British sector. The letter further stated that they would release him into the care of Dr Bernhard Roehder, the only surviving relative.

'I have to travel to Germany and bring my brother to Amboise' he told Susanne. 'According to the letter, he is desperately ill and needs constant care, but I won't know how sick he is until I can examine him myself.'

'Surely if he is desperately ill he needs hospital care?'

'Darling, he is the only family I have left. I must look after him. If Mutti were still alive I'm sure she would insist.'

'Bernhard, I am hardly qualified to look after a seriously-ill patient.'

'No one is asking you to. I am surprised at you,

Susanne. I have never known you to be so heartless. Hans has been through hell as a prisoner in Siberia and he deserves my professional help as a brother, and your compassion as a sister-in-law.'

'Who will look after him when you are at the laboratory? I might have been an ambulance driver during the war, but I only have basic first aid experience.'

'I will employ a day nurse to care for him. Yvette will prepare his meals, and I will keep him company in the evenings when I come home from the lab. Susanne, wouldn't we do the same for your family?'

Susanne was momentarily taken aback to hear him mention her family, having told him she was an orphan. She shook herself. He obviously meant Penny or June.

'How long will you be gone?'

'It will depend on the authorities and how soon it can be arranged. I'll join you as soon as I can.'

That was what he always said. There was always someone or somewhere more important he would rather be with than his wife. He only used her to accompany him to social gatherings or to preside over the many dinners they hosted. She shrugged her shoulders abjectly, wishing her marriage could be happier.

Bernhard was generous with his money. The South African shares he had given her from his mother were now worth a great deal, and added to this was the quarterly allowance he gave her for personal use. She loved the Mercedes he had bought her for a birthday gift last year. Through his generosity, she was slowly becoming financially independent, but there was a price to pay. They rarely spent any time together. If he wasn't rushing off to meetings he was working round the clock at the laboratory, and if a crisis developed he slept, showered and breakfasted there. Sometimes she would not see him for days, and when he was home he was often too tired to talk to her and fell asleep after dinner. Occasionally his secretary would telephone and ask Susanne to pack a bag and send it to the laboratory in a taxi, as her husband was jetting off again. When everything seemed to be going well at work and he had no urgent meetings, his regular game of golf or tennis with colleagues would take precedence.

Ten days after Bernhard left Amboise, he was back with an ambulance. He gave her a brief kiss, and supervised the ambulance officers carrying Hans upstairs to one of the guest bedrooms. Susanne caught only a brief glimpse of her brother-in-law.

Over the next few weeks Bernhard introduced a new system, and the household staff settled into a new routine. The nurse arrived each morning to attend to Hans' needs, washing him, changing his pyjamas and assisting him with breakfast prepared by Yvette. The patient appeared to sleep most of the day, until Bernard arrived home and went upstairs with an evening meal for his sick brother. Susanne was not required at all.

Her monthly lunch date with Emma Gordon was due, and as everything was running smoothly at home, Susanne saw no reason to cancel. Emma was married to one of the Scottish doctors on Bernhard's team. They went to a restaurant nearby, and were seated on a wonderful terrace, with a picturesque view of the Loire River. Susanne and Emma were enjoying an aperitif while waiting for the chef to join them to make his personal recommendation from the menu. This was a special service the restaurant offered to their regular patrons. They were still trying to choose from the menu when one of the waiters interrupted them.

'Madame, there is a telephone call for you at the desk.'

When Susanne put the telephone to her ear she heard Yvette asking her to please return home as soon as possible as the Doctor had been called away. She had finished preparing the evening meal and wanted to go home to her family.

'I will leave now and be with you as soon as possible. Susanne replaced the receiver, apologising to Emma she left the restaurant.

Susanne had scarcely opened the front door when Yvette came hurrying towards her.

'Madame Roehder, your husband has been called away. He asked me to give you this note and to wait until you returned. I have given the sick man something cool to drink. *Monsieur le Docteur* told me not to give his brother food until tonight, and so I left his meal in the refrigerator. There is also a seafood casserole for you, if you feel hungry. I will see you in the morning. *Au revoir*, Madam Susanne.'

After hearing the door close, Susanne went to her own room to change. Sitting on the bed, she opened Bernhard's note and read the familiar script.

Darling

I have to attend a symposium in Paris. They changed the dates at the last minute. I will be home at the end of the week. Please take care of Hans until I return. He can be a little abrupt. So do try and be gentle with him. I fear he hasn't got long to live. Will join you soon.

Bernhard

Susanne was angry with her husband. Not only had Bernhard gone off to Paris, leaving his dying brother in her care; he had told her nothing about Hans' condition or any medication he was to have. She just hoped the nurse would turn up in the morning. Trying to keep her feelings under control, she tossed the note on her dressing table and went to the kitchen to make a jug of coffee. Then she climbed the stairs and tapped gently on the door, just in case the patient was sleeping.

'Komm herein' said a weak voice.

She opened the door and stared open-mouthed at the skeleton lying in the bed. He was reed-thin, with sunken cheekbones, skin like parchment and dark eye sockets. One sleeve of his pyjama jacket hung loosely, and she quickly realised that his left arm was missing. Her heart went out to him. How he must have suffered in the Russian prison! This could not possibly be the handsome boy with golden curls and brilliant blue eyes she remembered from Mutti's photograph album. She felt sorry for him.

As soon as he opened his mouth her pity vanished.

'*Ach*, you are an improvement on that other *femme* – she had no *Arsch*, no *Busen*.'

He was mixing English, French and German words, together making her wonder if he was delirious. She chose to ignore his crudeness.

'I have brought some coffee,' she said, setting the tray down. 'I am Bernhard's wife. My name is Susanne, and if you could please speak English I would appreciate it.'

'You English expect us to learn your language because you are too lazy to learn ours. And you call us arrogant. Ha! My father made me study languages when I was a boy, and I practised English to pass the time. Come, come closer.'

She did as he asked. 'How do you feel?'

'You can see how I look. How do you think I feel?'

Susanne was startled not only at his rudeness, but the way he spoke and looked at her; but Bernhard had warned her.

'Is there anything you want, Herr Roehder?'

'You should call me Sturmbannführer Roehder.' His eyes travelled over her face and swept down to her breasts, an ugly leer appearing on his face. 'Once, I would have known how to answer your question, but now, it is too late. You are the first desirable woman I have seen for over ten years, I didn't fancy any of those fat Russian cows.'

Despite herself, Susanne felt herself blush. How was she going to cope with this awful man? Pouring a cup of coffee and placing it on his bedside table, she said, 'Well, I'll leave you now. I will see you in the morning.'

'*Nein, nein.* I have forgotten my manners with the ladies after all these years. Come sit with me. I would like to talk with you.'

His words pleaded for her to stay, and once again pity for him overruled her judgement. She relented and sat down on a chair, carefully pulling her skirt down and reminding herself to dress from ankle to neck whenever she came into this room in future.

'You must have suffered dreadfully.'

'I was in a prisoner of war camp in Siberia. I was there for over ten years. The Ivans worked us to death and gave us very little food. So we made stew with rats. There were many, many rats in the camp. They gave us one bucket of water a day for twenty men, which the Ivans pissed in it before they brought it to our hut.'

Revulsion ran through her. Once again she felt sorrow and sympathy for him over the treatment the Russians had subjected him to.

'Can you tell me what happened to you?' she asked, eyeing the empty sleeve.

'Shell blast. I was unconscious and taken to a field hospital. My left arm was hanging by a thread. So they amputated.' He sneered, 'That shell saved my life.'

She looked at him questioningly. He stared at her for a long time.

'I was a Sturmbannführer in the Leibstandarte SS.' His body stiffened into a proud, arrogant posture. 'You would call that a Major in the English Life Guards, but I was not a toy soldier sitting on a horse. Our regiment was the finest in the Waffen-SS. We were the bravest soldiers in the world. The Ivans were afraid of us, so much so that if they captured one of us, it was a bullet in the head. It was no use trying to change our identities, as we all had a tattoo of our blood group on our left arm, a fact that was known to the enemy. When the Ivans advanced and captured our command post, they were shooting anyone with a Waffen-SS uniform. I was stuck in a field hospital, and so I took the identity of a Hauptmann in the Wehrmacht who had just died. I stole his uniform and Soldbuch, and that's why I survived.'

Susanne was shocked to hear that Bernhard's brother had been an SS officer. She had seen the newsreels about the atrocities the SS had committed, especially in concentration camps. To actually be in the company of one of those monsters horrified her.

'It was lucky that our father insisted both Bernhard and I should learn languages, and it was because I could speak Russian that I was allowed to live and act as an interpreter for the German prisoners and the Russian guards. So, you see, I am lucky to be alive.' His face crumpled in pain. 'Why do you stare at me?' he growled at her.

'You look so ill and are obviously in pain. Shall I call a doctor?'

'I will have no frog doctor. Bernhard should be here.' He tried to sit up and grimaced, refusing to admit he was in pain.

She hurried over to the bed to give him some assistance. He held onto the sleeve of her blouse. Despite his weakened condition, he was surprisingly strong, and she could feel his grip on her arm.

'I have had many women, from many countries, but never an English rose' he said.

'I am your brother's wife. Please let go of my arm!' she said, pulling the material of her blouse. Eventually he let go. Susanne was relieved.

'I was shocked to hear that Bernhard had married one of the enemy. However, I have to admit he has good taste. You are a real prize. A few years ago, I would have overpowered you, ignored your screams, and fucked you, brother or no brother.' He smiled to himself as he visualised her struggling, begging and pleading for him to stop. 'The days when I took any woman I wanted, willing or not, are over. Now all I have are memories of what could have been, if the Reich had battered the British into the dust, slaughtered the Russians and sent the Americans home, bloody and beaten. Germany would have ruled the world.'

'I think you are vulgar and sick, sick in the head!' she snapped back. 'I am supposed to look after you until Bernhard returns and that is what I intend doing. So you can shut up, you, you awful man.' Susanne picked the jug up from the dressing table and banged it down on the table next to his bed, spilling the coffee. 'Help yourself.'

He had made her lose her temper, a thing she rarely did unless provoked, and she wondered why he had done it. Trying to calm herself, she deliberately made an unhurried retreat to show him that she was not afraid. Susanne slowly closed the bedroom door, his cruel, mocking laugh ringing in her ears. How could Bernhard have left that awful creature in her care?

Hans' laughter died away once she had gone. He did not want any female seeing him weak and helpless, especially a sweet little Englishwoman. He coughed and coughed, although it sounded more like a dog barking. Phlegm ran down his chin, and he wiped it on his sleeve. He knew he was slowly losing his grip on life and was glad he was going to die in a clean warm bed and not in that terrible rat-infested slave camp in Siberia.

Shaking more with anger than fear, Susanne hurried to the safety of her own bedroom and locked the door as a precaution. She took a relaxing bath and went to bed. She slept fitfully and woke up feeling anything but refreshed.

In the kitchen the next morning she made some tea and warmed some fresh croissants the baker had delivered. It was Yvette's day off and the nurse had been and gone. Susanne wasn't in the mood to prepare breakfast for the odious man upstairs. However, she gradually changed her mind when she remembered he did not have long to live.

Opening the bedroom door, she almost dropped the tray. He was sitting on the edge of the bed, his spindly legs draped across the quilt. He was naked.

'*Guten Morgen.* You are not too scared of me to bring my food.'

'No, I am not,' she said putting the tray on a small table with a casualness she was far from feeling. 'I expect Bernhard home soon.'

'My brother is a weakling. He kept enemy soldiers alive

with medicines, while I won the Iron Cross for killing them.' He told her how proud the German Army was of their early conquests in Russia. He bragged about the peasant girls who welcomed the conquerors with open arms and what happened to the ones that hadn't. She learned about the slaughter and carnage, and the terrible effect the winter snows had on both starving soldiers and civilians. Susanne had been through the blitz and heard other stories of warfare from Percy, and sea battles from Malcolm, but nothing like this. She was slowly coming to the realisation that the struggles and losses of people she knew and loved during the war had been worthwhile – even the sacrifice of her beloved Rick. Before her was a member of the 'master race' that had wanted to dominate the world. Thank God they had failed.

And now she was married to one. Susanne mentally shook herself. She knew Bernhard was not the kind of man given to wanton violence. The deathly pale man in bed was her husband's brother and both of them had blue eyes and blond hair, but there the similarity ended.

The next evening Hans started to reminisce about his days with the Waffen-SS. Susanne sat down, gripped with morbid curiosity to learn all the disgusting details, and was riveted to the chair. Contempt fought with compassion for control of her feelings. He was ill, as Bernhard had said, but Susanne felt he was mentally ill. Looking at him, she knew he was as weak as a kitten. Therefore she felt reasonably safe, but she dearly hoped that Bernhard would soon return.

Suddenly he coughed violently, his body arched with a spasm of pain. He sank back against the pillows and closed his eyes.

'I am tired, all this talking.'

Thankfully, Susanne rose from the chair, glad for an excuse to leave, but as she crept towards the door she heard him whisper, '*Danke*, Susanne.'

Each evening Susanne was drawn to the dying man's room. Her feelings alternated between pity for Hans because of the deprivation he had endured in the Siberian prison camp, and loathing for the horrific stories of terrible executions he and his fellow officers had presided over. He told her that when the Waffen-SS were ordered to clear a village, not even a cat or dog was left alive, and the village was burned to the ground. He seemed to be talking as if he wanted to get it all off his chest before he died. A kind of confession. He was getting weaker every day, and she knew he did not have long to live.

When carrying his evening coffee upstairs a few nights later, she knocked on the door. There was no familiar '*Komm herein*.' Entering the room, she saw him lying there motionless. His eyes were half-open, but she knew he was dead.

Feeling sad but relieved, she went to the telephone and called Bernhard's office. She was informed that Bernhard was staying at the Hotel Meurice in Paris. Susanne rang the hotel and was connected to his room.

'Allo,' a female voice answered the telephone.

'Est-ce que c'est la chambre du Docteur Roehder?'

'*Oui*, it is Paulette speaking, Madame Roehder.' Then Bernhard's voice came on. 'Hello, darling, my secretary is taking some dictation. How are you?'

Susanne told him about the death of his brother, and Bernhard assured her he would be home early the next morning. She spent a restless night alone, haunted by thoughts of the dead SS-Sturmbannführer lying in the room down the hall.

Chapter Twenty Three

'Dinner has been waiting hours, darling. Where have you been?'

'I got held up at the lab. What's all the fuss?'

'You could have telephoned to tell me you would be late. I was worried.'

'I've told you before,' he interrupted. 'Do not worry about me. You knew what my profession was when we married and you also knew that my work has priority. Nothing is more important, and that includes a late dinner with an irate wife. '

'How dare you! It is your complete disregard for our marriage that is the cause of the trouble.'

'Nonsense. It is your refusal to accept that I have something other than you to occupy my time. I just wish that you would find an interesting hobby. You got bored with the French lessons and stopped going to classes. Why not pop over to London and do some shopping? Just leave me alone.'

'I will go to London, and I may not come back. Or

perhaps I'll go to the villa at Golfe-Juan, but I refuse to remain here waiting for you to decide to grace the dinner table with your presence. Bernhard, I'm leaving.'

'Shall I ring for a taxi?'

It was the final straw. As she took a step backward and stared at him, disgust written on her face, tears were not far away. 'Please leave,' she said, before turning away from him and hurrying to the master bedroom, where she locked the door with a decisive click. Lying down on the bed, tears trickled down her face. How could he speak to her like that? How could he treat her like that? Perhaps he had been drinking. She knew some of the doctors indulged in a glass or two of the local wine, discussing current projects, before leaving the laboratory for the weekend.

When she had married Bernard, she had not been head-over-heels in love with him, but her love had grown as she had come to know him better. She had begun to idolise the man, his brilliant mind and his work. Susanne was proud of him.

Suddenly, the front door slammed, and she knew he had left.

The next morning while soaking in the bath, the ringing of the telephone had her reaching for a towel and hurrying from the bathroom into the bedroom, thinking it was Bernhard. Instead, it was her fifteen-year-old daughter's voice on the other end of the telephone. It had been months since Susanne had seen her, but she was kept informed of her progress by June. Penny was doing well at Kensington Girls' College and had passed all her examinations, including French and German.

'Hello, Mummy, how are you?'

'I am well, darling. I'm planning a trip to London soon. I'll leave a message with June, and we will meet for lunch.'

'Oh, super.'

She could sense that her daughter was troubled. 'Is everything fine with you?'

'I had another run-in with Daddy's wife. She really is awful. Everything I do is wrong, and I am unable to please her. Honestly, Mummy, I do try but she's so moody.'

'Perhaps you should avoid her, especially when she's in one of her moods.'

'She's always like that, and I do steer clear, honestly. I visit Aunt June as often as I can, and then I catch the train to Brighton once a month to visit Nana and Pop. I stay for the weekend and catch the Sunday train back to London. I try to keep away from her as much as possible. I call her 'Gloom and Doom' and it really suits her. Look, Mummy, the main reason I'm calling, some of the girls at college are going to Switzerland to do a finishing course, and I wondered if you would pay for me to go.'

'Don't you think fifteen is a bit young to go to a finishing school, Penny?'

'Gosh, Mummy, you are old-fashioned! I'm nearly sixteen and quite grown-up. Besides, Gaby is six months younger and her father, Admiral Walters, is allowing her to go. Oh, please, Mummy, say yes.'

'Gaby! What kind of name is that?'

Penny laughed. 'Mummy honestly, her name is Gabriele, but everyone at school calls her Gaby.'

'What does your father have to say about the finishing school?'

'Oh, the usual, 'Ask the Duchess. She can afford it.' You know what he's like, Mummy.' Penny mimicked Michael's accent perfectly.

'Very well, send me the details and I'll arrange it.'

'Thanks, Mummy, you're a brick.'

Susanne put the telephone down, wondering why she was paying expensive school fees to have her daughter say such things as, 'Thanks, you're a brick.' Pangs of regret and painful memories always surfaced whenever she thought about her daughter. Bernhard knew about Penny, but they had never met. Whenever Penny visited Amboise he was always away at a conference, and when she visited her daughter in London he remained in France. Susanne had never planned to keep them apart; it just happened that way.

Edward had never been to France to visit her, and Susanne did not know why. Each time she invited him, he just shrugged and said he preferred it when she came to visit him. He enjoyed living with the Millers and going to Tenterden College. It was an excellent boys' school, and the boarding fees were reasonable.

Susanne had always thought that the Millers had taken care of Edward's personal expenses, but when she told them she was now in a position to repay them for their generosity, she was astounded to discover that Harry had been paying all along. She had written immediately to Hayward Hall, only to have her letter returned unopened.

Perhaps Harry's wife, his mother or his awful sister had sent it back.

Then she wrote to his regiment and received a reply to the effect that Major Fortescue had resigned his commission and had given Hayward Hall as his forwarding address. Perhaps he was living abroad somewhere, or back in India; she just didn't know. Finally, Susanne contacted the school, took over paying the fees for Edward and sent the Millers a letter, asking them to forward any expenses they had incurred for her son.

This was of deep concern. How was she going to pay Harry back when she could not even get in touch with him? She had even written to Tom Marsh, the estate manager. He had replied that Harry was not at the Hall. The last he had heard, Master Harry was abroad, and he didn't know when or if he would be returning. She would have liked to keep in touch with Harry but she was married, and if memory serves her correct, he had married a Colonel's daughter in India. Maybe it was just as well she could not contact him.

She had just put the telephone down when Bernhard appeared in the doorway with an astonished look on his face. He rarely came home from the laboratory during the day. Susanne was suspicious and hoped there was not going to be another argument, like the previous night. She watched him walking to the French windows that overlooked the garden, and suddenly he turned towards the other side of the sitting room. Susanne stared at him with a look of concern on her face.

'What on earth is wrong, Bernhard?'

Completely ignoring her, Bernhard continued to walk up and down, throwing punches into the air with a clenched fist, repeating, 'I just can't believe it. I just can't believe it.'

'If it's about the argument we had, I would like to apologise for suggesting that you leave your own home.'

Laughing out loud, he said. 'You will not believe it. You will not.' He was acting very strangely.

'Darling, please stop marching up and down and tell me.'

He came to an abrupt halt. 'I cannot, until we have champagne. I'm off to the wine cellar. I will join you soon.'

His manner was very odd, to say the least, and she wondered if she should telephone the laboratory or call his general practitioner, Alain, who was a close friend. Perhaps Bernhard was having some kind of mental breakdown. He had been working long hours on an important project, and whenever she telephoned the laboratory she was informed that he could not be disturbed and could she leave a message.

'I've found a 1945 vintage. That was a good year,' he commented, wiping the dusty bottle. 'Get some glasses, quickly.'

Hurrying into the dining room, she unlocked a Louis XVIII cabinet, which displayed crystal glassware. 'A good year?' she mumbled. All 1945 had left behind was dust, death and grief. Returning to the sitting room with the glasses on a silver tray, she gave him a concerned look before resting the tray on a side table.

'Are you sure we should be drinking champagne so early in the day? Especially as you don't seem to be yourself.'

'Darling, whatever do you mean? I'm not myself? I will have you know that *Docteur en Médecin* Bernhard Roehder has just received the 'Magic Call' informing him he has been awarded the Nobel Prize.' He poured the champagne and gave her a glass. 'To your Nobel Laureate husband.' Then he started to tell her what the Nobel Prize presentation entailed.

Susanne could not wipe the smile off her face. It all sounded very regal. They would travel to Stockholm and she would be sitting in the auditorium when Bernhard was presented with his award by King Gustaf. It was a great honour for Bernhard as Director. Doctor Henri Lamboley and Doctor Angus Gordon were sharing the honour. The three men had developed a drug that would stimulate the immune system, attack and destroy parasites and dangerous bacteria, from poisoning cells in human beings.

'Congratulations, darling.' Susanne threw her arms around Bernhard and kissed him. 'I'm so proud of you. If anyone deserves this honour it is you, with your dedication and all your hard work and the many days and nights spent at the lab.'

'I didn't do it alone. Henri and Angus put as much work into this project as I did, and it was they who urged me to publish the findings. I have to go back to the lab now. Let's celebrate tonight and go somewhere special, darling. Telephone de Laval and book a table.'

After Bernhard had left to return to the laboratory, Susanne picked up the schedule from the coffee table and started to read. The awards ceremony would open the formal proceedings, followed by a formal dinner at the Royal Stockholm City Hall, with a grand ball to close the awards evening. Susanne was very excited, and had already started to think about having a gown made by the famous couturier Balenciaga of Paris. A small tiara would be almost mandatory at such a regal banquet, and as she had never worn one, she was determined to take advantage of the opportunity.

After looking at the calendar, she worked out that she had almost three months until the awards night. That would mean a few trips to Paris, choosing materials plus fittings. In addition, she had to buy matching evening shoes and purse, and made a note to discuss hairstyles with her favourite coiffeur.

The elegant ball-gown was a classic A-line in charmeuse satin, the same colour as her violet eyes, with the bodice of the gown encrusted with small sparkling crystals. It fitted her to perfection. There were silver-heeled shoes and jewellery. Her thick dark hair was swept up high on her crown into an elegant bun, encircled with a small silver tiara. Susanne had chosen Mutti's silver fox fur to wear, as she knew it would please Bernhard.

'Darling, who are you planning to enchant tonight? You look absolutely exquisite,' Bernhard complimented her, as he fiddled with his bow tie. 'Where are we meeting the others?'

She smiled at his approval. It had been a long time since he had offered any praise about what she was wearing.

'I believe downstairs in the cocktail bar.'

'Then let's go.'

'Before we leave, I would like to give you this.' She smiled and presented him with a silver cuff-link box with his initials engraved upon it.

'This is a wonderful gift, darling. I'll treasure it always.'

'I am thrilled that you are a Nobel Laureate.'

'Thanks darling, If they give a prize for the loveliest woman tonight, you will easily win.' Bernhard gave her a big smile as he opened their hotel room door and escorted his wife to the cocktail bar downstairs.

After they had been officially welcomed, Bernhard and the other Laureates were led away, leaving their families to find their seats in the body of the auditorium, with the help of an usher. Susanne gazed upon the floral decorated stage where red velvet chairs for all the Nobel Laureates were set out in symmetrical order. Slightly to the left was a special seat for the King of Sweden.

Just before the ceremony started, Susanne went off to the ladies' powder room, which she found empty. She had just closed the door of the cubicle when she heard someone entering the room.

'*Mon Dieu!* Susanne Roehder and her husband! I loathe them both.'

'You surprise me. I have always found Susanne to be pleasant and friendly, and very kind. '

'I disagree. She is just a powder puff. My Henri should have got the top job at the institute, not Bernhard Roehder. Little does the silly woman know that her husband and his secretary, Paulette, had a convivial meeting at the Paris conference – very convivial indeed.'

'I'm sure you are mistaken.'

'I was in Paris at the same hotel. And from what I saw there was no mistake.'

Susanne recognised the voice of Madame Lamboley, whose husband, Henri, had been overlooked for the Director's job in favour of Bernhard. She knew her to be both unpleasant and sometimes downright vindictive. Susanne had tried in vain at social occasions to make friends with her, but had been rebuffed each time.

The revelation about Bernhard and his secretary came as a shock, and Susanne had no idea whether it was true, or if that awful woman was just being spiteful. Bernhard, Henri and Angus and their wives had all travelled to Stockholm together. It was one of the worst journeys Susanne had ever endured. Adèle Lamboley had monopolised the conversation, leaving the rest of the group nodding their heads and trying to hide their boredom – except Bernhard, who had his nose stuck in a medical journal and completely ignored everyone. Eventually Henri Lamboley intervened, thrusting a magazine at his wife and telling her to read quietly. The atmosphere suddenly became peaceful.

The other voice belonged to Emma Gordon. At least she had tried to defend her. As Susanne heard the women leave, she went into the other room, washed her hands and sat down before the mirror. A small doubt lingered in her mind. Could there be some truth in that woman's malicious words? Her mind went into a spin, trying to come to grips with what Adèle Lamboley had said. What action, if any, should she take? She could start by checking his diaries both at home and at his office, and even telephoning the hotel to find out how many people had occupied her husband's room.

If only she hadn't been looking after his dying brother, she would have travelled to Paris with him. Susanne mentally shook herself as she heard the announcements being made, followed by loud applause, and hurried into the auditorium, taking her seat next to Emma Gordon to watch the presentations. Susanne sucked her bottom lip. Should she hire a private detective to get the information she longed for, yet dreaded?

'My dear, are you feeling unwell?'

'A minor headache, that's all.' She did not want to tell Emma that she had overheard everything in the ladies' room.

'Wasn't it wonderful to see the Laureates receive their prize from the King? Shouldn't we now be making our way to the Golden Hall? Oh, isn't this too, too exciting?' Receiving no answer, Emma said, 'Take these headache tablets, my dear, and let's go and find our husbands.'

Dropping the pills in her evening bag, Susanne smiled. 'I'll take them later.'

As the guests walked toward the foyer, Susanne came

to her senses. She would only ruin Bernhard's evening if she insisted on returning to the hotel. Banishing her misery, she put on a performance for the rest of the evening that would have rivalled the best actors in Hollywood. She laughed merrily at Bernhard's witticisms as they entered the banquet room, and gazed at the splendour of candelabra rising from the flower-bedecked tables. While the meal looked superb, she ate a little soup and the salmon but refused the beef and sipped a small glass of fruit punch. While desserts were being served, the entertainment started with students from the Swedish School of Music playing dramatic compositions of Ture Rangström. The three-hour banquet concluded with all the Nobel Laureates giving short speeches concerning their respective awards. Bernhard ended his by thanking the Nobel committee and then said that his wife deserved the biggest accolade as she had helped him enormously. A thunderous applause followed. Susanne was surprised, especially when Bernhard stretched out his arm to indicate the table where she was sitting, and many heads turned to glance at her.

'I wish Angus paid me compliments like that,' Emma whispered to Susanne. 'If I scaled Everest blindfolded, he wouldn't acknowledge me as Bernhard has just done. You are very lucky to have married such a considerate man.'

The orchestra started playing a waltz in the ballroom, and while some of the men remained in the banquet room sipping cognac others decided to join the dancers. When Susanne entered the ballroom she occupied a chair near a small buffet table that had been set up, she discovered, for anyone who was still peckish. Susanne could see no possible reason why anyone could still have an appetite after that sumptuous repast.

She was still brooding about what she had overheard earlier in the ladies' powder room and, was trying to decide when or if she would confront Bernhard. Obviously, she would not do it tonight. Her deep reflections were interrupted when Bernhard with a warm smile invited his wife to dance.

'I couldn't miss the opportunity of dancing with the loveliest woman in the ballroom.' Susanne summoned up a smile and thanked Bernhard for the compliment, but her mind was elsewhere. They continued to dance in silence.

Returning to the hotel, she yawned several times before saying she was tired. Excusing herself, she went to bed. Susanne did not want to spoil Bernhard's evening. She felt that if she remained in her husband's company, he would question her about the evening, her concerns would creep out, and the night would probably end in a blazing row. She had almost made up her mind to find some evidence before speaking to her husband about his secretary, or perhaps she should just ignore that awful woman's vicious accusations. Susanne decided to sleep on it and make a decision in the morning.

Chapter Twenty Four

Adèle Lamboley had been wrong about Bernhard and his secretary having an affair. When Susanne finally broached the subject, Bernhard told her that Madame Lamboley's words were nothing but a tissue of lies spoken out of jealousy. He further explained that Paulette had left the institute to marry a Swiss doctor. He even invited Susanne to the laboratory to meet his new secretary, a plump, middle-aged French woman called Maxine.

Shortly after Christmas, Susanne's daughter, now sixteen, suddenly appeared on the doorstep in tears.

'Mummy, can I stay with you for a while? I just loathe living with Daddy and his bitchy wife.'

'Please don't call any woman that, Penny. What about school?'

'I'm not smart enough to go to university. I left school and took a secretarial course. I hope to find employment doing some kind of office work.'

'I don't know what Bernhard will say,' Susanne replied, but she need not have worried. Bernhard was happy to allow Penny to live with them temporarily, and he was pleasantly surprised when Penny spoke to him in German. And, with her fluency in French, she had no trouble securing a job as a secretary to the manager of a wine wholesaler. She made some new friends and was even learning to drive. Her daughter was as happy and carefree as any girl of sixteen should be.

On Penny's seventeenth birthday, Susanne and Bernhard took her out for dinner to an exclusive supper club. After dancing with his wife, Bernhard danced with his stepdaughter. Penny had her first taste of champagne and caviar. Later, she opened a black suede box with the name of a Paris jeweller emblazoned upon it and discovered a gold bracelet resting on white satin. She hugged and kissed both her mother and her stepfather, telling them it was the best birthday ever.

Towards the end of the Ski season Bernhard booked one last holiday before the season ended, and the trio went to the French Alps to spend five days on the ski slopes. Unfortunately, Susanne caught a cold and decided to remain indoors for a few days. Bernhard took Penny on the slopes each morning to teach her how to ski. Throughout the following months the three of them were frequent visitors to the theatre and dinner parties, and most weekends during the summer were spent at Golfe-Juan sailing. During this time, Penny met one or two nice young men, and Susanne was happy for her daughter. Over the years, she had not spent a lot of time with Penny and now she was making up for it.

Stretching lazily, Susanne yawned. It was Sunday morning and very early, as the room was in semi-darkness. She slipped lower beneath the linen sheets, stretching and yawning, feeling the softness of the material against her skin. She was happier than she had been in a long time and sighed with contentment. She would get up as soon as it was light. They always had a casual lunch in a local restaurant every Sunday, and Bernhard preferred a light early morning breakfast, followed by a late lunch.

Gently moving her hand across the snowy sheet, she was surprised to find he was not in bed with her. Swinging her legs to the floor and slipping her feet into heeled slippers, Susanne opened the shutters to look out on a beautiful, cloud-free morning.

She knew Bernhard would be in his study working. Since he had won the Nobel Prize, his workload had increased, and she felt that if he carried on working non-stop he could make himself ill. He had received several job offers from pharmaceutical companies. The firm he was currently employed with had suggested increasing the size of both laboratory and technical staff and had offered Bernhard a senior management position, in charge of project performance and project success of all staff. Susanne was concerned about Bernhard's enormous workload. She thought he was taking on too much.

She decided to go to the kitchen and make some coffee. They could both go onto the terrace and spend some much-needed time together and enjoy watching the sunrise.

Not finding him in his study, she returned upstairs.

Hearing muffled sounds from Penny's room she went forward, opened the door, switched on the light - and screamed.

Her husband and her daughter were in bed together, naked and locked in a passionate embrace.

Shocked and distraught, Susanne could not confront them. Instead, she fled downstairs out onto the terrace, taking in great gasps of air. Disbelief made way for sadness, and she dissolved into heart-wrenching tears.

Susanne did not know how long she had been standing there. Time did not matter.

'Mummy, I'm sorry.'

Her daughter's words barely registered. Susanne's mind was reeling with the pain of seeing them together. Bernhard was old enough to be Penny's father! How immoral could a man be to seduce an innocent seventeen-year-old girl? She was full of loathing for him.

'Mummy, please.'

Wiping her eyes, she turned to her daughter. 'How long has this been going on?'

'Bernhard and I fell in love. He's so wonderful. I love him.'

'What do you know of love? He's despicable, and you should have repulsed his advances.' She could not bring herself to use her husband's or her daughter's name.

'I'll tell you what's despicable,' her daughter yelled back. 'When I was born you dumped me on Nana and Pop and ran off with an American. I heard all about you and Aunt June picking up men. I was spoiling all your fun. So you got rid of me. You never cared for me at all, did you?

'Who told you this nonsense?'

'Daddy.'

'I should have guessed. I did care for you, but I fell ill and could not take you with me. Nana and Pop offered to look after you.'

'I don't believe you.'

'I don't care what you believe. Go and pack your things.'

'I won't. I love Bernhard and he loves me and I'm staying right here.'

She stared at her daughter's mutinous expression. Tess had spoiled her, just as she had spoiled Michael. Penny was a tall, attractive girl with curly sandy hair and hazel eyes. Susanne could well imagine Bernhard turning her daughter's head, teaching her to play tennis, golf, sailing and skiing, eating in expensive restaurants, ordering the best champagne, dancing in candlelit supper clubs and whispering French and Italian love poems. Hadn't it turned her head ten years before?

'I love him, and I want to marry him just as soon as he can get rid of you!' she screamed at her mother before turning and running from the terrace.

By late afternoon Susanne's nerves had steadied. Bernhard had telephoned from the laboratory. He wanted to apologise and explain, but she told him that anything he had to say would have to wait until Penny returned to London. When he had rung off, she dialled June's number and asked her to catch the overnight train from London. Susanne would meet her at Gare du Nord, have breakfast with her in Paris and hop on the public transit service to Tours, where her car would be parked to take them to Amboise.

While Penny was out, Susanne packed her daughter's suitcase, stripped the sheets from the bed and burnt them in the basement furnace. Then she bathed, changed and telephoned Yvette to ask her if she could do extra hours the next day and look after Penny. Susanne wanted to get an early start if she was to meet June at the station, and she needed Yvette to keep an eye on her daughter until she returned.

Early the next morning she met June. The two of them went to a café and ordered croissants and coffee.

'Michael doesn't want her back – well, at least not to stay for any length of time' said June. 'His obnoxious wife has threatened to walk out if Penny is to live with them on a permanent basis. Don't worry, she can have a room with me until she gets a job, and then I'll help her look for a place of her own. It was a madhouse at Victoria Station…'

A sad look in Susanne's eyes stopped June in her tracks. 'Sorry for prattling on, blossom. What are your plans?'

'I really cannot talk to Bernhard while Penny is in the house. He owes me an explanation, and beyond that I really don't know.' She did not add that her husband had spent the night at the laboratory.

'If you ask me, it takes two to tango, and I don't think our Miss Penny is as innocent as you think. Michael was one for the ladies, if you remember, and his daughter, it seems, is a chip off the old block.'

'I know, but June, Bernhard's in his forties, old enough to be her father. You'd think he'd have more sense. And Penny told me she was in love. A mere slip of a girl, saying she's in love with a middle-aged man. It's preposterous!'

'When did men ever have sense where women are concerned? Especially, young, attractive, silly girls like Penny who are easily impressed. He'd only have to wear his prestigious Nobel medallion around his neck and nothing else. I'll bet most girls would drop their drawers. There's just no accounting for taste, I'm afraid.'

For the first time since catching both her daughter and husband in bed, Susanne smiled, something she thought could never happen to her again. June was as blunt as ever. Susanne liked her very much, and was grateful for the help she had given her on more than one occasion.

'Please take this,' she said, pushing an envelope towards June.

'Is it money?'

'Actually, it's two tickets to Nassau. You deserve a holiday, and I would appreciate it if you took Penny with you. I just want her out of the way while I deal with this awful mess. If she's in London she may try and phone Bernhard or me, or attempt to return to Amboise and I couldn't handle that.'

' I agree. Thanks for the tickets. I've never been to Bahamas. I'll take Penny with me, even if I have to drag her there.'

'Ten days in the sun, relax and enjoy it.' Susanne would love to get away too, but that would have to wait. 'Now we really must leave,' she said, finishing her coffee.

Later, when Susanne and June walked in through the front door, they discovered that Bernhard was in his study. Penny was in her room sobbing rather loudly, prompting Susanne to knock on the study door.

'What has happened?'

Bernhard called out that he was on the telephone, and a few minutes later joined his wife and June in the sitting room.

'Penny doesn't want to return to London, I told her she couldn't remain here and she ran off to her room.' He turned a sombre face to June. 'There's a train leaving at seven this evening. June. I know you've had a long journey, but could you please leave tonight with Penny?'

'Of course, Bernhard.'

'I took the liberty of booking and paying for you and Penny; you're in first class.'

'Darling,' he said, turning to his wife, who had her back towards him, gazing out of the window, 'I have some work to catch up on. I'll be in my study. Later, I will drive to the station to make sure Penny doesn't cause trouble.' Then he retreated into his study.

Yvette informed Susanne that lunch was ready in the dining room, adding in a low whisper that neither Mademoiselle Blore nor Monsieur Roehder would be joining them for lunch. Susanne asked Yvette to take a food tray to her daughter and to her husband. When Yvette had placed the serving dishes and a bottle of wine on the table she left the dining-room. June stopped talking for a little while and tucked into lunch, whereas Susanne barely touched hers.

Opening the conversation, June said, 'Bernhard seems very determined that Penny must return to London. Do you suppose they've had words? Perhaps it was only a casual fling.'

Susanne winced at June's remark. Ever since finding them together, her mind was numb, and her nerves were stretched to breaking point. She felt as if she was in some horrendous nightmare. Susanne thought there were no words to describe her world being torn apart. She just wanted to be alone, curl up in her misery and lick her wounds. Instead she murmured, 'If you'll excuse me, I must go and lie down. I didn't sleep at all last night.'

'Of course, blossom. I understand. I'll see to Penny.'

The meaning behind June's words was not lost on Susanne; she knew precisely what June meant. With Penny sobbing her heart out in the bedroom and Bernhard listening to the weeping girl in his study, anything was possible. Feeling exhausted, Susanne undressed. She knew Bernhard kept some sleeping pills, which he used occasionally, in the drawer of his bedside table. She had never taken a sleeping pill before, but there was a first time for everything. Swallowing the pill with a glass of water, she lay down on the bed and closed her eyes to blot out the pain of the past twenty-four hours.

'Darling, please wake up' said Bernhard. 'I have a tea-tray with some sandwiches. Yvette tells me you haven't eaten today.'

Food was the last thing Susanne wanted. 'I'm not

hungry, but the tea would be nice. What time is it?' she asked stifling a yawn.

'Five o'clock, we must to leave shortly. Or, would you rather stay here? I'll take them, to the station.'

The one thing she did not want was her daughter begging Bernhard for permission to remain in France.

'No, I'd rather come with you. I'll shower and change. Won't be long.' Swinging her legs to the floor, she went a little unsteadily into the en suite clutching the cup and saucer, leaving Bernhard still holding the tray. She had slept for several hours, but was far from feeling refreshed. Rather, she felt detached, as if this was all happening to someone else.

Susanne sat in the front seat of Bernhard's Jaguar while June and Penny occupied the rear, not a word was uttered until they arrived at the station, where Bernhard instructed a porter to take the luggage to the waiting train.

Dropping her shoulder bag to the ground, Penny stood behind her aunt, her mother and her lover. She felt unwanted and unloved, watching her mother and lover saying their final farewells to Aunt June and ignoring her. When the guard signalled imminent departure June hopped on the train, and waited for Penny to join her. Her daughter gave her a peck on the cheek, murmuring something inaudible. Then, turning and throwing her arms around Bernhard's neck and with tears streaming down her face, she said. '*Adieu*, darling. I will always love you.'

Bernhard pulled Penny's arms from around his neck, pushed Penny through the doorway of the train and slammed it shut, seconds before the train left the station. Susanne turned away, disgusted at the behaviour of her daughter, and walked out to the car, leaving Bernhard to follow.

'Darling, we need to talk' he said. 'Let's eat out.'

'I'm going home. You can go where you want.' She lifted her arm to hail a taxi.

He grabbed hold of her and turned her around to face him. His brow was furrowed, his shoulders were hunched and there was pain in his eyes.

'Susanne, let's go home together.'

Scalding tears of betrayal ran down her cheeks. Not only for her, but also for the man she loved and admired. He embraced her with tears in his eyes, and they both stood for a long time outside the station, Susanne wrapped in his arms. She had never seen a grown man cry before, but his tears could not soften her aching heart. Suddenly, he released her, saying they would discuss this at home. Helping his wife into the passenger seat Bernhard drove home at a furious pace.

'Can you tell me how long you and my daughter have been lovers?' she asked when they were seated on the terrace with a jug of coffee.

He winced at the question. Clearly feeling decidedly uncomfortable, he stood up from the chair and paced a few steps, rubbing his jawline.

'A month or so.' He knew exactly what the next question would be, and she did not disappoint him.

'Did you seduce my daughter?'

'If you must know, she flung herself at me.'

'Do you seriously expect me to believe that?'

'Yes, I do. It's the truth.' His voice rose in anger. He stared at her long and hard, and then said. 'Is it too much to ask for some loyalty – which, in ten years of marriage, you have never given me? Why didn't we have a family of our own?'

She was stung at both his words and behaviour. She calmed herself before saying, 'Bernhard, you have always had my trust, whether you believe me or not. And I thought children were the last thing you wanted. Your work came first, remember? I thought perhaps there was some medical reason that...'

'I am the doctor here,' he snapped. His words were glacial. 'I shall tell you why you never conceived. It's because all these years you have been taking precautions.'

'At first I did, I admit it. When we were married I didn't know if we would be happy together, but later I stopped. I foolishly thought you married me for love. I now know you married me to decorate your home, just like the Fragonard and the Monet hanging on the wall in the sitting room, and playing hostess your many dinners and cocktail evenings. I'll agree to....'

'I don't want your agreement, only your obedience,' he cut in fiercely.

She stared at him, hating the way he spoke to her. He was a clever doctor, but he was also quick-witted and arrogant when he chose. Whenever he was trying to get out of something unpleasant or distasteful, he would neatly turned the conversation around to point out her shortcomings and ignore his own. He wanted to blame both his wife and his stepdaughter for what happened. Susanne knew she could not win this verbal battle.

'I have to get away, Bernhard.'

'I'll take you anywhere you want.'

'I need to be alone.'

'Where will you go?'

'I thought I would go to the villa, and before you ask, I really don't know how long I'll stay.'

He gave a stiff nod. 'Golfe-Juan is nice and peaceful at this time of year. Take as long as you need, darling. When you return, our life is going to be completely different.'

There was a wealth of meaning in his words that she did not care to dwell on. Susanne just could not wait to get away from her crumbling marriage. She wanted to be alone to work out how she was going to deal with this disaster.

Golfe-Juan was beautiful, with sleek sailing boats bobbing on a shimmering sea. Napoleon Bonaparte had sailed from Elba to this famous place, and a hundred days later he had been defeated at Waterloo. She hoped she would not suffer Napoleon's fate. Golfe-Juan was not a big town, but it was quiet and restful, and Susanne enjoyed being there. Over the years she had spent a lot of time relaxing alone at the villa when Bernhard was too busy at the laboratory.

She called June occasionally to ask about Penny. However, she was totally unprepared when a couple of months later the telephone rang and she was informed that

Penny was pregnant. June told her not to worry, as she would take care of it. Penny was too scared to have an abortion, and June planned, with Penny's permission, to have the child adopted.

At this news, instead of returning to Bernhard as planned, Susanne remained at the villa. The emotional distance between herself and Bernhard grew. There was no hostility, but no warmth either. Whenever he telephoned they were polite and formal, like mere acquaintances. Susanne found his betrayal hard to swallow. Everything about him annoyed her. It occurred to her that she was somehow responsible for the lack of closeness between them over the years, but it was too late; the marriage was finished. All she had to do was to find the courage to tell him.

Bernhard was ignorant of Penny's condition, and the repercussions of revealing this to him did not bear thinking about. Susanne knew he had a few enemies at the laboratory, and she could imagine the gossip that would be circulated around Amboise by Adèle Lamboley, and the headlines in the tabloids if it were known. He could be struck off the medical register. Although he had seduced her daughter, she did not want his disgusting behaviour to become public knowledge, and sought to conceal her own shame and that of her daughters, as much as his. Bernhard had been very good to her financially, a fact, which her bank balance clearly showed. Susanne had to admit there had been lots of happy times together over the last ten years. Now, it was over.

She was hoping to go to London for the birth. However, June told her that Penny was refusing to have anything further to do with her mother. Susanne was so confused and had no idea how this would all turn out. Her husband had seduced his wife's daughter, who was now pregnant, and the baby would be both her stepchild and her grandchild; it was too ludicrous to think about. Susanne put on a jacket and went for a walk along the seafront to clear her mind.

A few weeks later Bernhard telephoned, telling her he was visiting Africa and South America on a lecture tour and asking her to accompany him. She told him she had organised a trip to England to visit some friends before returning home. He was delighted to hear she was coming back to Amboise, but she knew his delight would be short-lived when she told him she wanted a divorce.

Chapter Twenty Five

'Hello, Blossom. Why didn't you tell me you were coming? Penny has gone to have her regular check-up and then she's having lunch with an old school friend. I don't know when she'll be back; she didn't say.'

'I've been shopping and I thought I would call in on my way back to France to see you and Penny.'

'Lovely. Where are you staying?'

'The Cumberland, how is she, June?'

'A picture of health. Everything has been organised for the birth in a private nursing home near Epsom.'

'How much is it going to cost?'

'I'll let you know when the bill arrives,' June replied, leaving the room only to return a short while later carrying a jug of steaming coffee. 'It's nice to see you. How long are you staying? Sorry, blossom. I didn't mean it to sound like that.'

With a wave of her hand, Susanne dismissed June's tactless remark and smiled. She was feeling absurdly happy and was not going to allow June's rudeness to bother her.

As long as Susanne had known her, June had always overstepped the mark.

They discussed her journey from France, and June's holiday in the Bahamas and of her super bargains at the markets in Nassau. Susanne quietly listened, remaining silent about trip into Kent to visit the Millers earlier this morning. Her thoughts returned there as June went into the hallway to answer the telephone.

As soon as Susanne had arrived at the cottage, Rose Miller had thrust a letter into her hand saying, 'It's from Master Harry.' Recognising his familiar sloping style of writing, she had read that he was going to Paris on the morning of the twenty-sixth of September, catching the boat train from Victoria. He had asked the Millers for Susanne's telephone number or address in France. He had wished them well and hoped they would send him the information he wanted.

'John and I didn't know what to make of it. So I sent you a telegram. Was that the right thing to do?'

'Of course! It was, Rose, and thank you for telling me. I haven't seen Harry for years. Can I keep this?' She held up the envelope.

'Yes, yes, do.'

After a cup of tea and a chat, Susanne took her leave. She planned to have lunch with her son, near the business college he had enrolled in. Susanne had hoped he would choose university and gain a degree but he had registered to do a business course and she wanted to discuss it with him. Later, she would return the car to the rental company in London before going to visit June and Penny in Chelsea.

Twenty-four hours later, Susanne hurried along platform ten at Victoria station, glancing in all the first class compartments. Luckily, it wasn't busy, and she did not have to dodge luggage porters, British Rail trolley ladies or fellow travellers. Eventually, she found the first-class carriage she was looking for. It was empty except for one occupant, who had a window seat and was buried behind a copy of *The Times*.

'*Est-ce que ce siège est occupé?*' she asked, turning her back on the other passenger as she pushed her small suitcase into the luggage rack.

Discarding the newspaper, Harry slowly got to his feet, smiling inwardly. He would know that sweet voice anywhere, even in French. It was burned in his memory.

'The seat is not taken, but I hope you have a first class ticket' he said. Not giving her time to reply, he seized her around the waist. Lifting her into the air, he swung her around and released her just as the train guard's whistle blew.

'Harry!' she shrieked with mock surprise as she stepped back, hoping he would not be too angry with her for following him. Yesterday, when she had left June's Chelsea maisonette and returned to her hotel room, she had read Harry's letter three times before making enquiries at Victoria Station about a long-lost cousin taking the boat train the next morning. Finally, she had had the information she required and decided to catch up with him on the train. The disgusting episode between her husband and daughter was still too painful, and she did not want Harry travelling to Amboise or telephoning her home, especially with Bernhard in residence and her living at Golfe Juan. It might prove awkward.

'It must be fate, sweet Susie, that you and I are destined to meet on trains.'

She kissed him on both cheeks. 'Is it?' she asked, barely able to suppress a chuckle.

He lowered his brow and with a suspicious look said, 'Was this planned or accidental?'

'I was on my way home.'

'Lying hussy! You planned this, didn't you?' he admonished, trying to sound serious.

'Guilty,' she replied, holding up the envelope. 'Rose gave me your letter, and when I read it I wanted to see you so much. I was planning to return to France in a few days, anyway. I thought if we could spend even a few hours together catching up, it would be like old times.'

Taking her by the hand, he assisted her into a seat of the moving train and sat down next to her. The gentle touch of her fingers was familiar, and it brought back pleasant memories.

'Tell me everything that's happened since we last met – and I mean everything.'

Laughing, she said, 'Harry dear, it would take too long.'

'We have several hours before we reach Paris.'

'Where shall I start?'

'When we last made contact you were sharing a house with June in Brent, but then she moved and you married. Take it from there.'

As she spoke, Harry couldn't take his eyes off her. She was dressed in a dove-grey trouser suit, with a long fringed scarf draped over one shoulder. Her hair was shorter, in an attractive coiffure curling around her ears. During the war she had been beautiful, but now there was added charm and grace in both style and manner. To his eyes, she hadn't changed at all. Her skin was still flawless, and her laugh was like music to his ears. She was the most feminine woman he had ever met.

'Why didn't you contact me?' he asked.

'I did. My letters were returned unopened, and I asked around, but no one knew anything. I heard that during your posting to India you had met the woman of your dreams and you were getting married. I wrote to you at Haywood Hall, and I contacted your regiment, and got absolutely nowhere. How is your wife? And do you have any little perishers, as your father calls them?'

He tossed his head back and laughed. 'I am not married and I don't have any children. When I came back from India I tried to find you. I discovered June had moved and hadn't left a forwarding address. Then I remembered the name of the family you were living with in London, and with the aid of the telephone exchange I found Michael Blore. He told me you were married and living in Paris.'

Actually, as Harry remembered it, an angry voice had informed him that she had married a Kraut and was whoring around Paris with a Nazi. Harry had been angry at Blore's description and had told him so. He got the distinct impression that Blore hated Susanne: Harry did not want to mention it and possibly upset her.

'I knew you were in France and married, so I stopped looking. I went abroad with the Foreign Office and a few years later I went into politics. As I had a meeting in Paris, on impulse I wrote to the Millers to get your address. Blow me, you suddenly appear like a genie from a lamp.'

'I'm sorry. It sounds like I put you to a great deal of trouble to find me. I was shocked when I learned you planned to marry and thought it best I should stop writing to you. Six months later, I married and moved to France. When I discovered you had been paying Edward's school fees I felt guilty and tried to find you to repay the money, but you had left the Army, and the War Office weren't very helpful. I did wonder if perhaps you had returned to India. Harry, it was as if you had just disappeared and I needed some advice desperately,' she added dismally.

He caught the sadness in her voice and waited for her to say more, but there was only silence. He had a feeling she had many secrets that she would not divulge to anyone including him.

Standing up, he paced the short distance to the carriage door to hide his impatience. Then he turned around to face her.

'Sweet Susie, what was the advice you were seeking? There is something wrong. I can feel it. Can't you tell an old friend what happened?'

'My marriage is over.'

'May I ask why?

'He had an affair.'

'My dear Susie, lots of men run off the rails and then regret it. There's no chance of reconciliation?' Seeing her expression, he crouched down in front of her, and taking hold of one of her hands added, 'If I have embarrassed you, I apologise.'

With her head bent, Susanne eyed him from beneath lowered lashes. She could not possibly tell Harry the whole truth; it was too disgusting. However, she told him a little of her life in France and of her husband's medical work at the laboratory.

'There is absolutely no possibility, now or in the future, of Bernhard and me being reunited.'

From the tone of her voice and her choice of words, Harry guessed the affair must have been sordid indeed. He wondered what kind of a man would spurn a woman like Susie. Perhaps there was more to it than a mere fling. Knowing her as he did, she would never divulge it. He made a mental note to make some enquiries; being a Parliamentarian had its perks. He could make discreet enquiries about anyone, with the assistance of Scotland Yard.

He was pleased to hear that she had been shocked when told he was to be married in India. It made him wonder whether her feelings for him were more than mere friendship.

'I have an idea. Let's have dinner together in Gay Paree. I'm sure your French is better than mine, and living in

France for the last ten years, you probably know your way around Paris better than I do. You can give me a guided tour: places of interest, hysterical monuments, et cetera, et cetera.'

She laughed at his joke. 'It would be fun showing you around. When was the last time you were in Paris?'

'Before the war,' he replied, grinning wickedly. 'Where are you staying?'

His grin told her everything. She could well imagine him kicking up his heels in Gay Paree, as he called it. 'The Hotel Meurice, and you?'

'Georges Cinq. Now, sweet Susie, let's go and see if this train has dining service and celebrate our reunion with a glass of bubbly.'

Seated in the dining carriage near the window, Susanne just had to ask something that was puzzling her. 'When I entered your compartment you didn't seem too surprised to see me. May I ask why?'

'Sweet Susie, I would know you anywhere.' He did not add that every inch of her was etched in his brain.

Smiling, she said, 'I ought to tell you. Everyone in France, including my friends in London, calls me Susanne now.'

'Another name change! However, I still prefer Susie,' he said with a wink. Getting to his feet, he asked her what she would like to drink. 'It's far too early for me to drink champagne, Harry dear. Please may I have a cup of coffee with a slice of lemon instead of cream?'

After breakfasting together and spending the rest of the

morning being tourists, Harry arranged to meet her that evening in the columned foyer of the Georges Cinq. When she appeared, she looked breathtakingly beautiful in a black full-length gown with gold buttons all the way down to her toes and golden embroidery on the sleeves. His eyes followed her as she crossed the grand lobby. Her fluid movements and gently-swaying hips kept him riveted to the spot.

Suddenly she spotted him, and giving a small wave, she turned and headed in his direction. He was still bewitched by her, even after all these years. She was the most desirable woman he knew. Mentally shaking himself, he collected his thoughts before stepping forward to greet her with a kiss on her cheek. 'You look stunning,' he whispered before taking her hand and leading her to a set of silver-encrusted iron gates that swung open as they approached the restaurant.

'Votre table, Monsieur,' the *Maitre d'* said, pulling out a silver jacquard-upholstered chair for Susanne before going around the table to assist Harry.

'How are your family, especially your father?' she asked, after the champagne had been served and they were alone.

'He's still wheelchair-bound.' Twirling the glass between thumb and forefinger, he added, 'We were never close, my father and I.'

Sensing sadness in him, she changed the subject. 'As a Member of Parliament, can you tell me any state secrets?'

The corners of his mouth twitched. 'And be dragged off to the tower? Never.'

'You told me on the train about being groomed for the top position in government. When you become Prime Minister, will I have to curtsey and call you sir?'

'Most definitely,' he answered with a sly grin.

'Harry dear, I feel honoured having dinner with the future Prime Minister of Great Britain.'

'And you, sweet Susie, honour me just by being here. However, I shall only become leader if the current one loses his seat, and then we would still have an election to win.' He smiled. 'Shall we have some more champagne?'

Studying him as he signalled the waiter to fill their glasses, Susanne thought it was almost impossible not to like him. He was the embodiment of English sang-froid. Throughout the years she had known him, she had never seen Harry other than composed and controlled. Completely unflappable, he was charming to women and was not prudish. He loathed all levels of snobbery and had a natural style when speaking, not using an exaggerated 'posh' accent, as was the habit with some of the gentry.

'To us,' he said, lifting the glass to his lips.

'To us,' she repeated, sipping the champagne.

'Have you perused the menu and made your selection?' he asked.

'Be a dear and order langoustine for me please. There are thousands of butterflies inside me and they are all partying, from my tongue all the way to my toes.'

Giving her a fourteen-carat smile, he turned to the waiter and in faultless French ordered their meal. Susanne smiled inwardly at her trickery. She knew that his comment on the train about her knowledge of French being superior was nothing but a ruse to get her to dine with him. He probably knew his way around Paris better than she did, but she didn't care. Tonight she wanted to escape from all her troubles and be admired and loved for herself. Sitting opposite her was the man who could do that.

'Of course, when the title passes to me I will have a month to disclaim the peerage, if I want to remain in the House of Commons.'

'Whatever for?'

'It is not permitted for a Peer to be a Member of Parliament in the House of Commons. If I don't win a seat at the next election, when my father dies I will be given a life peerage and take my seat in the Lords.'

As they dined, he explained his position and his future in politics. He had been chosen as deputy to the current leader, and if anything untoward happened Harry would take over leadership of the party and aspire to lead them to victory at the next election. Then he would be Prime Minister of the United Kingdom. Listening attentively to the rich timbre of his voice as he explained the intricacies of political life and its pitfalls, she realised, not for the first time, that he was a good speaker. He never allowed anger to cloud his judgement, and his manner was easy and relaxed. Susanne loved the way he raised one eyebrow each time he made a relevant point or emphasised a word. She was in no doubt that he would make a superb Prime Minister. His personality would endear him to all classes of society, and his good looks would attract the women's vote. His chestnut hair was still thick and vibrant, with just a touch of silver at the temples, and his sharp grey eyes never missed a thing.

Suddenly he stopped speaking, and she caught his probing look over the rim of his champagne glass.

'Sweet Susie, where are you?'

'Sorry, I was just thinking that you haven't changed at all and you're bound to capture the women's vote.'

He chuckled, adding, 'You should be my campaign manager.'

'Not I. Years ago, when I was a naïve Nellie, I asked to see a Shakespearean musical. As I remember, it was entirely your fault.'

'My fault?' he exclaimed with an arched brow.

'On my first train journey you spoke about Shakespeare's *Twelfth Night* and said it was a good show. Shortly after I arrived in London, a member of the Blore family asked me to choose a musical. I picked *Twelfth Night* and made a complete fool of myself.'

He laughed so heartily she joined in. Suddenly, he became quiet, giving her a long intense stare.

'A man could drown in those eyes of yours.'

Feeling her cheeks redden, she dropped her eyes to the candles and flower petals in a glass bowl on the table. The atmosphere was heady, and not just because of his words; after several glasses of champagne she was feeling light-headed.

'Harry dear, I think I've had too much champagne. I have a sudden urge to dance.'

'I have a surprise for you,' he said, getting to his feet and extending his arm. He took hold of her hand and led her out of the restaurant and up in the elevator to his suite.

Harry opened the door with a flourish. On the far side of the suite, French windows opened onto a dreamy balcony festooned with flowers and candles. A violinist started to play *La Vie en Rose* while a waiter opened a bottle of champagne, put it on ice, placed it on a small table and withdrew. The balcony overlooked the city of Paris, aglow with lights against the night sky.

'Oh, it's so beautiful!' she gasped.

'Would you like to dance?' he asked, holding out his arms.

She went willingly, resting her head against his shoulder while his face nestled in her hair. They moved very slowly as the music filled the room, and were still locked in each other's arms when the violinist quietly left. They were completely unaware that they were alone.

Harry lowered his head, tilted her face to his and kissed her longingly. They continued to sway gently, although there was no music. He deepened the kiss and she responded. When his arms tightened around her waist, her heart started pounding. She was surprised at the fiery sensations coursing through her body. She was not only a little light-headed from the champagne, but completely intoxicated by him.

Lifting his lips from hers, he murmured against her ear.

'Let's be sensible. I'll take you back to Le Meurice.'

At this suggestion, she lifted her face to his; her eyes

spoke volumes, and no words were needed. 'My sweet Susie,' he murmured, lowering his head he covered her lips with his, while slowly guiding her towards the sofa. Harry removed her shoes before sitting down next to her, and between whispered endearments and passionate kisses, he started to undo the gold buttons down the front of her gown until it lay open, revealing black stockings, panties and bra for his eyes to feast upon. Releasing her suspenders, he rolled each stocking down to her ankle, tugging the flimsy material from her foot, and threw it into the air, leaving it to float noiselessly to the floor. The other one soon joined it, followed by her bra, panties and suspender belt. Now the black gown was the only clothing she had on. Harry swiftly but gently peeled it from her body, leaving her completely naked. Kneeling down between her legs he fondled and kissed every inch of her. Susanne could only moan; intense desire took hold, depriving her of speech.

Sweeping her into his arms, Harry carried her to the bedroom, elbowing the door open as he entered and slamming it shut with the heel of his shoe. Quickly undressing, he joined her on the bed. Raising himself above her, he saw the gold locket glinting around her neck. 'You're not still wearing this,' he said and taking hold of the chain he undid the clasp, easing it from around her neck, and tossed it on the floor. 'I want you to know that it's me making love to you and not a memory from the past.' Bending his head he kissed her until she was breathless. Then he slowly and skilfully joined his body with hers.

Susanne woke up and got out of bed. She found Harry's robe in the bathroom and tied it around her. Then she poured herself a glass of water and sat cross-legged on the sofa. Her response to his lovemaking felt like some kind of explosion throughout her body, and she remembered calling out his name. It had been a tumultuous coming together for both of them. She could not remember how many times they had made love, but he had been as relentless in his need of her as she had been with him. She sighed; never had she known anything like this. His expert handling of her brought her to experience new sensations time and time again, and left her wanting more. He was a very astute lover, mindful of her every need. Instinctively, he seemed to know when she wanted him to be rough and demanding, and when she needed him to be gentle and caring.

Sipping the water, she could hear faint traffic noises from the streets below and guessed it must be very late. Placing her empty glass on the small polished table, she leaned back, resting her head against the sofa.

She had scarcely closed her eyes when she heard movement and looked up to see Harry coming towards her, naked. He sat down at the opposite end of the sofa and smiled.

'You're magnificent,' he said, reaching over to pull open the robe and admire her once more.

'So are you. Where did you learn such skills? In India?'

A grin was his only answer. 'Darling, let's bathe together, and I'll show you how to make love in a bath,' he said, while caressing her nakedness.

'My mouth is a little swollen.'

'I do apologise. You tasted so delicious, and I couldn't stop kissing you.'

Sitting in the bath between Harry's legs, her back resting against his firm chest, she was scooping water over his kneecaps while he fondled her breasts. Her thoughts drifted back over the last few hours. This evening she had come to realise that one can love more than once in a lifetime.

'Harry, tonight, my body couldn't get enough of yours. You are a superb lover.'

'What about your heart? Can you find a place there for me?' he murmured against her ear.

'You have always have been there.'

'Have I?' he asked, somewhat surprised. 'My sweet Susie, when we were in bed, at one point you screamed, 'Harry, don't leave.' What was the meaning behind those words? Not to withdraw from you bodily, or never to leave you, ever?'

'Both,' she whispered.

'Are you serious about getting a divorce?'

'Why? Do you want me to become your mistress?'

'In my position, a mistress is definitely not an option. A politician has to have credibility, *sine qua non*. Any scandal for a Member of Parliament is catastrophic. You must become my wife.'

Stunned, she wriggled around in the water until she was facing him. 'Harry, is this some kind of joke? Is it just because tonight you feel you have to do the honourable thing? I am quite willing to become your mistress. I mean to…'

'Shush,' he pulled her closer to his chest and kissed the bridge of her nose, knowing her lips were a little tender. 'I've been in love with you since I was a schoolboy, on a train to London. When I found you again, you had fallen in love with someone else and were about to marry. During the war you were head over heels with another. And when I returned from India I discovered you were married and living in France. I just want to claim you before any more Don Juans whisk you down the aisle.'

She started laughing at this, and Harry joined in.

'Honestly, darling, you seem to have a knack for picking the wrong man' he went on. 'So, turn over a new leaf and pick the right one. Will you marry me? I asked this same question a long time ago. Do you remember when we waltzed around the family town house in candlelight?

'I don't remember.'

'Think harder. You tripped and fell into my arms. I kissed you and said, 'Marry me,' but you wanted me to get a taxi to take you home. I refused and escorted you to Chelsea myself.'

'Yes, I do remember us kissing and hearing you whisper, 'Marry me,' but I thought you had drunk too much wine and would not remember the next morning. So I dismissed it. To be honest, Harry dear, I think since I first met you I have always been a little in love with you. Tonight, my heart was aching for you to make love to me. When you carried me into your bedroom, I realised I love you and have for some time. Darling, I would be honoured to marry you.'

'My sweet Susie,' he said, hugging her, 'we'll have to wait until your divorce is finalised, but in the meantime I would like you to come to England at Christmas, spend a few days at the Hall and meet my parents. They are quite elderly, but their blessing will be paramount to your being received in society. I also have to get the Queen's permission. However, it is just a formality.'

'The Queen's permission?'

'Father's a distant cousin. If about two hundred members of the Queen's family suddenly died, he would be King, and I would be Prince of Wales,' he said, kissing the shell of her ear.

'You never told me.'

'You never asked. Now, can I be serious for a few moments? I am going to be quite busy over the next few months, but we'll keep in touch by telephone while you're here in France. One day, all this hard work may pay off and I will become Prime Minister. How would you handle being the wife of the PM?'

'I would just follow your lead, my darling, I know you'll be the best Prime Minister Britain ever had. I'd love to help you win the election.'

'I cannot allow you to help me until we are officially engaged, my love. The press would have a field day, especially as you are still married. And my career would take a downward spiral if bad press attached itself to me, as a Member of Parliament.'

She nodded, listening intently to his every word. Then it struck her that he had invited her to Haywood Hall.

'Harry, do you think your parents will like me?'

'They will adore you, as I do. I'm afraid politics keeps me extremely busy, but I will be able to see you more frequently than if I was still in the Army.'

She touched her lips gently against his, then added, 'Bernhard and I have a small villa on the Côte d'Azur. He never uses it, but I adore it there. When our divorce is settled I'm sure he will give it to me. He can keep the house in Amboise. Harry, our privacy would be guaranteed in Golfe-Juan.'

'Does it have a big tub like this one?'

'Afraid not.'

'Will you have one installed, my love, so we can bathe together just like this?'

She splashed him. 'The water is getting cold, and I would love some tea. Can you please ring room service, darling?'

'Your wish is my command.' He stepped out of the bath and flung a towel around his hips. With his hands resting on the side of the tub and lowering his head, he gently touched her lips with his. Susanne's hands lay on his forearms and she responded by sinking her tongue into his mouth as he had instructed her earlier in bed. He raised his head and smiled.

'You are a fast learner, my love. Which is excellent, as I have a lot to teach you.' Then he left and went to order room service.

Susanne wrapped a fluffy towel around her body and hugged herself. After years of disasters and disappointments, she had now found a man who truly loved her. She was so happy she wanted to shout it from the rooftops, but that would be unseemly in this hotel. She fervently hoped his mother would like her, but she had some misgivings. Harry was not snobbish, but she doubted that his family would be like him. She would do her level best to make them like her – not for her sake, but for Harry's. She would do anything to make him happy, and that included accepting and being accepted by his family.

Chapter Twenty Six

When Harry left Paris to return to London after the conference ended, Susanne went on a shopping spree, starting at Avenue Montaigne and ending at Rue Faubourg Saint-Honoré. She spent several hours selecting, being fitted for and ordering a complete new wardrobe, elegant enough to please both Harry and his family.

Upon returning to the Hotel Meurice in the late afternoon after a busy morning, she received a telegram, which had been re-directed. It was from Henri Lamboley informing her Bernhard was in hospital and asking her to return home immediately.

Doctor Lamboley met the train. His sombre face matched his mood. He said he would tell her everything when they arrived at her home. She did not question him further, but sat back against the leather upholstery and closed her eyes as the car sped along rain-drenched roads towards Amboise.

'Your husband suffered a severe stroke during a golf game and was rushed to hospital. I don't know how to say this.' He paused for a minute. 'Bernhard is unconscious, and the prognosis is bleak. I conferred with his doctors, and they informed me that Dr Roehder would temporarily have to give up his position as Directeur of the laboratory.' Henri stopped speaking, cleared his throat and continued. 'I am terribly sorry to be the one to break the news of your husband's condition. I will be taking over Bernhard's position until his recovery. Naturally the company will pay all medical expenses.'

'Thank you, Henri. I appreciate your taking the time to meet me. When will I be able to see my husband?'

'I have arranged for Bernhard's secretary to take you to hospital in the morning. She will pick you up at ten thirty, if that is convenient.' He did not add that his wife had flatly refused to take Susanne to the hospital, or that he had a meeting to attend. With Susanne's friend, Emma Gordon, in Scotland visiting her sick father, Henri was left with no option other than to ask Bernhard's secretary, Maxine.

Yvette arrived early the next morning, prepared breakfast and later selected a suitable outfit for Madam Roehder to wear to the hospital. She babbled on about how it had been raining non-stop, as she fastened a string of pearls around Susanne's neck and handed her matching earrings. The woman's chattering, barely registered, as Susanne was far more concerned with the condition of Bernhard.

Making small talk, Susanne and Maxine drove to the hospital in a heavy downpour.

'So glad you brought that umbrella, Madame Roehder,'

Maxine said, eyeing it on the back seat of her car. 'You're going to need it.'

'Usually the weather is pleasant around this time of year. Has it been raining long, Maxine?'

'*Oui, Madame*, almost seven days,' she replied. Turning into the car park at the rear of the hospital, she added, 'I will wait here for you.'

Susanne walked down the corridor with a nurse by her side. When she entered her husband's private room her hand flew to her mouth. She barely recognised him. Tubes connected his body to a machine, with winking lights emitting a high-pitched signal. Tears formed when she saw his emaciated face.

She remained at his bedside for twenty minutes before being called away to a meeting with his doctors. The news was all bad. Bernhard had suffered a massive stroke. He was paralysed down one side, and would need constant care for the rest of his life. Susanne knew he would never accept it. Bernhard loved his job at the laboratory and he did not work just for his salary. Money was unimportant to him. Since his mother had left him everything in her will, he had more than enough. Susanne did not know exactly how much Bernhard had invested, as he never discussed his finances with anyone except his accountant.

That evening Susanne wandered from room to room, picking up framed photographs and figurines displayed on the furniture. She had been married to Bernhard for ten years, yet she could not summon the tears of a wife whose husband was on life support. Susanne felt both guilty and shocked upon hearing how ill he was. How would he react when he regained consciousness and discovered he would be confined to a wheelchair, unable to play sport. Worst of all, losing his position at the laboratory, even temporarily, would be devastating for a man like Bernhard.

Susanne knew that she could not initiate divorce proceedings until Bernhard was released from hospital and was well enough to accept both paralysis and divorce. He would have enormous challenges to face and would need her support. She was his only family since Mutti's death. Susanne would look after him and give him the care needed. Perhaps Harry, Bernhard and herself could enter a kind of *ménage à trois* until the divorce was final and Bernhard was well enough to make his own plans. Susanne was sure Bernhard would agree. He was a practical man and would accept Harry visiting, in preference to being confined to a retirement home. However, Susanne could not imagine Harry's reaction.

A month later, returning home from the hospital she made some tea, and had barely taken a sip when telephone rang. 'I miss you, Harry.'

'I miss you too. How about Golfe-Juan, a week Friday, for a few days? I'll be in touch. Darling, have to go. A corridor crier is paging me. Love you.'

'Love you, too. Bye.'

Susanne smiled. She would do anything to please him, and if she were truthful with herself, the thought of living at Haywood Hall did wonders for her self-esteem, but more importantly, she would have the man she adored by her side.

Her telephone shrilled again. 'Harry, my love' she murmured.

'I beg your pardon? Mother, it's Edward. How are you and how is Bernhard?

'Edward, what a nice, surprise. I'm well.' She quickly told him about Bernhard's condition. 'How are you, Edward?' she asked.

'Actually, dear heart, I'm in a bit of a jam and need your help. Please don't lecture me about all the money I've borrowed from you in the past. I will pay you back one day, I promise.'

'How much this time?'

'It's a mere trifle, nothing for your bank manager to lose sleep over.'

'Edward, I will not give you any money unless you tell me how much.'

'I lost quite a lot of money on the horses. I borrowed more to pay my gambling debts and I have to repay it, immediately. To put it in a nutshell, I'm in a fix and I don't have any money. The good news is, I graduated from the business college.'

'What about the monthly allowance I send?'

'That's all gone too.'

'I am shattered.'

'Dear heart, it's not that earth-shattering. Besides, I've been thinking of selling my *pied- a-terre* that you kindly bought for me, and heading off to the States.'

'You're going to live in America?'

'That's where the big money is. They say the streets are paved with gold over there.'

'How much do you owe the bookmakers?'

'Twelve hundred pounds.'

'You're impossible.' She sighed deeply. 'Send me the details of your gambling debt. Edward, I will be in London at the end of the month, and we will discuss your future in America. I have a friend in Virginia, and since you love horses so much, I can tell you she owns a stud. Judy will probably help you until you get established. We can talk further when I see you. And Edward, I insist you repay me.'

'You're tops, dear heart.'

'Stay away from bookmakers! I cannot give you any more money. Do you understand? And before you hang up, do you still visit John and Rose Miller?'

'Haven't seen them for months, although we speak on the blower occasionally. Jade is now at grammar school, she came first in her class. Rose and John are over the moon about their daughter. In fact, John and Rose are in the pink, as they say. Dear heart, I have to love you and leave you. See you soon.'

A strange nostalgia came over Susanne as she put the phone down. Images of Rick surfaced for the first time in years. Edward was so like his father, with one exception; Rick had been careful with money, whereas his son was just the opposite. She remembered Rick relating a tale about his great-grandfather being a gambler who had won and lost fortunes in poker games. It seemed that her son was a chip off the old block, as June would say.

Her daughter, too, was very perplexing. Susanne knew that neither son nor daughter would ever repay the money she gave them, and it hurt that they treated her as a bank they could use whenever they needed cash. Neither of them sent her a birthday or a Christmas card, and she had grown to accept that, but Mother's Day always left her feeling unloved.

Penny never contacted her mother; all requests for money came through June. Susanne was disappointed with her two children. She made a decision that when she married Harry she would flatly refuse to give them any more money and would tell them to fend for themselves.

With this thought, the guilt returned. Hadn't she left her daughter in the care of Percy and Tess to give herself more freedom and a chance of happiness? And although she had paid Penny's school fees and other expenses, Susanne had not been there when Penny was growing up. Didn't she owe her daughter something, even if it was only money? After Edward's birth, she had been too ill with grief to take care of him and had left him in the care of the Millers, who had lost their child. She had visited the family frequently and paid all her son's expenses. Could she deny her son or daughter financial help when her record as a mother was so appalling?

Susanne was close to tears. She knew that the only thing that would cheer her up and drag her out of the doldrums was if Harry were to telephone and ask her to meet him at the villa. Since Bernhard had been admitted to hospital Susanne was now in charge of paying all the household accounts, which arrived in the post box with amazing frequency. She was finding it difficult to cope, paying the monthly and quarterly bills, and the household staff and arranging for her car and Bernhard's Jaguar to be serviced. With Jacques the gardener's help, she drove each vehicle once a week around the countryside to prevent tyre damage and battery failure, as advised by Jacques.

To the locals, the Loire Valley was the Garden Of France. Driving along the narrow roads she could understand why, as she passed picturesque fields abundant with crops, beautiful vineyards, orchards and rolling green hills. The hills always captured her attention, as did the streams below glistening in the morning sunlight. She sighed with the beauty of it all. She was having dinner with Doctor Gordon and his sister tonight, as his wife Emma was in Edinburgh nursing her sick father, who apparently did not have long to live. Thankfully, Bernhard seemed to be in a better position than Emma's father.

She fervently hoped that when Bernhard recovered and was released from hospital he would agree to a divorce without being difficult. Susanne had visited her lawyer the previous week and he had assured her that she had a strong case. However, she felt a little uneasy knowing how awkward Bernhard could be when things didn't go his way. She remembered him saying years before that anything he wanted he got. If he contested the divorce, the only option would be to tell the court about her husband seducing her daughter. Susanne shivered. She did not want all the sordid details to become public and hurt her daughter. Most probably Bernhard would be charged with statutory rape, and perhaps face a gaol sentence. However, if his paralysis did not end his career entirely, he might not dispute the divorce. Her mind was racing as she pulled the car into the garage.

She had barely taken two steps inside the door when the telephone rang. She was relieved to find Harry on the other end.

'Hello my love. I am leaving for Golfe-Juan Friday.'

'Oh, darling, how wonderful, I will drive down to the villa tomorrow. I am so looking forward to being with you again. See you soon.'

The precious days they spent together at the villa were always heavenly. Harry, as usual, was kind and considerate, catering to her every need. While lying in bed the morning after he arrived, she told him about her son.

'Edward is in financial difficulties again. I have to pay his gambling debts. Hopefully, he is off to live in America soon so this will be the last time I have to pay. I telephoned Judy and she told me Edward could stay at the stud until he finds employment. If he shows any interest, she will teach him to be a horse handler and if he's any good she will offer him a job.'

'I think that's an excellent idea. It may help him to grow up and learn to manage his own debts, instead of relying on his mother to get him out of trouble. How much is it this time?'

'Twelve hundred pounds.'

Harry gave a low whistle. 'He certainly knows how to lose money.'

'I've told him I will not give him any more money to gamble on horses. I'm sure he doesn't listen.'

'Shall I have a word with him? Sometimes advice from a man can carry more weight.'

'I disagree. Women can have the same influence.'

Throwing his eyes to the ceiling, Harry muttered, '*Au contraire.*'

'Darling, I do…'

'Can we please get back to the subject of your son?'

'Yes, of course, please advise Edward. I know he likes you, and maybe you will be successful where I failed. Shall I give you his phone number?'

'I have it. I'll get in touch with him when I get back to London and invite him to luncheon in the Members' dining room.'

'Dining in the House of Commons? Edward will be impressed.'

'Darling, he is not supposed to be impressed. He has to listen to what I have to say and hopefully start paying his own debts.'

Turning to Harry and leaning on one elbow, she gently outlined his face and then ran her finger across his lips. She always felt safe with this man. Without taking his eyes from hers he sucked her finger into his mouth, and nibbled it roughly. She squealed when he rolled her onto her back and raised himself above her.

'This is how I like you best, naked and in bed. Lady,

you are in my blood.' He growled lustfully, breathing in her womanly smell.

After making love Harry rolled onto his back, put his arm around her and pulled her towards his chest. Susanne smiled and snuggled up to him.

'Darling, with me in France and you in London, it is becoming unbearable' she said and then kissed him. Lifting his mouth from hers, he murmured, 'You are a temptress. I hope you're planning to spend the day in bed, with me.'

She whispered back, 'I give you my body, that we two might be one.'

After the idyllic days at Golfe-Juan, Susanne dropped Harry at the airport for his flight to London and drove home to Amboise. She was feeling gloomy. Upon her arrival home the first thing she did was to phone the hospital to inquire about Bernhard. She was informed her husband was still in a coma and remained on life support. She resumed her weekly visits to the hospital. It had been suggested to her a couple of months before that she should reduce her daily visits to once or twice a week until her husband regained consciousness.

Visiting him one afternoon, she told him quietly that she would be there when he woke up. As she spoke her eyes looked past the tube clamped to his mouth and wires snaking around from his arms, chest and skull into bleeping and blinking machines. He lay there completely unresponsive. However, the doctors had some good news;

apparently Bernhard's brain was still functioning. Perhaps, he will get well after all, Susanne thought.

She arrived home tired and worn out and was making herself some tea when the telephone rang. It was the hospital with an urgent call which sent Susanne hurrying back to Bernhard's bedside. She was met by one of the senior doctors with a sad look in his eyes. He explained that Bernhard had suffered another stroke and had died suddenly. He summoned a young intern to escort Susanne to her husband's room.

Her visit was quite short. Afterwards the intern directed her to a nurses' washroom where she could cry in private and rinse away her tears.

Susanne had just lathered the soap between her hands when she heard two women talking in French in the next room.

'Imagine Dr Roehder turning off his life support system' said one.

'Yes, I cannot understand anyone doing that' the other replied.

Susanne understood. When Bernhard had finally regained consciousness and become aware of his prognosis and the prospect of being confined to a wheelchair for the rest of his life, he had reached out of bed and pulled the plug. The concocted story that Bernhard had died from another stroke she did not believe for a moment. She knew the man and his pride.

During Bernhard's funeral service the rain was lashing against the church windows as Dr Lamboley gave the eulogy, Dr Gordon read the lesson and the Minister gave the blessing, ending with a prayer. One of Bernhard's favourite organ pieces was played: Albinoni's sombre *Adagio*. The guests, mainly from the laboratory, shuffled slowly down the arched aisle of the church to assemble a little later at the graveside. The rain was coming down in torrents and the funeral director was concerned that the burial might have to be postponed until another day, owing to the terrible conditions at the cemetery. Dr Lamboley, as acting director of the laboratory, insisted that the proceedings continue, and Bernhard's coffin was committed into the ground surrounded by a sea of mud.

Susanne stepped forward and placed a white rose on his coffin. Because of the torrential rain, nobody wanted to linger.

When Susanne arrive home she stripped off her wet clothes and had a warm bath. Then she lay on the bed and immediately fell asleep. A ringing noise woke her and reaching across the bedside table she picked the up receiver and sleepily answered 'Yes, who is it?'

It was June in a panic, telling Susanne that Penny's baby had been delivered, not in the private clinic with maternity staff as arranged, but by a midwife. The baby had been born in a flat at one Penny's old school-friends. She had given the baby up for adoption and left London.

'June, please calm down and tell me what happened' said Susanne.

'She told me a heap of lies about her pregnancy. First,

she was due to go into labour at the beginning of the month and not at the end of the month as she led me to believe. Apparently, she employed a midwife and she used a private adoption agency. Who, I understand, collected the infant. A few days later she left London.'

'Why didn't she confide in you? Where has she gone? Was it a boy or a girl?' Susanne asked, astonished.

'Evidently, Penny planned it all. She chose the adoption agency and the midwife and paid for it from the money you sent her to pay for the nursing home. If you ask me, you and I will only hear from her when the money runs out. All I got was a scrap of paper giving me scant details that I have just passed on to you.'

June did not add that she had told Penny that Bernhard had passed away and thought that was why Penny had left London. She knew that had Bernhard lived, Penny would have travelled to France and placed the baby in his arms and asked him to marry her. However, she made new plans when she knew he had died. June felt terribly guilty and wished she had not told Penny about Bernhard's death.

'I was going to telephone you today to tell you that Bernhard's burial service was held this morning. June, it rained and rained. I declined the invitation from the new Director to join the staff for memorial luncheon. I just wanted come home and remember Bernhard privately.'

'Oh, blossom, I am so sorry for interrupting at a time like this. Is there anything I can do to help?'

'It would be wonderful if you could make the rain go away, June, I have made up my mind to return to London soon.'

'I think it would be a good idea to come home. And blossom, I'll keep my fingers crossed about the rain. Please don't worry about Penny. She's a very independent young woman. I have to go now, my job. Well, someone has to pay for the Prime Minister's next pair of socks.'

Susanne smiled as she heard June's laughter before she replaced the receiver.

The rain persisted for three more weeks and low-lying areas were flooded. The conditions were very bleak, making Susanne wonder just how long it would be before she saw the sun. Rail and bus services had been affected and some schools had been closed because of the dreadful conditions.

Susanne's move to London had been held up too. A telephone call from the office of the furniture removal company informed her of a waterlogged bridge hampering progress. Eventually it eased off and people were able venture out. Susanne had an appointment with Bernhard's solicitor, which had been cancelled due to the weather and a new appointment made. Susanne hurried towards the office.

After discussing the terrible weather, he turned to the subject of the will.

'Madame Roehder, according to the Last Will of Bernhard Roehder, you are the sole beneficiary, executor and trustee' He said. He spoke at some length, but Susanne wasn't listening. Her mind was preparing to return to London. She suddenly became aware of a silence and looked at him.

'I was not concentrating. I do apologise' she said.

'It is a very distressing time for you, and I completely understand. If there is any other assistance my office can provide, please don't hesitate to call me.'

'I would like to sell the house and the furniture I don't want' she replied. 'I plan to return to London in the near future. Can I leave everything in your capable hands?'

'I will be pleased to act on your behalf. I will organise the sale of the property and furniture.' He stood up and offered her his hand. 'I met Dr Roehder at the golf club many times. Please accept my sincere condolences.'

She smiled and thanked him for his kind words. Rising from the chair, she wished him and his family good health and left the office.

Susanne was surprised to discover that all the assets Mutti owned had been left to her son. Combined with Bernhard's investments, they were worth a fortune. Before, she had been financially independent; now, she was enormously wealthy.

It took Susanne several weeks to go through all Bernhard's personal belongings. She had all his clothes packed in boxes and given to the needy. Several water-colours and four beautiful landscapes, including a small portrait of herself that Bernhard had commissioned, were being packed for her. Most of the Sèvres, Wedgwood and Dresden pieces she wanted to keep were all ready to be shipped across the Channel. Most of the furniture was being auctioned, except for two antique chairs and four silk Persian rugs which were particular favourites. Susanne was so happy to be going home.

Chapter Twenty Seven

The elegant Mayfair apartment Susanne had purchased was both comfortable and private enough for her and Harry to meet discreetly, whenever his Parliamentary duties allowed. Susanne had the main rooms painted in shades of peacock blue and cream and furnished with classical antiques. Comfortable wing-back chairs matched the plush drapes and hand-woven silk rugs complemented the polished floor. The only evidence of the twentieth century was a white telephone upon a rosewood table and a television set with sliding doors.

Susanne was delighted to be back in the city she loved, but most of all she was overjoyed about her future with the man she loved. With arms folded she gazed at the view across the city – the city that stoic Londoners had so valiantly strove to save from German bombers. Tears filled her eyes and she felt a knot in her throat. It always happened whenever she remembered those dark days. It was not easy to forget.

She mentally shook herself and turned to continue

packing. Harry had invited her to Haywood Hall to meet his father, the current Earl, and his mother. He would be picking her up in thirty minutes in the new Rover she had purchased for him two weeks before for his birthday. Glancing at her watch, she hurriedly fastened her small suitcase and placed it in the hallway. Then she went into her bedroom to change before he arrived.

As the big car swept through two large wrought-iron gates and up the driveway, the gardener touched his cap to Harry. Susanne sucked her bottom lip, reliving old memories and feeling a tiny bit nervous, as they passed the lodge she had occupied years before. The vehicle came to a halt in front of the imposing sandstone mansion.

When they were shown into the morning room, Harry guessed Susanne was feeling a bit apprehensive and gave her a wink and a smile as he introduced her to his family. His mother, Victoria, was tall, statuesque and every inch the lady of the manor, dressed in a fawn twin set and tweed skirt with a perfect set of pearls around her neck, her salt-and-pepper hair in a stylish French roll.

Seated in a wheelchair, his father smiled warmly and welcomed both his son and his future bride, while thinking Harry had made an excellent choice. She wasn't a simpering young thing who would need coaxing into bed. This woman looked both sensible and attractive. She would do her duty and provide the estate with a male heir.

When Harry introduced his sister, Elizabeth was cold and indifferent, snubbing her brother's future wife. To mask her disappointment, Susanne gave a weak smile and ignored her. She knew Elizabeth remembered her from their meeting at the Lodge at the end of the war and later at a Buckingham Palace garden party. Susanne was of the opinion that people should be accepted for what they were and not their lineage. It was obvious that Elizabeth did not share this view.

After tea in the morning room, Victoria gave her future daughter-in-law a tour of the manor and its grounds, going into great detail about the history of Haywood Hall. It had been built in Tudor times and had scarcely changed since then. Neither had the furnishings, Susanne thought. Suits of armour, crossed swords, bronzed shields and tapestry hangings of hunting scenes were displayed in the main rooms. Large oriel windows were simply beautiful. Lofty ceilings and huge open fireplaces, embellished with the family crest, all had the imprint of the Tudor era. The wood-panelled gallery above the banqueting room was decorated with family portraits from centuries ago, judging by the costumes.

However the Hall was cold and draughty and Susanne resolved to install a central heating system in the main rooms when she became the lady of the house. If they had to live in this time-honoured mansion, she and Harry should be warm and comfortable.

That evening, the Earl and his Countess gave a glittering reception to introduce Susanne to their kith and kin. Servants with trays of sparkling champagne weaved amongst the gathering, while others toured the reception rooms offering a selection of canapés. Susanne had difficulty remembering the names of all the people she been presented to. While some were members of the gentry, others were professional people, government officials or village worthies. Everyone was exceedingly kind, and Susanne was enjoying herself immensely.

Harry had not missed the slur directed at his future bride by his sister. Later, that evening while dancing with Elizabeth, he steered her into the library and closed the door.

'What the dickens are you playing at?'

'I have no idea what you are talking about, Harry,' she answered in a haughty manner.

He turned on her savagely. 'This morning you deliberately snubbed Susanne who, I may add, has done nothing, absolutely nothing, to warrant that kind of behaviour.'

Ignoring his anger, she retaliated. 'She's only after your money, and besides, she gives herself airs.' Her laugh was not pleasant.

'You are hardly in a position to express an opinion' snapped Harry. 'Unlike you, my future wife is neither penniless nor pretentious.'

Seething with anger, Elizabeth tried another tack. 'She must be good in bed. Harry, I'm only…'

He grabbed his sister's wrists and squeezed them tightly. Her eyes watered, but he didn't care; he was fed up with her meddling. He was in love with Susanne, had been for years, and she was in love with him. His sister's attitude could end up destroying his wedding plans, and that was something he would not allow.

'When Father dies I want you to pack your things and leave the Hall. I will not have you living under the same roof as my wife. Father has been paying your creditors for years. I will not. Go and look for a job and support yourself, or find a husband who will pay your bills.'

Tears brimming, she snatched her arms free from her brother's grasp and ran to the library door. She stopped, but did not turn around to look at him.

'Tell Mummy I have retired to my room with a headache' she hissed. Then she pulled open the door and hurried from the room.

Susanne witnessed Elizabeth's hasty departure from the direction of the library and then caught sight of Harry walking towards her. As always, the mere sight of him made her heart skip a beat. Imagine! At forty still feeling like a girl of twenty. She knew instinctively that they would always be happy together. He smiled, reached for her hand and led her onto the dance floor, sliding his arm around her waist. 'Happy?' he asked.

'Always, when I'm with you. I was thinking next week or perhaps the one after we could spend a few days in Golfe-Juan. Especially now that I have installed a tub that fits two. Do you think you could get away, darling?

'Sounds brilliant. If you travel Thursday morning, I'll catch an evening flight. Sorry darling I would rather be with you, but I have a late session at the House. Then we will be together for a whole week.'

Susanne smiled; he was so different from Bernhard. Harry was always apologetic whenever he was going to be held up and would follow it up with a small gift, usually perfume. 'Je Reviens', which he had bought her years ago, was still a favourite, although now she used several different perfumes, including Chanel.

'I saw Elizabeth going upstairs earlier. She looked rather upset. Do you think she is all right?'

'It's nothing important. Just brother and sister having a small spat.'

'Was it anything to do with me?'

'Good Lord, no! I merely told her to find a husband and not to rely on Father to finance her lifestyle. She excused herself, asking me to tell Mother that she was feeling a little off-colour, and has retired.'

As they circled the ballroom, Susanne gazed up at the gallery which led to the family bedrooms and wondered if Elizabeth was really unwell. Her intuition told her the spat had been about her, and she hoped Harry had not been too hard on his sister. Susanne was overjoyed in the knowledge that she was marrying a man who would support her one hundred per cent. This meant a great deal to her.

The next morning, when she joined the family for breakfast, Elizabeth was courteous and charming to Susanne, earning a warm smile from her brother.

Waiting in the library for Harry to arrive, Susanne was idly thumbing through a copy of *Country Life* when Elizabeth came into the room carrying a small leather pouch. She approached Susanne.

'I would like to return this to you. It was found at the

back of one of the shelves in the library of the Lodge you occupied when you were ill during the war.' She gave the pouch to Susanne. Puzzled, Susanne stared at it.

'How do you know it is mine?' She had difficulty recognising the small leather bag. 'What is it?'

'It is a birth certificate in the name of Edward Carlon, your son. I would like to apologise for suggesting the child was my brother's.'

Susanne was speechless. She could only nod as she removed the certificate from the pouch and stared at it. During the time of Edward's birth she had been so heart-broken grieving for Rick that she had not wanted the baby. Harry must have registered Edward's birth and left it in the Lodge for her to find before he had left for India. He was the only person she could think of. Susanne would ask him when they were alone. Her thoughts were quickly interrupted.

'I love my brother.'

'I love him too, and always will.'

Elizabeth smiled at her future sister-in-law. 'In order to make my brother happy, you and I have to become friends. For my part I will try.'

'So will I' Susanne said. She stood up and threw her arms around Elizabeth.

Just at that moment Harry walked in the room and came to a halt, grinning from ear to ear. 'Can I join in?'

At his sister's nod he went forward and embraced the two most important women in his life.

On her flight to Golfe-Juan, Susanne was daydreaming. It had been a wonderful party at the Hall, made even more so when Harry came to her bed and stayed until dawn. At forty-three, he was still as lean and firm as a Greek god. In his arms she had discovered pleasures she never knew existed. Susanne was as happy as a sandboy and so much in love.

After making love Harry wrapped Susanne in his arms. He confessed he had registered her son's birth and left the document in a leather pouch in the book room. According to Elizabeth, when the lodge had been refurbished the pouch had been discovered wedged behind a shelf. She had taken charge if it and put in her room, hoping to return it. Over the years Elizabeth had travelled in Europe quite a lot and completely forgotten all about the leather pouch.

Susanne let out a contented sigh at the knowledge that she had been accepted by the Fortescue family. Her thoughts suddenly switched to Virginia. She had heard from Judy that Danny had run off to San Francisco with his friend Kenny, leaving both Judy and her father shocked. Abe Carlon was ready to throw in the towel and was planning to sell the stud. Susanne had immediately replied to Judy with a lengthy letter and enclosed a copy of Edward's birth certificate.

Judy had telephoned as soon as she read the letter, saying both she and Pa would welcome Edward and were willing to teach him how to manage the stud if he was keen to learn. Pa had been upset not being informed about Edward's existence but understood Susanne's reasons for not telling him. Actually, Judy added that Abe was over the moon; the news of his grandson had breathed new life into him. Judy invited Susanne to visit real soon.

Edward's, gambling debts and airline ticket were paid by his mother, and she even popped a little extra inside a farewell card. The night before he left, Susanne gave a farewell dinner for her son at a London restaurant and invited Harry, John and Rose Miller, their daughter, Jade, and the estate manager, Tom Marsh.

Harry and Susanne went with Edward to the airport the next day, and with a teary embrace from his mother and a firm handshake from Harry, Edward left them at the departure gate. Susanne wondered when she would see her son again. Putting his arms around her Harry gave her a consoling hug, telling her not to worry.

'Now both my children are living abroad' she cried, enveloped in Harry's arms.

Walking along the foreshore in Golfe-Juan carrying a basket of plump peaches, freshly-caught seafood from the local market and some baguettes from the Boulangerie, the nicest and the friendliest bakery on the coast, Susanne was softly humming to herself while planning a romantic dinner. She was happier than she had ever been in her life, and could hardly wait until the man of her dreams arrived. When Bernhard had died she had toyed with the idea of selling the villa. Luckily, she had changed her mind. Harry loved the place, and so did she, for the privacy it afforded; he could escape from the corridors of power and relax.

Bernhard's small yacht was still tied up in the harbour, and she made a mental note to ask Harry if he wanted to use it.

Glancing at her watch, she scolded herself for daydreaming and hurried home with her shopping. After a quick shower and change of clothes she left the villa to pick up Harry at the airport.

Later that evening as they dined *al fresco* on the balcony of the villa, Susanne mentally sized up the area she was planning to redecorate.

'Darling, while you're here and when you have time, could you please drill some holes so I can hang a few flower baskets around here?' she asked, pointing to the ceiling of the balcony. She watched Harry put down his wine glass and lean across the table.

'Why are you staring at me like that, darling?' she asked.

'It has taken me a few months to learn to decipher what you mean. I take it you want the hooks drilled and the baskets hung immediately. Correct?'

'No, of course not, I wasn't even thinking about tonight.'

'Liar,' he said with a grin.

'How can you say that?'

'Darling, I know you. When you want something fixed or repaired, it has to be done immediately, doesn't it?'

'I suppose I do get a little impatient sometimes.' She rose from the table and seated herself on his lap, murmuring an apology. Then she kissed him. He nuzzled her ear and stroked her thighs, whispering, 'Forget the flower baskets. I'll do them tomorrow, darling. Let us get into the tub and make love.'

Three days after Harry arrived at the villa, he received a telephone call from London informing him that the party leader had taken ill. Harry was needed in London immediately to accept the leadership. On their return to London, Harry and Susanne were bombarded with cameras and microphones as they made their way to a waiting car. Several reporters and television crews pushed microphones into Harry's face, demanding a response to the recent announcement that he had been chosen to lead the party into the next election.

He also had to fend off questions about the woman with him. Susanne shielded her face with the magazine she had been reading on the flight to London but not before a few pictures had been taken. She almost fell headlong into the waiting car to get away from the newspaper reporters.

'Harry, how awful!'

'Don't worry, darling. We will announce our engagement as soon as I can arrange it. Leave it to me.'

Susanne would leave everything to him, except for one thing. She knew Harry and his parents desperately wanted an heir. She had thought that at forty her child-bearing days were over, but before she left Paris she had visited a gynaecologist. He had told her that in his opinion she would be able to conceive. Susanne planned to get a second opinion in Harley Street. Although Harry often said children were not important, she knew differently.

'I saw your picture in the *Daily Mail* and heard rumours about an upcoming engagement,' June said when they met in her favourite coffee house in Sloane Square. 'You are the luckiest woman on this planet, getting engaged to the Right Honourable Harry Fortescue MP, son of Earl Haywood. You know, Michael was a snazzy dresser. Rick was the perfect thoroughbred. Bernhard was smart and successful. Harry, well, he's got it all: rich, handsome, clever and a title. You must be damn good in bed, blossom.'

'You never change, June.'

'And you haven't changed either. You're so secretive, keeping it all to yourself and leaving me to speculate. For once in your life, be open.'

'If you really must know, he's the one who's good in bed.'

'Don't stop there. I want to know more.'

'That's it.'

'Honestly, you're impossible. I always tell you about the men in my life and the life in my men,' she joked with fluttering eyelashes.

'June, I love Harry.'

'I can see that. You're positively glowing. So whatever he's doing, tell him to keep doing it.'

'I love him too much to discuss our intimate relationship with anyone, and that includes you, June.'

'OK, let's order lunch and talk about the weather, shall we?'

June's flippant comment made Susanne smile. 'Actually, I wanted to ask if you've heard from Penny.'

'No, not at all, since meeting this Australian fellow, she's moved from the Bahamas and has gone to live in Queensland. From all accounts, her new love is a diving instructor on the Barrier Reef with his own boat.'

'Did you send her the money I gave you?'

'On both occasions, and I pleaded with her to write to you. She was grateful for the money and she knows where it came from, but she's not ready to contact you. '

Susanne's expression reflected her disappointment. 'Like her father, Penny has always been obstinate' she said. 'I'll just have to live with it, I suppose. The only thing I will never be able to understand is, why did she give her baby up for adoption? And why did she refuse to let anyone, even you, know the gender of the child, and then leave London without a word?'

June shifted awkwardly in her seat. How could she tell Susanne that her daughter had been head-over-heels in love with Bernhard and when he died she hadn't wanted her baby, her family or even her country and had fled abroad? Michael Blore had ignored Penny, but Susanne had not. She had paid all Penny's expenses, and she was still paying.

Returning from lunch with June, Susanne had just taken her jacket off when the doorbell rang. She hurried to answer it, hoping it was Harry so that she could give him the good news from Harley Street.

It was not Harry but a shabbily-dressed woman. 'Remember me, Susie Caddy?' she whined. 'I was Janet Bell. Now I'm yer brother's wife. We've got four young 'uns to look after. I see from the newspapers that you're knocking about with the son of an Earl. Well, you've come up in the world, 'aven't yer?'

The colour drained from Susanne's face. She stared at the shabbily dressed woman, totally dumbfounded. Then she heard herself say, 'Did my half-brother send you here?'

'Nah, Erik's a weakling, but I'm not, and neither is Michael Blore or his cousin June. They let me in on your daughter getting hersel preggers to your Nazi husband. I want ten thousand pounds from you, or I go to the papers and sell the story. Think what your hoity-toity Lordship will say if he reads about Ethel, your whore of a mother.'

'You wretch! You were a horror at school and you haven't changed. Now get out of here before I call the police.'

'Ifen ye does, that grand gentleman of yours will not want ye, when he reads the letter I've wrote but not sent yet. You tell the Old Bill 'n I'll post it. The shame of it would be too much and he'd most likely get kicked out of Parliament. Now wouldn't that be a shame?' She sniggered. 'Tell you what: I'll give you a few days to think on it. I want cash. I'll be back. Cheerio.'

Susanne closed the door and walked into her bedroom, her mind in turmoil. She paced up and down, sucking her lip and physically shaking. She had escaped from the dirt and squalor of her childhood, and now it had returned to haunt her. If she gave her half-brother and his wife the money to buy their silence she could still marry Harry, he could achieve his ambition of becoming Prime Minister, and they could have a happy life together. But surely blackmailers always became greedy and would demand more and more money?

Would Harry still love her if he knew the truth? How far would a man go for love? Would he give up his career and be content with a wife and heir? What about the gossip? She would never be accepted in society, and that would hurt Harry. Questions raced through her mind like wind through tall grass. Harry had told her that he did not want any scandal to harm his family or career.

A feeling of desperation seized her, and she moaned out loud as she visualised the headlines in the *News of the World*: 'Illegitimate Daughter of Prostitute Deserts Brave British Soldier to Wed Nazi. Will She Be The Next Prime Minister's Wife?' The press would have a field day, and it would destroy Harry and his family. In utter frustration, she picked up a perfume bottle and threw it at the wall. Then she flung herself on the bed and cried rivers of tears until she fell asleep.

Some time later she woke and went into the bathroom to wash her face. Then she began pacing between her bedroom and the sitting room, feeling lost, empty and utterly defeated. Her head ached, and a cold sweat was breaking out all over her body. She was feeling sorry for herself, but most of all she was feeling sorry for Harry. All he wanted was to marry the woman he loved and pursue his career, but he could not have both. The tears returned, and she sobbed brokenheartedly.

Then anger took over. She raged against the British class system, her mother Ethel, half-brother Erik and his wife Janet Bell, daughter Penny, son Edward, Bernhard and the Nazis. Above all, Michael Blore seemed to be behind all her ill luck. She couldn't appeal to his father, Percy. He had died last year, and poor Tess was in an aged care centre with dementia.

She would get little or no sympathy from June. When Janet Bell told that her closet friend was mixed up with this, Susanne could scarcely believe it. She always knew June was a little envious of her, but surely she wouldn't stoop to this level. It must have been June who told Michael Blore about Penny's baby; who else could it be? She wondered if June and that hateful Michael Blore would want money too.

'It's just not fair! But then, when has anything in my life been fair?' she muttered to herself as her eyes filled with tears again.

Susanne wrestled with her conscience to try and come to a decision. She knew she had to fight back, but most of all she wanted to shield Harry from scandal. Could she bring herself to tell the man she loved why she could not marry him?

Shaking her head, she resolved to speak to Harry. Yes, she would telephone him in the morning and pass on the good news the gynaecologist had given her. However, she would not tell him about the visit from Janet Bell; she would simply pay up and marry Harry. She felt happy with her decision and went into the kitchen to make a cup of hot milk.

Suddenly, she halted at the kitchen door. Suppose, just suppose, Janet Bell wanted more money. Would Michael Blore and June want more too? What then? Janet Bell's breath had reeked of alcohol, and if this awful woman got drunk in her local pub and her cronies asked where she got the money for booze every night, would she blab to everyone in her drunken state?

She would have to telephone Harry and tell him the truth about her past. She had told him months before that Penny was her daughter and that Michael Blore had hired a clever lawyer and won custody. Harry had been both supportive and sympathetic. She would tell him everything and ask him to decide their future. She wondered fleetingly if Harry could use his position to keep Janet Bell quiet, but she quickly dismissed that idea; it might lead to more trouble. How could she allow her past to destroy Harry's career and deny him his destiny?

There was only one course open to her. She would telephone him and ask him to cancel the announcement of their engagement. Then she would book a passage on the *Queen Mary* from Southampton to New York, leave her troubles behind in England and go to live in America. All those years before, Rick had told her that in the United States they had no class system to speak of; it wasn't who you were or where you were born that mattered, but who you became.

Judy had never married, and she had told Susanne that Abe had changed his will in favour of Edward. Her son would inherit Carlon Stud one day. Perhaps she could join him and live quietly. Susanne sucked her lower lip, wanting so much to remain in London and marry the man she loved, but that would wreck his life. Only by leaving could she help him fulfil his dream of becoming Britain's Prime Minister. The thought of leaving Harry and their life together in London was tearing her apart, and she knew if she went to Virginia she would be left with nothing but a mountain of regret. Tears flowed once more.

It was four in the morning before she stopped crying and stared into the bathroom mirror at her red, tear-stained face and tousled hair. 'What a dreadful mess you are!' she said to the swollen face that stared back. 'You have got to calm down, take control and find a solution. Do what is best for yourself and the man you love.'

She filled the bath with piping hot water and tossed in some perfumed salts, preparing herself both physically and mentally for the task ahead. Rubbing her face and neck with cleansing cream while the bath water cooled, she started to think rationally. There was no one she could approach for advice without revealing the very thing she wanted to hide. There was no one she trusted except Harry, but it would be inexcusable to place this burden upon him. His judgement might well be clouded because of his love for her, influencing him to make a wrong decision, which he might regret for the rest of his life.

Harry had sworn his devotion to her, declaring that marriage was more important to him than being Prime Minister. Even if he thwarted the blackmailers and resigned from politics to retire to the country, would he always feel that way, or would he grow to despise her?

Susanne stepped out of the warm bath, thankful it was the cleaning woman's day off. Outside, dawn was breaking. She went into the kitchen and made some tea. Picking up her cup and saucer, she walked towards the large windows that overlooked the city. Sitting down on the padded window seat, she watched the early morning sun bathe the city rooftops in coppery gold. Susanne had finally made up her mind; putting her cup and saucer down on the table, she picked up the telephone and dialled Harry's number.

THE END